SCRIPTURE

The Second Novel in the Rennsalaer Series

Michael Bradley

Manor House Publishing Inc.
www.manor-house.biz 905-648-2193

Scripture

Library and Archives Canada
Cataloguing in Publication

Bradley, Michael, 1944-
    Scripture / Michael Bradley.

ISBN 978-0-9781070-8-6

    I. Title.
PS8553.R226S37 2007   C813'.54   C2007-905314-9

Published Oct. 15, 2007, by Manor House Publishing Inc.
4522 Cottingham Crescent, Ancaster, Ontario, Canada, L9G 3V6
905-648-2193.... Fax: 905-648-8369
www.manor-house.biz

Printed and bound in Canada. All rights reserved.

Manor House Publishing extends special thanks to artist Gregory
Fromenteau for use on the front cover of his outstanding work The
Library (Night) and invites readers to view more of his exceptional art
at: www.mks-arts.com email: gfromenteau@gmail.com

We acknowledge the financial support of the Government of Canada
through the Book Publishing Industry Development Program (BPIDP)
for our publishing activities.

Novels of the Marc Rennsalaer Series
The Magdalene Mandala

Foreword

Civic upheaval and riots rocking the French countryside, gunmen with silencers, a bag lady Druid, a mysterious parchment, a damsel in danger, kidnappings, murders, high-tech weaponry, political intrigue and dark visions of death and destruction...

Welcome to *Scripture,* the second enthralling novel chronicling the Holy Grail exploits of Canadian-American adventurer Marc Rennsalaer.

Scripture continues the compelling exploration into secretive religious organizations and hidden truths that began with *The Magdalene Mandala*, Michael Bradley's captivating breakthrough novel, launching a series critics have acclaimed as *James Bond* meets *The Da Vinci Code*.

The story: Still nursing wounds from his last great adventure, Rennsalaer finds his dreams of a peaceful life are again swept aside as he becomes drawn into a deadly game pitting his wits, survivalist gadgetry and trusty Walther PPK against a determined and organized assault.

Bradley slowly, masterfully builds tension to the breaking point as he takes us deep into a clandestine world where nothing is as it seems, a world controlled by dark forces determined to keep the true origins of the world's major religions forever concealed from prying eyes.

With *Scripture*, Michael Bradley has crafted another gripping and suspenseful thriller – and a worthy successor to his critically acclaimed *Magdalene Mandala*.

- **Michael B. Davie,** author, *The Late Man*

For my wife, friend and companion, Joëlle Lauriol.

1

It was rising up in front of us, that black wall of water, but I knew it only because of its startling white crest of foam on top. Runnels of foam streaked down its front, too, and I could glimpse these because of the weak illumination of the lighthouse's beam to starboard from, I hoped, Dover... or maybe Hythe... or at least somewhere in Kent.

I had been taking no real care with navigation, only to stay relatively near the coast so as to keep out of the busiest shipping lane in the world. Was that true, I reflected? Perhaps now the Malacca Straits leading into Singapore was the biggest shipping lane in today's world. And then, too, I had recently read somewhere that the Strait of Hormuz leading into 'the (Persian) Gulf' from the Gulf of Oman had now become the world's busiest seaway. It was because of the oil, of course, if this were true.

Well, anyway, the English Channel was certainly still one of the biggest shipping lanes, at least, and like a highway and the Malacca Straits it was actually divided into two lanes through the Strait of Dover. I stayed as far to the right, but also as far from the coast of Kent, as possible in the hope Jester wouldn't be run down by an ocean freighter, giant oil tanker or container ship hurrying outward-bound south down the Channel in the darkness.

Black Channel rollers were coming directly at us, from the southwest, and Folderol Jester, somewhat to my surprise, lifted easily to this oncoming one as she had lifted to all the others – although her various hinges and folding joints squealed the mildest of protests. We surfed down into the trough where no lighthouse wand could reach us and where darkness ruled. Not that I greatly cared.

In these dark troughs the polycarbonate front windshield of the wheelhouse became like an obsidian mirror and my face was reflected back at me by the muted interior lights of Jester's instruments. It was a haggard face, and an even thinner one than just months before. I suppose this was due to the loss of weight from recovering from the Glastonbury injuries. It wasn't a handsome face, at least I didn't think so, but the face at least wasn't actually scared-looking any longer, not since I had learned that Jester rose easily to the Channel waves.

My height took up all but an inch of the 6-foot, 3-inch headroom – Jester had been designed that way – and so my nondescript mousy brown hair was partly cut off by the wheelhouse's frame. Only that unruly shock of hair curved down over my forehead and had to be brushed back from time to time so that the equally nondescript brown eyes could see. These eyes now gazed steadily back at me with new confidence in Jester's seaworthiness. The slight rippling imperfections in the plastic polycarbonate window-mirror emphasized the flatter, crushed right cheekbone and the lumpy right jaw line that the combination of a land mine and a Timor palm tree trunk had conspired between them to create. Jester rose out of the trough, crashing through the foam of the swell's crest.

True, at Margate, after throwing Mariko O'Shaugnessey's roses overboard at Gravesend, I had possessed the presence of mind to fold the cutwater plates forward and I had bolted the pointed apex where they met firmly together in overlapping steel plates – but all this was out of sheer habit. Then I had even, for some reason, bolted the folding floor of this cutwater to the steel flanges of the cutwater's plate sides at the bottom. This triangular cutwater extension of Folderol Jester's bow had never been intended to be watertight. Indeed, it had round holes drilled in its floor.

I had been experimenting with a Chinese refinement

when I had designed it. As I have made abundantly clear elsewhere,[1][*] I have never aspired to be a blue water sailor and I had therefore not permitted myself any lapse in weather watching to test the ancient Chinese idea.

And this was, in a word, to make the forward compartment of a vessel purposefully leakable, and drainable, to act as something of a shock absorber in serious waves. We were encountering serious waves now because I had suffered a lapse in weather watching back at Margate.

No, that's not quite true. I just didn't want to know about the weather at Margate because that Thames-side town was much too close to London. If I had learned of a late August Channel storm at Margate, well, commuter trains to London were much too handy.

I didn't think that Mariko and I could survive a second parting on the same day and I didn't want to spend any time at all in any lonely Margate marina. I also knew, and too well, that Mariko didn't want to see me again soon, or at least not for a long time. She was revelling in her long-deserved and new-found fame as a linguist, translating the Gospel of Mary Magdalene that we had supposedly dredged up somewhere, and rather vaguely, among the sunken islands of lost Lyonesse.

Given both the triumph and tragedy, the ecstasy and agony, that that adventure had cost us, I was already thinking of the summer's experiences as a parable with subtle depths. Privately, I always thought of the painful lessons we had endured because of that ancient parchment as The Magdalene Mandala. Something to be studied because of the perfect balance of its components, something a Buddhist might have kept spinning as a meditation prayer wheel. There had been the victory and retribution, the initial poverty and eventual comfortable financial viability, if not quite wealth, juxtaposed with such exquisite symmetry that

1   [*] The Magdalene Mandala

the wheel would have spun true. And in the central vortex of that wheel, around which everything else had revolved, was a scrap of parchment – well, vellum, according to Mariko – that weighed almost nothing and yet the impact of it might change the world.

After her tearful farewell at the Thames mooring, I thought it best not to return to her very quickly, if ever.

So I had put out into the Channel without turning on the radio and without learning of the impending 'early autumn' or (very) early equinoctial storm roiling up the Channel from the unpredictable North Atlantic.

I was feeling somewhat fey – perhaps the Celtic half of Mariko had gotten to me more deeply than I realized. And I was feeling more than a bit fatalistic because the Oriental half of Mariko had most certainly gotten to me.

I didn't greatly care what happened to me.

Of course, that half of Mariko O'Shaugnessey, the Oriental half, had the reinforcement of decade-dead Mei Ling, now at the bottom of the Sulu Sea in the storm-twisted wreckage of an Indonesian orembai just like Folderol Jester.

As Jester rose easily to the next black wall of water – a wall I estimated at about fifteen feet high – one part of my brain wryly whispered a more vulgar version of 'folderol'. To wit, horse shit.

Mei Ling's orembai had been a traditional one of bamboo and teak planks held together with ages of skill but only bamboo-plaited ropes with which to express it. Jester's main two folding hulls were welded steel up to their gunwales and from there up she was welded in 6061-T6 aluminium-magnesium alloy. Jester's outriggers were of the same stuff, as were most of her internal bulkheads. Her outrigger struts were not Indonesian bamboo, but oval stainless steel pipe. Jester was about twenty times as strong as the Brunei orembai that Mei Ling had fished from and died on, maybe more.

The realization that I was infinitely more fortunate

than Mei Ling – and perhaps even luckier than Mariko O'Shaugnessey, come to that – dissipated my feyness and fatalism pretty quickly.

In short, I donned a life jacket and clipped a nylon safety harness around me. Then, I climbed out of the wheelhouse and into the 'bracing' wind. It was maybe a little more bracing than the half-gale naturally made it because Jester was making about ten knots under steam power and almost directly into the wind, at that. All four masts were up, but the sails had not been hoisted for over two months. They were still securely furled by nylon straps.

I noted that the wind was not yet strong enough to blow the crests off the rollers, so it was not even a full gale, as blue water sailors might disdain it. But it was a strong wind, stronger in the gusts and also whenever Jester topped a wave. I held onto the wheelhouse hatch until I had clipped the safety harness to the brass knee-high rail around the rear hull that contained the cabin.

I sat on the great stainless steel hinges that held the two hulls together and let my legs dangle down into the almost empty ice-cube tray of Jester's forward hull. I saw that Ivory – which Mariko had first re-named Achilles and then Victory – was securely bound to the deck just below me by its stainless steel 1x19 wire cables and stainless steel snap-shackles to eye-bolts TIG-welded to the very frame of the hull. Ivory rocked forward and aft a bit with every wave, but the vehicle wasn't going anywhere soon.

I noted, with some amazement, that the flower shop's paper, in which Mariko's roses had come, and which I had wedged between the smokestack and one of the thinner whistle-tubes, was still in place. A substantial piece of the paper had folded over the hinges and all of the paper cone had apparently been held there by the sheer force of the wind. Even as I watched, this folded piece tore away and was whirled aloft into the black sky. The piece wedged between the smokestack and the whistle-tube somehow stayed in place a few moments longer. As I watched it, however, it performed a wild gyration.

It had been definitely creased in a straight line, either by the flower shop's counter edge when Mariko had bought the roses and they had been wrapped, or else – and less probably – when the conical paper container with the roses had been carried down, crushed against Mariko's chest, to Jester at the Thames-side quay. And now this creased paper arose, like a thing alive, and began to flap like a bird's wings along the crease-line beside the smokestack. As it flapped, it began to rotate, slowly at first, and then faster and faster. Finally it stopped flapping and closed in an aerofoil curve caused, I suppose, by some cello tape stuck length-wise inside it, and rotated even faster. Fascinated, I watched it soar upward alongside the smokestack until it disappeared aloft into the blackness.

I imagined that its strange antics were caused by errant drafts of the wind that were distorted by the smokestack and the two brass whistle-tubes flanking it. Strange things can happen in wind. I remembered seeing in Florida, after a hurricane, old-fashioned broom straws stuck completely through telephone poles. I doubted that the newer plastic broom bristle-whiskers, ubiquitous only a few years ago, but once again becoming supplanted by natural straw because of the energy and petroleum crisis, could pass through a telephone pole even with hurricane force behind them.

I remembered these aerial antics of the rose wrapping in the back of my mind as I looked forward toward Jester's cutwater.

I knew that the strength of it, and the Chinese idea, hinged, very literally, on the strength of its vertical hinges that were welded to the sides of Jester's steel front hull. Of course, these hinges had more than substantial stainless steel pins. And, in the approved Chinese manner, I had drilled holes in the cutwater floor that were smaller in the front and became progressively bigger toward the landing-craft type ramp-style door that, squeezing plastic-covered edges together tightly, denoted the truly watertight section of the front hull. A foot thick layer of Styrofoam under the plywood deck ensured that this rectangular front hull of Jester would not sink even if it were flooded. Any water in excess of about six tons would simply drain out through the screened (stainless steel) scuppers at deck level, or find its way back into the sea a bit more slowly through the doors covering the well between Ivory's rear wheels.

And these vertical hinges welded integrally with Jester's steel hull had held, so far, even when cascades of a comber crest had occasionally curled aboard and had splashed up against the truly watertight vertical ramp wall. The water seemed to recede quickly enough from this strange cutwater, too.

Jester rose and fell easily to each oncoming wave, but not abruptly. I had tried to follow ancient Chinese depictions and it seemed as though I had done a tolerable job. The only thing not really done in the ancient Chinese style was to have simple rounded holes of progressively larger diameter in the cutwater's floor rather than diamond-shaped holes of progressively larger size. This would have required extra machining and thus extra cost and I had long since decided that the Chinese refined things beyond the dictates of sheer practicality.

As politically incorrect as I was, I attributed this to, probably, genetic inclinations of Oriental humanity. The ancient Chinese believed that the diamond-shaped fenestrations (as the French called these holes from the French word for window, fenêtre) created 'living water'. Perhaps they were right, but the round holes had worked very well... so far. I had left Yin and Yang at that in my design drawings intended for my Toronto welder.

Jester seemed to be working very well in conditions I had never dared (consciously) to try – like the passage from St. Nazaire to Hoedic or worse, the passage back from Hoedic to the Vilaine River, both with Mariko during the last summer solstice. The waves then had been only four-to-six footers and even so I had been a bit worried. Now, my feyness or fatalism at Margate had plunked Jester and me into waves three times as high, at least.

With even the last paper reminder of Mariko O'Shaugnessey's roses gone from Folderol Jester, as it were, I started to become once again my own man – as it were. I sat up there, on the break of Jester's poop, with the strong hinges beneath my knees emphasizing my reality. Mostly, I was re-running last summer's vignettes of Mariko-as-anima. Surprisingly, I must have thought (and didn't do it very often) of C.G. Jung, and the primal strength of the female anima on the male psyche. I sat there, I suppose, for some hours, not feeling much of anything, but seeing the enjoyable and also the not-so-enjoyable mental vignettes. The first stages of that oft sought, but never truly grasped, emotional closure, you see.

On the other hand, because I suppose Jung happened to cross my mind when the day had begun to lighten, maybe I had been looking in the wrong place for that elusive anima.

I could discern the barest smudge of land to the southeast because of a few twinkling lights. I noted that no such lights glimmered toward the northwest, so I must have been steering automatically all that time. This barest smudge of land must be France, assuming that I was still in the North Atlantic, that is. And I was fairly sure we were. I cautiously turned Jester to port, noting with satisfaction that the boat ascended the diminishing waves – greenish-looking rollers in the wan dawn and looking about ten feet high now – with her outriggers almost parallel to the waves. From my perch up on the hinges where Jester's two hulls joined, I could view my boat more objectively than I had for the full ten years since she had been made.

At fifty-eight feet long with the cutwater extended and twenty feet in total width, Jester wasn't about to capsize even in this cross-chop on the unconscious course my mind had chosen. Not with the eight tons of free ballast on her bottom, the impeller tubes of always-moving water alongside her wide keel.

Finally, turning more to port, the wind and waves pushed me toward France just on the horizon. I guessed from the chart that the smudge must be a part of Normandy. So, since I was back to normal, more or less, I steered a bit more westerly for Brittany. Sooner or later, when I made landfall, I would find out exactly where we were. The main things were the distant horizon of land over the bow and the fact that the sonar had run out of enough fathoms with which to express the depth of water beneath the keel. The Eagle 5000 portable sonar was good for a depth of over 400 feet, about 70 fathoms, so things couldn't be all bad. In fact, things were relatively good.

And as the grey dawn light steadily became stronger, I realized that I truly felt very good too – except for some slight aching in the neck, spine and ribs that had probably truly awakened me from that pleasant miasma of Jung-and-anima nostalgia. I'd been told that my neck and ribs would always cause 'mild discomfort' (as doctors like to put it). So, I was not particularly surprised at the ache, but gratified to learn that it had required some hours in a cool breeze to start it up. All that physiotherapy back in London had done some good, after all.

And I had discovered, through carelessness back at Margate, Folderol Jester was much more seaworthy than I had ever dared to test. Not that I hadn't designed her that way, but it was good to verify the theory with practice.

With my newly found confidence in Jester as an offshore boat, and with an ever-brightening day that promised to be sunny but blustery, I decided to take a stab at more serious navigation. After some concentrated study of the chart, and figuring that the winds had created a current of two knots against us during the night, I finally decided that the distant glimmering lights far abeam were probably Dieppe. Taking this as a reasonable assumption, I turned Jester a bit to starboard, heading more south and west for the tip of the Cotentin Peninsula and Cherbourg.

It, or some headland, duly rose above the horizon dead on the bow by late afternoon.

If I left Cherbourg and crossed the Gulf of St. Malo to coast around Brittany and Poitou down to the Gironde, it would take Jester about two weeks to reach Aiguillon. But with a dangerous lee shore all the way and the season turning to notorious September in the Bay of Biscay. If, once reaching Brittany, and sailing its southern shore to once again enter the inland canals at St. Malo or further east at the Vilaine River, the same trip would take about three weeks. And it would be as safe as houses. I found that with twenty-four hours between Mariko and me, I was looking forward to being 'home' – although I had no idea what awaited me there or even precisely where home was. Oh, Raoul and Joëlle had given clear enough directions, but I had never actually seen the place.

There, somewhere off the mouth of the Seine, with Cherbourg nestled in a headland muted with distance ahead of Jester, I succumbed to temptation. On a whim I braked the wheel and ran Jester for some minutes under unchanged power while I hoisted sail. I hoisted both mains and mizzens, and on both sides, not forgetting to rotate the port masts forward. The full-battened and vaguely Chinese-shaped sails turned Jester into a genuine orembai again, as she had not been since the summer. I also raised the Western-style jibs (or Genoas) on the fore stays – except that they, too, had full battens of carbon fibre slats, cut from sheets of the stuff.

The three pairs of sails each were tethered together by an aluminium tube; so only three sheets came back to me atop the poop and hinges. The wind was coming out of the west; call it about 15 knots and in the gusts a bit more. When I had these six smallish sails (or three) depending on one's point of view, correctly trimmed to my satisfaction, I reached down into the wheelhouse and valved the steam engine down to 'simmer', as I called it, and de-clutched its chain drive from the impeller.

Jester had already heeled over a very few degrees toward the low coast of Normandy to port. But now she was making about 15 knots – if not a bit more in the gusts – and I was using only a trickle of fuel to keep the boiler hot enough for fairly quick usage.

As the sun sank toward the west in the late afternoon, I noted that the smudge on the horizon over the bow was becoming much more definite. I knew also, without having to look at any chart, that the harbour and town of Cherbourg must be snuggled behind this headland.

Home? How could one have a home without knowing its precise location? Its smells? Its trees? Its views from cozy windows?

Mariko, when she had chided me on that last – was it only yesterday afternoon? – Thames-side parting had said with too-feminine certainty that I had a perfectly good permanent address at Aiguillon with Joëlle. But Mariko had really known nothing of the seven-year relationship between Joëlle and myself.

I had never told her.

Firstly, because I had known too well that *any* knowledge that Mariko had beyond her own theft might have proved dangerous to herself, and would certainly have proved dangerous to Joëlle. Not to mention Raoul, Philippe and their wives. And secondly, because the strange relationship that existed between Joëlle and me was ours alone, not to be shared with anyone, not even with Mariko O'Shaugnessey.

Joëlle, during the seven years we had been together since I had first come into France, had gradually become more of a daughter to me than a womanly peer consort.

And also, in some strange way that she herself had insisted upon, and perhaps *was*, Joëlle had also become a timeless Earth Mother, a spirit of the Haute Garonne. And it was simply a fact that her family had lived for, perhaps, 10,000 years where the Lot River flowed into the Garonne River, not six miles from Aiguillon where Raoul had so conveniently found the warehouse that my money had made it possible to buy. So, by some unlikely quirk of fate – or *was* it coincidence? – Joëlle was once again living at the confluence of the Lot and Garonne Rivers, just where her entire family had resided since, maybe, the close of the last Ice Age.

And, aside from securing, *almost* outright buying the warehouse itself, had I not sent some 17,000 Euros to Joëlle out of the bounty gained by the Magdalene Gospel from Stewart and Ibn Da'ud? Then, she had the motorized tricycle that I had constructed for her in Narbonne seven years before. It had been made of steel and aluminium, yes, but its major components had been infinite care and concern. It would sustain Joëlle for longer than she could reasonably expect to live, or be able to ride on it. Its driving mechanism would never wear out, it seemed. There were Velocette mopeds still running in France that had been made in 1930. Its 25cc engine had not changed at all from 1930 to 1997, when an upscale refinement to 35cc had been introduced. Even its tires would last for a decade, if cared for.

So, I owed her nothing. Nothing, except, of course, those obligations of my heart. She was, after all, *female*, and in the world as it seemed to be disintegrating day-by-day, this fact alone made her as vulnerable as little Lucy the Australopithecine some 2-3 million years ago. Once again.

As I looked aloft at the superbly-drawing Chinese sails… I realized that *Folderol Jester* was my real home, and not Joëlle and 'my' (or the communally-owned) warehouse at Aiguillon.

Could Joëlle understand that I had changed? That there was no automatic 'chivalry' or 'obligation' in my heart, beyond what I had already done for her, any more? Somehow, 'the Magdalene Mandala', as I chose to call it, had burned that sort of emotional commitment out of me – again – just as Mei Ling's death had burned it out long before.

I didn't know what Joëlle could, or could not, understand.

I did know that in the very late afternoon, almost sunset, the Cotentin Peninsula was close abeam and I steered for its westernmost tip, the Pointe de Barfleur. Long before actual sundown I dowsed the sails, furled them with the strong nylon straps again, and, once rounding the first headland, steamed at a stately 5 knots up past the Grande Rade breakwater into Cherbourg. I threaded the narrow channel between the Petite Rade with some care and disdained the Chantereyne Marina – more like an upscale Western-style boat city, really, since it could accommodate some 12,000 yachts – and I noticed that it was much less than half full even at the end of August.

As the sunset flared into reddish-orange in the far West, I turned past the Government Wharf and into the much more modest breakwater of the Club Nautique Sportif. It felt a little odd to be back where Mariko and I had started our Channel crossing to Weymouth and Glastonbury just two months earlier.

2

I must admit that when I reached the pontoon-supported docks of the Club Nautique Sportif, I just picked the first available slot and moored Jester immediately. I didn't visit the office and take care of mooring fees. On the other hand, the Club Nautique Sportif knew me and Jester because of a couple of previous visits, including last summer's, and I figured that the business manager, Matilde, would not be upset if I didn't make an appearance until the morrow. Being suddenly very tired indeed, I had just flaked out on one of the two bunks in the cabin and was almost instantly asleep.

Naturally, I woke ravenously hungry, and naturally at my habitual time of sunrise. Old habits die hard. Sunrise was just before six o'clock at this time of year. I took a quick and refreshing hot shower and then dressed in a shore rig of jeans, flannel shirt, my disreputable Nikes and my only windbreaker, a rather heavy one because of the dictates of winter barging in France, since the wind off the Atlantic was cool. My plan was to walk up to the familiar Pâtisserie Paris and get some breakfast as quickly as possible. I walked down the pontoon-supported boardwalk and left a note under the office door for Matilde assuring her that I would return later.

Walking back to take a last careful look at Jester's mooring lines, I noticed that the Club Nautique Sportif was proportionally much smaller than the giant Chantereyne floating city not too far away, but was proportionally much fuller. And I also noticed something else that should have intruded long before. Had I really become that sloppy? How had I ever survived the events of the Lac des Doigts and Glastonbury?

All around the perimeter of the concrete breakwater leading to the Club Nautique Sportif was a new chain-link fence. And at the end of the boardwalk leading onto the breakwater was a sturdy chain-link gate. And at this gate stood a uniformed guard – armed, I saw, even from Jester's mooring – and he was gazing in my direction.

Only the water approaches to the Club Nautique Sportif were unfenced. Surely, all this had not been put in place since the bare two-and-a-half months since Mariko and I had last been here?

Had things gotten so much worse? Of course, I reflected, while giving a casual wave to the guard and kneeling to pretend to examine the hitches around the bollards more closely, we had been in something of a cocoon in London. I had hardly seen a newspaper, or television news all during July and August. The manuscript, and the increasingly hopeless relationship, had more or less obsessed both of us.

Mariko had her small apartment in the Kensington Arms Hotel and I had my upscale Thames-side mooring among trendy houseboats and converted 'narrow barges' painted in bright neo-Gypsy livery. And all this had been paid for by the ever-helpful Malcolm Stewart and his associates, according to the contracts and addenda executed in Salisbury's King's Arms.

Come to think of it, Mariko had seldom walked anywhere alone, not even to the nearby museums on Cromwell Road. There always seemed to be a car waiting for her, not necessarily a limousine, mind you. As for me, they let me walk to and fro to visit Mariko, but perhaps my performance on that Glastonbury sidewalk, not to mention the boat jetty, had impressed them. Or maybe I was just less valuable to the parchment's translation process. That seemed much more likely.

In any event, the chain-link fence and the guard made me quickly forget my hunger. I wasn't going anywhere, obviously, without some kind of receipt and recognition from the Club Nautique Sportif's office. And I wasn't going anywhere until I knew more from Matilde.

Therefore, I went calmly aboard Jester again and, for something to do on the way, I checked the lashings on the aluminium grab-bucket that I had had fabricated in Britain. This aluminium grab-bucket was temporarily stowed in Ivory's truck bed. It supposedly replaced the one lost when we had dredged for yet more artefacts on the fishing banks of lost Lyonesse after we had already recovered the reliquary containing the parchment. As I bent to check its lashings, and I might as well really do it, I wondered idly whether it would ever prove useful. Of course, from one point of view, it had already proved extremely valuable, having earned several thousand times its cost.

My inspection of the grab-bucket confirmed what I had seen last night in the black mirror of the wheelhouse front window, only reflected now in rather dull and weld-distorted aluminium alloy rather than obsidian. My face was still somewhat haggard looking, but not so much after a night's sleep without worry about the relationship between Mariko and I. And there was even a shine to the eyes after Jester's performance. And did the somewhat too wide and sensuous mouth (some women have said) have a slight curve of confidence at the corners of a tentative smile?

Surely, there was something I could eat in Jester's galley?

There was, indeed, and it turned out to be not so bad. I found the makings for two Havarti cheese and English roast beef sandwiches. And I made two cups of Colombian coffee from my own mixture of beans from Harrods's best. And this was considerably better than I would have gotten at the Pâtisserie Paris where I would have been served the rough Arabica-based coffee that only French stomachs can accept early in the day.

I dawdled over the second cup until it was almost 8:30 a.m. when the office was supposed to be open. Before seeing Matilde, I collected my passport and my Walther

PPK. Lying in the drawer I saw the Beretta .25 that had once been 'Annie Oakley' Mariko's and might now be Joëlle's. I decided to don a tee shirt under the flannel one, and to hide the Walther discreetly under both the flannel shirt and the bulky windbreaker. I didn't know what was going on, what with the new fence and new guards.

I read and understand spoken French much better than I can speak it myself and besides, Matilde spoke fairly good English like any marina manager in Cherbourg. Most of their clientele was British, after all.

Prices had gone up a bit since we'd been here last summer. Matilde accepted my mixture of Euros and Francs, while explaining that the price hike was to pay for the new security features – the chain-link fencing and the 24-hour armed guards. She gave me a plastic card in exchange for my money. It was supposed to work the electronic lock on the gate. This had all become necessary because of the late summer's rioting and looting. Rioting and looting?

Yes, hadn't I heard?

Well, no. It was the rising unemployment and the simultaneous freeze on welfare. Marinas and yachts had become a preferred target, at least in maritime Cherbourg, of the desperate and disenfranchised. They figured that anyone with a boat was fair game. Boats must mean money. Money they didn't have. Boats and boating people – if they looked like yachts and not working craft and crew – had become an emotional symbol of economic disparity in maritime-oriented Cherbourg.

In late July, a virtual mob had stormed down the breakwater and had broken into several yachts. Some crews had been badly beaten, and one woman and two men had died from their injuries. Not at the Club Nautique Sportif, but over at Chantereyne, you understand. Here, only three yachts had been vandalized. And no one had been injured.

Jesus, so it was starting. Maybe, come to think of it, it

had already begun back in November of 2005 when riots and arson raged for ten days throughout the suburbs of most major French cities, including Paris. Jacques Briac had managed to restore law and order, just barely, without calling out the army. He had to deputize many more gendarmes and give the prefects wide powers of arrest and curfew.

I had heard nothing of all this recent summer's violence in Britain, although perhaps something similar had occurred there and I had simply not read about it. Of course, the French are popularly thought (in Anglo-Saxon minds, anyway) to be more volatile in nature than the British, but they are also more no-nonsense with their military... and private guards. I had no doubt at all that the Club Nautique Sportif's guard was armed, and with real bullets in his holstered automatic, and no doubts either that he would shoot to kill if he deemed it necessary.

So, the fence and the guards, not to mention the soldiers patrolling the streets, had quelled the waterfront's violence with sheer force during what remained of the summer 'tourist' season.

People would have to learn that times had changed. The good times were gone. And no country in the Western world had the means to care for its citizens in the democratically equal manner that everyone had become used to. That would only be possible if Western countries became totally and enthusiastically Socialist, but the political trend seemed to be going the other way.

Now, once again, there were the definite haves and the have-nots, as there had always been. The police and military worked on behalf of the haves, of course, as they always had. Nonetheless, I thanked fortune that I was one of the 'haves' – of course, I had planned for that and had worked for it.

So, up with the fences and bring on the armed guards.

I thanked Matilde for all the news and told her that

I would probably be leaving early tomorrow. So, I paid for the extra few hours, amounting to a 'day', in advance, to forestall any trouble with whatever guard might be on duty. Matilde marked me down on the 'departures' board so that the oncoming guards could be briefed. I watched her do this, marking 'Payé', and then I thanked her.

Given Matilde's news, I went back to Jester yet again and double-checked that the sliding hatch on the wheelhouse was securely locked. Jester's wheelhouse framing was of steel and her windows were polycarbonate. Once locked, no one could get in without a blowtorch and plenty of time.

When I was walking past Chantereyne a few minutes later, I saw the same kind of chain-link fencing, and guards. I also saw that I had underestimated its occupancy rate in the near darkness and because I was concentrating on the narrow channel between the Grande and Petite Rade breakwaters. I saw now that actually much less than a third of its moorings boasted yachts, albeit most of them were large and luxurious. Perhaps the violent events of the summer had played their part in scaring some people away. There were other factors to consider.

The Cotentin Peninsula, of which Cherbourg was by far the major port, was a primary terminus for ferries from Britain and a prime destination for yachts bound for France from Britain, Holland, Belgium and Scandinavia. It was also, of course, a major commercial port.

The problem was that it was really only that – a port of entry. The Cotentin Peninsula of Normandy held few attractions in its own right compared to Brittany to the south and the beautiful inland canals on which one could reach any part of France, including the Mediterranean coast. Although the local tourist board was doing its best to promote Cherbourg and the Cotentin as an alluring tourist destination, it had not quite succeeded.

In this, the promoters of the huge Chantereyne Marina

had miscalculated. And, of course, in common with everyone else, they had been caught in the now decade-long oil crisis, which had, perhaps, officially begun in September of 2000 with the gasoline and truck diesel shortages that had virtually brought Britain, France and Germany to an automotive halt. Things had seemed to be up and down since then, but a careful observer could see that the situation was really always getting worse.

And now, no one, not even the rosiest optimist, could deny that fuel, heating oil and gasoline prices were three or four times higher than the 2000 level. And that had been considered ridiculously unacceptable. All of Western so-called civilization was declining because of its total automotive dependence on Middle Eastern oil.

Of course, even last year, the heating oil problem had begun to be partly alleviated because coal oil, once obsolete, had come onto the market in barrel quantities. Coal mines in the United States and Europe were once again being worked with pre-World War II frenzy. The problem with coal oil was that while it could be converted to heating oil that would work in some modern home furnaces (others had to be modified to burn it), it could not be cracked to a sufficiently high octane to replace gasoline. Jester's boiler usually burned coal oil, now that it had become more readily available, but it could burn wood and even cardboard in a pinch.

Some countries had committed themselves heavily to nuclear power years before. France was one of them. There was sufficient electricity, if rationed, unless some reactor went critical and poisoned the environment for thousands of years. So, it really boiled down to a crisis in personal transportation and the transportation of goods.

Of course, some petrochemical industries, like plastics, were directly and drastically affected by the petroleum crisis. In the meantime – that is, now – there was increasing unemployment in some industrial sectors and in the transportation industry.

There was also some substantial absolute loss of agricultural productivity because that 'industry' had become so mechanized. So, actual shortages and distributional shortages, combined with rising unemployment, were causing social problems – like the summer's riots and vandalism.

As far as boats were concerned, they used a lot of fuel, and unless you happened to be a fisherman or a part-time bargee like me, boats didn't get you to work. Assuming you still had a job, that is. Most people had long since sacrificed their day-sailers and motorboats as unnecessary luxuries. And such local would-be weekend sailors were the real bread-and-butter of a marina like Chantereyne. Only the relatively few truly wealthy local people could afford their yachts now, and they now represented Chantereyne's remaining clientele. Perhaps, they even flaunted being Chantereyne's clientele and enjoyed reliance on fences and armed guards.

I carefully crossed the broad Avenue Millet, though there wasn't much traffic at this hour. For that matter, there wasn't much motorized traffic at all. I saw many bicycles and dodged them politely. I still headed for the Pâtisserie Paris in Place de Gaulle. This would be open, and, in fact, seemed never to close so far as I could tell. Boat people had known of it under the same name for over forty years, although the probability was that it had changed management several times.

Mind you, my agenda had changed. I was no longer in search of breakfast but looking for an Internet Café I had noticed nearby last summer. The breeze off the Atlantic, remnants of the Channel storm, made the Club Nautique Sportif's water too choppy for my satellite dish. Aside from that, though, Matilde's news had brought me to a decision about Joëlle. In many ways, it was a surprising decision, even for me. But perhaps it suited the new times.

The Internet Café was still there and, walking toward it, I passed ordinary gendarmes and the occasional tough

French paratrooper patrolling the sidewalks of Cherbourg. Beggars asked me for 'spare change' on the way, but they did it politely and were not bothered by the flics or the military. One got the impression, however, that if anyone tried to snatch a purse, for example, he or she would be gunned down without much ado. I couldn't decide whether I favoured this policy or not.

Many of those begging looked able-bodied, but they did nothing except beg. Probably, they had never contributed any creativity or beauty to society but had lived on welfare and the generous French unemployment supplements during the good times.

I purposefully stopped in front of a strong-looking but spare-framed middle aged woman who was playing a Breton harp with her case open for donations. Her long black and clean-looking hair was neatly braided and moderately streaked with grey. She was putting her heart, or soul, into a Breton tune that I had vaguely heard before. Her closed eyes looked dreamy and she swayed to the music, as she played in jeans even scruffier than mine.

I stopped and listened appreciatively for some minutes, I suppose. Then I tossed a two Euro coin into the harp's open case and, listening some more while studying those eyes and strong jaw quite carefully, stepped closer as if truly enraptured with the music. And I was enraptured. I glanced around and saw no one paying any attention. I then shoved a 50-Euro note, letting her suddenly opened dark brown eyes see it in my partly closed palm, into the pocket of her tatty windbreaker as I supposedly bent to tie my Nike. She nodded.

On sheer impulse, I asked: "Voulez-vous voyager à Brittany… er… Bretagne… par bateau?"

She looked puzzled for only a second at my atrocious French, then missed a chord on the harp, looking me up and down. My eyes looked at her guilelessly because I was, indeed, guileless. She was not particularly attractive, and I was still some years too young to settle for someone like her. Behind her was a shopping cart filled with plastic bags. I didn't know whether they belonged to her or not.

"Mais, oui," she said, but cautiously.

"Il y a beaucoup de travail, bien sûr," I said, "mais pas de lourd."

She gave a ghost of a smile, but said, "Maintenant?"

"Non," I said, looking at my watch, "restez ici une heure jusqu'à je retournera."

"Oui." She said it firmly, and nodded. And smiled.

In the Internet Café, I first e-mailed Joëlle in Aiguillon, both to her personal address and to her workplace in Agen. I had been composing it since I had spoken with Matilde in the Club Nautique Sportif. It was in English, the language (these days) of commerce, since Joëlle was fluent in English, albeit in a strange way sometimes, being a Business Administration graduate.

Dear Joëlle:

I am in Cherbourg headed for Aiguillon.

Left London yesterday because Mariko and I decided, mutually, that things could not work with our differing plans.

It may be a time for children, if ever there was one, not a time to hold off for better conditions. They won't get better. They will get worse. In some ways, I wish I could say I want to marry you and have children. I cannot say this, or do it, because my heart has been broken once with Mei Ling and again with Mariko O'Shaugnessey. There is not a whole heart left for you and I, for one, will settle for nothing less in a marriage.

However, I am willing to make financial provision for you as my sole beneficiary and very generous provision if there should be any children of our union. And I expect you to work, as you have been doing, until and unless children come of our union.

That is, things would continue as they were in Narbonne

and Moissac, except that some financial security for you would be spelled out in a legal Agreement.

Emotionally, a 'marriage under the Goddess and Greenwood', would be satisfactory and meaningful for me, so long as it is equal-equal. That is, I am willing to pay a certain amount for you, and you must be willing to demonstrate that you're mine sexually and in terms of life commitment, such as I can manage a life commitment.

I must be free to roam, as always and as before, and there will be from me no promise of fidelity, as I expect from you. I will take care of you and our children to the best of my ability always, by the Goddess.

Otherwise, Joëlle, I will return to Aiguillon, to the home I secured for all of us and occupy the room you earmarked for me and the position in the partnership I have earned, free to choose anyone as a public consort. You would be welcome to stay at/in the warehouse so long as you pay your way in the partnership.

Please reply at your soonest convenience.

Marc Rennsalaer

Now, I admit that this was not a stellar composition as love letters go, but I was rushed. I looked up on Lloyd's, and also on the Cherbourg website, the outward-bound cargoes available. Finally, I discovered that there was a cargo of Calvados available at the commercial wharves in Cherbourg and it had been waiting there for three weeks. The telephone number and e-mail address of the shipping agent were given on the Cherbourg 'waterfront cargoes' website.

Eventually, with e-mails back and forth, I provisionally bought four and a half tonnes, almost five tons, of Calvados out of a 10-tonne total consignment on the wharf. It was going for what I thought was a very reasonable price from a small local vintner – subject to my random testing of each crate of bottles to determine whether the contents were actually Calvados of a fair quality. I knew very little about Calvados, certainly not what constituted good or bad Calvados. I knew the bare basics.

Calvados is apple brandy. It is distilled from apple cider and is produced mostly in the Calvados province of France, which is near Normandy. Some is also produced in Normandy and Brittany. Now, I had learned two things from my seven years of carrying cargo on the canals of France. The first was that Jester, without a barge to push, was herself limited to only about five tons of useful carrying capacity and had to carry high-value cargoes. The second thing, learned from Bouchard, was that the southern French preferred wines and spirits from the north, while the northern French preferred wines and spirits from the south or the Midi.

Since I was ultimately headed for Aiguillon, almost in the middle of the Midi, as it were, I wanted to ship a five-ton cargo of some northern specialty. Like Calvados. I needed someone who knew something about Calvados. That's why I had approached the woman playing the Breton harp. Anyone who knew that tune really had to be from Brittany, and any intelligent Breton knew more about Calvados than I did. And I knew the harpist was intelligent. Her eyes had been bright, appraising and friendly but worldly wise.

By the time this was all arranged through the Internet, Joëlle had responded. It was simple: "I gladly choose the Goddess and the Greenwood, if that's all I can have. And a legal agreement incorporating financial security for any children that may come from our union. And I understand your conditions."

I noted that she had written from her workplace. It wasn't a stellar acceptance of an odd relationship, either, but perhaps she had also been rushed. Then again, she had always been businesslike. My reply was even more businesslike.

> Probably arriving Aiguillon with 4.5 tonne cargo of Calvados. Assure my share of warehouse space. Try to get buyers through Philippe, Raoul, Bouchard or your

own contacts. See you about three weeks.

After sending this romantic billet doux to my… er… consort or girlfriend, I left the Internet Café and strolled back toward the source of rare Breton music.

Half expecting my Breton harpist to be gone, I was somewhat surprised to find her still where I had left her. Seeing me approach along the sidewalk, she gathered her money from the case – and actually she had made a fair amount of it – and carefully stowed the harp down inside it, handling it like a baby.

Perhaps babies were on my mind.

She snapped the case shut and, checking the snap-locks very carefully (an action I liked), she lifted it up and put it in the top of a shopping cart that otherwise held orange plastic bags and began to walk beside me. So, I had collected a street dweller.

"Votre nom…?" I asked.

"Mélusine," she said.

"Certainement," I said, "c'est un nom… er… de plume, ou de théâtre. Pas le vrai."

Mélusine was the legendary daughter of legendary King Gradlon of Lyonesse. When the sea level rose and flooded Lyonesse, Gradlon was forced to relocate to the Brittany mainland, then called Cornouaille, and established his capital at the town of Quimper. This was supposed to have happened about the 6th century, or roughly about the time of King Arthur. There's a monument to King Gradlon in Quimper to this day, although I had never seen it.

Mélusine, however, was drowned in the flood. She was supposed to have been a fairy with marine inclinations. She could transform herself into a fish.

"Oui. Je suis écrivaine… et aussi une professeure."

"De quoi?" I saw her wince.

"L'histoire orale de la Bretagne…" She paused. "And

why don't we speak English," she said slowly in a very thick accent. Nonetheless, it was probably much less thick than my own.

"The oral history of Brittany?"

"I am from the Ile de Sein off Cornouaille. I am an acknowledged expert – by some, that is," she smiled wryly " – on the folklore and mythology of la Bretagne… Brittany. No degree or formal academic credentials, you understand. I taught for a time at the University of Western Brittany in Brest," she said proudly. "I also taught the Breton harp."

"But were one of the first to get laid off. No union card."

"Exactement… Right."

"Mélusine, do you mind if I change the subject rather abruptly? Do you know anything at all about Calvados?"

"My family used to make a little of it every year. Just for a winter solstice treat. We had only a few apple trees. I know a little. Why do you ask that, of all things?" she added.

"Because I've just bought four and a half tonnes of the stuff and I wouldn't know Calvados from turpentine."

"I can tell that much, at least."

"I can open random bottles in the cases, of course," I said, "to check the quality of the cargo. I wouldn't know if it was good or bad."

"I will know if it is good or bad if I can just sniff a bottle," Mélusine said.

"I figured that a native of Brittany would know at least that. And that's more than me."

"When do you have to… collect…? this cargo?"

"Tomorrow morning early at Wharf…" I took a scribbled note from inside the windbreaker, down in the flannel shirt's breast pocket, "… at Wharf P 19," I finished. I showed her my note. "What do you like to eat? I guess we should stop and get some groceries."

I should explain that Mélusine's shopping cart was not from any supermarket like the equipment preferred by North American street people. Supermarkets do exist in France – they are called 'grandes surfaces' – but they are not ubiquitous. And their carts are jealously guarded and well marked. These days, it might well be that a stolen supermarket cart in the hands of a street person would rate gunfire.

Mélusine's shopping cart was one of those two-wheeled lightweight affairs owned by almost every housewife in France. And this one had been scavenged, I suppose, because one of its wheels wobbled much more than the other under the load it was never designed to carry. Not knowing what I might face on the morrow with roughly 150 boxes of Calvados (24 bottles to the box), I looked around for a quincaillerie – a hardware store. One was just up the side street off the Place de Gaulle.

I bought one of those two-way dollies, but a very heavy duty one. It would serve as a vertical two-wheel dolly with pneumatic tires or, if the push-bar handle were relocated, it would serve as a four-wheel pushcart. I bought two packages of assorted bungee cords. I figured that these items would be useful in the Aiguillon warehouse anyway.

Right now, though, with a large plastic-topped plastic storage bin bungee-corded to the dolly in four-wheel pushcart mode, Mélusine's belongings fitted loosely inside with much room for the harp and for some groceries. We hung her folded-up old shopping cart from the push-bar handle with shorter bungee cords.

I managed to find some few examples of dehydrated food in a general grocery market, but we had to buy fresh vegetables, fruits, some pork chops and stewing beef. I found some canned Danish butter. At the boulangerie we got our loaf bread and croissants.

"Where are you going?" Mélusine asked. "Brittany is only a day's sail from here."

"I'm going first to Brest and then around the coast to Bordeaux. From Bordeaux to my home in Aiguillon on the Garonne près d'Agen."

"Ah," said Mélusine. "Now I understand all this food."

"Right." I added, "I have a refrigerator aboard so some of this stuff should keep. I want you to have a few really good meals... while we talk of many things."

"Like what?"

"Your Breton harp. Quelle sorte de bois? And why was your Ile de Sein the last place to be Christianized in Europe? And why were the Breton women's headdresses so much taller there? So that they became the model for our idea of a witch's hat?"

She was silent for some time after we had left the last shopping stop, with my Pirate beer from the Netherlands secured low down in the large cargo box on the dolly, but cushioned from the all-important harp.

The sun was almost at the local meridian, I estimated, when we headed back toward the Club Nautique Sportif. Mélusine didn't realize our destination, although she might have guessed it, until we crossed the Avenue Millet and ventured out onto the complex of concrete breakwaters. If I had chosen a bag lady, well, I wanted the guard to see a seaman-like dolly and not a shopping cart with wobbly wheels.

The Club Nautique Sportif's guard paid us no notice whatsoever as I inserted the plastic card and trundled over the boardwalk to *Jester*. When we came to my mooring, Mélusine stopped and took a long puzzled look at the boat. It was when she looked over the front hull's gunwale and saw Ivory with the grab-bucket in the truck's bed that she said in her accent accentuated by definitely un-French slowness of speech: "I have seen this before, this very picture of the mind."

Me, I climbed over the gunwale, around Ivory, and up the

few steps to the level of the wheelhouse on *Jester*'s rear hull. I saw that no one had tried to enter the cross-wheelhouse hatch, so I unlocked it.

"I am a seer, you know. They say I have the Sight."

"Did you maybe catch sight of some newspaper stories about two months ago? *Le Monde*, *Paris Match*, *Le Figaro*, *The International Herald-Tribune*?"

She looked up at me from the dock, perhaps a trifle angrily, but then some memories tickled her brain's synapses. "Merde!" she exclaimed. Then she smiled somewhat sheepishly up at me. "*Paris Match*. Almost the same photograph," she waved an arm inside *Jester*'s front hull, "but you… *you*… were in the picture beside *that*." She pointed to Ivory and the grab-bucket.

"Hmmm." I suppose that the photo must have been one of those taken in the Weymouth yacht club. Probably a wire service shot. Chivalry dies hard in me. I waved her brusquely aboard as I slid the wheelhouse hatch back now that it was unfettered by both mechanical and electronic locking mechanisms. I went back to clamber over the gunwale to the Club Nautique Sportif's dock. I tossed the orange garbage bags to her out of the box on the new dolly, finishing with the harp that I held very reverently and carefully out to her. "Take all that stuff below, through that hatch." I pointed. "Put the stuff that needs it into the fridge."

"The beer gets a very high priority, Mélusine," I chided, "and then use the shower at the very back of the boat." She glanced my way just once, and then bent to grasp the various plastic bags and disappeared up onto the poop and into the wheelhouse. "Watch your step," I called loudly, but as I heard no shrieks or splats of plastic bags, she was already doing that.

Me, I dismantled the dolly back to its most unobtrusive proportions and manhandled it over the gunwale. I finally just lashed it and the plastic bin down with bungee cord beside the grab-bucket in Ivory's pick-up bed.

Did Joëlle *really* believe in her Goddess as a 'Supreme Being' any more than she believed in the more usual Judeo-Christian God as a similar entity?

Once, not long after I had first met her in Narbonne, when I had first arrived in France, she had answered "Of course" to my direct query on this matter. Later she had admitted: "Not really, but the Goddess and her Good Shepherd consort is a more psychologically satisfying belief for most people. Monotheism, at least with a male 'God', makes people aggressive. Or maybe it is more true to say that aggressive people invented that God."

At last the dolly was secured to my satisfaction. I knew it wouldn't disappear overnight. Not with Matilde's fences and armed guard.

3

That night, the first of September of the year 2011, it rained in a cold, clammy and miserable drizzle.

Mélusine and I were as snug as two bugs in a rug in our bunks aboard Jester. It was undeniably true, however, that Mélusine must have been a bug that was considerably more tired than me. On the other hand, I would have to load four and a half metric tonnes of Calvados early in the morning. And I wasn't at all certain how this might go, given the events at Glastonbury and the subsequent physiotherapy. Not to mention the aches that had made themselves manifest just about twelve hours previously.

Once having the assumed luxury of a long and hot shower, she asked me about the Club Nautique Sportif's Laundromat. I told her it was next to the office down the long dock boardwalk and that she would have no trouble using it so long as she spoke first to Matilde in the office and explained that she was aboard Folderol Jester with Marc Rennsalaer in slip F18. I refused to believe Mélusine's assertion that the handle of Jester's chemical toilet was broken, or 'busted', as she finally put it and that the contrivance wouldn't flush properly. I showed her how to pull it out to get a flush, not try to pull it up. That got the usual flush. Jester's toilet was an expensive specimen of its kind. And surely there could not be another busted flush at slip F18.

Given the change I had seen her retrieve from the harp's case, I was gratified she didn't ask me for laundry money.

Anyway, she returned about an hour and a half later with her orange garbage bags looking more symmetrical and I could see folded items making their imprints within them.

During this time I had the opportunity of consulting one of the twenty favourite books that actually had covers and pages, as opposed to the almost infinite library digitally entrusted to Jester's CD-ROM library. One of these was Robert Graves' The White Goddess in its original Methuen edition of 1947. Within those pages, just as I thought I had remembered, was mention of the Ile de Sein.

It was not off the Seine River that runs though Paris as the name might suggest, but off the coast of Brittany just northwest of the entrance to Brest. According to Graves, it was the very last place to be Christianized in Europe, a deed that was done in 1654 by a shipload of Jesuits from France. They had been inspired to stamp out the few sorcerers and many more sorceresses who lured Brittany ships to crash against the Ile de Sein rocks. Graves noted that the women's traditional Brittany headdresses on the Ile de Sein were, in his time (the 1930s) still the tallest in Brittany.

Although Graves himself never said it that I know of, I had come to the conclusion that the Brittany headdresses were based on depictions of Isis with her horns that long predated 'Ancient Egypt'. Just like the Brittany Carnac long predated the Egyptian one and the name of the Ile de Ré (or 'Ra') off the Gironde estuary was older than any mention of the supposedly Egyptian sun god.

The Ile de Ré, I knew, also boasted scratched depictions of boats or small ships on some rocks, probably curraghs, which were thought to be as old as the similar ship-glyphs of Böslund in Sweden. If so, these glyphs dated from about 4000 BC, about the time of Carnac, but in the Egyptian scheme of things, Ra was a relative religious stripling dating to about 2500 BC.

After verifying my memory in this way with The White Goddess, and at least part of my own ruminations, I had sketched out a vertical axis 'windmill' or 'aeroturbine'. It had been inspired by that scrap of Mariko O'Shaugnessey's rose-wrapping paper that had performed such crazy gyrations in the Channel storm. I resolved to reproduce this configuration in Dacron cloth and aluminium tube just as soon as I could.

That meant Aiguillon. If there was anything to it, a whole host of possibilities lay behind that crazily flapping paper. Just like the scrap of parchment, or vellum, this, too, could change the world. Today's here-and-now world, at any rate.

I had finished my rough sketch of the 'wind-motor', as I called it, just as Mélusine returned with her laundry. I casually slipped the notebook-sized drawing pad into my bunk drawer with the Beretta .25 and I set Mélusine to the task of cooking dinner from the groceries we had bought. After all, waiting for machines to do laundry wasn't hard work and the 50 Euros I'd given her was a good day's salary for, say, a full professor these days.

Now, Mélusine wanted to talk after our meal of pork saddle, Brussels sprouts, cauliflower, wax beans, garlic bread and coffee.

I wanted only to go to sleep, the previous day of 36 hours, 24 of them at the helm, having depleted my resources somewhat. And the day to come promised to be difficult. So, I begged off conversation, rolled down my slatted aluminium privacy partition, and went to sleep like a log.

I didn't know Mélusine. I didn't really have to know her.

She could not get into the computer compartments aft of the galley and extending to the head. She could steal all the food she wished from the refrigerator, even my beer. Being French, she didn't like my coffee very much anyway. So be it. She could leave with her laundered clothes, a good meal, 50 Euros and not much else – unless she took a liking to the aluminium grab-bucket or the fairly heavy new dolly. In the night, I didn't think she could get them past the guard at the gate. She was welcome to her own shopping cart.

I must have gone to the head during the night. Some of the muscle relaxants, painkillers and anti-depressants that had been prescribed for me had that sort of side effect, although it seemed to be wearing off now. And I must have forgotten all about Mélusine's being aboard. That's the only explanation

I can give for crashing back in 'my' habitual bunk at some wee hour without pulling down the privacy partition and snicking its simple tab lock. It was another indication that my concentration had slipped during the secure days and nights in London.

At any rate, I woke up at my usual time to the delightful smell of Colombian coffee, flat on my back on my bunk with the usual male morning erection. I opened my eyes at once – I'm not one of those people who seem to need to doze in bed, half-awake, for anything from five minutes to half an hour – to find Mélusine sketching me on a large pad of drawing paper that was balanced on her knees. I opened my eyes just as she had glanced at me and was in the process of re-focusing on her work. My right hand moved in an instinctive attempt to cover myself.

"Non, s'il vous plaît," she said. "Vous êtes d'une beauté exquise… juste comme vous êtes." She smiled and sketched briskly. "Do you mind not moving for another minute or so? You are… beautiful… just as you are. I'm almost finished."

So, I just lay there, feeling somewhat embarrassed, but going along with it. My erection didn't seem to get any smaller, but harder. "Even with this?"

"Mostly because of that," she said. "Totally male… and very beautiful." She busied herself with scratching that sounded to me like a charcoal pencil on rough textured paper. I noticed that she was dressed for the kind of work I had described: clean jeans, a spotless shirt collar and a bulky knit sweater, with Nikes a lot less disreputable than my own.

She stopped her scratching with the pencil and regarded her work at arm's length. "Voila," she said. "Not too bad. You have too many scars," she added. She handed the sketchpad to me casually and arose from the bunk to disappear the few steps beyond the bulkhead into the galley. I heard coffee being poured. Mélusine's drawing of me was at first somewhat embarrassing because it was unashamedly anatomical and accurate. The line was extremely economical while yet conveying form and texture – and something more. She had depicted me in a somewhat troubled sleep, not comfortable relaxation. And she was right about the scars. My latest acquisition, the hole in the shoulder from the sharp end of a boat hook, no longer bled or leaked clear fluid. It had closed up, but was still pink. That was another thing I would have to watch while loading the Calvados.

She came back from the galley with my coffee creamed and sweetened as she'd seen me do it last night. I swung my legs off the bed, still looking at her sketch and still with a substantial erection. I took the cup and handed her back her drawing pad. "I'm really no judge," I said. "I think it is more than just very good. It is rather … exceptional."

"Do you want me to get rid of it?"

"The drawing? Of course not."

"Thank you," she said. "I would like to keep it." She folded the pages over and set the drawing pad beside her on the bunk. "Do you want to keep it," she asked, nodding slightly but unmistakably between my knees.

"Mélusine," I said, "the fifty Euros were not for… er… services rendered." She looked puzzled, so I said, "n'était pas pour les services rendus."

She still looked a bit puzzled, but then she smilingly shook her head. "I know that… very well…" she responded in her thick accent. "It would be my… fun… où plaisir. After all," she smiled again, "I stole a model. And I am very good with the hands."

I discovered that I was getting embarrassed. "Not this morning, thank you," I said. I stood up, which brought me closer to her in Jester's narrow central corridor and handed her my still-full cup. That was to keep her hands busy. She looked at me unabashedly, ignoring the cup. "Vous êtes très, très beau," she said. "Mais beaucoup de douleur… how do you say… much… pain."

That, perhaps, was true enough. I turned away from her and rummaged in my bunk drawers for some clean underwear. And then, taking the cup from her, I went the few steps into the galley and set the cup down on the small counter space.

"Les couilles, the balles, elles semblent très… très… dûres," she said.

That was also true enough. I went on down the corridor to the head and revelled in a short, hot shower. It was impossible, even ridiculous, to try to be politically correct in French. Even male and female body parts sometimes have the opposite gender as words. Even something less personal, like, say, the name of the early medieval king, Pepin the Short, would become 'Pépin, le verticalement défié' – or roughly Pepin the Vertically Challenged – in English politically correct translation. But in French it makes absolutely no sense whatsoever. The closest you can come is 'defied by verticalness' as if Pepin were trying to climb a wall. And Anglo-Saxons think that the French are over-emotional?

By the time I had my shower, and then peed, the erection was largely gone, of course, and the underwear bulged only a little. Mélusine shook her head slightly when I returned, but said nothing when I stretched into my jeans and started to dress. Armoured, as it were, I retrieved my coffee and drank it at the counter while making another Havarti and roast beef sandwich. I ambled back toward the bunks, chewing a bite. Mélusine shivered slightly at the sight of the sandwich. I saw the remains of a croissant on her drawing pad.

"Sorry," I said, pointing up. "There's a table that can come down between the bunks. A bit more civilized, but I usually don't bother with it. I forgot." I reached up, not all that far with bare headroom, of course, and swivelled the spring-loaded table down between the bunks. It covered at least part of the length of the two bunks. It was a barrier of sorts between us. Still without a plate or saucer, I transferred my sandwich to the table's wooden surface and squeezed past the end of it to get another cup of coffee. Mélusine was looking at me, I saw her shrug, and transferred her cup and croissant to the table too. On impulse, while in the galley, I collected two saucers from the small cupboard and returned with them. The remainder of our breakfast was, indeed, more civilized. She asked, and I recounted, much of the same story she had read in Paris Match. I told her only the story that had been in the newspapers, the one that Mariko and I had concocted, then had analysed for flaws and then had rehearsed for days and days and days on the Brittany canals en route for Weymouth and fateful Glastonbury. Mélusine asked many questions, none of them very insightful or threatening to the much-published canon.

Apparently the reliquary and parchment had been of great interest at the University of Western Brittany when the story broke. Some faculty and students had wondered, not very politely, if the parchment had really been recovered from Brittany waters and not in international ones. Perhaps it really belonged to France?

If they only knew the truth.

I assured Mélusine that the treasure had truly been discovered in international waters, just like the papers said. And I told her that as far as I knew, Mariko O'Shaugnessey's translation would be out in good time for Christmas, probably sometime in late October. I could tell her truthfully that Mariko's first crack at translation had long been done and that her second polishing and revisions were almost finished.

And then it was time to find Wharf P19 and load the Calvados. I asked Mélusine to go on deck and admire the scenery while she studied the harbour map and tried to locate P19. I had to unlock my secret cache and retrieve enough money to pay for the cargo. I put the cash in a money-belt and threaded that under the flannel shirt. I came on deck with the Walther under the bulky windbreaker.

4

As it turned out, finding Wharf P19 proved to be harder than actually loading the Calvados. The wharf seemed to be stuck into the back corner of the big commercial harbour and it had obviously been intended for smaller boats. For all I knew, it was intended for local fishing boats and the very smallest of coastal freighters. At least, that was the impression I got from the fishy smell of the wharf and its modest height. It also had a concrete ramp from the water level up to the concrete and stone wharf and a covered warehouse behind a modest open expanse used for loading. This was perfect for Jester and Ivory.

Now Ivory, painted dark blue, was an anagram for 'Integrated Vehicle On Rennsalaer's Yacht'. It was powered by compressed air turning a modified two-stroke motorcycle engine. It was amphibious and versatile. Mariko had called it Achilles when it had been powered by the old modified Norton 500cc single-piston that tended to rust a bit after every immersion. It made, she had said, 'a fearful clatter of arms' – the Homeric epithet of Achilles – every time it started up. Achilles, too, had been reluctant to enter the fray, in his case the Trojan War. With the engine transplant to the all-aluminium Kawasaki made in Roche Bernard during the past summer, it clattered on start-up no more. All I had to do was undo all the ties that held the dolly and grab-bucket and newly-acquired plastic bin, remove all three, find somewhere out of the way for the grab-bucket and bin, and throw the dolly in the back of the vehicle's bed again.

I drove straight off Jester and up the ramp. Mélusine met me at the working level of the wharf and clambered over the doorless side. I explained to the wharf foreman what I was after. He pointed down one of the long aisles of the warehouse to where a stocky figure stood already waiting, and looking at his watch impatiently, beside a modest ziggurat composed of cardboard cases. We wuffled off, as directed, in his direction.

We passed cargo like debarked and trimmed lodge pole pine logs about twenty feet long, fence rails or ceiling beams, cartons of farm-preserved bottles of whole tomatoes in oil, local homemade (or farm-made) pâté, and many stacks of local bottled wine in cartons. There were more stacks of grain in cloth bags than anything else – wheat, barley and oats – and these grains contributed the dominant smell of the warehouse. And a nice, earthy and wholesome smell it was, too. None of the stacks of goods was very large. This was, indeed, a wharf for very local produce.

Me, I revelled in this warehouse and these kinds of cargoes. There was something timeless about it. Things had been much the same on the wharves of Sumeria five thousand years ago, on those of Rome two thousand years ago and on medieval wharves right here in France until about a hundred years ago. This warehouse and these small cargoes were the way of the future, although they were still overshadowed now by the huge ocean freighters carrying 50,000 tons of wheat from Canada, the United States, Argentina and Australia.

This would gradually cease and, in fact, was declining daily as anyone could read on Lloyd's website. North American agribusiness was already so mechanized that the fuel crisis was cutting deeply into production. And the soil of North America's prairies, once (for a brief time) the breadbasket of the world, was so depleted by chemical fertilizers that the yield-per-acre was already declining, and was propped up only by ever-newer chemical combinations and genetically modified grain that could accept them as nutrients. The entire 20th century house of agricultural cards was folding in upon itself, and had been doing so for some years.

It was this local produce, using little mechanization, fewer chemical fertilizers and disdaining genetically specialized strains of age-old organisms selected only by nature and human knowledge of it, that would survive to sustain the next century, the 21st, ours. The unknown answer to the unspoken question was a simple one. How many people could the old-new agriculture sustain? The old-new transportation methods, like Jester? I had given this a great deal of thought.

I had concluded that the present world might, if we were very lucky, represent the level of about 1930. If we were not so lucky, we could sustain a level of civilization and living of, perhaps, 1850-1870. In the first 'very lucky' scenario, only about half the present population would have to die. In the second, not-so-lucky scenario, two-thirds of the population would have to die.

Whether it would be the 1930 or the 1850-1870 scenario depended largely on the strength of Socialist politics and Socialist sentiments. That is, whether in a political movement to save as many people as possible (whether they had contributed anything or not beyond their over-rated sheer existence) we would fall from 1930 to about 1850-1870.

I figured that if we were courageous enough to accept the losses of mostly useless people now, we could hold the line at 1930 more or less. Misguided policies of 'humanism' to alleviate the shortages with 'equalization' would definitely and inexorably push us back to about 1850-1870.

No matter what, I had long ago resolved to be part of the surviving population, that half to one-third. At the end of my cogitation, I saw that it was really a genetic battle.

I thought that my genes and being, since I had been a soldier, writer and inventor, were worth more to humanity's present and future than the genes of anyone who had not contributed any courage, creativity or commitment to the world.

I always kept in mind that this attitude had to be softened by appreciation for the kinds of courage, creativity and commitment that I did not happen to manifest within my own psyche and behaviour. That's why I had proposed a long-term agreement to Joëlle. That's why someone who claimed to be named Mélusine was beside me in the passenger seat of Ivory. For lack of a better word, I called this 'Chivalry'. It was tempered by open-mindedness and as much humility as I could manage.

The little man, in a somewhat rumpled suit and a ragged moustache proved to be the shipping agent. We said a few words of hasty greeting, shook hands, and started checking out the Calvados. The agent had already borrowed one of the wharf's ingenious manually operated and purely mechanical light-duty forklifts.

I took a very careful look at this clever contraption composed mostly, it seemed, of bicycle sprockets and chains. It required no fuel except muscle-power, but was a wheel-supported forklift that could lift a skid of 250 kilos (call it 500 to 550 pounds). I studied it carefully, thinking of the warehouse at Aiguillon, while Mélusine asked the agent to open a bottle in a case with his corkscrew. He'd also brought a bag of many extra corks and a cork-inserting tool.

Mélusine came up to me while I was more or less memorizing the forklift's innards. "This is very good Calvados," she whispered. "In fact, I have had far worse in good restaurants. It has preserved the true aroma of the autumn, as Calvados should."

So, as Mélusine sampled a bottle from each case, and as soon as the corks were replaced, I took a load of ten cases back to Jester tied up at the ramp. I had to stow the cases so that they would not shift. This took a few minutes with each load so that by the time I returned another load was usually waiting for me. I noticed that Mélusine did reject some cases and they were stacked to the side of the principal pile. Once, when I came back for another load, I had to wait while the corks were replaced in the bottles of two or three cases. "What's wrong with those," I asked, pointing to the apparently rejected cartons.

"They smelled bitter to me," said Mélusine. "I think they were from apple trees that grew on a side of the orchard near a road or highway. The trees, they were not happy breathing car exhaust. They made bitter cider. So, bitter Calvados."

I had to drive nineteen times back and forth to Jester before all my cargo was loaded. The agent perched aboard Ivory with Mélusine as we wuffled the last trip up the long aisle toward the rectangular glare of sunlight at the far end of the wharf's warehouse. It was getting warm, but I just unzipped my windbreaker. His count and Mélusine's tallied: 157 cases. At our agreed price, the cost of the cargo was a bit less than 12,000 Euros. I went into a far corner in the shadows and counted out the exact amount from my money-belt. I kept a firm hand on it and stuffed it down into my jeans.

The agent took the wad, counted it carefully, and gave me a floridly stamped Bill of Sale denoting the 157 cartons of 24 1-litre bottles each of Calvados. Another stamp, this time from his pocket, said 'Cherbourg' in grand letters over his signature. And so we parted, shaking hands again, and I took his business card. On the back of it he wrote the name of the vintner – if that's the proper word for someone who produces apple cider and Calvados. The whole transaction and loading had taken about three hours.

Mélusine and I were careful with the huge plastic-weave tarp I selected from my collection. This cargo of neatly rectangular cartons made a welcome change from this past summer's crazy cargo of Marcel Bouchard's small wooden wine casks. Ivory was invisible and unobtrusive, being loaded with cartons itself while others were stacked close beside it and all around and then as far forward as the ramp-door of the forward hull. We fitted the corners of the tarp at each corner, and wrapped the nylon belts around the whole lading, until it was maybe the neatest cargo I had ever shipped. It made a compact kind of wedge inside Jester because I had stacked most of the weight up near the rear hull, of course, to keep Jester's proper trim. This manner of loading effectively used the rear hull's flotation even though no cargo was stacked in the cabin.

Under power, I backed Jester away from the warehouse's ramp. Mélusine helped to secure Jester's landing craft-style ramp door and fold out the cutwater extension again. I let her bolt down the Chinese floor since my back and shoulder were starting to ache. When we were through, I decided, on impulse, to head back to the Club Nautique Sportif. I knew they had plenty of berths and the sky in the west was building up some clouds, I thought.

"How much is it worth," asked Mélusine beside me up on the poop with her knees over one of the great hinges.

"My guess would be about 40,000 Euros in Bordeaux, Agen or Narbonne," I said. "But it would have to be sold in very small quantities to get that price. Carton by carton, almost bottle by bottle. To restaurants."

"And how much did it cost just now, if you do not mind my asking?"

"A very little less than 12,000 Euros," I said.

"That's quite a lot of profit."

"Is it? On the other hand, I have to get it there in one piece. To Narbonne? Call it 600 kilometres from here. I usually travel by canal – for safety's sake – and that's fuel all the way. Still," I conceded, "if you're careful, lucky and shrewd, you can make a good living. That's more than most people these days."

"Yes."

"I thought about these times coming over ten years ago. So I worked while others played. I had this boat made and I came here where, I figured, I could work along the canals when the bad times started."

"Yes, I know." She paused. "When are you headed for Brittany?"

I pointed toward the west where some potentially troublesome clouds were assembling, as if for attack. She followed my pointing finger. "Tomorrow, if the weather's good. I cannot take a chance on the hundred miles across the Gulf of St. Malo with this cargo. Do you feel how heavy the boat seems now?"

She nodded. "I think that would be wise."

When I came back into the Club Nautique Sportif, I eased into a berth. Mélusine squeezed past me down the hatchway. I tied up securely and went to explain everything to Matilde, saying that I would pay for another day's mooring if it did not look more promising by nightfall. I then went back to Jester, looking at her trim and computing all the intangibles I had learned in the Channel storm. She was down by the bows, of course, by almost a foot, leaving three feet of freeboard forward and not the usual four. Was it foolish to do what was in the back of my mind? And, of course, it was now September – that time of the year.

I went below to find that Mélusine had washed the few dishes from this morning, made up both bunks into passable day beds and was cooking a big lunch. She had gotten a pot of coffee going, too. I pulled the table back down so that we could enjoy luncheon in a civilized manner. Until the lunch materialized, I took out a chart and began some measuring. Mélusine glanced at me every once in a while.

Now, I could coast along the southern shore of the Cotentin Peninsula, with the Channel Islands of Guernsey and Jersey (and many smaller ones) as something of a breakwater against the open Atlantic weather, and enter the Brittany Canals at St. Malo. This would be the safe and prudent passage. From St. Malo, I could eventually reach Aiguillon by an all-inland canal route. The operative word was 'eventually'. I estimated that this route would require about three weeks, if I pushed it. The odds were very heavily in my favour, almost certain, that I would actually reach Aiguillon with the Calvados.

On the other hand, given Jester's newly discovered seaworthiness, I could, just possibly, take several chances.

First, I could sail direct for Brest across the mouth of the Gulf of St. Malo. This would still not be too dangerous because it was only about a hundred miles to Brest and I could always run into the Gulf of St. Malo in threatening weather and find a haven in the lee of several islands, some large and some small. This passage would take about eight to ten hours, with a good Atlantic breeze. It could take as long as 24 hours under sail, the same 10 hours under power – but that used fuel, coal oil. That was the minor temptation.

Then came the horrible temptation, the Devil's own concoction.

Dare I sail direct from Brest to the mouth of the Gironde? Across the notorious Bay of Biscay? When the season had just turned to equally notorious September? This was the month of equinoctial storms. It was a damned fool idea.

But one could have good weather luck, even in September in the Bay of Biscay, especially if one paid very close attention to the forecasts. The chart said that Brest was about 28 hours from the mouth of the Gironde – if Jester could make ten knots, that is.

And perhaps only a craft like Jester could be expected to make ten knots laden. An Indonesian orembai was a sort of cross between a mono-hull and a multi-hull. Lightly loaded, it was a multi-hull. Heavily loaded it was virtually a Chinese junk, a mono-hull. I had rendered this concept in steel and aluminium and specifically, the long wide keel under the forward and rear parts of the hull worked to trim Jester. I could blow compressed air into several compartments in this keel under the front hull and force part of the free water ballast out through small holes in the bottom. If the welds were still air tight.

This would raise Jester's front hull. In theory, it might raise the front hull sufficiently to reduce the surface friction considerably. With this load, Jester could not become a true multi-hull. She could almost become a multi-hull. Perhaps she could make those ten knots – with a good and constant breeze of about fifteen knots out of the west.

The trouble was, I had never tried it. Not once during the past ten years. If it worked as I had designed it so long ago, I could possibly make Aiguillon in about seven days instead of three times as long. The Chinese cutwater extension had worked in the Channel storm.

The down side of this diabolical plan was that I would not make Aiguillon at all, being somewhere at the bottom of the Bay of Biscay for eternity instead of on the inland canals for three extra weeks. I figured I should be able to ride out almost any storm if I jettisoned the Calvados cargo. Of course, the cargo of Calvados was intended for Aiguillon, and in several ways. And did I have the sheer strength to jettison this cargo quickly enough if worse came to worst? Altogether, it was a pretty problem of probabilities. It kept me occupied until Mélusine asked if she could serve lunch.

I talked to her about this while we enjoyed her rice-and-onion-stuffed spicy tomatoes with a delicious cheese topping and, once again, equally delicious garlic bread. I showed her the charts and the distances, giving her the dividers. "Mélusine," I said, "you are a truly excellent cook."

"Ah, but you have truly excellent… pots…? pans?"

"Call it cookware." I had bought some extremely upscale copper-bottomed thick stainless steel cookware when I had outfitted Jester almost a decade ago. This alone seemed to have cost a minor fortune. And I had bought a few other implements since that Joëlle had recommended from time to time. And I had used them. The Magdalene Mandala adventure had interrupted my self-taught course in Languedoc and Roussillon cookery that had even impressed

Mariko O'Shaugnessey.

In London, we had eaten to live and not the other way around in the approved French manner. We shopped at the giant Tesco supermarket a long block westward from the Kensington Arms at the intersection of Earlscourt. I had to admit that Tesco's stock of ready-to-cook prepared meats and prepared vegetable ensembles far surpassed anything I had seen in the United States or Canada. The mix of tastes was well chosen and nutritious, the basic and all-important quality of the vegetable components was very high, the seasonings added were imaginative and piquant without being over-bearing and the packaging was both thrifty and highly practical. During seven years in France I had never seen a supermarket even remotely approaching Tesco's high standards.

Nonetheless, even Tesco's pre-prepared dinner components could not compare with Mélusine's productions. These bordered on true gastronomie.

Mélusine glanced up from the charts. "I understand the... chance... the gamble," she finally said. "Do you mind if I try something?"

"Go ahead," I said. "I am interested."

She closed her eyes and spread her hands out, finger extended. She held her hands out just above the surface of the chart and moved them back and forth over the two legs of my course. First, from Cotentin to Brittany. Back and forth, back and forth. This went on for some time and I would normally have become impatient, but I remembered that I had nothing else to do this afternoon except for watching cloud accumulation. Finally, she finished and looked at me. "The... voyage from Cherbourg to Brest will be no problem... but we will leave unexpectedly tonight. You will be in Brest all day tomorrow, however."

Then she turned her attention to that crazy Brest-Gironde crossing of the entire Bay of Biscay. This took even longer, and her expression was sometimes pained, but it gradually brightened. She looked up at me and her eyes seemed troubled. "It is like this," she said. "On the whole, it will go well, if you set out when a storm is approaching Brest. It will… go away… but only for a day or longer because it will go to the south. Then it will come in your direction here…" she pointed at the mouth of the Gironde. "If you know this, you will try to get into the Gironde as quickly as possible."

"I would do that, for damned sure, anyway," Mélusine.

"Yes, but you must make every effort from here…" she pointed offshore of the Ile de Ré "… or there will be a disaster. I see death, perhaps."

I swivelled the chart toward me and pointed as I spoke. "The Cherbourg to Brest leg…"

"La jambe?" she said, obviously puzzled.

"Er… part… segment," I said slowly and saw her finally nod. "Well, I had already figured that it would be pretty much like that – without the Sight – just with navigation. It is the Brest to the Gironde… *jambe*… that bothers me," I said.

"Yes, I know that bothers you. But this journey is all one… one… movement." She shrugged, but I nodded. "We must leave Cherbourg when the weather seems threatening because that is part of the same storm that will move comme ça…" her finger scrolled over the chart in an arc to the southeast, "… to hit you there." Her finger stabbed precisely where she had indicated previously – some miles northwest of the Ile de Ré. "That is why, even if the weather seems good there, you must make all energy to get to here." Her finger tapped inside the Gironde estuary.

Now, although Mélusine probably did not know it… except, perhaps, from ages of lore on the Ile de Sein… what she was describing was a weather pattern I had intuited from the occasional Bay of Biscay weather report I had happened to hear. The Atlantic coast had not been my area of operation during my years in France. I had stuck to canals, from Bordeaux to Narbonne, mostly, with the odd trip as far as Marseilles. I had noticed, or had seemed to notice, that some (not all) Atlantic storms seemed almost to hit the Cotentin Peninsula and then sort of bounce off the land to arc southeastward to hit hard at about the Ile de Ré. They made a mess of the Bay of Biscay en route. I had seen a photograph once that still provoked nightmares. A 60,000-ton battleship awash back to the bridge in huge waves with the mild caption: 'Heavy weather in the Bay of Biscay.'

I regarded Mélusine speculatively across the table.

"Oui?" she said.

"Well, if you are correct about the first leg, you get to Brest tomorrow and that's that. If you're wrong about the Brest to Gironde jambe, I'll probably be lost at sea with Jester and the Calvados. If I take this crazy gamble, you'll think of me from time to time, won't you?" I smiled.

Then she really surprised me. "I will go with you from Brest to the Gironde," she said. "Besides, you will need me. I must play the harp and enchant the storm here," she pointed northwest of the Ile de Ré again. "So that you can get safely there." And her fingernail moved down into the Gironde again.

"If this is witchcraft…"

"Wicca."

"– it sure takes at least some of the luck out of being a successful trader."

"It always did, in the old days," she said, regarding me steadily. "A good trader always needed luck too. But that is the… ah… département… of a capricious god, not a judicious goddess."

"Hmmm." I paused for along minute. "Yes. Loki."

"We do not often speak of Loki. He is… how do you say…? A bump… in the patterns."

"Okay, Mélusine, how will you get back to your beloved Brittany? Of course, if this works it will save me a lot of money and time. Time is money, come to that. I will give you some train fare and some extra living money."

"Thank you, Marc Rennsalaer, I know you by now and I trust you. There are bigger patterns at work here than you can see, I think. It may be that I shall not see Brittany for a very long time. There is a college of dru... of... us, in Bordeaux, so I shall not be lonely in the south. You need me now, I think. Also..." she sounded puzzled, "... there is a woman somewhere in this pattern. She is very special, but she does not yet know what she is. She has had no teacher." She said this in a sort of sing-song and dissociated way. Maybe she was just mildly deranged. And I was considering taking on the Bay of Biscay in September with someone who would 'enchant' the storm with a bog oak harp? I was the one who was deranged, and not mildly. Perhaps Mélusine was contagious.

"Hmmm." She was correct, in a way. For I was feeling some sort of urgency about reaching Aiguillon, an urgency I could not quite define. It was a sense of great peril – for Joëlle? – that caused me to consider the crazy plan at all.

I went topside and had a long look at Jester and Ivory. The reason why the vehicle was 'integrated' was that Ivory carried all the tanks for compressed air. The compressor itself was aboard Jester and was run by the steam engine. Ivory's tanks of compressed air were 'fuel' for the vehicle, but also a reservoir of 'fuel' or 'propulsion' for the air-cannons in the whistle-tubes that flanked the smokestack.

These air-cannons had won the battle of the Lac des Doigts against the Scandinavian Sleipnir attack helicopter. And Ivory had saved our lives off Le Croisic – when Mariko had renamed the vehicle 'Victory' – 'Vehicular Integrated Compression Tanks on Rennsalaer's Yacht'. This had been a peace feeler against my American penchant for anagram-assault.

Crouched beside the wheelhouse, I turned on the

compressor – I always left the steam engine ticking over on 'simmer', about 50 revs. The thing had enough torque, God knows, to take the extra load of the compressor with only a minor upward adjustment of coal oil to the boiler. Even though Ivory was covered by the tarp, I could see from the compressor's gauge that the air pressure was building up toward 175psi in all the ten scavenged scuba tanks.

Atmospheric pressure was only about 15psi, give or take, so I valved some of the air from wheelhouse levers into the floodable compartments of the keel under Jester's front hull. I had never tried this, except when testing the boat when it was first launched back in Toronto almost ten years ago, during my seven-plus years on the French canals. I had covered all the air hoses with 'Longlife Rubber Conditioner' religiously every three months and I had checked the bicycle-type valves of the rubber nipples at the same interval.

Now, came the acid test, with five tons (more or less) of Calvados in the front hull, but with (as I have explained) most of that weight snuggled up against the immense flotation of the rear hull. The great stainless steel hinges, plus the vertical stainless steel box-sections joining the two hulls in stainless steel sleeves, took the stress of this weight.

I clambered down to the dock and saw bubbles all around Jester. The front hull came up out of the water several inches. She was no longer down by the bow, but at least partly supported by the orembai keel. Finally, the actual flow of bubbles seemed to increase markedly. I took this to mean that all the water had been expelled from the inflatable tanks in the keel, so I clambered back aboard and up to the wheelhouse and cut off the flow of compressed air. I went back to sit on the dock, pseudo-lotus fashion, and contemplated the front hull's waterline.

After an hour of TM (Transcendental Meditation) on air leakage I discovered that my unused air connections did leak – but not much. I could keep the front hull even in an upward trim with a zap of compressed air every hour or so.

No, the air in the available hollows in the keel under the front hull would not convert Jester into a true multi-hull. Not with almost five tons of Calvados aboard, but the air did bring the front hull up in the water so that the wetted surface of the larger steel sides of the bottom barely kissed the water – at rest at the Club Nautique Sportif's berth, that is. And the air would have to be topped up every hour or so. There was some slow leakage from somewhere, either through the welds of the aluminium or through the disused rubber-tire fittings to the tanks. More likely from these neglected fittings than from the welds, I thought.

"What do you think?" This came from Mélusine now sitting on the poop beside the wheelhouse.

"Mélusine," I said. "I am gratified to find that the flotation tanks leak only a little. I tend to think it is the fittings, which have not been used for ten years, and not the actual aluminium welds. Jester's a bit up by the bow, not down like she was before, and she can be kept that way. She is almost a multi-hull, not quite, but I believe that the surface friction will be reduced considerably. In short, Jester may well make the desirable ten knots. Not anything compared to magic, of course, or witchcraft."

"Jesus," said Mélusine. "Can I come down there and... er... presume... to educate you?"

"Not unless you bring a beer." But I looked up into the sky, and especially into the west. The clouds looked black and purple out over the Atlantic. Not so good.

After some few moments, I heard Mélusine clamber down over Jester's gunwale, a movement punctuated by a tasteful 'gong-like' sound as one of her Nike's banged on the steel hull. I imagined Zen Buddhist monks drawn to prayer from Japanese rock gardens. After a while, I felt the cold can of beer pressed into my hands while my eyes were yet surveying the heights. I popped the tab of Pirate, not a good beer, but cheap and all that was now available in some places in Europe. It came from the Netherlands, had an illustration of Long John Silver and a Parrot on the label, and could be found most anywhere. I find that the better European beers, like Stella Artois, Union Spazier and Amstel have a slightly soapy taste after one has sampled Molson's Canadian.

"There are many kinds of magic, Marc Rennsalaer." I said nothing to that, and so she continued. "This boat is magic. That vehicle – Ivory? – is magic. You yourself are magic. You shouldn't be afraid of women's magic. It is no more or less than your own. We only pay attention to different… ah… proportions and… ah… relationships. You pay attention to weights, measures, capacities and the relationships between them. We pay attention to different weights, measures and the relationships between them. That is all."

"Hmmm."

"Those weights, measures, capacities and relationships are… how do you say… emotional ones, not physical ones, and yet they are just as real as the truths that have dictated your life. The… ah… tragedy is that too few men can understand women's reality – et… and… I sometimes… pense… think, even fewer women can appreciate men's reality."

"That's why men think of women's reality as witchcraft, or 'women's intuition.'"

"Précisément… but this boat is 'men's intuition', and magic, at least to me and I am accounted a Seer." She paused. "If we live, Marc Rennsalaer, it will be because of your magic – which I don't understand – and mine, which you don't understand."

"Perhaps, "both kinds of magic may work together."

"That was ever… always…? our only chance," she said.

"Well," I said, somewhat dryly, "if your magic is true, then we should leave pretty soon."

I looked up at the sky and, although it was still angry toward the west, the clouds no longer drifted toward us.

They seemed to have stopped heading eastward and were being propelled southward. I naturally attributed this to a clockwise cyclonic storm system that had somehow been deflected off the Cotentin Peninsula and southward along the coast. Perhaps a rising column of hot air from the Peninsula had done it. Maybe the Brittany Peninsula would hold it at bay, for a few days or hours in confusion, but the open Bay of Biscay would invite it into the southeast corner of Atlantic France.

"You are correct. Our pattern is... begun… starting."

Mélusine scurried below. As for me, I watched the clouds veering sharply southward and then went aboard Jester to check the compressor – the belts had not been used since the Lac des Doigts – and backed Jester out of the Club Nautique Sportif. I steamed rapidly between the Grande and Petite Rade breakwaters this time, since there was no oncoming traffic (I suppose that the threatening weather had caused the local boats to scurry for shelter hours earlier).

Like an idiot, once we cleared the southern headland, I turned Jester to port for Brittany and Brest. And, just to make the idiocy complete, I de-clutched the engine, reduced the revs to 'simmer' and raised the three starboard sails. Occasionally, I fed bursts of compressed air into the forward keel. I estimated the wind at about 15 knots from the west, 25 knots in gusts, and Jester was making about 9 knots on a virtual beam reach. It was going to be a long afternoon and a longer night. The sky to the west was full of low, black clouds and the sun was now behind them. So, the afternoon was dark.

Knowing very well that I should have been heading the other way, toward the shelter of Cherbourg and not out of it, I decided to complete the folly. I raised the portside main and this gave Jester another knot. In the gusts, I had to free the sheets considerably, and then haul them in again. On the whole, Jester seemed stable enough.

5

We had cleared Cherbourg about three o'clock in the afternoon in a confused chop with waves about six feet high, but no real pattern to them. The swells were rebounding from the coast and, somewhere out in the Atlantic they had once been driven in some other direction by a strong wind. At sundown I began to see a sprinkle of tiny lights far off to port. Some of them were extinguished from time to time and I took these for Guernsey and Jersey changing position relative to Jester sailing past.

When the sun actually sank, it was as if a black velvet wall came down around Jester. I steered a little west of due south by the softly glowing binnacle. Not too much west because I didn't want to run up against the Ile de Sein myself. After all, I needed no sorceress ashore. I had one on board. I rather hoped that I could thread the channel between the Ile de Sein and Cape Finistère at the western end of the Brittany Peninsula. There were supposed to be powerful lighthouses on either shore.

And, sure enough, by 11 o'clock that night, I thought I could see the faint wand of light every few seconds from the lighthouse on Cape Finistère off the port bow. A little later, I picked up the barest finger of light every few seconds from the light on the Ile de Sein. It was a little too fine on the starboard bow for my liking, so I steered a bit more southerly. Of course, there must have been a current setting out of the Gulf of St. Malo toward the west. I had not consulted Blondel's tide tables for Brittany because I had read in too many boating books that Blondel's predictions were invariably wrong. It was a stupid thing to try to thread between Cape Finistère and the Ile de Sein, at night, when I knew very well that a storm was just to the west out in the Atlantic. The two suggestions of lights gradually became actual dim beams, and then stronger ones.

Mélusine stayed with me, in a manner of speaking. Every hour or so she came into the wheelhouse and asked me if I wanted anything. She also said that she could steer a boat. And at about 11:30 when the two beams were a bit more definite I let her steer between them while I, on a lifeline snapped to the toe-rail around the cabin, relieved my bladder to leeward. She brought me some hot chocolate after that.

By midnight, Jester seemed equidistant between the two slowly pulsating lighthouse beams. And by 1:00 in the morning, the first pair of leading lights peeked at me coyly from behind a headland of Cape Finistère. All I had to do was follow successive pairs into Brest. I called brusquely to Mélusine and she came into the wheelhouse at once. I told her to take the wheel and steer directly for the two lights. Me, I turned on a pair of masthead lights to flood the deck with wan light, although this wasn't strictly nautical.

I dowsed the sails, starting with the port main, and then worked to windward with the three starboard sails. So many sails (six) might seem cumbersome, and it was sometimes, but they were all identical and they were all small. And, being all full-battened variations on a Chinese lug, they came down like window blinds. In spite of the fact that there were six of them, I had never experienced any difficulty in raising or lowering these sails. As a single-hander most of the time, I had resisted the temptation to have fewer but larger sails. These worked very well, and one didn't have to use all six. I only had to furl four, for example, tonight.

I took the wheel again, and steamed at ten knots under steam power along the rather convoluted channel, past the several protecting breakwaters, into the heart of Brest. I decided to tie up alongside the government dock. This offered, so the Pilot Book said, storm mooring behind the breakwaters to any vessel, any time. For ten hours I had been afraid of the storm, if not actually running before it. Maybe this counted. And I was happy to see two other boats – one seemed like a fishing boat and one seemed more yachty – tied up further along the mole.

As soon as the tire-fenders were over the side and I had double-checked the mooring lines, I locked Jester and went into the cabin. I was more than tired; I was exhausted. So, I just sat on the side of my bunk and drank another cup of Mélusine's hot chocolate. She had put the table down. It had been washed off spic and span.

"We did it," she said, and smiled.

"Yes… And maybe we were very, very lucky. I don't know if I… we… should tempt fate like that again."

"Is there a yacht club here?"

"Several. There's also a commercial harbour and many moorings for fishing boats and barges." Brest, too, like St. Malo, was a terminus for the inland canals. Some canal barges that never put to sea did unload their wares in the safety of Brest's well-protected harbour. As a registered barge, I could use the commercial moorings if I could find a place there. It was much cheaper, too, a nominal fee.

"We must stay at Brest today, you know," she said. "The storm will hit here and then… how do you say…? rebondir…"

"Bounce off."

"Yes… bounce off… Brittany and go back out to sea. When it has gone, that is when you must leave."

"If I don't choose the inland canals."

"Yes. That is so." Then she paused. "Where is the University of Western Brittany – from here – do you know?" I didn't, but she had a folded chart beside her on the bunk. She placed it on the table. I pulled it toward me and saw that the government wharf where we lay was only a few blocks from the University. I pointed with my finger. "Not far, as a matter of fact," I said. "Look, regardez, a matter of ten minutes walk."

"How long can you stay here?"

"I don't really know. A day or so, I would imagine."

"Good. That's all you need, I think."

Perhaps. I had to think very carefully about that. I squeezed past the end of the table and rinsed my cup, putting it into the ridiculously small wire drain board beside the sink. The galley was spotless. I returned and raised the table up to the ceiling. I fumbled with my belt and Mélusine withdrew discreetly toward the head. I was glad that she did because I could shrug out of the Walther's shoulder holster and the money-belt beneath the windbreaker and flannel shirt. These items I temporarily stowed beneath the foam mattress under my pillow along with the Beretta from the drawer, as an afterthought. I had had no time to open my cache in the keel. I smoothed the pillow to look just as it had before.

Mélusine returned after a fairly decent interval, I admit, but it was to find me stretching out of my jeans. I stood up in my very brief French-style briefs and peeled the tee shirt over my head. "You know, I think I'll take a shower," I said. Then, remembering the Walther, Beretta and money-belt under the mattress under the pillow, I shocked her by saying, "Want to come along?"

"Ah… oui… bien sûr… si vous voulez."

"I do."

As it turned out though, Mélusine sat on the toilet while I stripped out of the briefs in the shower, and showered. I also washed out the briefs while I was at it. I hung them over the steering shaft, as was my wont. One thing about a steam engine with a boiler: you seldom ran short of hot water, although I always conserved it. With the engine ticking over at about 50 rpm, there was also electricity from the generator, using the minimum of coal oil.

I stepped out of the tiny sit-down shower stall nude and after I had towelled off the front of me, I handed Mélusine the towel and turned my back to her.

Presently, she kept those hands busy and dried me off. She patted my legs apart, somewhat imperiously, I thought, and was very thorough with the towel. "Les couilles, elles sont très dûres... Your... ah... balls are very... hard", she said. "Comme des pierres." By the time she was finished, I had the erection that I had been getting, off and on, all day.

"Thanks," I said. I hung the damp towel over the steering shaft, letting her see everything there was to see, and padded off toward the bunks.

"I haven't looked in your bunk... closets..." she said.

"Drawers. I know."

"How?"

"Well, Mélusine, you've cleaned everything else, but you didn't clean those." I knew this because my notebook and other items had not been moved – and some had been balanced securely, but purposefully.

"I could have looked," she said.

"Did you?"

"Non."

"I didn't think so." The notebook had been lightly wedged inside the lip of the drawer. If the drawer had been opened, it would have fallen flat inside. The other two drawers had similar impromptu devices.

"Then why did you invite me into the shower?"

"To give you a thrill."

"... Trill...?" I heard her mumbling right behind me.

"Un petit frisson..." I said.

She laughed as I sat down on my bunk. "Mélusine, do not doubt that I will tell you to go into the wheelhouse or into the head... er... bathroom or on deck when I want to do something private, like hiding money." She nodded. "In fact, you have the choice of the bathroom or the wheelhouse now. Make it the bathroom, I said as an afterthought, it's probably warmer in there." She nodded, and left.

I unlocked my secret cache, which I have described at

length elsewhere, and deposited the Beretta and the money-belt inside. This took only a few moments, but I also took the opportunity to check the action on the AR-15 and to look at the clips and cartridges to see if there were any signs of rust or corrosion. There weren't, but then I had given them a light coating of oil in London. I checked the much-depleted air-cannon magazines, too. I would have to fabricate some more projectiles in Aiguillon, since I had not wanted to do that in London. With the spate of suicide bombings that had forced Britain out of America's ongoing and ill-fated Iraq war, the British police were understandably touchy about anyone fabricating terrorist-like munitions. They kept a discrete, but highly effective, watch on the sale of certain nitrates.

When I had re-locked the cache, keeping a selection of Euros and Francs for immediate use, I called to Mélusine that she could come out. I heard the… bathroom's… door unlock noisily, presumably so that I would know that she had really closed it, and she rejoined me at bunk side.

"Would you like me nude or barely covered," I asked.

"Nude, s'il vous plaît."

I lay down on my bunk and switched off my private little reading light. Jester's cabin was dark, but for her reading light. "About your hands…" I said.

"Oui?" she answered.

"You are truly good with them?"

"Yes. Very." Then she hesitated. "Maintenant?"

"No. Surprise me, Mélusine… if you really want to, that is."

She giggled, an odd sound for a middle aged woman to make, I thought. Looking at her across the narrow corridor of the thick keel that worked the magic of an orembai to give standing headroom in a low hull, I saw that her face was handsome, in that lighting, at any rate. It was the fine bones of her face that did it, the brightness of her frank eyes, her flawless skin except for laugh-lines around her mouth and eyes, and her smile. "Bien sûr," she said. After some moments she asked, "We are fairly secure at this mooring?"

"Very."

"Then, if you don't mind, I will undress as if we were."

"Not at all." I knew what she meant. Last night, she must have slept in her jeans, as I often did, against the possibility of having to move quickly. Her concerns may have been because of an unknown personal situation, not primarily the weather or an external human threat.

At length, her own light clicked off and I think we were both asleep very quickly. It had been a long day.

6

Mélusine surprised me, all right, but not in the way that I expected.

When I awakened – and my privacy partition had been rolled down – I saw that she was not in the opposite bunk. I saw that it had been neatly made up. Automatically, I checked that the Walther and the money were still beneath my mattress beneath my pillow and head. They were. I refused to believe that even with my lack of concentration, assisted by medication and the security-giving guards in London, that anyone could get beneath my head without suffering grievous bodily harm.

Then I saw that her orange plastic garbage bags were still stowed away in her upper bunk, bunks I used to hold miscellaneous items of all sorts. Ordinary storage space was scarce on Jester, a natural result of the orembai concept. It had so many other advantages, that I had long since accepted the few, but very real, limitations. And then I also noticed the lovely smell of fresh-brewed Colombian coffee. And after that I saw the head of the bog oak (as I had learned) Breton harp peeping around the pillow that secured it carefully in the upper berth. So, Mélusine would return.

In the process of getting my coffee, though, I felt Jester shuddering a little. This could not be wave action, not with that protecting maze of breakwaters spaced at intervals along Brest's rather estuary-like harbour approaches. This was wind, and it was gusting. Given that, I dressed quickly before even sampling the coffee, and went topside to check the mooring lines. As soon as I left the shelter of the wheelhouse, slanting cold rain assailed me from the west. Jester tugged at her moorings and tried to frolic ponderously at the concrete mole. There were now two other boats tied up to the government wharf and room was becoming limited.

As un-seamanlike as I can be, on occasion, I actually tied a square knot atop the bollard hitches. I don't trust hitches, for some reason, although I had once used a Blackwell hitch around a crane hook just to show off for Marcel Bouchard.

Then, I looked very carefully at the hull. It was a bit difficult to tell with Jester's slight motion, but I thought she was down by the bow again. Thankfully, I went below and, while going through the wheelhouse, gave a burst of air to the keel compartments. I had discovered a way of telling when the water was expelled – the air pressure began to drop more rapidly than it did when there was still some water to be blown out through the holes in the bottom of the keel.

I went back into the cabin though the uninviting steel door that had once belonged to a refrigerator in a Toronto meatpacking plant. Not knowing what the day might bring, I slipped on the Walther's shoulder holster and put on another, and even bulkier, denim 'shirt'. This was something of a 'jacket' itself, it was so thick, but I thought that the day deserved it. And I kept the bulky windbreaker close to hand if I had to venture out again.

Finally, I got to the coffee. And I soon discovered that Mélusine had made a Havarti and roast beef sandwich – that was the last of both – and it was waiting for me in the refrigerator. How had I missed all this activity? I must have been more worn out than I thought. On impulse, I glanced at my Seiko and discovered that it was, indeed, seven-thirty. The day outside was dark enough for six-thirty and it had not alerted me.

No witchcraft, Wicca or sorcery was needed to dictate staying at a snug Brest mooring today. So, I pulled down the table and again contemplated the lunacy of sailing across the Bay of Biscay in September. Maybe I was getting fey. It didn't look any saner with all the measuring I could do. But something was pushing at me. The Devil? I found that I was fretting about staying in Brest for the day and I had the temptation to head for the canal entrance and be heading for Aiguillon somehow. I knew, in some way, that was an even bigger waste of time.

By about nine-thirty, I heard muted voices speaking rapid French and felt Jester heel a fraction to port. A few moments later, I heard the hatch slide back and then Mélusine's Nikes squeaking down the aluminium ladder into the wheelhouse. The door opened. Her tatty windbreaker was streaming rain and she held a plastic bag in her hand. She had one of those accordion-plastic rain bonnets over her head. I also heard someone else coming down the ladder, but slowly, uncertainly and in leather-soled shoes.

Mélusine glanced back and, seeming flustered, darted back into the wheelhouse and I heard the hatch being closed firmly. Then I heard the sounds of wet clothing being placed on the hooks and more rapidly whispered French. She reappeared in the cabin doorway. "I hope you do not mind," she said. "I have brought someone who wants to meet you. Le professeur, Docteur Pierre Falardeau," she said proudly. "De Paris… from Paris."

"It's alright, Mélusine," I smiled.

She waved the plastic bag. "I found some Havarti," she said, "but could only find Schwarzenwalder jambon… er… ham." She went to the fridge.

Falardeau followed her in and I rose politely, while lifting the table up to the ceiling. I tossed the chart and dividers onto my bunk. He seemed a fairly tall – about my height – but dapper man with a trim salt and pepper moustache and a carefully shaped beard. His concession to informality was an expensive casual jacket, shirt and knotted tie and whipcord-looking trousers, rather soaked and definitely upscale.

I held out my hand. "Professor Falardeau."

He shook it. His handclasp was firm. "Captain Rennsalaer." He looked around and finally did the obvious. He sat down on Mélusine's bunk.

As for Mélusine, she lowered the table again. "C'est bon… okay…?"

I nodded and smiled. Presently, almost immediately, she put a cup of coffee in front of Falardeau and then me. I noted that she even provided saucers. To my surprise, she put cream and sugar containers on the table between us. I had forgotten that I had any. I heard her making a new carafe-full of coffee.

If Falardeau disdained my Colombian, he didn't show it. "Captain Rennsalaer, to save us both time, let me tell you that I know most of what the newspapers reported about you and Mariko O'Shaugnessey. But," he added, "I know O'Shaugnessey because I am doing the French translation of her English text of the Magdalene document."

Here, he withdrew a letter from his inside breast pocket and handed it to me. It was, indeed, a letter confirming his translator's role and it bore Malcolm Stuart's genuine signature, which I had reason to know well. I read it carefully, nodded, and handed it back across the rather narrow table. It confirmed, also, because of his international stature as an academic, that he would not just be translating Mariko's English text. That would save time, but he was free to differ from her English rendition with his own translation from the original Anglo-Saxon-based language.

"I also met Mariko O'Shaugnessey once at Oxford two years ago," he said. "She must have remembered me when the question of a French edition of the book came up, as it inevitably would, although my work confirming hers about North African linguistic elements in the Book of Ballymote was well known to her. I was always impressed with her work and, ah, sympathetic to her… ah… situation. I have spoken recently with her by phone."

He looked at me while he creamed and sugared his cup of coffee. "By the way," he said, "she warned me not to under-estimate you if ever I should meet you." Falardeau's English was fluent and without any discernable accent at all.

"I'm flattered."

He nodded. He paused and studied me. "So, taking O'Shaugnessey's advice very seriously – what would be your reaction if I told you, Captain Rennsalaer, that a version of the Pentateuch may exist which claims to have been authored by Akenaten?"

I took my time answering. Then at last I said: "I would say that such a thing would be highly dangerous to whoever has it." I creamed and sugared my own coffee. "The Mossad had better not find out about it."

Falardeau laughed. "Right to the point, just as Mariko O'Shaugnessey said."

Now, Sigmund Freud back in his 1939 book, Moses and Monotheism, had been the first to suggest that supposedly Jewish Moses had really been the Pharaoh Akenaten, who had tried to introduce a form of Monotheism to Egypt. This was a highly unpopular move for the majority of Ancient Egyptians, they eventually rebelled against Akenaten's intolerance and fanaticism, and he was deposed. It had more recently been suggested, on the basis of some intriguing evidence, that Akenaten's wife and queen, the exquisitely beautiful Nefertiti, had been a victim of the popular uprising. Akenaten fled with his supporters and this was 'The Exodus'.

More recently, various scholars had both amplified and supported this notion with linguistic, historical and geographic research. Kamal Salibi, Chaim Rabin, Bernard Leeman and Ahmed Osman had all fleshed out this idea. I was familiar with some of it. Scholars had managed to publish some books, but so long as there was inordinate Jewish ownership of North America's mass media, no newspaper article along these lines would ever get published. I had never even bothered to write one ten years ago when I was working as a Toronto freelancer.

According to these scholars, the Israelite 'Promised Land' was not in Palestine, which was solidly held by the Philistines at the time of the Exodus, but somewhere on the Arabian Coast of the Red Sea. Chaim Rabin and Bernard Leeman had pinned the location down more exactly, and Leeman had provided a map in his Queen of Sheba and Biblical Scholarship published in 2005 by the Queensland Academic Press of the National University of Australia.

"I take it this... document... must be in Sabaean?"

"Actually, no," said Falardeau, "although you've just saved me a lot of background. It is Ancient... very ancient... Coptic."

I raised an eyebrow. "So it is a copy or a copy of a copy... maybe more."

"Right."

"How do you know that it is genuine?"

"Because, according to my colleague... colleagues... on the spot, it has been in the possession of Coptic monks for at least a thousand years. They've kept it secretly hidden. It is very probably genuine for that reason."

Now, such an unlikely person as Thor Heyerdahl had visited the Coptic monks at the source of the Blue Nile when he was researching reed boats for his 'Ra' expedition to sail a reed ship across the Atlantic in the early 1970s. Heyerdahl was also looking for a good source of papyrus because no papyrus then grew in Egypt because of modern Nile pollution. The Papyrus Institute in Cairo babied a small pond of papyrus with which to make Ancient Egyptian paper.

Tourists bought copies of tomb paintings on this paper – at fairly exorbitant prices too, because the supply was severely limited. Heyerdahl needed twelve tons of papyrus for his reed ship replica and he found it in the Rift Valley lakes at the source of the Blue Nile. In The Ra Expeditions, Heyerdahl had mentioned the priceless manuscripts in the possession of Coptic monks who lived, for safety's sake, on islands in those lakes. He had seen the books with his own eyes.

"On which island in which Ethiopian lake?" I asked. Mélusine had sat down beside Falardeau by now. She was gazing at me in some surprise, but Falardeau burst out laughing.

"Lake Zwai," he said.

This was one of the southernmost of the Ethiopian lakes, if I remembered my Heyerdahl correctly, not too far from the border of Kenya. Only Lakes Rudolf and Turkana were closer to Kenya along the Rift. Little Lucy the Australopithecine hailed from near Lake Rudolf and the early Homo erectus 'Turkana Boy' was naturally from Lake Turkana. Now, as it happened, Heyerdahl's The Ra Expeditions and The Tigris Expedition were, along with Graves' The White Goddess, among those treasured twenty real books of mine aboard Jester.

"Mélusine," I said and pointed, "in that shelf beside you, there's an old paperback book called The Ra Expeditions, by Thor Heyerdahl. It has a white cover… I think." She knelt on the foam mattress to get a better view, and finally took the book out and laid it on the table. I pulled it over and thumbed through to the chapter 'Among Black Monks at the Source of the Nile'.

"No one knows about this," said Falardeau.

"Hmmm."

I finally located Heyerdahl's forty-year-old account of the manuscripts he had seen on Lakes Tana and Zwai. I selected the pages and passed the open book over to Falardeau.

He read about how Heyerdahl had illicitly spent the night on one of the monks' sacred islands precisely so that he could see their sacred manuscripts. Their existence had been rumoured since the 1850s. Me, I sipped coffee. "Mon Dieu," he said. "I thought only scholars knew about these manuscripts."

"Just goes to show you," I said.

"But it says nothing about this Pentateuch specifically," said Falardeau.

"True enough. If you think the Mossad would miss a broad hint like that, someone is sadly naïve." I saw Mélusine stiffen. "Heyerdahl was an immensely popular author," I said to soften my remark somewhat, "his books sold in the millions of copies, and in at least twenty languages."

Falardeau, himself a bit shocked, recovered quickly and eased the situation by saying, "You're damned right." Mélusine relaxed, but looked at me oddly.

"Remember," I continued, "that book" – I nodded – "was published… when…? Sometime back in the early 1970s?" I saw Falardeau looking at the publication data in the front pages.

"1972. And this is the paperback. The hardcover would have been when? 1971?"

I nodded. "That's reasonable. Okay. And what was Israel doing then, in Ethiopia?"

"Involuntarily airlifting the falasha back to Israel."

"Hmmm. And why were they doing that, I wonder."

"Under the guise of 'repatriation'… to gather up any source of Ethiopian traditions of the Exodus among the Ethiopian Jews."

"Bingo."

"That means that my… colleagues… are in grave danger."

"Not really," I said. "Not unless they try to take an old book off one of those islands. You can bet that the Mossad has all the islands under surveillance. And if you'll read Heyerdahl there you'll see that it wouldn't be too hard to keep track of who comes and goes. The monks themselves make it easy. They don't welcome visitors."

"Captain Rennsalaer… they already have taken the… document… off of an island in Lake Zwai."

"Where are your... ah... colleagues now?"

"That's the problem. I don't know. I had a message that they had reached Addis Ababa en route for Cairo. I've heard nothing since."

"How long ago was this?" I asked.

"Four months."

So, it was just before Mariko O'Shaugnessey had dropped into my life. "They're dead," I said flatly, "... most probably, anyway, and if they had a manuscript like you describe, well, it's in Tel Aviv by now." I stopped, then continued, "What did you want... of me...?" I asked cautiously.

"To help them. Like you helped Mariko O'Shaugnessey."

"I'm afraid that's out of the question, Professor Falardeau. For one thing, someplace like the Eastern Med is just too far from home. And, anyway, I have some extremely pressing personal concerns now. In France. The answer is a definite no." I stood up.

Falardeau seemed in something of a daze as he stood up. He extended his hand, but somewhat vaguely. "Thank you... Captain Rennsalaer," but he sort of mumbled it. Mélusine rose from her bunk to help him out. He stopped at the door of the cabin. "If I hear from them again, Captain Rennsalaer... if they somehow made it... out... can I contact you again?"

"You are at the University of Western Brittany?"

"Yes."

"Well, Professor Falardeau, I must admit that I am intrigued. I am interested in history, as you know. I will contact you by e-mail once I reach Aiguillon. If your... ah... colleagues... er... surface, please do let me know."

"Do you really think they are... dead?"

"Almost certainly," I replied, "... if this entire story has any truth to it, that is. Which is to say, if it isn't bait for a trap."

Falardeau regarded me oddly for a moment. I thought that

either he was genuinely puzzled or a consummate actor. Was that probable with a noted academic? "Oh… yes… I see," he said at last. "I believe that I have been rather foolish about this matter…" Then, a bit more briskly – "Thank you," he said. He rummaged in his jacket's pockets and finally found a card.

I took it and nodded. It had as much contact information as anyone could want.

"I can't promise anything," I said. "I have neglected my personal affairs much too long as it is."

He nodded, again vaguely, as he disappeared into the wheelhouse. Mélusine was busy clucking over him, like a French mother hen.

The real question, of course, was whether Professor Pierre Falardeau was himself a Mossad agent. Perhaps… perhaps… his 'colleagues' had managed to get the manuscript – if it really existed – somewhere. Perhaps… perhaps… they had succeeded in giving the Mossad the slip because they suspected Falardeau. But perhaps I was also being uncharitable.

Yes, the Mossad, Israel's secret service, was the main contender among possibly interested parties in this particular case, but there were other candidates. The Vatican? After all, the Magdalene document had struck a grievous blow against the Judeo-Christian Tradition, but a Pentateuch by Pharaoh Akenaten would pretty well finish it off.

Not that either would make any immediate difference in public opinion. But attitudes were already changing as the world was changing. Gradually, such revelations would percolate down to the mass of people. Two thousand years ago there had not been any such thing as the Judeo-Christian Tradition. Two thousand years from now there might not be any Judeo-Christian Tradition either – especially since it almost daily seemed to be the biggest religious hoax ever perpetrated on unsuspecting humankind.

And I also wondered… and not for the first time during the past two months… whether certain organizations might hold grudges. Why else had Mariko and, to a much lesser extent, I been guarded in London? But, I thought, any danger would be truly past once the book was out. Unless someone could hold grudges, that is. I actually doubted that. Pragmatic organizations like the Vatican and the Mossad could not afford to hold grudges.

Yes, a Pentateuch by Akenaten was more than just possible. It was probable, if Chaim Rabin, Bernard Leeman, Kamal Salibi and Ahmed Osman were right.

And it was probable, too, that if such a thing existed it would most probably turn up in one of two places. It would either be somewhere beneath the sands of Yemen or among Coptic monks at the sources of the Nile.

7

"Professeur Falardeau said that you had… er… waked him to the seriousness of the situation," Mélusine said when she came back. I was somewhat apprehensive that I'd offended her. I had had no intention of doing so. Sometimes the obtuseness of academics offended me, a lesson I had learned from Mariko O'Shaugnessey. On the other hand, she had learned a lot from me… and I from her.

"Awakened," I said. "And yes, I believe that is probably very true."

"He said that he had… been… talking to too many people," she added, as she put a small plastic bag into one of her bunk drawers. It clunked. "He was truly shocked to think that his… friends… might be dead. He told me to thank you for the… ah… warning?"

"Did you walk with him all the way back to the University?"

"Yes. Have you eaten?" she asked.

"A couple of your sandwiches. And that reminds me." I stood up and took another fifty Euros from my pocket. I put the bill on the table and she transferred it to her pocket matter-of-factly.

"Thank you, Mélusine. I was interested to meet Professor Falardeau. Was he one of your supporters at the University?"

"Oui… Yes… But it didn't do any good with the Administration." I heard some of the bitterness in her voice. She was one of the truly knowledgeable in her field, perhaps, but she lacked that all-important degree. From a professor herself, to the streets. I imagined, but I did not ask, if that was why she had gone to Cherbourg. I could almost feel the embarrassment of busking with her harp in her own University's town. She could show her face now, with Marc Rennsalaer in tow.

"How long have you known Falardeau?" I tried to make my voice casual.

"About three years," she said, sitting down. "He is a very notorious… notable… linguist. He was one of those most interested in the Gospel."

"One of those who thought it might belong to France?"

"No. Not Falardeau. In fact, he once said that the original possibly came from England or Friesland. Because of the language."

I remembered a snatch of an old rhyme 'Good butter and good cheese is good English and good Friese' – maybe Falardeau was right. "Mélusine, how much of all that did you understand?"

"All of it. Pierre explained much in French."

"And what do you think?"

"I think you are probably right. They may well be dead, as you say, and it is very far away. You could do nothing."

"Well, if Falardeau doesn't know where his… er… colleagues are, how can I be expected to find them?"

"You cannot, of course. They are not only his colleagues. One of them is his daughter, Danielle, and the other is her fiancé, Gérard."

"Jesus. Perhaps I could have been more tactful," I admitted. Then, I had been uncharitable, at least where Falardeau was concerned.

"Oui, possiblement. It awakened him." She smiled. "Do you want to… how do you say…? make up for it? He is giving a talk… lecture… at the University later this afternoon. À quinze heures… three o'clock," she said. "Only an hour… it is about the Gospel."

I glanced at my watch, it was just noon. "Certainly," I replied. I thought I knew how much Mélusine would appreciate that .

"Then, do you mind going into the… ah… bathroom…?" she said. "I would like to dress."

"Not at all," I smiled.

"And you might as well take a shower," she said. "To give me a… trill… It will also give you something to do."

I was just towelling off when Mélusine knocked on the door. I opened it and she came on in. She was in an ankle-length black dress with a colourfully embroidered bodice. It was traditional Brittany attire that I had seen only in photographs. It was worn mostly for tourists these days. She reached for the towel and she turned me around and started on my back. Again came that imperious patting of the thighs – and again that very thorough drying.

"Tournez, garçon… turn around, boy."

I turned, more than a little embarrassed, and it began to show very clearly. She laughed. "Ah… bon… good," she said. "I want to leave some wet on the front… for the… shine." She patted me on the front, leaving a sort of sheen. But she drew the towel softly around the testicles and my very erect penis. She brushed the top and giggled as it jiggled back upright and vertical.

"I want to do something very… artistique… with you. Come… venez." She turned me and, taking my hand, led the way down the short corridor toward the bunks. I didn't mind going with her, leaving the Walther under a heap of clothes.

She considered angles carefully and then propped the pillow of my bunk on end in the corner of the hull and my bookcase. She shoved me gently down, leaning me against the pillow. "For a while you will be Prometheus," she said. "I thought about how to use your scars for the best. They will be the scars of Zeus's eagles… où… or the female… ah… harpies? Whichever you like." She put my right leg straight out on the bunk, and bent my left leg over the edge as if I were sitting. "Put your arms up above your head."

"I can't hold them up for too long," I remarked. It was the shoulder, of course. From my position, I could see a tall Brittany headdress tossed aside on her bunk. It had proved too tall for Jester's bare six-foot-three headroom.

"Then clasp your hands behind your head with your... helbows... up."

"Voila," she said. "Now close your eyes. They have been pecked out, you see... Good... Very good. Now, I will begin."

I heard her sit down and the rustle of her drawing paper. Then the scratching as she worked with the charcoal pencil. This went on for a while. I heard her getting up. "Now, I have to see something. Do not move." Suddenly, she grabbed my right thigh high in my groin and squeezed. "So that is how the flesh looks... how do you say... pushed in."

"Indented...?"

"Yes. As if by a claw." I heard the scratching again. It went on for some time. "Now, again... do not move..." She grasped my right testicle and pulled at the scrotum... "Ah... the balle... bag looks comme ça. And... the... how do you say... beautiful fore... skin looks comme ça if it is nipped by an eagle's beak... or a woman beast." I felt the foreskin being pulled sideways and down, the glans exposed. Then she went back, I heard her sit down again, and the scratching began. I remembered the pull of the testicle and foreskin and I moved.

"Ah... very good... very... delicious."

"Mélusine... please..."

I heard her get up and then her hand grasped hard on my left thigh. "What is it, garcon? You want this..." and, suddenly, unbearably slippery fingers engulfed my penis, peeling the foreskin down, and squeezing the bared glans. I must have thrust toward her and she waited for the whole arch before I felt fingers squeezing both testicles, milking them as others worked my penis.

It didn't take me long to gush, and I felt hot splatters on my belly, but she didn't stop. She laughed or cackled, but she didn't stop, and I felt myself squirting again. Then I felt her lips close around me and pull me, by the balls, into her mouth. I throbbed and gushed again. She mouthed the semen and swallowed, and then licked my penis with her tongue.

"I like that," she said. "You are very beautiful... naked. You need much more of that."

I opened my eyes. She was smiling, and she looked pleased, and she offered a hand to help me lean up.

"Would you like to see my sketch?"

"Very much."

As artistic pornography, I must suppose it might have been first rate. I had never seen any with which to compare it. She had drawn Prometheus chained to his rock, writhing in agony as the eagles... or women harpies... worked on him in eternal punishment for bringing the gift of fire to humanity. His eyes were already pecked out, he had a deep wound on his shoulder and another across his ribs where hits of tattered flesh protruded – my scars. She had used them well. One hideous eagle-woman pulled greedily at a testicle while perched with her talons sunk deep into one thigh. Another harpy was perched on the other thigh with equally cruel claws and was pulling the foreskin and penis with it, as if to bring that unbearably sensitive morsel toward her beak. Prometheus was restored every night, to suffer the repeated horror again every day.

"What do you think?"

"I don't know what to think."

"Eh... bien..." she said. "Then I think I have done well. A Freudian drôlerie, n'est-ce pas?"

I leaned up further off the pillow and into a sitting position. "I think I will take another shower."

"Bien sûr," Mélusine said. "You have… how do you say… boy juice all over you. You… ah… squirt like a fountain."

"You truly like that?"

"I love it," she said. "And I will check myself for boy juice while you shower. Mais… but a few more drops of it will not hurt this dress."

"More drops?"

"Of course. On the Ile de Sein, I had most of the boys on their first time."

"In that dress?"

"That is vraiment… really… what it is for, and other ceremonies."

"What… was it you used to make me… er… squirt?" I was half imagining some exotic potion known only in certain Brittany circles, gathered at midnight and consisting of unspeakable ingredients that, perhaps, had unwelcome side effects.

"L'Oréal hand crème," she said. "It was the cheapest. You have nothing like that on this boat, so I bought some near the University."

I must admit that I felt a lot better, albeit a bit embarrassed, with that release.

Mélusine didn't seem embarrassed at all. It also felt very good to close the door and lock it, (I heard Mélusine giggle at this) knowing that the Walther and the money were in the collection of clothes.

8

Falardeau's lecture proved to be nothing very new, but I suppose it would be interesting to someone who had not lived out the whole thing. We sat at the very back of the lecture room – and this was in one of the modern concrete and glass buildings of the University, not one of the 15th century stone ones – and Falardeau saw us, nodded and smiled. I had dressed à la mode Grand Capitaine – grey flannels, my double-breasted blue blazer, shirt and one of my few ties, glowingly-polished black Gucci loafers – all for Mélusine's sake.

Although I was a bit embarrassed about it, I had also donned my Greek fisherman's cap for the occasion. Ordinarily, I wouldn't have been caught dead in it. Thankfully it looked as if it had been stomped on a few times. And its nautical braid above the small cloth-covered visor was the same colour as the cloth of the cap itself, not brassy. It had no 'nautical' insignia of crossed anchors or anything like that. At least I didn't think I looked like a Sunday sailor. I kept this shore rig clean, pressed and ready for emergencies in 'my' skimpy hanging closet, all that Jester could offer. The last time the entire ensemble had been worn had been at the King's Arms in Salisbury last June. However, that had been to meet 'HRH' Malcolm Stuart with Mariko and to sign contracts in the Cavalier Room where Stuart's own ancestor had planned the military disaster of… Nasby…? Well, one of them. HRH had a sense of humour.

Mélusine was a bit proprietary with me in her Brittany tourist get-up, complete with her tall headdress. There had been no rain when we left Jester, although the western sky was that puce-purple that gives even Grand Capitaines the heebie jeebies. And the wind still gusted strongly, sending a low overcast scudding over us, so Mélusine didn't add the headdress until we were safely inside the building. Hunched over and holding my Greek fisherman's cap in one hand and Mélusine's hand in the other, I saw precious little of the University of Western Brittany's campus.

For an hour we listened politely to the media canon of our story about discovering the reliquary. The only twist was, as Mélusine had said, Falardeau's opinion that the original language had been either a primitive form of Anglo-Saxon or an equally primitive form of Friesian. He projected PowerPoint slides and pointed out these telltale linguistic indications to the audience. Although I had given Mariko the basic idea for cracking the parchment on the night of the Summer Solstice – and I remembered the fallen monolith all too well – his (and Mariko's) expertise was far beyond me. Very thankfully at the end of his lecture, Falardeau did not, as I half expected, invite me to say a few words. I think that Mélusine had actually been hoping for this.

Nonetheless, Falardeau did make his way slowly toward us, answering presumably student questions en route, and finally came up to me. Mélusine was nearby, chatting to a small knot of former students or acquaintances.

Falardeau extended his hand. "Good to see you again, Captain Rennsalaer. I'm glad that you could make it."

I shook his hand for the third time that day and said: "I believe I owe you an apology, Professor Falardeau. I regret giving my opinion so… er… forcefully earlier this morning. Mélusine told me that your… ah… colleagues… were actually your daughter and her fiancé."

"How could you know?" he said reasonably. "As I remarked to Mélusine, you opened my eyes to the seriousness of the situation."

"If you'll pardon me, I've observed that linguists… er… academics tend to think in terms of pure… ah… science and not so often in terms of geopolitical ramifications of their work. Sometimes ramifications can be fatal… or nearly so."

Falardeau raised an eyebrow at that, but then put a friendly arm around my shoulder and guided me out of the lecture room. He looked around to see if anyone marked our exit. "Am I to understand that, perhaps, the previous adventure with our mutual... acquaintance was not so straightforward as the media coverage would lead one to believe?"

"That would be an understatement, Professor. But that is for our mutual acquaintance to tell – if she ever decides to. Not me."

"I suspected that there might be more to that story."

"But, as for your own... story... I would be very concerned. I wouldn't go to the police and I wouldn't force any French enquiry with the Ethiopian Embassy. Not yet."

"What would you do?"

"Wait. But only for another month, say. Remember where your colleagues," I smiled reassuringly, I hoped, "were operating. Travel is difficult there, and slow. And there may also be the need for great caution in making any move. And," I emphasized it, "I would not talk to anyone about this. Not with the current... ah... Le Piniste revival in France. Israel has much interest in that, as it did back in 2002, but more so now that Le Pin's popularity has soared. The Mossad has agents literally everywhere for the very good reason that all French Jews are potential agents."

"I didn't think of that in my anxiety. I have already been somewhat indiscreet, I'm afraid, Captain Rennsalaer."

"Well, don't compound that mistake. Wait for a month and, in the meantime, say nothing. If the Mossad... or other interested parties like the Vatican, for example, aren't already on the trail... then they may make it out yet."

"I think that is very good advice," he said, nodding and smiling casually.

"What was their plan after Cairo, do you know?"

"Vague. But the most often discussed plan was to try to get from some port near Cairo to either Crete or Malta... by fishing boat, perhaps. Do you want a drink?"

"Sure," I replied.

"Good. There's a student brasserie nearby." He glanced back as we left the building. "Mélusine will know where to find us."

There proved to be enough noise in the brasserie to preclude all but the most professional audio surveillance but, of course, video surveillance would show Professor Falardeau with Marc Rennsalaer and that would be enough for any self-respecting Mossad agent. But I shrugged. I wasn't involved… yet… and Falardeau had probably already alerted every real, professional Mossad agent within miles.

Israel kept an eye on students and Universities through the Hillel organizations on almost every campus in the Western world. This was to monitor the growth of anti-Israeli sentiments, if any. And to monitor the growth of pro-Arab or pro-Palestinian sentiments, if any. But this was very low-priority stuff in terms of actual surveillance by trained agents. All the information anyone wanted to know was usually covered by student newspapers.

Falardeau bought us a couple of beers. I could hardly hear myself over the strident voices from nearby tables.

"Do you want to move to a quieter spot?" Falardeau asked.

"Not on your life." I paused and sipped my Amstel. And wiped foam off my mouth. "And from Crete or Malta?"

"Then to France by regular commercial airline."

"If they are still alive, and if they made it that far, I sincerely hope that they have developed the smarts to forget about that plan. I would try to take a small coaster – there are more of them operating now and with little regulation so far – to Italy or Sicily. And then another one around to Nice, Béziers or Narbonne. How are they fixed for money?"

"Quite well, I think… I know. That was, of course, a major concern in planning our… project."

"Get in touch, discreetly, with Inspector Bernard Gabereau, Head of the Canal du Midi Police in Carcassonne." Falardeau started to take a notebook from his inside pocket. "Don't you dare," I said pleasantly and sipped the Amstel. "Gabereau, Bernard." I spelled it. "But don't phone or e-mail. Take a trip. Tell him you know me, the truth about how we met. You'll probably be able to get him alone if you do that."

"How much do I tell him?"

I considered this carefully. "I think I would tell him everything... so long as you can speak with him privately, that is. That doesn't mean in his office with the door closed. It means, say, in Le Cheval de Septimanie in Old Carcassonne. Better yet would be a supermarket aisle, but Gabereau might not go for that. Canal cops, even Inspectors, don't make all that much money. Gabereau will probably want some sort of treat for his time. Le Cheval de Septimanie would be a treat he cannot have sampled too often. "

"Everything?"

"Everything. Then he will know what boats to look for. That's his specialty. I would say that you can trust Gabereau. Perhaps especially in this matter. There are other forces at work in this world than perhaps you know," I said.

"Forces?"

"Yes." I paused and sipped, but I didn't look around. "Another possibility, after Gabereau, would be to speak... again discreetly... with Mariko O'Shaugnessey and her... ah... associates."

"I had already considered that."

"Of course, but not yet. Wait another month. Give your colleagues a chance. See Bernard Gabereau."

"You are interested in this... ah... project?"

"I said I was. I have an interest in history, particularly recent history. It may be an old manuscript to you, but if it is genuine it has geopolitical... ramifications... that speak volumes about the ongoing Middle East crisis since, say,

1948. In fact, that is its major value… or threat… depending on your point of view, of course."

"Yes," said Falardeau, "I knew that, of course, but it seemed… far away and not quite real… compared to the importance of dating the book and language."

It was my turn to laugh. "Hmmm."

"If Gabereau cannot help… will you?"

"I'll tell you what," I said. "If they make it to say Italy or Sicily, somewhere closer to home, perhaps I can do something. God knows what."

About that time, Mélusine sailed in holding onto her Ile de Sein headdress for dear life. She scanned around and spotted us quickly. "We have to go now," she whispered in my ear over the clamour.

"Would you like a drink, Mélusine," Falardeau asked.

"No, thank you. I really don't think we have the time."

I rose and extended my hand for the fourth time. "It's been a pleasure, Professor."

"Thank you, Captain Rennsalaer. Mélusine…" he nodded. She bobbed a little curtsy.

We scurried out of the brasserie and back toward Jester with the wind strangely lulled. There were still gusts, but they seemed both less fierce and less frequent. And the overcast was breaking in places, in jagged rents. At least it looked that way, but at this time – about five o'clock – latitude and season, it was getting on for dusk. Mélusine grasped my hand, almost dragging me along. "Thank you for that," she said, "it mattered a… lot… to me."

"My pleasure," I said yet again.

9

Impossibly high. Jester could never climb that hurtling black wall. And she didn't. Jester crashed through the top of the comber and water smashed into the wheelhouse. I could see nothing through the polycarbonate, but I could hear the sound of metal being wrenched and tortured. And, my God, Jester wasn't rising. She couldn't rise. Not with that weight of water cascading over the front hull. Not enough water could flow out of the scuppers quickly enough. We were going down… down… down…

Water sprayed into the wheelhouse past the rubber seals. But the hatch held. Mélusine screamed and then put her hands over her mouth. The whites of her eyes showed all around.

"I'm coming to you, Mei Ling," I yelled. "You've been calling to me for so long… from your watery grave…"

"It is all right… c'est bon… it is all right now."

I awakened suddenly, and shook my head to dispel the nightmare. Mélusine was bending over me, and she was smiling. "It is all right now," she said again.

"Jesus." I sat up and looked around. I was in Jester's cabin. I was in my bunk. "Sorry, Mélusine," I said. "Where are we?"

"Royan, of course."

Jester's motion was still somewhat disturbed, but nothing like the nightmare. Then I remembered, and all too well, that it wasn't exactly a nightmare. Not entirely. It had really happened. Only Jester hadn't gone down, and that was the worst part – in a way. Somehow she had risen, and water sluiced off the wheelhouse windows. The beam of the lighthouse at Pointe de la Coubre had almost blinded me. The giant combers – twenty feet? Twenty-five? – had followed us into the wide Gironde estuary.

And there they got worse, steeper, as the Atlantic rollers tripped over the Banc de la Mauvaise – the Evil Bank. Jester was buried alive many times and we felt the horror of being buried along with her. She didn't go down. I didn't have the – peace? – of joining Mei Ling. After Jester struggled up once, and then again, I had to struggle again, even though I was so tired…

"Royan?"

"Bien sûr."

"What day?"

"Le six septembre. The… ah… six, sixth."

It all started coming back. Yes, once truly inside the estuary, the swells had fairly quickly become smaller until it was clear that Jester would swim. I had then run into the small marina at Royan on the eastern side of the estuary where the west wind was pushing us anyway, barely a few miles within the yawning mouth of the river. I hardly had the strength to tie up, but I had help from Mélusine and the proprietors. They came quickly once they saw Jester struggling though the heavy chop at the marina entrance. They had refused to believe that anyone could have come in through the Gironde channel – it wasn't very wide and you had to aim for the light – in that storm. And they expressed astonishment that anyone had sailed direct from Brest. Maybe they thought no one could be that stupid. They helped me to climb back aboard Jester and said to worry about payment when I could.

"I have paid the manager, I hope you do not mind."

"When?"

"Today. An hour ago."

I reached for my jeans on the end of the bunk. Mélusine must have taken them off, and my heavy denim shirt. However, I noted, at least she had not taken off my tee shirt and briefs as well. I patted the pockets of my jeans and felt the bulge of money.

"Non. From my money," Mélusine said. "And your… ah… pistole. It is in your drawer with that leather thing."

"The sixth. What time?"

She laughed. "You have not been asleep that long… Marc. Only about fourteen hours. It is about noon."

I rubbed my eyes to try to erase visions of the nightmare. "Is there any coffee?"

"Non… no. The pot is broken. It slid off." She paused. "I can get some from the office."

"Thank you, I would appreciate that. Here," I handed her the jeans, "take whatever I owe you for the mooring." I walked, and none too steadily, toward the head. Jester's motion was disconcerting, but the motion I was still reacting to, I suppose, was far worse. I felt better after a short, hot shower, but not much. When I heard Mélusine close the cabin door again as she returned, I decided I'd better have a look at Jester's hull. The noises had been a good part of the horror. Jester had shrieked almost as much as Mélusine – but maybe I had screamed too, for all I know.

I came back into the cabin, noticing en route, that the carafe had indeed slid out of the drip coffee maker. Its plastic handle and assorted glass was stuffed into a plastic bag. Not much else in the galley seemed to be damaged. No dents in the cookware. The saucers, plates and cups were all thick Melmac plastic bought in Canada long ago, unbreakable and apparently non-biodegradable.

The coffee Mélusine had brought back was, of course, bitter, strong and French. Maybe that was all to the good this morning. Mélusine was obviously delighting in it, from the smile she wore. I diluted it somewhat with lots of powdered whitener and some sugar. I found some non-sweated briefs in the usual drawer, but I didn't put them on immediately. Now that I had been introduced to it, I found I rather enjoyed being a sex object. At least, it made a change from the usual female expectations. Mélusine genuinely seemed to like what she saw of me naked. After a decent (indecent?) interval of giving Mélusine her 'trill', I dressed.

"Mélusine," I said, "could you go into Royan while I check Jester for damage?"

"Of course," she replied, getting up from her bunk to follow me topside.

"And bring what's left of the coffee carafe."

On the marina dock I dispatched Mélusine into Royan, a picturesque huddle of buildings that began about three hundred yards from the marina. I asked her to replace the Moulinex coffee carafe – she should have no trouble with that – and to buy some groceries to replace those we had eaten since Cherbourg. Then I turned back to Jester.

Now that it was daylight, though not bright daylight with the scudding overcast, I had seen some damage just as soon as I stepped up and out of Jester's wheelhouse on the central hull. I had been too exhausted to notice anything... was it really only last night? ... in the dark and with the driving rain. I saw it now. The outriggers' decking. From what I could see quickly, the cargo was still in place although the tarp wasn't nearly so neat as it had been. In places, it sagged and moulded itself to the cartons beneath, and in those places there were puddles. I figured that the strapped down tarp was probably all that was holding the cardboard cartons together. They must be soaked. I decided to leave well enough alone for the moment. The wedge of the cargo still retained its basic shape and maybe the cartons would eventually dry out.

The plywood outrigger decks on both sides had cracked, sagged and some of the retaining bolts had been pulled through the wood. And mind you, this was three-quarter inch ply with a coat of fibreglass. However, none of the all-important outrigger struts looked damaged or bent. I went over these as if I were Sherlock Holmes, especially the bolts and flanges at either end of the struts. The forward flanges were a bit bent on both outriggers. The forward-most bolt on the starboard outrigger had sheared. That would have to be replaced immediately and before Jester ventured from Royan. Otherwise that outrigger would start to wobble, even at canal speed, and the whole outrigger would eventually break off when other bolts sheared.

Inside the central hull, I felt up and under the plastic tarp and learned, to my great surprise, that the cartons were wet, yes, at least the outermost ones, but really only in places. And also some places were badly soaked. Thank the gods that I had packed most of the cartons on some of the wooden skids that had supported them in the wharf's warehouse. Only a few of the cartons, those immediately around Ivory, actually rested on the deck itself – and those were the ones that seemed soaked the worst. Most of the others were about four inches above the deck on the skids and so water had flowed away from them fairly quickly.

I could do nothing about this because I dared not take off the many nylon tie-down straps. The whole cargo might literally fall apart. I checked those straps carefully, every one. A few needed to be tightened. I discovered, and I hardly believed it, that one of the straps was broken at the ratchet. It was supposed to take a load of three tons. Maybe chafe had weakened it considerably. I replaced this strap and ratcheted it down tight.

Also, I saw, peeking under each outrigger deck, that one of the guy wires had parted, also on the starboard side. The break had probably happened when the bolt had sheared and the wire suddenly took most of the stress. That would have to be fixed too.

For reasons of space I could keep very few spares aboard Jester. Since this had become apparent early in the design phase, I had simplified things as much as possible. There were only two sizes of truly structural and critical bolts on Jester and only one size of steel wire. This meant that some things looked a bit over-built but this was all to the good.

I could therefore make the repairs myself by using one of the four or five spare high-tensile strength stainless steel bolts and the Nicopress tool and its sleeves for the quarter-inch wire.

But, naturally, there were complications, as anyone who has ever had a boat will know too well. For one thing, I had to turn Jester completely around at the dock in order to reach the afflicted outrigger – and Mélusine returned while I was doing this. It took some time before she could go aboard because I went very slowly so as not to put undue stress on the starboard float. Then, of course, and all according to Murphy's well-known laws, I could just barely reach the bolt from the dock. The alternative was standing in eight feet of water. Without working frantically – I was feeling that sense of urgency again – I was finished by about three o'clock.

I then examined the plywood outrigger decks very carefully. They were obviously cracked, but jaggedly in a way that the wood still had some strength to hold itself together, and they sagged a bit but they, the port one at least, had already borne the combined weight of Mélusine and me. Although a few of the retaining bolts had torn through the displaced wood, the central ones, over the central strut where the plywood could not bend, were still as tight as ever. The outrigger decks weren't going to fall off or actually disintegrate any time soon. They could wait until Aiguillon.

On the way back to the cabin, I checked that the bolts holding the steam engine to the floor and ceiling were not sheared. They weren't, but one of the deck beams looked slightly twisted. The engine, as always, was ticking over and I watched it like a hawk in the bright lighting I had insisted on for the tiny engine-room flanking the wheelhouse. It was turning smoothly and there was no rhythmic displacement of it that I could see. The deck beam – yes, it was twisted a bit – didn't vibrate.

On the other side of Jester, the squat boiler seemed

solid enough too. That was the other heavy object, besides the steam engine, that could not be allowed to come loose under any circumstances. So I had designed them to be very strongly tethered at both the bottom and top, floor and ceiling. Just for curiosity, I looked to see if the deck beam above the boiler might be twisted in the same way as the one above the engine. If it was I couldn't discern it.

So, when all was said and done, Jester had escaped relatively lightly. I prided myself, this was also due to the design and careful attention to detail. And, I reminded myself, it was also due to good luck. Well, perhaps that expression was inappropriate under the circumstances. Mélusine had not spoken of Loki very highly.

The real question, and the one I could not answer, was whether Mélusine and her harp had really held the storm off us for those critical few hours off the Ile d'Oléron? Now, it seemed as if the squall line was held at bay all around us so long as Mélusine played. And she plucked her fingers to the bone until the storm finally engulfed us off the mouth of the Gironde. Then, nothing could help us except Jester's strength and my grim determination to try to keep her running straight and true before the fury of the gale. But what if the same wind and combers had overtaken us just an hour earlier? I didn't like to think about that, except for Mei Ling, of course. It had been certain enough that we seemed to have been in a pocket of relative calm that had moved with us toward the Gironde. I saw the squall line fore and aft and all round to seaward. Of course, that was impossible… wasn't it?

Nonetheless, it was off the Ile de Ré, just north of the Ile d'Oléron, with the sky still clear and the wind just steady and strong enough to give Jester the necessary ten knots that Mélusine had said with fear and great urgency in her voice: "Marc, we must go now. As fast as we can."

So, I gave her the wheel and ventured out on the sun-bathed deck, barely squeezing past the cargo, and took in the sails.

And I took great care – even with the apparent urgency – to wrap them securely in their nylon straps. Then I returned to the wheelhouse and gave Jester everything the steam engine had. This was also about ten knots. And then the storm had rapidly swooped in on us from the Atlantic while Mélusine had sung and played that uncanny calm around us.

I had to admit that her timing had been perfect, I suppose, in retrospect and from the safety of a dock. She had been right in Cherbourg, Brest and off the Ile de Ré – if, as she had put it, each had been but one stage of the same journey. We had made it, just barely. But what else could one expect from such a foolhardy gamble?

I was just about to open the steel door to the cabin, when my brain niggled at me that I had seen something that was not quite right. I turned back to the engine room cubbyhole first and spotted it. The chain from the engine to the big generator was too slack. By looking carefully, I could see that some impact had caused it to slide against its locating bar, overcoming the adjustment bolt's pressure. This frequently happens even with automobiles, and from much less stress. It was a five-minute job to lever the generator back to its proper position and tighten the bolt again. But it was a job that needed the engine shut down for safety – and I had already gotten away with some chances. I didn't want to get caught up in a whirling chain and sprockets.

I opened the cabin door to the smell of a delicious ragoût. Mélusine was stirring it at the stove. "Mélusine," I called out, "no electricity for about five minutes. I have to adjust the generator. So, no lights. There's candles under the sink."

"No… problem," she said and nodded. "It is about ready," she added. "Five or ten minutes."

And that's how long it took. I checked the generator with extra care to see if one of its bolts had sheared. Then, on an impulse, I went into the grandly named boiler room – or cubbyhole – and checked the Calor (Propane) gas tank that had a closed cubbyhole to itself with a tiny door. I didn't like the idea of gas in close proximity to the flame of a boiler, but Jester's design gave me no choice.

I had insulated the gas as much as possible with its own more or less airtight steel compartment. Of course, if it ever did explode, the compartment would make a fine casing for compression. Like a bomb. Knowing this, I had consoled myself with the reassuring sight of several ABC fire extinguishers hanging on the bulkhead. And I checked their pressure and charge religiously, possibly because this ritual was also reassuring. If the gas ever did explode, the fire extinguishers were a joke. I would never get to them. And, by some miracle, if I did they would not do much against a Propane fire.

The only thing I could do, and I did it, was to have an external through-hull fitting so that the Calor or Propane could be refilled from the outside. The hole to allow the brass fitting to poke through Jester's steel skin was lined with close-fitting rubber and was about four feet above the waterline. The idea was that with the gas compartment's door firmly locked, any explosion might choose this through-hull hole to blast through. Jester's side might be blown out, but the entire cabin would not comprise the bomb. That's another reason I had that steel door into the cabin.

My concern now was the brass fitting through the hull. Had enough of it protruded to be bent by the sheer water pressure of the combers that had broken over us? It seemed unlikely, but I checked it very carefully. It didn't seem to be bent, and I smelled not the slightest whiff of Propane. I checked the gas tank's retaining straps and bolts too before I finally left the potential bomb and dogged the little door to the gas compartment top, bottom and centre.

The wheelhouse was getting dark when I came back to it. I supposed that it was about four o'clock of an overcast day. I reached up and locked Jester's hatch.

I stepped over the raised lip of the cabin door to enter a cabin replete with savoury smells and barely filled with gentle yellow candlelight. I suddenly realized that I was starting to get a little tired around the edges. I couldn't be surprised. I had been at Jester's wheel for thirty hours, from Brest to Royan. And the last five hours from the Ile de Ré had been hell. I had pains up and down my back and in both arms and legs from keeping muscles virtually locked in position in order to steer against the pressure of giant (to my mind) waves overtaking us.

I slid behind the table that, I noted, had its own candle in a weighted and squat holder that would not turn over. Having a rubber bottom, it wouldn't slide very easily either.

"How is the boat?" Mélusine inquired while setting the table with real plates, and my 'good' stainless steel knives, forks and spoons. These had unbreakable plastic inserts in the handles and the style was Tandoori Indian. It was a somewhat downscale version of some 'Marco Polo' flatware that had once caught my eye, but the teak inlays in bronze were not too practical for a boat.

"She's seaworthy – at least for the Gironde, Garonne and up to the canal. I wouldn't like to try the Bay of Biscay again immediately. There's some damage and I hope the cargo dries out."

Mélusine served me a bowl of ragoût on the plate that was already laden with Scandinavian rye flatbread, a selection of sliced cheeses and a generous dollop of pâté. "What's the occasion?" I asked, "the last supper?"

Mélusine looked a bit puzzled as she served herself. She took the ragoût pot back to the galley and brought back a bottle of vin rouge that she poured into two Melmac cups.

While she was doing this, my eyes alighted on a small package laying on my bunk. I picked it up. "What's this?"

"A present. Vous étiez… you were… magnifique pendant l'orage… in… the storm."

"I was scared to death," I said. I opened the package. Three pairs of briefs: black, white and red. And they were very French briefs as I learned when I removed a pair and held them up. A smallish triangle made into something of a pouch was in front, a somewhat larger and pouch-less one comprised the rear, and these were held together by two ephemeral straps around the hips. The material was thin and would leave little to the imagination. Any one pair could have fitted into a cigarette pack. I held the black pair up as Mélusine sat down across the table.

"But maybe I'm more afraid of these." I looked especially at the front pouch and tested the tension of the straps. The elastic was laughably weak. "Mélusine, if I got even a suggestion of an… er… erection… well, some balls would fall out."

"Oui… yes," she said. "But of course that is the… whole… idea."

"Jesus, Mélusine, thank you but I'd be too embarrassed to wear these – even with you. How much do I owe you?"

To my utter astonishment, she choked back a sob and put her hands over her face. I saw tears running down her fine cheekbones. I noticed that in the candlelight, at least, the streaks of grey in her black hair shone like the silver inlay on the black plastic handles of my Tandoori flatware.

"Mélusine," I said firmly, maybe too firmly, "I'm not about to deal with that. I'm too tired. If you have anything to say, say it."

"You… do… not… understand."

"What don't I understand?"

There was a long pause, then she looked up, brushed her eyes, and tried to smile. It wasn't a very successful effort. "It was… très important… for you to get here… er… quickly. Yes?"

"Yes."

"So, Marc, I worked to make that happen. Et… and…

we made it, because of my magic and yours. And because of your strength… that you did not really have, except for your determination."

"Yes."

"But it took a great deal out of me… too. I am depleted. I must feed in my way, just as you must feed in yours." She gestured at the ragoût. "I know this about you. But you do not know about my nourishment."

"I see."

"Yes… and just now you ask me about the last supper…"

"Ye…ss" I said cautiously.

"Now, perhaps, since I have been… depleted… you want me to go."

"I thought you wanted to go back to Brittany," I said, puzzled. "You can get a train from here, from Royan. I'll give you enough money."

"Enough money… for a life?"

I could see her point. What could she go back to? Busking with her harp on the streets of Brest?

"What do you want, Mélusine?"

"To be a part of your… pattern, that we have risked so much to do."

"I am going to Aiguillon to marry someone I have lived with for seven years. Where do you see your place?"

"As your… Druid. There… I have said it… to help with the children, for there will be some, and to help with your trading… as I have already done with both, Marc Rennsalaer."

That was true enough – if she had enchanted the storm off the Ile de Ré and the Ile d'Oléron. I then remembered what that oft-used word enchanted really meant: to control, or influence, by the act of singing. Well, she had certainly done that. Singing, that is, from the Ile de Ré to the mouth of the Gironde where she had at last succumbed to the raw terror we had both felt.

If I was feeling that inexplicable sense of urgency in getting to Aiguillon, one could say that Mélusine had saved me two weeks of precious time. Under ordinary circumstances, which too many people did not truly understand, time was about the only thing that could not be created, made up for or saved. And yet it was more valuable than money. I often said 'Time is money' and that is true enough in its own mundane way. Time is also the very stuff of which life is made.

So, from that point of view, then we had already saved much time and – if my sense of urgency was valid – that might prove to be more precious than gold. If so, her 'nourishment' – which was not at all unpleasant to me anyway – was a very small price to pay.

"This is a very good stew, Mélusine, and if I were you I would eat it." I took a spoonful, broke off a piece of the Ryvita and added a slice of Boursin. "Now, I will give you your nourishment. I think I understand."

"I need your… juice… to contend with Loki. He almost won, vous savez? I must be in control of something to be able to contend…"

"If I am not daft… er… crazy, I think I understand." I took another spoonful of the ragoût and helped myself to more light Ryvita, this time with Cheddar. "Okay. But I will not continue to pay you fifty Euros a day, more or less. I will give you an honoured place and provide for you. There are six of us – seven with you – and Joëlle has worked out some sort of share structure. You will have an equal share with us all. And," I smiled, "you will get your special 'nourishment' in return for your special services."

She inclined her head to me. But she started to eat, which was what I wanted to see. "Yes, my Lord," she said.

"Geeze, Mélusine, we are not extras in a medieval movie."

"Extras…?"

"Actors."

"Are we not, Marc Rennsalaer?"

In truth, of course, I had thought the very same thing the last time I had seen Joëlle at Le Port Romain restaurant in Moissac. She had been wearing a 'sexy' outfit for my homecoming. She had bought it locally, and probably cheaply – knowing Joëlle and her frugality as I did, but her outfit had had a definite medieval ambiance. Certain authorities had proved that fashion foretold social and economic reality in some uncanny way. From 1900 to about the 1990s, women's skirt lengths had accurately predicted the GNP of all Western nations – but two years in advance. Broby-Johansen's Body and Clothing had illustrated this with graphs. Broby-Johansen had discussed other, and more subtle, correlations between fashion and socio-economics.

I had often thought that if economists could get away from their columns of figures for a second and just look outside their office or university windows, their predictions would be a lot more accurate. And think of what might happen if the governments of Western nations encouraged or subsidized fashion trends in order to mould the economy? Shorter women's skirts to stimulate an economy, longer skirts to dampen an over-inflated one.

None of this, of course, was too difficult to understand. Men, mostly, ran the economy. Shorter skirts stimulated more male expansiveness. Longer skirts put a psychosexual damper on things. And what did shorter or longer skirts (and Broby-Johansen's more subtle indicators reveal)? Well, the goal of money and power – what was between women's legs – that's what. It was really that simple and only about two or three million years old, as far as humans are concerned.

So, judging from Joëlle's last 'sexy' ensemble – ankle-length voluminous skirt, but with slits up to the thigh (obscured, partly, by the fullness of the skirt), upturned 'fairy' shoes and medieval-style laced bodice and wide sleeves – we were heading for a generally medieval economy with great economic opportunities for some (the thigh-high slits).

"Dost thou agree, Mélusine, to cook for seven – I will buy the cookware and can save money by buying groceries in bulk – and otherwise look after the kids, none so far, of three couples?"

"Okay," she said, and smiled.

That smile outshone the candles. "And dost thou agree, Mélusine, Druid and oak-seer…"

"They mean the same thing," she said.

"I know," I said, "but don't stop me, I'm on a roll. Where was I?"

"Oak-seer."

"Right. Druid and oak-seer… to contend with Loki, insofar as your powers are given nourishment, in order to enhance the welfare of the realm? My realm."

"I do," she said. This reminded me uncomfortably of a marriage vow. "But this is what Druids have… toujours… always… done."

"Then, we have made a bond."

"Yes," she said.

"But not tonight – for the nourishment part – maybe tomorrow morning?"

"Okay." She smiled, and giggled.

10

To my mind, some of the rivers of southern France are misnamed. I think of the Gironde as being merely a continuation of the Garonne, the funnel-shaped estuary of the Garonne, which is about twenty miles wide, where it enters the Bay of Biscay at Pointe de la Coubre five airline miles north of Royan.

However, for the French, things are different. The Dordogne River enters the northward flowing Garonne from the east at the city of Bordeaux. And from this confluence the differentiated Gironde theoretically begins. It is about sixty miles long.

The Garonne continues on to the southeast, where it is still mightily tidal up to the huge sea-locks at the town of Castets-en-Dorthe, another thirty-five or forty miles southeast from Bordeaux. The beautiful and famous Canal du Midi begins at these locks and it follows the route of the Garonne to the southeast past Toulouse to Carcassonne, far into the foothills of the Pyrenees. From Carcassonne, the Canal du Midi forsakes the Garonne and follows another river system, the Aude, as far north as the Rhône and Marseilles.

The conceptual problem is that north and west of Toulouse a 'tributary' of the Garonne called the Tarn flows into the Garonne at the ancient town of Moissac. And actually the Tarn is almost as wide as the Garonne at Moissac and it is considerably longer, for it flows all the way from the foothills of the Maritime Alps in romantic Provence.

So, when all is said and done, I have always thought that perhaps the Garonne should really be called the Tarn and the Tarn, in turn, becomes the 'Gironde' at Bordeaux. These names are a hint that the rivers were named locally by people long before anyone knew their actual relationships and before the people had wide geographical horizons. These names may be as old as the end of the last Ice Age. And there are plenty of indications along the rivers and canal that this may indeed be true.

The tides are convenient for navigating the Gironde and Garonne Rivers up to the huge locks at Castets-en-Dorthe where the Canal du Midi begins. Four times in every twenty-four hours the tides basically reverse the flow of the Gironde and Garonne. Boats can go north or south in six-hour bursts of speed that can be disconcerting. Jester's engine was powerful enough to breast the tidal stretch of the rivers if necessary – but only with a considerable and unnecessary waste of fuel.

Riding the tides instead of opposing them to Castets-en-Dorthe was not only much faster, but also much cheaper. The engine merely had to supply enough power to give steerageway – a boat going downstream with the current has to go a bit faster than the current in order for the rudder to work. So, the engine must supply only, say, one or two knots of speed while the tidal flow supplies from three to five knots more speed for free.

From Royan, we rode the tide thirty miles upstream, or south, to the small town of Pauillac, waited for six hours during the ebb, and then rode the floodtide south again for another five hours into Bordeaux. We made a speed of six or seven knots, most of it almost fuel-less.

In the two floodtides from Royan to Bordeaux along the 'Gironde', we passed through the eastern fringe of the Landes to starboard, flat land that was in reality a vast mud bank deposited in the corner where France and Spain meet. Anyone who looks at the Gironde on a map will immediately see that the river takes the form of a huge runnel through mud. And the Landes says much about the tumultuous end of the last Ice Age – not that many scholars want to hear it.

The mud bank isn't ordinary mud. It is finely ground-up pumice, once the dejecta of volcanoes. Now this was learned in the 1850s when a serious attempt was undertaken to make the Landes productive. Before that, this vast flatland grew only coarse marram grass and a few struggling pine trees. Fledgling science of the time discovered that the Landes was composed of ground-up pumice. That's why it grew nothing but marram and pines. The soil was alkaline. But by a concentrated program of reducing the alkaline content of this soil by adding some acidity to it, by 1920 the Landes was supporting vast orchards of apples, peaches, apricots, and pears.

Now there are volcanoes in France, but none are supposed to be active like Vesuvius and Stromboli in Italy. However, the problem is that all the ancient and extinct volcanoes of France put together cannot have supplied enough pumice to form the Landes.

A German scientist named Otto Muck – perhaps appropriate for the Landes – proposed an explanation for all this volcanic mud in the 1950s. It was, he said, the result of floating pumice ejected by doomed Atlantis when the Mid-Atlantic Ridge suffered a direct hit from a meteorite and blew up in gigantic explosions of multiple volcanoes. Some of the floating pumice got swirled into the corner between France and Spain by eddies of the newly flowing Gulf Stream.

Formerly, during the so-called 'Ice Age', the mid-Atlantic landmass of Atlantis had blocked the Gulf Stream, said Otto Muck, and had turned it back to the Caribbean so that it never reached Western Europe. This had accounted for the cold weather of the last Ice Age. But when Atlantis went down in the gigantic tectonic upheaval, it no longer blocked the Gulf Stream. This warmed Western Europe and ended the Ice Age.

Eventually, Muck put it at a thousand years, the floating pumice from the explosion of the mid-Atlantic ridge was ground down into mud by wave action that caused the floating carpet of pumice stone to jostle together. It settled as mud to form the Landes. The Garonne River had to cut its way through all this mud, accounting for the funnel-like Gironde. Muck pointed out that only a gigantic mid-Atlantic volcanic disaster could have supplied enough pumice to form the Landes. He was, of course, completely correct – and completely ignored.

He also pointed out that floating pumice not only collected in the corner between France and Spain, but in the similar corner between Spain and Morocco – the Straits of Gibraltar. That was blocked, also for about a thousand years, by chunks of floating pumice tightly packed and about 300 feet thick. Muck calculated this amount based on the pumice ejected by the much smaller Krakatoa volcanic eruption. This much smaller amount of pumice actually impeded sailing ships in 1883. They had to try to sail around the floating carpet of pumice stone.

Until this huge mass of pumice at Gibraltar was converted into mud by wave action, and then slowly dispersed by ocean currents, the Straits of Gibraltar were impassable. The only way into the Mediterranean from Western Europe by people exploring a changed world was through southern France – and that was a much shorter route anyway. Which is to say along the Gironde-Garonne-Tarn river system, the age-old route of the Canal du Midi today.

But was there any cultured humanity at that time some 12,000 years ago?

The Dordogne River joining the Garonne at Bordeaux supplies the answer. In the Dordogne region was the 'Magdalenian Culture' that produced the famous cave-paintings. It is now known that some symbols in these cave paintings actually constituted an alphabet. And some scholars think that the paintings of aurochs indicate domesticated cattle. They had been able to accumulate only a rudimentary material culture, maybe, but the Magdalenians of about 10,000 BC were every bit as intelligent as humanity in 2011.

Come to think of it, maybe more.

We spent an entire day and night at Bordeaux to get a good sleep and not mere naps between floodtides. And we went shopping. I bought Mélusine a good-looking windbreaker and an equally good water-repellent ankle-length coat with a zippered lining that would be suitable for the mild fall and winter in the Midi. I also bought her a good pair of tall leather winter boots.

After all, I couldn't have my Druid going around in street-lady clothing – noblesse oblige, and all that. But she refused to eat moules marinières in any Bordeaux restaurant, saying that she could make just as good – or better – herself aboard Jester.

Mélusine and I talked of such things as the Landes as we navigated between Royan and Aiguillon. The tides forced us to wait twelve hours of every day between Royan and Castets-en-Dorthe. And navigation on the canal is supposed to cease at seven in the evenings, so we had many hours of conversation during the five days or so until we could reasonably expect to reach Aiguillon.

I had long suspected, and Mélusine insisted, that much of civilization had actually come from the Atlantic west to the Middle East, and not the other way around. Anyone who travels the Canal du Midi with curiosity as part of his or her cargo must eventually come to much the same conclusion. The 'Light from the East' dogma of civilized beginnings was purposeful propaganda and always had been. That myth had supported the pretensions of a 'certain' ethnic and religious group. This myth also bolstered the 'truth' of the Bible. These were the same people who were probably after Falardeau's 'colleagues'.

We had already had more than enough time for me to tell my life story and tell how I had met Joëlle. And to tell how I had met Mariko O'Shaugnessey. I had related that story in Bordeaux at the very same Ancre bistro where I had supposedly met Mariko. That is, according to the media canon. And at the Ancre, Mélusine refused once again to have moules marinières in any restaurant because it was a waste of money.

A day after Castets-en-Dorthe, Jester arrived at Marmande on a beautiful warm Midi evening in mid-September. Mélusine had steered and navigated most of the way to Marmande. She had said that she could 'steer a boat' – and she had done so for brief periods, a few minutes, when I had to do something else. I rather suspected that this only meant that she could hold a steady course that was pointed out to her.

I discovered, as I thought, that she had no knowledge of what buoys meant and she had never seen a chart. If she was going to be 'my' Druid, a trader's Druid, she had to learn the basics of canal navigation at least. She seemed to accept this. I had never attempted the same thing so far with Joëlle because she had always worked at a computer job. I worked the canals.

Things seemed to be changing now and Joëlle might have to become more acquainted with the basics of the business that justified all her accounting expertise. She might have to stand in as a crew member from time to time. I figured that teaching Mélusine could be considered a preliminary to teaching Joëlle. Or, better, if Mélusine learned, then she could teach Joëlle.

So, I showed Mélusine the rudiments of the international canal buoyage system – which is to say to keep red buoys to starboard (the right side of the boat looking forward) and green buoys to port. That delineated the safe navigation channel. And I told her the old 'red to right returning' rule, with the complication that at the top of a canal or summit level, the buoyage system reversed itself and boats going the other way were considered to be 'returning'.

I also said that some buoys indicated hazards of some

kind. And I showed her how to read a chart and become aware of the hazards on either side of the supposed channel. On a river like the Garonne, the channel could be changed in a day by a storm and a spate of water that created new sandbanks. Trees could float down at any time and constitute a hazard, especially if they became waterlogged, sank and became invisible on the surface. I showed her how riffles in the current indicated various underwater hazards regardless of what the safe channel buoys might suggest.

She picked all this up fairly quickly and I wasn't surprised. She actually not only steered but navigated into Marmande. And, of course, in keeping to the marked channel, except for detours around uncharted obstacles that she mostly picked out, Mélusine had to become intimately acquainted with the way Jester's engine worked and her steering characteristics. With the five tons of Calvados, even with an air burst to raise the bow every hour or so, Jester could be a bit sluggish in a tightly curving channel. By the time Mélusine berthed Jester at Marmande, she was understandably proud of herself.

Mélusine and I were sitting up on the poop beside the wheelhouse enjoying a last cup of coffee. We were looking at the first fat Midi stars and the planet Venus blazed brightly as the evening star just above the western horizon to starboard.

"Do you know what Marmande means?" Mélusine said.

"No."

"It means 'men from the sea'. Do you know what Aiguillon means?"

"No."

"It means… a long… ah… pole for herding cattle."

"Like they still use in the Camargue?"

"Oui. Exactly. The people here were… how do you say…? the first cowboys," she said. "Cow… pokers?"

"Cowpokes."

"Ah… yes… cowpokes," she repeated.

"And they came from the sea?" Marmande was not all that far from Aiguillon, so it seemed reasonable that the two place names might be related. Aiguillon was only a day further south and east along the canal. We would be there tomorrow, perhaps by early afternoon if there wasn't too much traffic and waiting at the canal locks.

"You know," I said, "come to think of it, Joëlle did tell me that once, but it was five years ago when we were living in Narbonne. I must have forgotten. She said this whole corridor, from the Atlantic to Narbonne on the Mediterranean, along the Garonne had been settled by people she called the Elysians. They had come from the Atlantic."

"Elys was the original name of Atlantis. Elysians were what the Atlanteans called themselves. Some of us have never forgotten that."

"Hmmm."

"Why else is the Champs Élysées the most famous street in Paris? Why does the French president live in the Élysée Palace?"

"Hmmm. Because the French came from Atlantis, I suppose?"

"Oui… some of them… long ago. And some of us remember."

"Yeah, right," I said.

One thing about the French that I have never liked, and would probably never accept, was their natural arrogance. They will cheerfully inform you that almost every aspect of Western Civilization had once either originated in France or else had been preserved there when other peoples had abandoned them. Joëlle had learned to temper this national chauvinism, at least she did in my presence. And Mélusine would have to learn to do the same. Otherwise, she could hit the streets again, as far as I was concerned.

Thankfully, in most cases, this arrogance was only skin-deep. If challenged, even the French could be more objective.

Most Anglo-Saxons became too outraged and too emotional to challenge the arrogance, at least not in polite company where the French are at their worst. So, they never learn the truth, which is, unfortunately that the French are largely correct in their views.

France will survive and preserve the essential elements of, say, democracy when the other nations of Europe and their transatlantic offspring have all at one time or another betrayed it. That's why, after all, I had abandoned my once proudly held American citizenship for French citizenship after a period of socio-political purgatory in Canada. Living in Canada had awakened me to other opinions about U.S. policies and had prepared me for the even more critical European attitudes about America's international antics.

So, I had to call Mélusine's arrogant bluff now, or I would have no peace. She already knew that something was wrong, perhaps seriously wrong, because of my protracted silence. So, since she did not want anything to destroy the start of her new life at Aiguillon before it had begun, she was looking at me with some apprehension. If she really was a Druid, maybe she was reading my mind. If so, I hope she understood every unspoken word.

"If we are speaking of refugees from Atlantis, I would think that Ireland, Wales and Cornwall and the Channel Islands of Lyonesse would have received their share of these refugees too, maybe even more of them, because these havens were closer to Atlantis."

She laughed softly and a bit nervously, I thought. "I admit that is true," she said. "I think Atlantean culture was probably preserved in Ireland, Wales and other places in Britain better than in France – at first, anyway."

"But…?"

"The problem is that the British Isles are just that – islands. Later invasions by many peoples forced the Atlantean refugees into smaller and smaller… er… enclaves…? And on islands they had smaller territories and no place to retreat. So, the Atlantean … heritage…? Yes, heritage… became either debased and diluted or it was… ah… plowed under…? The people may remember… ah… fragments… of their true history… but not the… whole story."

"But in France…"

"There was a larger land, and many mountainous regions, where the refugees could maintain their independence for much longer. And with more land they could also become more… populous… so that they could stand against invaders better, or absorb them. Until now, in some places, the old ways are truly remembered."

"Where?"

"Brittany, for one. It is an obvious landfall for Atlantean refugees too – and for refugees who had to leave Ireland, Wales and Cornwall. Also, parts of Brittany are very rugged so that invaders are… stopped… and defence is easier. Some… offshore…? islands around Brittany were even more… isolated… from invaders. Like the Ile de Sein where I was born. Much lore is preserved there that was lost in other places."

"So, the preservation of Atlantean culture in France is not due to any special quality of the French, but only to geography."

"Of course that is true," she said.

See? The French can be reasonable and objective – if you act like a lion tamer with a whip, chair and pistol in the early stages of their training. "Now, according to you, Mélusine – and Joëlle, for that matter – these Atlanteans were a matriarchal culture…"

"And a maritime one," Mélusine added. "They had to have boats in order to be refugees from Atlantis."

"Joëlle stressed the same thing once in Narbonne," I said. "I have a question, Mélusine." She sat there waiting in the glow from Venus. "Now, as I understand it, Druid means an oak seer, roughly."

"That is so."

"But the oak is supposedly a tree belonging to the sky gods, thunder-and-lightning gods, like Zeus and Jupiter who were the chiefs of the gods. And they were gods of the patriarchal Indo-Europeans. You said yourself that your harp had to be made of oak in order to have any... er... power... and yet that is a 'male' tree sacred to male Indo-European gods."

She laughed softly. "Yes," she replied, "you have certainly read the... er... conventional textbooks."

"I used to write newspaper feature articles back in Canada, so I had to read a lot, once I decided to stop being a soldier."

"The land mine gave you no choice."

"Don't change the subject, Mélusine."

"All right. I will not." She paused. "It is true enough that many people still think that the Druids were a Celtic religious priesthood or class of wizards, bards and... brehons... judges. And it is true that for them, the oak tree was sacred. And it is also true that the oak was the tree of Zeus, Jupiter and other sky gods of the Indo-Europeans or Indo-Aryans." She paused for a fairly long minute. "But the oak was not always, and not... originally... sacred to male sky gods," she continued. "That was an Indo-European distortion of the oak's original symbolism. You see, Marc, long before people learned to plant peas and grains in the earliest Neolithic, they made their staple food – a kind of bread – from acorns. Some people still do this, in times of famine, in Greece and Italy mainly."

"I didn't know that, Mélusine."

"Yes. In Hesiod's Works and Days, he says that long ago, back in what he called the Golden Age, the Pelasgians or Arcadians lived mainly on acorn-bread. Since Hesiod is thought to have lived about 700 BC, then a long time ago for him was very ancient indeed. The Pelasgians, sometimes called Arcadians, were the pre-Greek inhabitants of Greece. They were also called Proselenes… because they supposedly flourished before the moon was in the sky." She paused again, but not so long. "So, the oak was originally a female tree and represented the Great Fertility Goddess because of the food it provided."

"Is there any proof of all this? Any evidence?"

"There is," she said, and giggled. "You, in a way."

Again I said nothing, waiting for her to continue. "What was the most sacred plant for the Celtic Druids?"

"Mistletoe."

"They called it 'all-healing'," she said. "But according to modern science, mistletoe has no obvious medical properties at all. That didn't matter to the Celtic Druids. Do you know why?"

"No."

"Because the juice of mistletoe berries looks and tastes just like… boy juice."

"Semen."

"Yes," said Mélusine, "I suppose that… semen… is a more polite mot… word "

I said nothing, so she continued under stars that were considerably brighter with the fall of night and little competition from city lights. Marmande was not a metropolis and the town itself was beside the Garonne, a fair distance from the canal. "So the Celtic Druids' reverence for mistletoe growing on oaks proves that the oak tree itself must once have been regarded as female, a representation of the Goddess. If the mistletoe growing on an oak supplies the… semen… then the tree itself must be feminine in order to be seeded and produce the staple of life – acorn bread."

"I suppose that make sense," I said.

"And at Marseilles in the famous Druid oak grove there, the oaks have been carved into representations of a female divinity, the Great Goddess. Why is that if the oak was considered a male tree sacred to Zeus and Jupiter?"

"So, in your opinion, the Celtic Druids represented an Indo-European spin... er... distortion of the original Druids and oak-worship. And it was already in place when the Celts came and was much, much older."

"Précisément... Right," she said. Then, with some urgency that was surprising under the circumstances, she said: "Marc, what is that? Straight ahead." She was pointing but I could barely see her arm. I looked directly over the bow where Jester was also pointing. Some miles ahead, but obviously somewhere near the canal route, the southern horizon was barely illuminated by an orange glow. It flickered.

"It looks like a fire," I said.

"And it must be close to Aiguillon."

"Yes..." I said. "It must be. But I can't do anything until the canal locks open at seven in the morning."

"Perhaps it is just as well that we took the gamble across the Bay of Biscay," Mélusine remarked. "Perhaps we will arrive just in time."

Remembering Matilde's tale of the summer's riots at Cherbourg and the additional gendarmes and occasional soldiers we'd seen from Bordeaux to Marmande along the canal – to guard the locks? – I wondered if Aiguillon or Agen was experiencing riots too. Joëlle worked in Agen and lived in Aiguillon. "I hope we are not too late," I said grimly.

We hurried below and I tried to raise Joëlle on her cell phone, but it wasn't activated. I left a message on the answering service. Since I could do nothing more in the way of trying to establish contact in order to learn what was going on, I asked Mélusine to make some coffee. I turned on the radio and tuned to the canal police channel. I could barely make out the bursts of rapid French anyway, but the static made it worse. Jester was moored with high-tension lines from the reactor near Marmande between us and the nearest relay station at Agen. I tuned to the ordinary FM broadcast band from Bordeaux in the other direction and got clear classical music. Ravel's Bolero seemed to escalate my anxiety in tasteful stages.

"Mélusine, listen for the news – on the hour – maybe they will mention something."

"Oui, Marc. I will listen carefully."

There was something I could do. Not knowing what kind of situation I might face at Aiguillon, I could prepare Jester for the worst. I could set up the air-cannons and double-check the AR-15 once again. That would take up only part of the night, and it looked like it would be a long one.

11

Some things aboard Jester were not exactly, or only, what they seemed to be and the two skinny brass whistle-tubes flanking the central brass smokestack were a case in point. To be sure, they were whistles and they did, on occasion, use steam from the boiler. One tube had a high pitched whistle and the other a lower pitched one and Jester's Toot-Toot was very well known all along the Canal du Midi from Bordeaux to Narbonne, my usual back and forth route. The occasional puffs of steam along with the tooting proved they were just steamboat whistles, right?

These whistle-tubes were whistles only by virtue of two tonal inserts that were screwed into their very tops and which could easily be unscrewed out of their ends. When that was done, the 2-inch inside-diameter, 3/16-inch wall thickness, brass tubes could be pivoted down to horizontal on the central smokestack, up and away from their supposed supporting flanges atop the deckhouse. And, the smokestack being an 8-inch diameter brass pillar, they could be swivelled around it to point anywhere along the horizon. Of course, it would be somewhat awkward to scramble around the wheelhouse, not to mention over it, but it could be done.

I had tried to draw the eye away from this obvious possible or potential relationship between the whistle-tubes and the smokestack by adding two visual distractions. First, the ends of the whistle-tubes and the smokestack had crowns of Mississippi steamboat-like brass fretwork flaring slightly outward all around.

Second, affixed to the smokestack mainly, but also to the whistle-tubes with odd hinges, was a largish oval 'brass' plate with a cheerful intaglio reading 'Folderol Jester' in staggered letters. And the staggered letters were painted bright blue and red and tasteful black. This plate extended out past the whistle-tubes on each side, but when the tubes were being lowered to horizontal, a rather complicated system of rods and hinges connected to the back of the plate caused its two ends to open like clamshells and to close together again when the tubes were finally horizontal.

Thereafter, so long as the tubes were anything but vertical, the plate pivoted up and down with the tubes and also swivelled around the smokestack with them. This plate then formed a travelling shield for the person operating the air-cannons. Because it was decidedly convex-curved on the outside, it would deflect almost anything, certainly any handgun or hunting rifle bullet.

Of greatest interest to me was the deflection of 7.62 (Eastern bloc military, but widely available) or 5.56 (Western military and special police, but not so easy to get in Europe) calibres. The 7.62mm I was never able to test, but with my own AR-15 I had been able to try out the 5.56mm on various pieces of curved brass. Since this bullet travelled at 1400-plus yards per second, it possessed immense penetrating power, at least at short ranges. I discovered that only 3/16-inch thick curved steel would deflect the 5.56 at twenty-five yards. Hence, the plate was steel and was only brass plated, but thickly so.

One had to observe things, and not just look at them, to discover that the first 'o' in Folderol and the last 'e' in Jester were not raised intaglio or painted black, but were cutouts in the 3/16-thick plate of jaunty brass. Both the 'o' and the 'e' had tiny brass cross-straps – but they were needed to support the letters, weren't they? Especially the 'e'. They were also sight lines for the air-cannons – in manual mode, that is, and they converged at about 100 yards. They were painted with luminous paint on the inside in case I had to shoot at night.

Naturally, I kept all this brass highly polished and the painted letters touched up. Keeping the shine bright whiled away the hours at canal lock moorings by giving me something to do – and made it virtually impossible for casual observers to imagine any other use for the smokestack and whistle-tubes. This brass, along with the knee-high (fold flat) brass railing around the rear deck, was a source of much pride to me.

No one except Raoul had ever noticed that the two whistle-tubes were not precisely perpendicular when flanking the truly vertical smokestack. No one but he had ever examined the letter cutouts. And no one except Raoul had ever taken a long look at the attachments of the brass plate to the smokestack and the whistle-tubes. When he had done so, and this was back in Nantes during a hasty breakfast with much of Mariko O'Shaugnessey to look at instead, he said nothing and merely smiled. That's why, or partly why, Raoul was one of my partners in Aiguillon.

What with the brass plate and the virtually bulletproof wheelhouse of steel and polycarbonate, the cannoneer was almost completely protected from small arms.

As cannons, the tubes used compressed air from Ivory's generous storage capacity. The projectiles were brass tubes slightly less than 2 inches in diameter for most of their length, which was 6 inches. They were roughly football-shaped at each end, with four fins at one end and two strips of high-density felt spaced apart around their midriff. At the nose of each was an epoxy glued-in Ramset .22 calibre blank. This set off a charge of home-made, high-nitrate-fertilizer-and-black-powder mixture, that would pretty well demolish something the size of a Volkswagen on impact and would open up something the size of a city bus like a sardine tin. Unless the something was armoured, that is, in which case my projectiles would only leave an unsightly scorch mark.

The range was about 500 metres with the 500psi pressure I normally used and about 1000 yards with 3000psi that I could attain, but only with a grievous use of the engine's torque. I decided that, in the present circumstances, Jester's mobility was limited by the canal anyway and I might need cannon range more than motive power. Besides, the compressor above the generator in the engine room had all night to put air into Ivory's tanks. So I turned up the fuel a bit and the engine began running at somewhat more than simmer. The compressor began to wuffle loudly and rapidly enough to be heard.

The brass magazines down below in my secret cache were rather large and heavy because each had originally held 10 of these brass footballs. They fitted into the tubes' support flanges on top of the wheelhouse and were held in place by lengths of bungee cord affixed by their middles to the magazines themselves. This left the bungee cords with their hooks dangling.

As I have said, Mariko had used about half of the projectiles needlessly at the Lac des Doigts. The Sleipnir helicopter was mortally wounded some seconds before she had registered my command to stop shooting. The flames and explosions must have rattled her. By my count, and it was very careful, there were only 12 projectiles remaining.

I went below and told Mélusine to go into the... ah... bathroom. She went. I heard the door close and the lock snick. I removed the two magazines and the AR-15 from the cache under part of the wheelhouse floor. Its access was disguised by the three carpeted steps leading two feet down into cabin and the wide keel that served as Jester's floor-corridor.[2*] I carried the magazines very carefully up to the poop and with equal care fitted them into the supposed support flanges for the whistle-tubes.

They looked like buttresses to the flanges when they were in place. So as not to cause talk in the morning, I decided to keep the tubes vertical until we were in or much closer to Aiguillon. So, although I had removed the tubes' retaining pins while in the wheelhouse, I stretched the bungee cords

2   * See The Magdalene Mandala.

into the most forward of the two available positions on the wheelhouse flanges. This kept the tubes vertical, but the cords could be re-positioned in literal seconds to hold only the magazines in place and the tubes could then be swung to horizontal.

I had already re-routed the cannons to use Ivory's compressed air instead of steam, and I had already unscrewed the tonal inserts. I had also fired a few test phutts with the tubes still vertical to see if the simple bolt-action of each cannon was working properly. There was always the chance that the Atlantic combers off Pointe de la Coubre had bent the tubes enough to cause the bolt mechanism to bind. I didn't think this was likely because the breech was well protected by the supporting flanges on the wheelhouse roof and these were of steel. Salt in the mechanism was much more likely. Phutting meant simply pressing the brass gas station-type air lever like you use to fill a tire. And test phutting made me think that the bolts sounded a bit reluctant and scratchy. Salt. There was a 'safety' of sorts on these two levers, just a captive through-pin, and I put it on.

The cannons used an air blowback system to operate the loading mechanism. The air was taken from near the muzzle after it had done most of its propelling job but with the projectile still inside the tube and acting like a stopper. These smaller tubes were 1/4-inch diameter thick brass brazed to the aft (or top, when horizontal) side of each whistle-tube and at 3000psi yielded 196 pounds of operating power.

This pressure violently raised a piston (a Toyota brake cylinder) and this caused one of the locking lugs to be thrown up and out of its stop in its groove. And the curve of the groove itself caused the brass bolt to be thrown back toward the breech. A projectile rolled into the tube by gravity feed from the magazines, the brass bolt was returned by a strong spring in the breech, and the cycle was completed for the next phutt. Each cycle took about one and a half seconds, because of the length of the projectile and the consequent length of the bolt's throw, but there was no need for any ejecting mechanism because there was no spent cartridge to get rid of.

There was also virtually no noise and no telltale muzzle-flash or smoke from a cartridge. But, of course, there was still some recoil from the energy required to launch a roughly 3/4-pound projectile into flight. This recoil was merely taken by the smokestack with no springs or hydraulics to soften it. The smokestack, also of 3/16-inch thick steel brass-plated tube, had an X-shaped support of steel plate TIG welded inside. It had cost a small fortune to fabricate. And its strength was doubtless why it had not buckled in the storm when, I had reason to believe, some waves must have washed over the lower part of the smokestack at least.

As for the AR-15, I stuck it onto the wheelhouse steel wall with its taped-on ceramic magnets. Then I went back for the two 5.56mm banana magazines for the assault rifle and stuck them on the wall, but resting on the floor, below the weapon. Mélusine, I thought, could be allowed to see this armament if she was to be my Druid – but maybe not the air-cannons unless there was great need.

I had always preferred Eugene Stoner's original AR-15 design because of its lightness and simplicity to the refinements that most of the Western world's armies had insisted on for most military models. I have described the AR-15 elsewhere at length, but anyone can read about it in easily obtained library books. Mariko, after ten minutes of instruction with Stoner's 'unimproved' original, had proved to be sufficiently adept with it to save my life.

I knocked on the extreme aft of the cabin roof, or on the deck, whichever you prefer and called out to Mélusine that she could come out now. With the portholes partly open because of the warm night, I figured she could hear me.

Presently, I heard the haunting and slightly otherworldly

sound of her harp while I sat on the poop watching the distant fire subside slowly but steadily, judging from the diminishing orange glow. Then Mélusine came out onto the poop and sat down next to the wheelhouse. She brought a cup of coffee for me. And she brought my windbreaker for later with the Walther and shoulder holster wrapped up in it. It took no Druid to foresee that I would be awake all night.

"I cannot see anything harmful or critical to you or yours in this distant fire," she said. "It may be an accident unrelated to your pattern." She paused. "Along with the pistol, I put your passport and the Calvados Bill of Sale into a pocket of the coat. They were in the same drawer."

"Thank you. Come to think of it, in the middle drawer is the registration for the pistol. Could you bring it up as well – if you come up again?" I hesitated. "But are you always right, reading your patterns?"

"No, that is true, Marc, but I am mostly right."

"So, I can put away the assault rife and the ammunition?"

"No. I would not say that." She hesitated a long while. "There is… something… odd and violent unfolding, but I cannot see what it is. I think you may need that gun."

"Was there anything on the news?"

"No, not yet. There was mention of food riots in the north: Lille, Brussels and, of course, Paris."

"That figures," I said and sighed. Paris was naturally the best-fed and best-wined place in France. The government had allocated generous and highly subsidized rail and highway transport to ensure this. But could Parisians, hearing of distant riots, resist any excuse whatsoever to indulge in their own? It was almost a Parisian hobby – aux barricades! "Well, we can only see what tomorrow brings."

"Yes," said Mélusine. "There seems to be a sense of urgency, but not for you and your… ah… realm," she laughed softly.

I busied myself for the remainder of the night in oiling (once again) the breech mechanism of the air-cannons and all the hinges and bushings associated with them and the smokestack. Then, in the dim lighting from the canal dock and the dark shadows it created because of the 250-ton barge moored in front of Jester, I needlessly serviced the AR-15 and the Walther yet again.

About three in the morning when a slight mist was rising from the still and dark canal water, Mélusine brought me another cup of coffee along with the Walther's registration. Presumably she had set an alarm. "I guess I haven't stopped being a soldier," I said, setting down a can of light machine oil and a soft rag so I could take the pistol's registration form.

As she handed the cup through the hatch, she smiled. "No, but you are not a soldier now. That implies someone else's organization and fighting on someone's orders. You will always be a warrior, Marc," she said, "for now you have much to protect. And it must be so."

"Thus spake my Druid."

"Yes, of course," she shrugged with that and disappeared. I heard the door to the cabin close. It was getting nippy. I stretched into the shoulder holster and donned my bulky windbreaker. The coffee was very good.

12

It was evident, by the time Mélusine reached the vicinity of Aiguillon – I was letting her navigate and steer again – about one o'clock the next afternoon that the fire had been there. We had seen the smoke rising even more definitely when we had cleared Marmande. There was still a wisp of smoke rising from somewhere in the neighbourhood of Aiguillon. It must have been a fairly large conflagration, as we saw last night, but it was only smouldering now.

I was standing on the poop, holding onto the starboard whistle-tube so as to keep clear of Mélusine's view through the wheelhouse's front window. I could speak clearly to her through the open hatch, her head being about level with my left knee.

We were in the Garonne River, not in the canalized part of the waterway, because the Lot River enters the Garonne at Aiguillon – just north and west of the town's outlying houses and buildings. The Lot is navigable some distance up into the Massif Central – or specifically into the Dordogne region – whichever way you want to view it. It is navigable north to the town of Villeneuve-sur-Lot and a few kilometres beyond.

This place is noted for its very high arched and brick-built bridge across the Lot. It had been constructed by the Angevins, English invaders or titular owners depending always on the point of view, sometime in the late 14th century.

Although I had never actually been in Aiguillon before, I was somewhat familiar with it because of its strategic location and I had traded up the Lot River once. So I had at least seen maps of Aiguillon en passant, as it were, and knew it for a small town, not just a village.

Both Raoul and Joëlle had said that 'our' warehouse was on the Garonne side of the spit of land that sticks out like a spear point between the two rivers and on the northeastern bank of the Garonne. That would put it on the southwestern shore of the spit of land itself. And it was just above, meaning upstream of, the point of the spit. That is to say, it was just south of the spit's point. We were nearing that point of land now and Mélusine again read the channel buoys correctly and steered to starboard to keep us in the Garonne and not heading into the Lot instead.

We could still see suggestions of smoke rising off the port quarter, somewhere in the small town of Aiguillon – or actually on the point itself? Joëlle had mentioned, in one of her e-mails to me in London, that instead of commuting between Aiguillon and Agen twice every day, a matter of almost thirty kilometres by twisty road, on her tricycle moped, she had taken a small room in Agen during the week. She only travelled the eighteen miles to Aiguillon on the weekends. This had seemed reasonable.

If so, Joëlle should be in Aiguillon, this being a Saturday. So, I scanned the south shore of the oncoming spit of land with the binoculars, trying to match what I was seeing with the hand-drawn map Raoul and Joëlle had digitalized and e-mailed. I told Mélusine to keep on going south toward Agen… but only fast enough to best the current by a knot or so.

The problem was the trees. The point seemed thickly wooded, at least beside the river, and I had expected nothing so picturesque. There were the inevitable scattered palms that one expects in the Midi, but also many ashes, beeches, oaks and pines. The leaves of the ashes, beeches and oaks were turning yellow, orange and copper according to their respective species. I had expected nothing so colourful either, and it was some seconds before I actually picked out a building among the trunks. Raoul and Joëlle had said that it had probably been made in the late 1800s or the early 1900s and was a low building of stone with a couple of newer and decrepit concrete silos on two corners, presumably for holding local grain.

And suddenly I realized that the spit of land between the Garonne and the Lot had a sort of rounded mini-point of its own that bumped out into the Garonne. Just to the south of this, just upstream, that is, and in the lee of the gentle mini-cape, a narrow inlet suddenly opened and I could see one long side of a low building – a warehouse? – running alongside it. And there were two rather incongruous silos at the far end of the building. Moored beside a ribbon of cracked concrete that served as a wharf, I saw Raoul's barge Mer-Cedez – he had actually painted the name across the stern. He had said that we had an inlet and wharf.

"Hard to port, hard," I shouted down into the wheelhouse to Mélusine. "And steer across the current into that inlet there." I pointed. Had she not shown so much acumen and promise as a helmsman… er… helms-person…? I would not have trusted her to perform such a manoeuvre because it was a bit tricky. The current of the Garonne tried to push Jester northward, of course, but Mélusine, after an initial surprise and a few swerves, took us across only slightly crabwise. Most of the Garonne's vehemence had been tamed by many canal locks by now, especially the sea lock back at Castets-en-Dorthe. In the slight lee of the little point the current diminished and Mélusine was able to slip into the little inlet that ran alongside the warehouse.

"Can we make it?" Mélusine called out.

I knew what she was asking. Mer-Cedez was alongside the narrow concrete wharf just inside the inlet. I thought there was enough width to the inlet for Jester to slip past Raoul's barge without colliding either with it or with the bank opposite the wharf. I happened to know that Mer-Cedez was exactly 8 feet wide. Jester was almost exactly 20 feet at maximum beam. I judged the inlet to be slightly more than 30 feet wide.

"Dead slow," I said. "I think we have clearance. Barely. And there's no current here."

We slid slowly past the iconoclastic blue, white and red barge that had once been the top four feet of a fibreglass transport truck trailer. We also slipped past the side of the warehouse. It was truly of stone, but again not what I had expected. I had automatically thought of those square blocks of light grey stone-looking cement of which so many utilitarian buildings had been constructed in France, especially during the first decades of the last century.

This low one-story building had been made of local Lot-et-Garonne rather dusty rose-coloured granite, but it was dark and grimy with the dust of a century. I think it is granite. As if to compensate for this unforeseen charm, a round cement silo rose from the corner of the building at the end of the wharf and another like it apparently rose from the far corner of the warehouse we could not see.

To my further surprise, I saw that the inlet turned a sharp left past the warehouse and its corner silo. "Dead slow, Mélusine, and hard to port again."

Someone had rounded out and enlarged the outside bank of the turn so that it posed no real challenge to navigation. Mélusine horsed Jester around it, using reverse only once, and a new vista came into view – and the drama. The smoke was still rising from the right side of this inlet – that is, across the inlet from 'our' warehouse, and it was wafting upward directly overhead.

First of all, the new inlet seemed to extend in a straight narrow ribbon of water northward to the end of the spit of land between the two rivers. My guess was that this northward 'canal' or backwater probably gave onto the Lot River because I had not seen any evidence of any other entrance on the Garonne side. Along the new vista on 'our' side were one or two other warehouses, and all of them looked much more derelict than what I believed, because of Mer-Cedez, was ours. These other buildings were effectively just ruins.

The reason for this dilapidation was equally obvious. The entire complex on the spit between the rivers had originally been planned during the canal era, and last added to when local canal commercial traffic was still viable – say 1950, at the latest.

First the railways and finally transport trucks had all but killed small commercial canal transport. The warehouses on 'our' side of the spit had suffered the most because the inlet to both the Garonne and Lot rivers had effectively isolated it from Aiguillon and the railway and roads serving it. This had accounted for the low price of the property. As far as I could see, the long and narrow backwater was crossed by only one bridge and it was a high hump-backed affair of ancient wrought iron. It had been designed about 1870 or so and had been intended to give small canal barges clearance. I figured that Jester might barely squeeze beneath it with the masts and smokestack down, but with them up it would be impossible.

I didn't have to try to pass the bridge, for the drama was taking place at the hump-backed bridge itself. A small and angry crowd was still knotted on the Aiguillon side of the bridge, but they could not cross it. It was evident that the crowd must have been much larger last night and had vented its fury by first looting and then setting fire to the few, somewhat less decrepit, buildings on the Aiguillon side of the bridge. These fires had unfortunately also spread to some nearby trees beside the gutted buildings. Sad and blackened skeletons of these trees remained and smoked like spent candles. The fire had not jumped to our side of the long backwater. The canal must have acted as a firebreak.

The scene reminded me forcibly of November 2005, almost seven years back, when many cities of France had experienced ten days or more of arson and rioting until Jacques Briac had called in the police in brigade-strength and empowered the prefects to enforce a curfew. Briac had stopped short of calling out the army. Even the suburbs of Paris had blazed by night. Joëlle and I had been in Moissac by then and the riots and arson had affected that smaller city too.

Of course, the riots and fires of November 2005 had had a slightly different cause. The major protagonists were youths of North African origin who had never been assimilated into French life. On the other hand, they had never striven to assimilate themselves within French life because they were mostly Moslems. The rising power of the Le Pinistes had since made the Moslems and Jews assimilate – or else. And many had, but many had returned to North Africa. As for the Jews, those who could afford it had, of course, emigrated to Israel.

The riots and arson of late 2005, just like the riot in Cherbourg during the late summer of 2011, were a foretaste of things to come. In both cases, people could also feel the winter coming on and were concerned with sheer survival on reduced Welfare. The almost-forgotten Club of Rome had predicted, back in the late 1960s and early 1970s, that the years from 2010 to 2015 would begin the violent change to another social order because of energy and food shortages in the Western world.

The scene at the humpbacked bridge reminded me that our veneer of civil law was perilously thin compared to the fundamental and possibly also religious concerns of people.

I saw immediately that the reason the crowd dared not cross the bridge was because Raoul Doucet and Philippe Beaupré prevented them. Laying prone behind an impromptu barricade of cereal sacks and wooden cases at 'our' end of the bridge, they wielded weapons of some sort – rifles, shotguns? Obviously, they had been shooting at, or overhead, of anyone appearing over the hump-backed middle of the span from the Aiguillon side.

"We cannot go under the bridge, Mélusine. Get to the wharf, to port again."

The angry knot of people across the water and Raoul noticed Jester at the same time. Raoul turned to face this new threat, one that outflanked them, and I saw him turn and aim at me. About the same time he recognized Jester. He obviously doubted his senses. He lowered his weapon, and I thought he squinted through a veil of smoke that drifted between us, but the shotgun or rifle was ready for instant use. Jester bumped into the concrete wharf at the front, I suppose you would call it, of the warehouse. Mélusine kept Jester there by side-thrust of the impeller.

I turned and bent around the wheelhouse to the air-cannons. It took only seconds to re-position the bungee cords and raise the breeches of the tubes to horizontal. Seeing the clamshells open and close up, Raoul knew there was no doubt that Jester had arrived.

One could not very well fire air-cannons directly into the small knot of people, but I could scare the hell out of them. This crowd was spent and tired. They were hanging on out of sheer French stubbornness and whatever embers of French passion remained in them from last night. They were ready to disperse. I wanted to encourage them.

Aiming carefully at the wall of a smouldering ruin, I squeezed the lever. The almost immediately following explosion and flames caused heads to turn, some shrieks and a loud gabble of voices.

"Mélusine," I said. "Hand me up the… gun."

Up came the AR-15. I had already loaded one of the banana clips. Of course, I didn't want to waste any ammunition. For theatrical effect, I fired a very short burst directly under the bridge, being rewarded by SFX in the form of much loud coughing of the AR-15, much spray from the water's surface and the whine of multiple ricochets. The people started running away from the bridge in all directions through the trees and haze of smoke. I watched and let them run. Raoul also came running from the end of the bridge. His face was blackened and he smelled of smoke.

"Joëlle…?" I said.

"She didn't arrive last night… or this morning… how could she?" He waved an arm. "I think she would be in town." He pointed toward Aiguillon.

I asked him to tie Jester up and vaulted over the gunwale onto the wharf. I handed the AR-15 to Philippe at the barricade. "Comment ça va?" I asked.

"Bien," he said, grinned in a smoke blackened face like Raoul's and took the offered assault rifle. Philippe had been a paratrooper. I knew I left Stoner's brainchild in good hands. Putting my right hand on the Walther beneath my windbreaker, but not drawing it, I walked over the bridge toward Aiguillon.

Immediately on the other side of the bridge, a road began or ended, depending again on one's point of view. The bridge was too narrow and antiquated to accommodate motorized 20th century traffic. It could possibly handle light trucks or cars on a one-way-at-a-time basis. It had been left as a footbridge and apparently it had not been considered economically worthwhile to construct any newer bridge and a continuation of the road onto the spit. Within minutes, signposts revealed that this road was the Rue de Larousse and, from the increasing frequency of buildings and houses, it led into town.

I kept a steady right hand on the butt of the Walther because I could see people ahead of me jogging away along the road. However, the occasional glances over their shoulders were more apprehensive and furtive than threatening. The French are tigers – so long as they are victorious, that is. But when a French mob, or army for that matter, is defeated, well, it is defeated. My observation was nothing new. Caesar had said the very same thing two thousand years earlier.

Now, the Canal du Midi, the new one constructed in the 1950s and 1960s, often departed from the course of the Garonne. This was because, by then, highway truck transport had largely superseded canal-barge commercial transport. And the four-lane highway called the 'Autoroute des 2 Mers' carried goods much more rapidly between Bordeaux and Narbonne than canal barges could ever hope to do. Even the smaller Garonne towns could be served much faster by roads off the Autoroute. So, the canal engineers of this later era often made their Canal du Midi depart from the original 1687 route beside the Garonne and made it detour far into the beautiful countryside. This not only made a swath of physical room for the new Autoroute but also offered tourists one of the most romantic and scenic experiences of France imaginable.

Nonetheless, the canal engineers of the 1950s and 1960s were obliged to make the Canal du Midi swing back to the Garonne River at towns like Marmande, Aiguillon and Agen. These places had been established long before the canal had become mainly recreational and touristy. They had been established along the Garonne before anyone had ever conceived of canals… or highways. And even tourists needed a break from unrelieved rustic beauty.

Therefore, the Canal du Midi still curves into the heart of Aiguillon, just northeast of the railway station, and relaxes in a big basin where barges and yachts can tie up for as long as it takes to sample all that Aiguillon has to offer. This is not much. Aiguillon owes its visit by the canal to its geographical position at the confluence of the Lot and Garonne, not to its size or cultural attractions. Some yachty tourists wanted to sail up the Lot, an incredibly picturesque twenty kilometres or so, at least as far as the famous bridge.

By now, a big plume of largely dissipated smoke was rising over Aiguillon, directly overhead. There must have been a food riot here as well as in Lille, Brussels and Paris.

But Aiguillon was much too small to get reported by France 2 radio. That's probably why the warehouses on the spit between the Lot and Garonne had been targeted – that, and the fact that they were a fair distance from the Aiguillon police station and there could only be a few gendarmes in Aiguillon anyway. And these few were not about to challenge an angry hometown crowd. Not for the sake of some old warehouses.

Mélusine had reminded me of my passport and the ship's papers and had brought them up to the poop last night in one of the windbreaker's pockets, including the Bill of Sale for the Calvados cargo. If I encountered any gendarmes or soldiers on the streets, they might be a bit touchy and the identification might keep them from insisting on a search and thereby discovering a concealed Walther PPK in a shoulder holster.

And, not only heeding my Druid's advice but improving on it, I had also asked her to collect the very legal registration for the handgun from one of my beneath-bunk drawers. She had brought that up to me in the wee hours at Marmande. Barge owners had been allowed to carry handguns for the past two years under French law. But soldiers can still be touchy. I might still get stopped, perhaps arrested, but I would be released fairly quickly.

The streets of Aiguillon – and there seemed to be very few of them as towns go – seemed deserted, deserted by soldiers and gendarmes anyway. The shops were open, of course, and merchandise spilled onto the sidewalks. Most of the people seemed busy and friendly. It was as if there had been no drama at all in the night, but one gradually gets used to the French.

And perhaps there had truly been no drama. It was perfectly possible that some people in Aiguillon had merely wanted to ape their betters in Lille, Brussels and Paris. For all I knew at this point, the ruined buildings had already been that way before the fire. However, I could well imagine that the thought of strangers at work refurbishing an old warehouse and apparently filling it with foodstuff and wine might have incited the envy and wrath of the less responsible townsfolk. A stranger was anyone who had not been born in Aiguillon or who had not lived there for a few decades, I imagined. Small town people are the same all over the world, only the small town French are more so.

I finally found Joëlle in the Hôtel de Ville, City Hall, down in the basement where the only police station in Aiguillon was located. I had seen her candy apple red tricycle from afar, and supposed that she had sought a haven from the fire at the police station. After checking that the tricycle was all right – it was chained to a wrought iron fence, and not even a tire was flat. I followed the 'POLICE' signs downstairs. I saw her across a crowded room, as the song goes, or at least a semi-crowded one, but I wasn't quite sure how to approach her.

The last time I had seen her, about three months earlier outside the door of Le Port Romain restaurant-bistro in Moissac, she had been pedalling away on her tricycle moped. Then she had been in a laced-bodice thigh-high-slit dress that vaguely recalled medieval attire and was quickly becoming the new fashion. She had bought it as a sort of sexy homecoming present for me after one of my canal trips. This was one of our traditions.

And then, of course, my infatuation with Mariko O'Shaugnessey – oh, and the manuscript, of course – had been between us. Manuscript, yeah, right.

But... had I not slain three dragons in Glastonbury? Had I not earned a maiden's undying love...? But maybe I had better not go into that too closely. Had I not sent much money back to Joëlle from these adventures? Had I not braved the perils of the sea to reach Joëlle more quickly than she could ever have imagined? And had I not earned a Druid's loyalty? Come to think of it, maybe I shouldn't go into that too closely either. Anyway, I was a hero... wasn't I? Then, walk like one, Rennsalaer.

She wasn't in that medieval dress now, but in sombre workday attire – a blue skirt suit, conservative blouse and sturdy shoes for pedalling. I thought that her office higher-heeled pumps were probably in her tricycle's lockable carrying compartment. This skirt was a little looser on her than I remembered. She had lost weight – not that Joëlle had ever been exactly plump – but she had one of those buxom and sturdy figures that one associates with Girl Scout leaders, the most energetic of cheerleaders and serious nature lovers. Her honey-brown hair was still in that shortish cut that made me always think of a field of ripening wheat. I saw, in profile, her rather sharp-bridged nose that bespoke immense amounts of determination and endurance. Her definite chin confirmed what the nose proclaimed.

But, as I had immediately observed, she had lost some weight and seemed somehow to sag in her clothes. Perhaps that subtle aura of dejection came from a night without sleep in the police station. The benches were hard wood.

This made things easier, somehow, Joëlle not being in sexy clothes, that is.

Accordingly, I gently shoved my way though a crowd and came at last beside Joëlle where she was apparently waiting in a straggling and confused French excuse for a queue in order to fill out some police form or other.

"Hello, Joey," I said. "I am glad to find you alive... and safe."

She whirled toward me. "Marc?"

"As ever was."

And to my great relief, she broke down crying, buried her head in my chest, and so I was able to put my arms around her and be stolid and comforting – just like a real hero should be. "There, there," I said, "you're alive, I'm alive and so nothing can be all that bad."

13

Sparks showered onto the cement from the tiny British-made Sun MIG welder and, what with the sizzle of the welding machine and the darkness inside the fibre welding mask, I didn't hear Joëlle approaching until I heard her voice. I finished my bead, tricky in aluminium because it doesn't change colour when it melts, and then broke the arc from the aluminium wire.

"Marc," she said more loudly. I pivoted the mask up.

"What's up," I said from the floor, taking the long leather welding gloves from my hands. I unbuttoned my shirt from my neck. Radiation from aluminium welding is harmful to the skin.

"The mail has come. There's a heavy package for us from Mariko. It came by special delivery too."

"Did you give the postman a cup of coffee for his effort?" Packages, especially heavy ones, were understood to be an 'extra' to the meagre government salary and thus deserving of a little extra attention from the recipient.

"Postperson, in this case," said Joëlle. "And, of course Mélusine gave her a cup of coffee, not to mention a scone. I had to sign for it, either me or you, no one else."

"Hmmm."

Now, I suppose I should mention two things here. First of all, most of this conversation, like most of the following ones, took place in French. Since the English of Raoul and his wife Christine, and of Philippe and his wife Marie-Thérèse, was even more rudimentary than my French we stuck to the common tongue that everyone spoke – more or less, in my case. After all, we were all in France and when in France, do as the Romans do, right?

And the second thing is that our time was an exceedingly strange one. The world was generally returning to an earlier system of social attitudes and values because, of course, of the ongoing oil crisis. Of that there could be no doubt. There were many fewer cars and trucks on the road. Some industries had almost disappeared altogether and many more people were unemployed.

The transportation industry in which we were intimately involved had begun to revive the canal commerce of an earlier era. Heavily mechanized 20th century 'agribusiness' had been hard hit by the petroleum shortages and so there was also an absolute shortage of some foods, especially in major cities where the populace depended on nourishment formerly trucked in by roads and highways. There were continual food riots, but mostly in large cities, as I have related, and they were of a more or less serious and valid nature – as I have also related.

Airline flights had been severely curtailed and minor airports had closed down. No one took flying for granted anymore; it was a luxury and an adventure – like it had been back in the 1930s.

On the other hand, some aspects of the 20th century, and especially the late 20th century, were flourishing. Space communication satellites had been in orbit for years, and there was sufficient electrical power from hydroelectric dams and nuclear reactors to keep television and radio stations operating. Therefore, those who already had cell phones and computers could call up or e-mail a friend in, say, Paris when actually getting there might be a two or three day expedition.

Mail service had actually improved. That was one way that governments could usefully employ people. And useful employment was a social priority. It not only kept otherwise idle people busy, but it contributed to holding society together. I will not pretend mail efficiency had again attained the efficiency of England in 1920, but even in France it was very good.

There was an increasing emphasis on law and order and the corollary social value that unbridled individual 'rights' had to be commensurate with social contribution. There was some increasing social deference paid to those who seemed to be contributing more. Welfare, as such, was getting almost impossible to get – except for certain categories of people like single mothers. On the other hand, either the government or private business was starting to offer many more menial jobs as people were again taking the place of machines whenever possible. And people were increasingly expected to take these jobs – or starve.

As Dickens might have put it, and did, I think: it was the best of times and the worst of times. And like every time in fairly recent human history, ours was definitely a time of transition.

This is all to explain why I wasn't surprised that the mail had come.

I got up with minor aches from my prone position beside the tubular wind-motor frame on the cement floor, turned off the welding machine and put my mask and gloves on top of it. "If it's heavy and from Mariko O'Shaugnessey," I said, "it must be a copy of her book."

Following Joëlle across a fair expanse of concrete and then through the old kalamine fire door with an 'EXIT' light that no longer worked above it, we went into the combined and quite large kitchen-dining area of the old warehouse. This area was dominated – and that is the word – by our most recent décor acquisition. It was the warmest and best-smelling place in the whole building because Mélusine was almost always cooking something on the huge ex-restaurant stove. And whatever it was, it was always delicious. This time it was a stew – ragoût – in a five-gallon pot.

I sat down at random in one of the ten chairs at the huge

oak table that Philippe had spotted last month right here in Aiguillon, of all places. It had once been the pride of the local Masonic Lodge and a carpenter's nightmare. All six of us had had a devil of a time lifting and balancing the round expanse of it aboard Ivory's willing but too small truck bed. We'd had to rest part of the table on Ivory's trailer.

And you can imagine the fun going over the top of hump-back of the bridge when Ivory was going down and the trailer was mostly still coming slightly up, while the table top was wider than the bridge's wrought iron railing and had to be lifted up on alternate sides. It had been a case of going very slowly and being very careful, for any injury these days could be a serious matter.

Actually, once we had gotten it through the warehouse's loading door, someone insisted that it simply had to come apart somehow. Although it had been under a tarp in a vacant yard behind the Masonic Lodge, which was being demolished at the time when Philippe had spotted it, the thing had obviously not been constructed in situ in the Grand Chamber. Raoul and I discovered its secret connections at about the same time, and then it had been not too much trouble to take it apart. It had been made of pie pieces with rounded ends that met in the centre.

"Well, aren't you going to open it?" Mélusine and Joëlle demanded.

The package from Mariko was on the edge of the table, simply because no normal human being could bend and reach into the middle of it. Indeed, once it had obviously accommodated two or three more chairs. Probably the canonical twelve – or thirteen? I knew nothing of Masons and their lore. Perhaps some of the chairs had got broken over the years, presumably by overweight Masons. I saw that the package was, indeed, addressed to me.

"Now, Joëlle," I said piously, "… and Mélusine… a great many things will be revealed unto you."

"Not if you don't open it," Joëlle said.

This took some doing, what with the tape, twine and thick cardboard holding the bubble wrapping together. It was hard to get bubble-wrap these days. The package was heavy and it was bulky too. Gradually, it became apparent that the uncreaseable Mister Stuart and his associates had spared no expense with the book. It was intended to look like a two-foot tall ancient holy book and the cover was either mock leather or real leather, I couldn't tell, dark ancient brown with The Gospel of Mary Magdalene stamped on it in a reverse intaglio. I admit that I did wipe my hands very well on my jeans when I saw the stunning presentation.

"My god," Joëlle breathed, "it's beautiful."

This was a numbered first edition of 10,000 copies. Mariko had sent two copies. Mine was numbered 00001 and Joëlle's 00027. Little slips of paper were tucked into each book with these numbers prominent. I pushed Joëlle's copy over to her, still nestled in the wrapping because we had still not been able, even with two weeks of off and on sanding, to get the oak table's top glossy-smooth. I was looking at Mariko's inscription to me on the title page, also numbered, of very thick, glossy and mock-parchment paper – blue ink and a too familiar hand: *For Captain Marc Rennsalaer, perhaps the last knight errant.* I read it out loud.

"What does yours say, Joey?"

"I'm afraid to open it."

"Why?"

"I don't want to injure it."

"Hmmm. I doubt that HRH would like that reaction in most consumers." On the other hand, I reflected, perhaps that reaction was precisely what he had intended. Readers would approach the Gospel with the reverence it warranted.

"HRH?"

"Never mind."

She very gingerly opened the book. "Jesus, look at the paper…"

"Jesus… is the entire idea, Joëlle," I said unctuously.

"For Joëlle, who accepted so much on faith." Her voice

cracked at the end.

"Is that true?" I asked.

"Yes," she whispered and I saw tears skittering down her cheeks.

Women.

In the best tradition of Barnum and Bailey, HRH had told the media almost everything there was to know about how the new Gospel had been found and how it had been authenticated. There had been personal sketches of Mariko and myself. Indeed the media had reported everything – *except what the Gospel actually said*. The only thing that Mariko and HRH would reveal was that the new Gospel was shocking in its content and would cause the origin and meaning of Christianity to be re-evaluated.

Even in this time of crisis, anxiety and trepidation, this had kept curiosity and perhaps mild fear along with stronger hope alive among thousands, perhaps millions, of newspaper readers in the Western world. The Gospel had managed to remain a tantalizing media event over the course of almost four months.

Now, of course, with the release of the book and its content out of the bag, there would be television documentaries, not to mention scores of radio and television interviews. Thankfully, Mariko O'Shaugnessey would have to cope with these. I did not think she would mind all the hoopla. Revenge is sweet.

The Vatican had already declared the Gospel to be a forgery and a fake – and in any case heretical. This was more than HRH could ever have hoped before the text was actually published. A sort of 'Banned in Boston' from the horse's mouth, as it were. Possibly this alone had justified a more lavish product than what might have been originally intended.

"How much do you think each copy costs?" asked Mélusine.

"At least a thousand Euros," said Joëlle.

"Try half that... or four hundred," I said. I knew a little bit about book publishing myself from *War Crimes*, my memoirs and observations on Somalia, Desert Storm, the Philippines and East Timor. It had not done too badly and, in fact, had largely paid for the building of *Folderol Jester*. The book had gotten us both to France and had subsidized the start of my life as a canal bargee operating hesitantly out of Narbonne.

"Anyway, it's beautiful," Joëlle said again.

I noticed, as I turned the pages carefully with my fingertips, that the first few dozen glossy pages covered The Discovery, The Authentication and The Translation illustrated with superb colour photographs. There was even one of me and *Folderol Jester* and I remember well signing the release for it in the King's Arms. Then a page was blank except for: The Text of The Gospel of Mary Magdalene. Thereafter, sumptuous colour photographs filled each left-hand page with a fragment of the actual parchment – vellum, according to Mariko – on a rich royal magenta background while the corresponding English translation was on the facing right-hand page. The book reeked of age, sanctity and authenticity.

Pierre Falardeau had been given the Afterword – a lead-in to the French edition, of course. It would be translated into almost every language in the world and in editions of shrewdly calculated ever-diminishing price. HRH and his associates would make a fair return on their investment. And so would I. Mariko had wanted to give me half the royalties as well as half the advance – plus that $10,000 against my expenses. I accepted the half of the advance and the expenses, but I knew that half of the ongoing royalties was too much and would sooner or later become a source of regret for her.

I wanted no regrets for either of us because the cost of the Gospel had already been immense in the coin of pain.

I insisted on only a quarter of the ongoing royalties and a copy of the first edition. This was also finalized at the King's Arms. The only things I had forfeited by leaving London and Mariko were Mariko herself and, by contract, any responsibility of Stuart & Associates to keep paying my expenses and mooring fees until the first royalty instalment was payable. I had not contracted for two copies. That was, I supposed, Mariko's gift to Joëlle.

"Okay," I said, "back to work. Joëlle, would you mind taking my copy into my bedroom? My hands are a bit dirty."

Joëlle and I had signed a legal agreement within a week after my arrival in Aiguillon. It was simple in intent, if not in legalese. Joëlle would try not to get pregnant and we would both be equally responsible for the use of contraceptives. If she did become pregnant and bear a child of mine – on the evidence of DNA, blood and other tests recognized by French law, in the opinion of a duly constituted court – then I undertook to provide for the child with a bulk payment at birth and provisions for reasonable support thereafter to the age of 21.

Joëlle would retain the share-interest she currently held in our organization headquartered at Aiguillon. We were both free to dissolve our agreement and, if we wished, marry someone else. Joëlle's uncle, Hervé, had witnessed the document on her behalf, as had Christine and Marie-Thérèse. Raoul Doucet and Philippe Beaupré had been my witnesses. Mélusine wasn't present because she was back at the warehouse cooking a modest feast and baking all sorts of traditional cakes and sweetbreads. We regarded this as a wedding *of sorts*, anyway, or at least a social and financial union of two consenting people.

Joëlle and I had exchanged rings in token of this agreement and, after almost seven years, we felt – at least I did – somewhat more bonded. Our celebratory kiss did not hold much passion, maybe, but it was symbolic of already-proven commitment. More than anything else, however, the agreement legally protected Joëlle and any children of mine as my heirs under French law. As we kissed, Joëlle whispered in English – and it was typical of her – "And I have not forgotten the other conditions, Marc."

It is understandable that we all wanted to return to the warehouse as quickly as possible. The local nastiness of only a week earlier had made us all wary and uneasy. So I went back immediately from the lawyers' office with Raoul and Philippe. We went in Ivory with Hervé following with the women in his small car. By then, Ivory had negotiated the hump-backed bridge several times. Hervé's car barely squeezed over it.

We had a small and sober celebration what with the Calvados and the various wines in the warehouse to set off Mélusine's cassoulet. We kept things simple. We were really looking forward to our 'Greenwood marriage', as I had called it, and I had wanted to celebrate this as quickly as possible too. Both Mélusine and Joëlle, sharing some quick and secret glance between them, had nixed this idea.

No bonding was likely to bring good luck near the close of the year and Samhain was fast approaching. A proper bonding had to be celebrated in the spring, at Beltane. Since they both agreed on this with such vehemence, and since they both seemed to know what these terms meant, I let it go. Needless to say, Joëlle and Mélusine had also bonded, and at first sight. It didn't take *them* seven years. On the other hand, their close rapport was to prove short-lived with intervals of mere off-and-on mutual tolerance.

This is all to explain why Joëlle and I had separate bedrooms. I am in favour of this anyway. Couples need their separate spaces. Joëlle had been true to her word of last summer when 'we' had acquired the warehouse. I had maybe the best room in the whole building. It was on the front corner of the warehouse and what had once been an office window overlooked the inlet from the Garonne and the wharf and therefore offered a view of the widened-out corner turning pool. It also incorporated the best of the two silos, the one that hadn't leaked. Exactly what to *do* with this silo was another matter.

Before I had arrived, they had all agreed on the distribution of space. Raoul and Christine, and Philippe and Marie-Thérèse, had small apartments contrived from the existing 'front office' space. We had a communal bathroom – or rather two of them, once 'Hommes' and 'Femmes' back in the 1950s perhaps. And they had made a true bath room near these with a four-person huge plastic tub (and shower) bought in Agen and barged downstream by Raoul. This had been acquired from the money I had sent Joëlle from HRH's largesse. Getting water, hot water and then electricity had been, I gathered, a protracted and frustrating matter. Raoul and Philippe had had to lay an electric cable over the bridge (that is, under it) in order for the town to agree to hook up the electricity from the end of Rue de Larousse. By the time I got to Aiguillon these things had largely been sorted out. Originally they had made do with some appliances donated by Joëlle's uncle, Hervé.

Since mid-September with the advent of Mélusine and me to what might have passed for a hippie commune of the late 1960s, I had gently suggested some modifications. I proposed that Mélusine become our full-time and communal cook. There was no argument with this since Joëlle, Christine and Marie-Thérèse were all late 20th century women who didn't like cooking anyway. For them it was a chore, not a delightful outlet for creativity. I liked cooking, but the nature of our joint venture made it inevitable that Raoul, Philippe and I had to be away much of the time.

The financial efficiency of this suggestion also commended itself. Mélusine could buy local produce in fairly large quantities and one of us could transport it all back to the warehouse from Aiguillon in Ivory. Mélusine kept track of who was and wasn't available to be fed at any given time.

This had led to the acquisition of large restaurant-style appliances and pots and pans. One or the other of us had located this stuff in one of the canal towns we visited. And this policy of communal eating of Mélusine's nearly-gourmet offerings had inspired Philippe to react to the oak, well, monstrosity that now plainly ruled the dining area.

But the biggest change in our lives had been wrought by the wind-motors.

Once Mariko O'Shaugnessey's conical paper rose wrapping had been rendered in aluminium tube and Dacron cloth, the inevitable problems solved in theory, practice and finally refined, I discovered that it actually worked. By discussing the matter, mainly with Philippe and Raoul, we refined the design still further and decided to make a larger one. We eventually settled on twenty feet high and five feet in diameter as a kind of standard model. I have included a diagram of it because anyone can make one. This size of wind-motor could turn an automotive generator or alternator and supply from 1 to 3 kilowatts of electricity depending on the wind speed. It would start by itself and it didn't matter which way the wind blew. It was simple, and it was cheap to make. Since all the mechanicals were at the bottom of the wind-motor, it was easy to do maintenance and to effect repairs.

The one I was currently welding was the frame of number 6. We produced about one wind-motor a week in addition to what we would ordinarily do. One of the women would sew up the simple vanes on the old Singer pedal-operated sewing machine. It was a good thing that these vanes were simple, because the women were no better seamstresses than they were cooks.

Because it was within our means, we had called a

moratorium on anyone going out to work. The problem with the local crowd had decided me firmly that Joëlle was no longer going to commute long distance anywhere. Not until things had settled down locally and perhaps more police had been assigned to Aiguillon. Philippe and Marie-Thérèse had been helping Raoul and Christine to work their barge for three months anyway. We would expend most of our energy and our resources until the New Year in establishing our security and self-sufficiency within our warehouse. Then, we would begin trading again in earnest, but from a more efficient platform.

The other five wind-motors were already revolving merrily up on our warehouse's flat roof. With the prevailing wind generally funnelled down the inlet from the Lot River, from the west roughly, we were already producing from 5 to almost 15 kilowatts of electricity. This was stored in scavenged car batteries, of which there was an almost unlimited supply nowadays. Raoul said he would be able to convert most of our appliances to DC so that we could use this power. Electricity was a profound mystery to me. The welder, for example, ran directly off wind-motor power and 12-volt battery power because, according to Raoul, it already incorporated something called a transformer.

The most valuable potential thing about the wind-motor was that it would, at least in theory, work on a canal barge just as well as on the roof. We had to prioritize things, and 'critical path' planning had been Joëlle's profession. After adding wind-motor number 10 on the roof, she had calculated, we would have enough electricity production – if we could scavenge or buy more batteries – and could start applying the wind-motors to the barges. We would also continue on the roof-mounted ones until we reached the maximum of twenty that the roof could accommodate.

We had discovered that each wind-motor needed a certain amount of room around it – and we had also discovered that some wind-motors turning clockwise while others turned counter-clockwise seemed to feed each other somehow.

But we didn't know exactly how. Someday, through trial and error, we would discover the most efficient way to arrange them. For now, we were satisfied to weld up the frames to alternate the direction of rotation equally. Joëlle and Christine worked this production schedule out as well. Christine had once been a warehouse inventory clerk in a Bordeaux trucking firm. We had to buy the cloth, available at yachty sail-makers in Bordeaux, and for the moment there was enough of this too. We also bought old sails and there were plenty of these available. Eventually, though, we would have to use cotton or light canvas instead of Dacron. We were always on the lookout for automotive generators and old bicycles with their sprockets and chains.

Now, the problem, if it was one, was that Raoul and Philippe had both been truckers up until 2011. For that matter, Philippe was still technically a trucker since his trailer had not yet been converted into a barge in the way that Raoul had pioneered. As truckers, they were naturally used to having a lot of horsepower available. Only Raoul had gradually discovered that on mostly level canal water, just a few horsepower went a long way. I once explained that one man could comfortably tow 60 tons all day, once it was got moving, that is, and man-towed barges had been a common sight in England until 1900.

I loaned Raoul and Philippe my copy of *Requiem pour une Garonne défunte* by Pierre Vital. This book had been a present from Joëlle when we lived in Narbonne. The author had illustrated sail-powered barges in use on the Garonne until about 1900. We had already discovered that the wind-motors used wind more efficiently than an ordinary sail – I *thought* – and had the added virtue that one didn't have to know how to sail. And they had still another and greater virtue, as far as barges are concerned: they produced power but also continually spilled the wind. Wind-motors would not tend to heel a boat over.

The problem with wind-motors on barges was, of course, what to do when there was no wind? However, this situation was seldom encountered along the Canal du Midi because the valley of the Garonne was the weather corridor of the prevailing westerlies off the Atlantic across southern France. And, thankfully, the river current went the other way, against the wind. Still, could wind-motors supply the power that would satisfy ex-truckers? Probably not, but they could supply as much or more power than sailing barges of the early 20th century. Maybe we had no choice except to settle for that.

I finished the frame of number 6 by nightfall. It was time to sample Mélusine's ragoût.

14

Philippe was the lucky one, or the guinea pig, whichever way you want to view it. Since he had not had the chance or financial resources to convert his truck into a barge as Raoul had done, we all decided to try out the wind-motors first on Philippe's barge-to-be.

The first thing was to cut off the top four feet of his fibreglass 40-foot trailer 'à la Raoul' and to drop some wooden supporting frames inside. Following my suggestion to Raoul last summer, we converted the open rear end of the trailer into a ramp-style landing-craft type door like Jester's. We left two feet of hull that could be submerged when the barge-to-be was fully loaded, an estimated 15 tons or so, much more than Raoul's because of the more compact and barge-like arrangement.

We could not find any Styrofoam for the flotation under the deck, except for a few pieces of old packing-carton fillers for television sets and the like, so we finally used lots of 2-litre plastic bottles with their caps epoxied tight. Over the layer of plastic bottles, including some smaller ones to fill in all of the gaps between the 2-litre jugs, we screwed a 1½-inch plywood working deck to the wooden frames.

It was Raoul who had suggested that the new barge have three archways, each about 2 feet wide, from side to side across the 8 foot width: one near the bow, one near the middle and one near the putative stern. These archways, not unlike our hump-backed bridge and perhaps inspired by them, supported three 'standard' (by now) wind-motors at their centres. Now, I had refused to use any of my nearly priceless stainless steel wire and Nicopress fittings for the wind-motors on the warehouse roof. They were guyed by plastic-covered wire clothes line, rope, and just about anything that came to hand.

But for Philippe, I did offer the stainless steel wire and we set up the three wind-motors properly with open-barrelled turnbuckles from Agen. The one in the middle rotated counter-clockwise, the two end ones clockwise. They turned automobile generators attached to the underside of the light steel tube and plywood archways. This was to give them some protection from the rain. The archways also supported, underneath, an I-section beam of steel that took an old chain hoist that Raoul had. So much for the loading crane.

Christine, Marie-Thérèse and Joëlle designed, measured and sewed up a tarp that covered the entire cargo area and which used these archways as ribs and the I-beam as a ridgepole. The tarp rolled down from the middle to either side. This had been what Raoul had intended all along.

I convinced Raoul and Philippe that an impeller was more efficient than any propeller because the water had no place to go but out the thrust tubes. With a conventional propeller, water could escape off the ends of the blades. Therefore, we constructed this impeller housing and thrust tubes from plywood covered with fibreglass and epoxy resin, which was now almost literally worth its weight in gold. We constructed this submerged impeller system carefully and included ducts for reverse and side thrust. There was an advantage to impellers: thrust could be taken from around the housing and avoided the need for a transmission.

From Bordeaux, on one of my quick and infrequent trips to sell some of our Calvados there and to buy Moroccan flour cheaply, always with either Raoul or Philippe, we acquired a nominal five horsepower electric motor. We launched the barge, checked for leaks and then wrestled the electric motor aboard. With the storage batteries just arranged on the deck for the moment, we slid the barge around to the front of the warehouse near the bridge in order to get the full benefit of the wind coming down the inlet. We left Raoul to it, for a few hours, and he managed to connect the wind-motors to the generators, the generators to the batteries, and the batteries to the 5 hp motor.

The next day, Raoul declared the wind-motors to be working, the batteries to be working and the electric motor to be working. Since he had by far the most experience with this sort of barge, he took it out onto the Garonne. The wind-motor powered barge could not go under our bridge. Jester shadowed the new barge like a mother hen. Raoul wore a life jacket and I kept a life ring ready to toss.

It was quickly evident that the new barge was a theoretical success. The wind-motors would move it fairly well. It didn't heel very much, but the windage of the windmills pushed it sideways and not always where Raoul steered it with the plywood and fibreglass rudder. I should have thought of that, of course. However, I assured everyone that the trouble could be solved with the addition of plywood and fibreglass leeboards, like those on Dutch Zuider Zee barges (but better). These took two days to make and they solved the problem.

We now come to something of a disagreement between Raoul and Philippe on one side and me on the other. I had suggested that the barge might make do with wind-motors alone. Raoul and Philippe adamantly refused. They would not trust to wind power alone, and I suppose I couldn't blame them. I had wanted a steam engine on Jester, and so did Philippe. We discussed this around the oak table, and finally came to an agreement. We would try to duplicate a less powerful version of Jester's engine, say 5-7 horsepower, for use when there was no wind. With the usual wind, this gave a total of perhaps 10-13 horsepower if someone wanted to use the fuel.

The question was: could we do it? We looked at Jester's engine, which could produce about fifty horsepower, and discussed ways of copying it with the tools we had. It had been the simplest steam engine I could design, short of the rocking-cylinder design of toys. Our tools were, in reality, very good – my DeWalt rechargeable saw, grinder and several drills and all of Raoul's wrenches and sockets – but we could not manage fine-tolerance machining. As the ideas flew, it gradually became apparent that we could use already-machined parts. The idea was the main thing, and that had been done for us long ago by James Watt.

So we made a simple steam engine from stainless steel pipe, an automotive piston that fit inside – with some honing using a hand drill and a brake cylinder attachment. This took several hours. We used an automotive connecting rod, cut in the middle, with both ends welded into a length of steel tube to fit the stroke and flywheel, which was a 12-inch Citroën wheel weighted (at first) around the rim with through-bolted pieces of scrap steel. The engine thus had a stroke of 12-inches and a cylinder bore of 3-inches. We naturally used automotive valves and springs and the cam was a carefully contrived bump on the wheel rim. I have included a drawing of this engine in case it should prove of use.

We made a boiler from a scavenged industrial-sized Calor (Propane, in Europe) tank that was rusting beside an abandoned restaurant. We bought safety valves in an Agen welders' supply store. The firebox was an old kerosene stove in which we burned coal oil.

All this took about a month-and-a-half of dedicated, but not full-time, labour. Sometimes we worked late into the night because we knew we were working for ourselves. Finally, the big day came, in late November, for the steam engine. It was only a single expansion affair, much simpler but less efficient than a triple-expansion engine, and basically a modified copy of Jester's. After all, we had plenty of water all around us and could afford to use it only once for steam, exhausting the steam into the atmosphere where it would only condense back into water again. Now Raoul and I both knew, even if Philippe did not, that this steam engine would work. The question was: how long would it work?

We naturally fed it steam very slowly and cautiously. It began to turn over on cue, but at about 30 rpm it became noisily apparent that our flywheel was not balanced correctly. Gradually, by re-arranging the scrap weights and adding (and then subtracting) a bit, we got the thing running very smoothly. The only real problem was the lubrication. Like the early steam engines and even some up to the 1920s, it had to be given a drop of oil manually in various places.

Eventually that same night, we took it up to 200 rpm, which was about all we thought it was safe for. And, again for safety reasons, we limited the boiler pressure to just 100psi. And we had to balance it again because a vibration set in at 150-200 rpm. By my calculations this engine produced 4.2 horsepower at 200 rpm and at only 100psi of boiler pressure. Then the next day we added three automotive generators run by bicycle chains and sprockets off the flywheel. It may have looked like one of Emmet's or Rube Goldberg's creations but it worked.

We were all somewhat disappointed with this power, so we arbitrarily upped the boiler pressure to 200psi since the Calor tank (new and in factory condition) was supposedly good for 1000psi. Ours was old and superficially rusty, but we thought it should take 200psi. Then, by my calculations, we could get roughly 8.4 hp from it at 200 rpm. This satisfied Raoul and Philippe.

Between us three taking turns looking after it, and oiling it, we ran it for 24 continuous hours and finally judged it successful.

As Raoul remarked, now came the tedious part.

Raoul and I went over all the electrical and mechanical parts again in order to upgrade everything from a 'cut-and-fit' prototype into a finished production model. This is often the most difficult stage. Once Philippe had decided on the cabin and wheelhouse location and layout – at the traditional stern with the wheelhouse extending well above the aft-most archway, partly supporting it and being supported by it, Raoul arranged the batteries accordingly. He made proper plywood shelving for them in a large and sturdy enclosed cabinet or locker, not forgetting a top vent for the hydrogen gas that batteries give off.

As for me I replaced the scraps that had temporarily balanced the steam engine with a tapered bulge of lead cast from old battery plates and a few large lead fishing line sinkers. This plug fit snugly into the Citroën wheel rim and was bolted in securely with cotter-pinned nuts. And naturally I made it just a bit too large and heavy so that the plug could be progressively ground and cut away until it balanced 'perfectly' at 200 rpm.

While Raoul and I were doing the electrical and mechanical work, Philippe and Marie-Thérèse painted their new barge blue and white, just liked Raoul's barge, with the mechanicals picked out in red, again like Raoul's colour scheme. In a new and modernistic twist, Philippe, as I have said, extended the actual wheelhouse well above the cabin roof in order to have vision above the three archways and the cargo-covering tarp. This wheelhouse was also streamlined so his barge looked nothing like a traditional canal barge.

The new barge looked quite modernistic with its three archways and wind-motors. It didn't look 'traditional' at all. And Raoul showed Philippe how to operate it, imparting his own rather recent canal and river lore to Philippe. I had another book, one of the cherished twenty, called The River's in My Blood that also explained the way to handle a barge in current when approaching bridges and curves. True, it had been written about the Mississippi, but the essential principles were the same among all the rivers of the world. Unfortunately, though, it was in English, so Raoul and Philippe got more from the diagrams than from the text.

In conformity with our much-discussed strategy around the round oak table, Philippe had made the stern cabin small and functional for two people, himself and Marie-Thérèse as the usual crew. The cabin had two bunk-beds to conserve space, but they were comfortable with good foam mattresses, a small galley with a travel-trailer Dometic refrigerator from Sweden and a coal-oil stove for minimal travel cooking, and a chemical toilet. The boiler, just alongside the cabin on one side, and the engine alongside the cabin on the other, provided sufficient hot water for washing dishes and persons. The steam line through the cabin provided some heat during the mild and short Midi winters – and de-fogged the raised wheelhouse's large windows. The steam line could be re-wrapped with foil-covered insulation during the summer when any heat was superfluous. These windows were of automotive shatterproof glass.

The round-table strategy we had discussed so much involved short-term trips to Bordeaux on the Atlantic side of the Canal du Midi and to Narbonne on the Mediterranean side. From Bordeaux one could obtain red Bordeaux wine, apples, apricots, peaches and pears from the Landes, plus incoming Moroccan flour in small freighters at Royan.

From Narbonne, one could obtain citrus fruits from Spain and the Narbonnais, plus incoming leather goods from Spain, Italy and now, the Adriatic countries of Serbia, Croatia, Albania and Montenegro.

From about the middle of the Canal du Midi, where we were, there was upland honey, oats, barley and some wheat from the valleys of the Massif Central to be had up the Lot River. Here were also potatoes, turnips (fresh or pickled), and a good supply of pâté, some pigskin and some limited amounts of white wines and even much more limited amounts of champagne.

All over and everywhere, of course, there were a great variety of cheeses. And thankfully, as with wines, the people of France mostly preferred cheeses from anywhere else but their own region. Thus, from our more or less central position in the south of France, there were brisk opportunities for canal trade.

Actually Aiguillon was a bit too far west of the middle of the canal route to be the optimum location. Moissac would have been a more central position but Raoul had never found a warehouse there that we could have afforded at the time.

But there was one advantage to our location. Not having the fisheries of the Atlantic and not having the sunshine and allure of the Mediterranean, the Lot-et-Garonne was something of a depressed area and so it was cheaper to live there. On the other hand, it had had to be self-sufficient for thousands of years and so these uplands had developed small family farming, mixed farming, in order to support its population. And this population had traditionally been rather small because the more ambitious younger people had migrated away to the Atlantic or the Mediterranean.

Therefore, not only was it less expensive to live there, but there was always a sufficient quantity of mixed produce to sustain life, even if there was not a great excess of anything. The 20th century's mechanized agribusiness had affected the Lot-et-Garonne less than other places.

Joëlle mostly developed our trading strategy. Christine contributed her invaluable help from her long experience as an inventory clerk in a Bordeaux trucking firm, hauling goods from Bordeaux to Narbonne and back again, and stopping in towns all along the route from the Atlantic to the Mediterranean. This strategy basically evolved into one of short hops from our 'nearly' central position in Aiguillon. We would go up the Lot River into the highlands of the Massif Central. Then we would go east or west to either Bordeaux on the Atlantic or to Narbonne on the Mediterranean.

The goods acquired in these places, so long as they were not quickly perishable, could be sold at a profit where such goods were in greater local demand. Since we had a warehouse that could store non-perishable goods, at least, we could wait until the demand for a certain product was peaking and sell at a higher price than we had bought it. Trading, in short. Joëlle and Christine kept computerized track of what products were available in which areas and what products were in demand in other areas.

By early December we had three barges – in theory. Philippe's new barge was assigned to go up the Lot River and brought upland produce down to the warehouse at Aiguillon. This would give him relatively safe experience in using a river instead of a highway. Raoul had the Bordeaux to Aiguillon run and Jester was putatively assigned the Aiguillon to Narbonne run. As long as I was not otherwise engaged in personal adventures, that is. Raoul would take over the east-to-west run from Bordeaux to Narbonne route temporarily should 'opportunities' arise, my adventures having more than paid their way so far. Indeed, my adventures with Mariko O'Shaugnessey and the Gospel had largely supported us and financed the construction of the wind-motors, Philippe's new barge and much else.

By early December, too, it became obvious that Philippe's new barge was a cost-effective commercial success. Using wind for fuel about 85% of the time, except for the ongoing costs of maintaining the wind-motors, Philippe and Marie-Thérèse decided to name their barge Véronique, which was a short form (more or less) of 'camion mécanique environnemental'. After Philippe and Marie-Thérèse had made two short and quite profitable trips up the Lot to Villeneuve-sur-Lot, mainly because of the savings in fuel, Raoul expressed his determination to make Mer-Cedez into a copy of Philippe's barge.

Raoul's barge, as I have described elsewhere, was a cobbled-together affair using his original Mercedes truck engine converted to a two-stroke steam engine by a special cam and using an old heating boiler from an apartment building to generate steam. It was paddle wheel powered using the Mercedes tractor axles with welded paddle wheels in the wheel rims. It worked, but not very efficiently.

Around our oak table, his request – or demand – was unanimously approved. And so we set to the task immediately. This used some of my quickly diminishing financial cushion from Mister Stewart, but Joëlle's spreadsheets and projections showed that another wind-motor barge would add greatly to our future profits.

Now, having done it once for Véronique, converting Raoul's barge was not such a headache. All of the problems had been solved with Philippe's barge. The only difficulty was going into Bordeaux to get the necessary components. Some things were in short supply and were, of course, much more expensive than formerly.

But we discovered that the Western world still did produce top-quality stainless steel wire, welding wire (steel and aluminium), inert gasses like argon, stainless steel turnbuckles, Nicopress sleeves and 5 hp electric motors – even if these items were somewhat slower in getting to market. This is another way of saying that some high-tech items, after an initial shortfall, were again becoming available but in lesser quantities. One sometimes had to order certain items and wait for delivery.

In fact, we found 5 hp electric motors with aluminium cases from Belgium, and not with steel ones, and so these motors weighed 200 pounds less than the one we had used on Philippe's barge. Two hundred pounds less weight was either two hundred pounds more cargo or some extra speed – and time was still money. So, we bought three… one for Philippe, one for Raoul and one for another barge-to-be.

A little less than two weeks before Yuletide, Philippe, Raoul and I had finished Raoul's barge to Philippe specifications. Raoul then replaced the four-stroke cam in his beloved Mercedes engine and we parked his truck tractor cab beside the warehouse and next to Philippe's GMC truck tractor cab alongside the warehouse. Maybe things might yet change for the better and they could become truckers once again. We all knew that trailers for the tractors were no problem.

Hundreds of them littered the countryside in every garage lot and, sometimes, in house driveways. I noticed that both Raoul and Philippe protected and maintained their truck tractors as if they were shrines. And, of course, they were. The Mercedes and GMC tractors parked neatly by our warehouse were, in reality, the old gods of a vanished social order and I begrudged no homage to them.

The matter of an Ivory-like vehicle for Raoul and Philippe had come up in discussion as early as November. So, during the first hectic two weeks in December, we had made two more vehicles from double-axle boat trailers we had been able to find. We failed to standardize them with Kawasaki motorcycle engines like Ivory, but we used one Citroën 2CV and one Honda engine instead.

However, it was to take three more months before the full complement of scuba tanks had been collected and, in the meantime, Raoul and Philippe had to make do with less than 50% of Ivory's road range and loading-endurance capacity. But these vehicles were fully amphibious – and, unlike Ivory, did not leak at all.

That was because they could be made in one piece because their length would never have to be extended for use as a trailer on their barges. This fact speeded up their construction. Ivory could be lengthened to become a highway trailer for Jester. Indeed, the desperate escape from Carcassonne over the Massif Central with Mariko was how I had first met Philippe Beaupré and his GMC truck. I had known Raoul Doucet a little longer.

To bring their vehicles up to Jester-like specifications we also had to find sufficient lengths of herring-bone pattern conveyor belting. Two lengths of conveyor belting fitted around the two rear tires converted the vehicles from road and highway capability into half-track ATVs. The herring-bone conveyor belt pattern with the '>' tread facing forward provided some propulsion in water.

The vehicles enabled one man to load or unload a barge in half the time that it would ordinarily take two or more people to do the same job.

While all this was going on, Joëlle and the other women had already determined (by computer analysis) that our three powered barges would be more cost-effective and much more profitable if they also pushed a 25-foot long by 8-foot wide non-powered barge. Given a generous safety margin of, say, two feet of immersion with a gunwale of four feet, this extra scow or barge would increase the payload-per-trip by a safe 10 tons.

I had insisted on a ramp-style landing craft-type door in the front of each barge and a working deck over a 1-foot flotation chamber consisting of Styrofoam and/or empty plastic bottles in the manner of Philippe's barge. The ramp-style doors meant that the vehicles could be used to load and unload these unpowered barges as well. The flotation meant that we might lose a cargo, but we wouldn't lose the barge along with it. I also insisted on a Dacron or canvas cover over angle or tubular steel hoops in order to protect any cargo.

Accordingly, I had drawn up the plans for such an unpowered barge, to be built of plywood and fibreglass. This type of barge used only polyester instead of epoxy resin. This was somewhat less expensive.

The three women made three of these unpowered barges between the beginning of October and the third week of December. They were also painted blue and white. Not having any mechanical parts to speak of, they were spared the red. I saw this lack of red, along with Raoul and Philippe, and then we all agreed that the cleats showing above the gunwales just had to be painted red. These unpowered barges were not given names, but they were at least dignified with numbers – 1, 2, 3 – also in red.

In fact, Philippe and Marie-Thérèse made their last trip of the year up the Lot to Villeneuve-sur-Lot with such a barge and had brought back to our Aiguillon warehouse almost all the home-bottled pâté that had been available. There had been a good deal of cargo space left over and they had filled it with home-smoked hams and sausages.

Me, I doubted strongly that any of these products would have passed once-modern bacterial scrutiny. But they were what the people of the Lot-et-Garonne had lived on for several thousand years, with their several thousand fatalities per year, which beat famine fatalities by a significant degree in terms of the total numbers of deaths per annum.

Naturally, part of some cargoes stayed in our warehouse as provisions for ourselves, such as flour, pâté and small quantities of the more exotic fresh fruits, like Spanish oranges. Once we had three on-board vehicles operating it was easier for Mélusine to buy the fresh provisions we needed in Aiguillon. The vehicles of Raoul and Philippe did not yet have their planned complement of scuba tanks, but they held enough compressed air to manage the two kilometres into Aiguillon and the two kilometres back.

I remember that Yuletide as being a particularly eventful one, but maybe that is only because of the drama that happened so soon after the turn of the year. About a week before Christmas, our approved registrations for the handguns arrived in the mail. These had been stamped by Inspecteur Bernard Gabereau as Chief of the Canal du Midi Police in Carcassonne.

We had agreed around the oak table that the men would carry 9mm automatics while the women would carry .25mm Beretta automatics. This was to standardize ammunition as much as possible. I have already mentioned that barge owners or captains were permitted to carry handguns. This was because of the ever-increasing possibility of violence involving barges carrying food.

Joëlle had structured a corporation in which all of us held shares, hence Christine was a barge owner as well as Raoul and Marie-Thérèse was a barge owner as well as Philippe, Joëlle as well as me. Consequently, the women could carry firearms as well as the men. Indeed, we made it a rule that the women carried their guns at all times off the spit of land where our warehouse was located and at all times when on a barge. Mélusine devised thick leather holsters for these handguns and sewed them up on the venerable Singer. I stuck with my old shoulder holster and the Walther PPK.

Mélusine was registered as a barge-owner too, of that barge-to-be represented by that third electric motor with the aluminium casing. This was a polite fiction, but it must have seemed reasonable to Gabereau that she would crew on one of our barges from time to time – as indeed she had. Therefore, Mélusine got her Beretta too. We agreed on regular target practice beside the warehouse and behind the two parked truck tractors. The noise did something, I'm sure, to deter any thoughts of further 'riots' directed against us. Philippe and I taught the others 'safety first' with a handgun. It is too easy to shoot oneself, or someone in close proximity, by 'accident'. There are really very few genuine accidents. Almost all of them can be traced back to carelessness.

I have never liked handguns for this reason – although I admit they have their uses. I suggested around the table that we should buy one kind of rifle for all of us, and we discussed this. Since I, with the possible exception of Philippe, had the most experience, I suggested the cheapest and most basic .22 rifle we could get, so long as it wasn't a single-shot and had at least a 5-round magazine. A .22 Long Rifle will kill or wound almost any human being at any reasonable range – I put this range at about 50 yards (or metres) in most defences against a crowd.

There was no recoil that a woman couldn't handle with a .22 and the ammunition was plentiful and cheap. Philippe agreed. So, between Bordeaux and Agen, we found seven identical French FN (Fabrique Nationale) downscale models of a .22 that would take Long Rifle ammunition and had a magazine capacity of 10 rounds. I insisted on downscale but very strong and perfectly adequate nylon-strap shoulder slings for each rifle.

The bolt-action mechanism was sticky and badly machined with five of the rifles, but we remedied this situation with judicious Dremel grinding and buffing with rouge. Philippe and I were in charge of this and we weren't satisfied until the actions worked like butter. We also bought seven spare magazines and 20 boxes, or 1,000 rounds of Long Rifle ammunition. In France, one did not yet require any license to own a rifle or shotgun.

But that Christmas season was also busy for another reason. To soften the sheer SFX impact of the daily target and safety practice with both the handguns and the rifles, Joëlle and Mélusine had approached the Aiguillon Social Services (such as it was). They volunteered to prepare a Christmas dinner for everyone who was hungry, unemployed and/or a single mother. The Social Service workers were responsible for assessing who was qualified to get fed and where this would take place. They also had to feed the people from the dishes, cutlery and pots and pans of food we provided. We would wash up.

This had also been discussed and approved around the oak monstrosity and we thought we could go so far as to provide a soup kitchen twice a week at the City Hall from January to March, during the depth of the mild Midi winter. The town thanked us for this 'generous' gesture and, in return, complied with our request to provide a police escort for the food and personnel back and forth to the Hôtel de Ville.

Naturally, this also gave our organization the aura of *being on the side of the powers that be in Aiguillon* – a perception that might greatly reduce the chance of another nastiness as had happened in mid-September. I did not take peoples' gratitude too seriously as a deterrent.

So, Mélusine was busy in the week leading up to Christmas. And she sometimes took a load of baked goods, pots and pans into Aiguillon in one of the vehicles, usually Ivory, after the vehicle had warmed up overnight in the warehouse and had been recharged with compressed air using 12-volt current generated by the roof array of wind-motors. Joëlle, Christine or Marie-Thérèse usually accompanied her.

It was during one of those outings some days before Christmas when Raoul and I became restless and, almost by unspoken common consent, tackled the two large jobs we had originally scheduled for doing before the end of the year.

The first job was the hump-backed bridge. Since mid-September's unpleasantness, we had been discussing the possibility of making it into a drawbridge. Both Raoul and I had hit upon the same idea, the obvious one. To put steel-plate flanges beside both bottoms of the large wrought-iron tubes on our side of the inlet. These tubes supported the bridge's wooden floor. We would then put strong bolts through the flanges and tubes, and only *then* cut the tubes below these bolts.

As for the Aiguillon side of the bridge, we would just cut the wrought-iron tubes off near their bases and weld some sort of curved steel 'tusk' onto each stump. The idea was that the pointed ends of these curved tusks would enter the bridge's wrought-iron tubes and then guide the lowering bridge to its proper position on the stumps. As for raising it up, a Toyota Land Cruiser winch in the far (western) silo would wind up a steel cable attached to the hump-backed middle of the bridge.

Raoul and I, with hardly a word spoken, went to work

almost as soon as Mélusine and Christine had wuffled off toward Aiguillon with the promised gendarme riding on Ivory's gunwale.

The job took two full days because we did it well. Being the designated welder, I had to fabricate the thick flanges that were, in reality pivots or 'hinges' on our side of the bridge. While I was doing this, Raoul cracked the concrete with a sledgehammer and a punch, removed the cement pieces and dug two 3-foot deep holes into the turf of the inlet's bank just inside the retaining wall.

The flanges were welded to long bolts and pieces of steel scrap and were set down into the holes that were then filled with cement. And I had to fabricate the two curved tusk-like steel guides that fitted into the tube bases on the Aiguillon side. Most people say that you cannot weld steel to iron, but you certainly can if you take your time. We planned the work so that the bridge was actually out of service for only four hours.

And the bridge was really much lighter than we had thought. The curve of the humpback gave it its strength and although the structural wrought-iron tubes and the decorative fretwork along its balustrade looked heavy, the bridge proved to weigh only about two tons, or so we estimated. Because of the pivot, we had to lift all of this weight initially, but the weight became increasingly less as the bridge came up.

This was well within the Toyota winch's 5-ton capacity – we weren't nearly so certain of the strength of the silo's wall. Nothing seemed to crumble away on the first attempt. We had always suspected that the two silos had once been made of reinforced concrete. We decided that someday we would rig up a system of counter weights hanging vertically down the inside of the silo to take some of the sideways stress off the silo wall. An application of grease and the pivot bolts stopped their terrible initial squealing. By test, the Aiguillon side of the bridge could be lifted nine feet, or what a tall man could possibly jump, in about thirty seconds. The guiding tusks worked very well because there was almost no play in our pivots. This bridge could be lifted toward the vertical sufficiently so that one of the wind-motor powered barges could squeeze past if it stayed close to the Aiguillon side. *Jester* could more easily do the same. We therefore now had direct access to the Lot and the Garonne, and at least some further protection from any future crowd.

The second job that had been a subject of round-table discussion was to install one of Jester's two air-cannons somewhere at the top of 'my' silo, the one on the eastern side of the warehouse's front. Access to this silo was in a corner of my room through a curved wooden door that had been made when carpenters had still taken pride in their work.

We finally decided that putting a floor on a level just above the warehouse roof would be best. This was near enough to the top of the stubby silo and meant that no holes had to be cut into it. The cannon could just wheel around to shoot anywhere over the parapet. That meant putting in a floor at the right height inside the silo. And meant making steps leading up to a trap door in this floor.

In spite of the few hours of extra time entailed, I insisted on steps that clung to the silo's inner sides, and a trap door that also opened alongside the silo's wall. I didn't want to waste space. We finally decided that a curved fire-escape-like angle scaffolding was the best solution. With Raoul cutting as I welded, things went fairly quickly as all the steps were identical. From our collection of angle, tube and pipe we had gradually collected on our excursions in the vehicles and further afield in the barges, we found enough pipe to provide columns for the outside of the steps. For the inside supports, we drilled the angle and then used masonry bits to wrench in self-tapping carriage colts.

The silo already had a heavy-gauge galvanized sheet steel roof, a kind of 8-sided dome. This was bolted to a flange of angle so that it wouldn't blow off in the wind. We used the existing angle as a runway for supermarket-type rubber caster wheels welded to the nine ribs of the dome. And I welded our own flanges from the caster wheels down to hook beneath the curved flange that had been part of the silo and was now a runway. This was done when the wind had died down in the evening, and we modified the casters one at a time around the dome, working from the warehouse's roof. We didn't think it would ever blow off.

Now the dome would rotate on top of the silo. Raoul and I selected the worst of two adjoining panels of the eight galvanized curved sheets that comprised the silo's domed top. We pounded out the dents with rubber mallets. And, since we had discussed it all before, we welded these two sheets onto a short length of steel tube. This tube was intended to be dropped over a length of smaller tube that once connected all the panels of the dome at its apex.

Hanging this curved double-panel over the dome's original tube took much of our combined strength, a lot of profanity and several attempts working from the warehouse's roof. We secured this double panel with rubber-wheeled casters welded onto extensions so they, too, would fit on the original flange around the top of the silo and would not blow off... we hoped. But someday, this movable panel's edges would have to be reinforced, finished and edged with rubber or plastic to seal it better. These 'someday' refining jobs were accumulating at what seemed to be a geometrical progression. The list of them was becoming very long.

Nonetheless, when it was finally in place, this double panel that rolled aside from the revolving dome itself gave us a very wide field of fire and a wide aperture up to an almost vertical view. I remarked to Raoul that this dome was now a great place for a telescope... someday.

The air-cannon was mounted on an old shopping cart. This cart also carried two scuba tanks from Ivory's collection.

Another job: these two tanks would have to be replaced, found somewhere, somehow – along with the tanks needed to bring Raoul's and Philippe's compressed-air vehicles up to Ivory's specifications.

We finished the silo-mounted air-cannon about noon on Christmas day, just as Philippe and Marie-Thérèse returned from Villeneuve-sur-Lot with the first tryout of pushing an unpowered barge. This was the very profitable load, mainly of pâté, referred to earlier. After we all helped to unload the barges, we washed up for Mélusine's Christmas feast.

15

Unfortunately, there could be no rest until I did something about those silo stairs. They were a tragedy waiting to happen. I also had to do something about the curved door otherwise my room would be too cold for any comfort at all. None of us had been in Aiguillon during a winter and Mélusine had predicted – from reading caterpillar hairs in the fall – that this winter would be unusually harsh as Midi winters go.

I rummaged through our well-stocked junk pile, finding some rather crooked lengths of 1-inch steel pipe and many assorted lengths and sizes of steel angle. I was just about to start carrying this stuff into the silo when Raoul – and this was typical of him – heard the slight commotion, for I was trying to be quiet, and joined me.

"Bannister for those stairs?"

"They're a death trap and we don't need any accidents."

"You weld, I'll cut… and straighten out this pipe." He eyed along several lengths.

I rolled the welder into the silo while Raoul paid out electrical cord. Then we went back for the tube and angle. Then we went back for the tools we thought we would need. While we were doing this, I said that I wanted the handrail to be 33-inches tall – and very strong. He began cutting the angle into 35-inch lengths in order to compensate for the thickness of the 2-inch stairs. We had 26 stairs. It took an hour to weld on all the angle uprights with Raoul holding for me to get a tack and then I welded good beads while he cut.

If we welded three pieces of pipe together, we had enough for a banister and by the time I got to doing this, Raoul had straightened all three pieces.

"I guess we should weld first at the top and then bend and curve the pipe down to the bottom, tacking as we go." It is not hard to bend 1-inch pipe if you have a long length of it.

So, we began this, eyeing the pipe as we went down in order to get a good curve with the pipe resting on every upright. About this time, Philippe found us, took one look and left.

He returned minutes later with my DeWalt rechargeable grinder, a wire brush attachment and a pair of safety goggles. Squeezing past us and starting at the top, he wasn't in the way of our efforts further down. He ground down all the rough spots and then brushed all the welds smooth.

When Raoul and I were finished, I put some weight on the banister and shook it. It wiggled. "What about some pipe bending overhead and screwed into the cement?" said Raoul. "That should make it strong enough."

"I think you're right," I said. We started measuring.

We put five such supports up the stairs. We gave head clearance of 6-feet 3-inches because Philippe was taller than I am by almost an inch. We welded the overhead supports to the handrail, bent them in a curve to the wall where drilled plates could be screw-bolted into the cement of the silo wall. Again, Raoul cut and I welded. This time, the banister didn't move with our full weight thrown against it. It vibrated nicely, but it didn't really give.

Raoul and I knocked off and went into the kitchen for some breakfast which, Mélusine was making. As soon as Philippe was finished grinding and brushing, he joined us.

"One thing I've been wondering ever since I started barging," said Philippe.

"What's that?"

"Are there any fish in these rivers?"

"In theory," I replied. "There's the largest freshwater fish in the world in the Garonne, Danube, Rhône and Rhine."

"No shit?" said Raoul.

"None," I answered. "This is a kind of catfish called a 'Wels'. Their mouths can be four feet wide and they can be about 12 feet long and weigh 1200 pounds... 600 kilos."

"What do they eat – people?" This was Philippe.

"Other fish, ducks, geese. Only two reports of a child getting eaten – that I know of, that is." I added. "But that was along in the Danube during the late 1800s."

"How do you know such things?" Raoul grinned.

"I used to write offbeat newspaper stories in Canada."

"And then there are supposed to be big sturgeons in the Garonne," said Philippe. "I think I saw one once. Now, wouldn't that be fun, going fishing," he added.

"Maybe we could build a simple skiff," said Raoul. "Then we could fish. What kind of license do you need?"

"About the license I have no idea, but Joëlle or Christine could look it up on the Internet." I said. "And why do we need a skiff? Where we are, the fish should come to us… and from either river. Why not fish from the bridge?"

"You think they'd come into the inlet?" Philippe asked.

"I can't see why not," I said. "It's certainly wide and deep enough and I doubt that anyone has ever fished here, at least not for the past half-century or so. It might be just the place for a big sturgeon or catfish to lurk."

"I would like to try that," Philippe said enthusiastically. "I'll tie a line to the bridge."

"There are some hooks aboard *Jester* – hooks, bobbers, weights. Everything you need."

We finished our coffee and croissants. I pushed my chair back. "Anybody know if we have some white paint left?"

"Lots," said Raoul. "Left over from the new barges."

So we went back to the silo and Philippe set to painting the steps with metal primer and, once that was done to the bottom, the top was dry and he began again on the steps and handrail with white enamel. Raoul and I tackled the curved door. It needed rubber weather stripping on both sides of the door. We had bought some for the barge cabins and there was enough left to seal the door. By the time we were finished no wisp of a cold draft came from anywhere around the door.

"The problem is there's no light in this place," I said.

"We can rig one easily enough," Raoul replied.

"Let's think this through," I suggested. "Right now we can screw a fixture into the ceiling fairly easily. It is a long way up, about 16 feet but a 100-watt bulb should give enough light. And if we ever want to add another floor under that one, then another light fixture will serve for that room."

"Who would want to live in here?"

"Maybe not live, but use for various purposes. Remember, I mentioned the idea we could put a telescope up in the dome?"

"Hey, man, that would be great," Raoul said.

"And if we ever put in another room, we could use it for a library."

"That would make the ceilings about 8 feet high – high enough," said Raoul.

So, with me holding our longest ladder, Raoul screwed a light bulb fixture into the middle of the ceiling. And secured the electric cord across the ceiling (or floor) over to the silo's wall and down to my doorway. Here he put a switch and ran the cord, after drilling a small hole in the silo wall, back into the warehouse somewhere. About the time Philippe finished painting the steps, handrail and supports white, Raoul came back and said "All hooked up. Try her."

I flicked the switch and things were much better. The steps were bright white and couldn't be missed.

I must have under-estimated the seriousness Philippe's desire to fish, for later, around one o'clock on this dark afternoon, I saw him in the middle of the bridge looking down. He was wrapped in a coat and his breath came in white puffs. Shrugging into my windbreaker, I went through the warehouse's front doors and called out "I'll bring you some tackle."

My fishing tackle-box, such as it was, was somewhere in the bottom of a closet. I found it finally and trotted it back to Philippe on the bridge; trotted because it helped in the cold.

"Help yourself to what's there," I said. Then, "Oh, damn."

"What?"

"I forgot the most important thing," I grinned.

After five minutes I returned with the huge aluminium-handled Canadian landing net. It must have been designed for the largest Muskellunge that had ever lived. I had never caught anything large enough to deserve it, but it had caught crabs at Hoedic last summer.

By now, Philippe had a line out from the top of the bridge. A bobber was already in the water with the end of the line tied in a big loop over a wrought-iron tendril of vine leaves. There was something of a current in the water now with the sharp prevailing west wind blowing along the inlet from the Lot. Philippe's bobber was drifting toward the enlarged turn at the corner of the warehouse where our now deadly silo overlooked something of a pool.

"What are you using for bait?"

"Mélusine's ham."

After you got used to it, the cold was bracing. One gets used to a warm climate in the Midi. So as not to disturb Philippe's concentration, I leaned on the opposite balustrade and looked around. The front of the warehouse once had double glass office doors. Sometime before I arrived, Raoul and Philippe must have replaced them – maybe the glass had cracked – with faceless, but strong steel-clad fire doors. I knew the doors had handles on the outside and panic bars on the inside. You *could* open them from the outside, if you had a key, but they could be secured inside with beams set vertically inside the panic bars.

I saw that some attempt had also been made to put wooden shutters on all the windows – some of the panes were broken and taped over with thin ply, some panes had been replaced – and these shutters could also be locked by setting beams across them. I already knew that the three large loading doors giving onto the wharf from the warehouse were of articulated steel plate of modest thickness and had hook locks set into the cement floor to keep them from rolling up. They had done the best they could with what they had before I arrived and before I decided to commit the rest of my money to Joëlle and the warehouse commune that sustained us.

What they had already done before I showed up did much to explain everyone's willing and even frantic work once I had joined them, bringing an infusion of resources. We all knew, without saying anything very often, that firm establishment of ourselves now meant survival in a future that was likely to become grimmer.

My eye was teased upward by the wind-motors whirling on the roof in a somewhat dizzying effect because some were whirling one way while others whirled another. Christine had been right. They would have looked better if they had been made from coloured Dacron in horizontal bands – but we couldn't find enough coloured Dacron in Bordeaux, only sailcloth white, and time had been pressing. Just how pressing was proved by Philippe watching his bobber from the bridge that was now a drawbridge.

Raoul and I had completed the drawbridge when we did because our twenty wind-motors up on the roof had, just a week before, made us independent of Aiguillon's electricity supply.

Marie-Thérèse asked if she could try welding just for the fun of it, and I had let her have a go. As it turned out, she had excellent hand-eye co-ordination and was able to run a good steel bead within ten minutes. I then switched to the aluminium wire and argon, telling her about the special difficulties of welding aluminium – the danger of the radiation given off and the fact that melted aluminium doesn't change colour. It took her half an hour to get the hang of it using scraps of various kinds of aluminium – some tube, some angle and some sheet.

She also had an intuitive grasp of the current to be used

with various thickness of metal. So, it was Marie-Thérèse who welded up the last five wind-motor frames, which, with the addition of the Dacron vanes sewed by Joëlle, Christine and Mélusine, completed our roof array.

Independence from Aiguillon's power saved a great deal of money every month because electricity was no longer cheap. The wind-motors were reliably producing, along this prevailing wind corridor, from 20kw to 60kw. This was more than enough for our needs and, in fact, more than our storage capacity at the moment.

In order to forestall any envy, and therefore the enforcement or invention of some regulation requiring the purchase of electricity from the local grid, Joëlle had got on the Internet and informed the French government in Paris of the wind-motor. We offered plans of it for free, and even offered to make a few prototypes for copying. The Aiguillon, Agen and Bordeaux papers did big stories, with photographs, Joëlle did most of the talking and Marie-Thérèse was photographed welding. I was mentioned as the inventor but, being away in Agen, was unavailable for comment.

Once the vehicles were completed and painted, we promoted and offered their designs too as being transportation using compressed air that, in turn, used electricity to compress it. This concept wasn't ours. It had been pioneered by Guy Negre, the racing car designer, in his 'Evolution' automobile of 2002. We had made Negre's high-tech design work in a low-tech way.

And just then, I don't know why – maybe it was Philippe the ex-paratrooper near me on the bridge – I looked at the wind-motors revolving crazily on the warehouse roof and suddenly realized what I was *also* looking at. I pretended cold, wished Philippe good luck with his fishing, and hurried to *Jester* in order to sketch the thing before I lost the essentials.

16

Mélusine proved to be right (again). After Christmas, the weather turned colder than anyone had remembered for almost forty years. Ice about two inches thick formed over our backwater inlet. This had not happened since 1936. We could not venture out with the barges, as we had planned for the New Year because they could not power through such ice and besides, any attempt to do so would damage their hulls at the waterline.

However, the impellers came into their own in this situation because the outlet ports could be set to keep a small thrust of water going for and aft and from side to side. I had insisted on this added work when we made the impeller housings. Raoul and Philippe had thought me crazy, but now they thanked me. Canadian experience. And, though people in the Midi like to think they live in the tropics, a glance at any map proves them wrong. A continual and gentle upward roil of water surrounded the barges – so long as the steam engines were kept ticking over – and kept the ice at bay all around the hulls.

As for the unpowered barges, we hauled them up our quickly improvised mud boat ramp onto the wharf. Their covers kept the snow out.

Mélusine and the other women more than redoubled their efforts and supplied a soup kitchen at the Hôtel de Ville every day at noon so long as the deep freeze lasted. We had a fair stock of dried peas, potatoes, lentils, radishes, turnips and barley in our warehouse. And we had more than a fair stock of Moroccan flour. We had a fair store of butter. Ten gallons of soup per day barely put a dint in our sacks of trade goods. Mélusine made many loaves of bread. The only things we seriously depleted were butter for the bread and some sort of meat to put in the soups. Here we used almost all the wind-dried 'Parma' ham before the weather broke and we even cooked sausage for the soup.

The less fortunate people of Aiguillon probably thought that they would be abandoned on days when the snow blew and drifted and when ice made the roads slippery. Even the social workers were often late, but we never were. Ivory in half-track mode with the conveyor-belt treads would go though almost anything that Canada had to offer, much less the Midi. Ivory's light-duty trailer could be up-ended to form a cap for the truck bed and so the food always arrived hot – especially as we wrapped the pots with towels, sheets and even duvets. True to our policy, the women arrived with side-arms and their rifles. I wanted to give a double message, and in no uncertain terms.

Since we couldn't trade, we turned to the things we could do. I proposed an agenda that, first, refurbished all the window shutters with a layer of 1/8-inch steel plate welded direct to the hinges set in the concrete of the window sills. This meant, in practice, every one of the office windows in the front of the warehouse, now our living quarters. With all of us men working, this required three days, partly because we had to drive Ivory into Agen for enough plate.

Then I proposed some better and faster locking beam for the front double doors rather than just loose beams though the panic bars. Between us, we devised a system whereby a thick beam was pinned by a big bolt through the central door frame at an angle, but when it was positioned horizontally it also pivoted the vertical beams to lock the doors in three ways at once, top, bottom and across. This system was always held in place by guides or straps around the beams and could be operated in seconds. Then we reinforced the beams themselves with angle-steel corners.

The next item was the dome on 'my' silo where the air-cannon was. We had already made a good floor of plywood supported by beams set into the silo walls. We added 2-inch thick planks to this foundation and reinforced the beams with angle brackets screw-bolted into the silo's cement wall. We duly reinforced the sheet metal revolving double-panel on the dome that gave us our field of view – or fire. And we covered the edges of this roll-aside port with rubber weather sealing to reduce the cold. Unfortunately, we could not do anything about the cold air coming in between the sheet-metal dome, its steel supporting flange, casters and the cement wall of the silo.

Once we had these essentials done, I confided my idea to Raoul and Philippe, but I obtained their oath of secrecy first. The women were not to know – for the moment. I explained how two wind-motors, one clockwise and one counter-clockwise, could be reassembled using opposite-side vanes into one ultralite-type biplane. I showed them the sketch I had made when I had left Philippe to his fishing on the hump-backed bridge.

"Jeeze, Man, it's unbelievable," said Raoul, grinning and rubbing his head.

"No way," said Philippe.

I took them through the stages I myself had gone through. First, from a conventional tractor airplane with the engine and propeller in the front. Then, a canard design with the wings at the rear where the weight was and a pusher-prop in the back. And finally a canard again, but with no propeller at all – just two small-diameter squirrel-cage fans inside the wings run by a central engine.

"Now, what I want us to do while this cold lasts is to incorporate all this," I tapped the final sketch, "into two standard-sized wind-motors with this wrinkle." And I turned the page to show two floats at the rear of the canard under the biplane wings and one float at the front of the canard... "And all this to be fitted to Folderol Jester as mizzen masts – the ones at the stern."

They bent over the sketches that were arranged on top of

the welder.

"These control surfaces can be incorporated, no problem," Raoul commented after a moment. "Just extra aluminium tube as frames. No one would notice, or they would think it was an improvement of some sort that you're trying out."

"What can we use for the squirrel cages?" asked Philippe.

"What about those lightweight fibreglass forms used as column forms for cement?" I asked.

"The ones I've seen are about eight-inches in diameter."

"Then these wings will have to be that thick."

"Why not a conventional propeller?" said Raoul.

"We may have to fall back on that," I said. "But the squirrel cages have some theoretical advantages – theoretically," I grinned.

"For one thing," Raoul was musing, "the air pressure inside the wing will inflate and fill out the wing so there won't be ridges at every wing strut."

"Bingo. That means a lot more lifting capability and less drag for more speed."

"This thing has to have very good guy wires. The best." This was Philippe.

"Right. I would like to use 1/8 or 3/16 stainless."

"Better 3/16-inch," Raoul emphasized.

"Here's a finished drawing I've done. What do you think?"

They pored over it. "Let's see if it works," Philippe shrugged. "You and Raoul can get started on the frame and I'll go into Aiguillon or Agen and see if there are any fibreglass concrete forms around."

"Okay, do that… Philippe, you were a paratrooper. Can you fly a plane or did you just jump out of them?"

"I got to fly a couple of times, not exactly official but I knew the pilot. I didn't land or take off and that's the hard part."

"I guess we'll learn as we go," I said.

For Jester we decided to reverse things a little insofar as wind-motors were concerned. She already had two mizzen masts twenty feet tall and they were unstayed hollow fibreglass tubes of great strength but lightweight. Unfortunately, both had Decca radar fittings on top and the main masts carried a digital wind speed indicator (starboard) and a digital wind direction indicator (port). We switched the positions of mains and mizzens, which meant rerouting the Decca cables eventually and (eventually) also setting up the foresail stays to the new main masts beneath the complex Decca fittings. But I thought that I would need wind speed and wind direction on an aircraft more than Decca. Of course, I could have used both. But sometimes one has to choose.

So, instead of the central shaft of the wind-motor turning, as on the 'standard' rooftop and barge models, in Jester's case the wind-motor would turn around a stationary fibreglass mast-tube. That meant thin stainless collars around the masts on which some bearings could turn. I have included the sketches here just like the ones I showed to Raoul and Philippe.

Philippe got the fibreglass cement forms and we split them lengthwise into six vanes, leaving 8-inches at the end of each tube not split and reinforced. Into one end of the tubes we forced an aluminium disc with a tapered 1-inch pin sticking out that would take a standard wheel bearing. At the other end was an aluminium wheel with tiny inward-pitched props as spokes.

Now, I had thought of a Kawasaki 4- or 6-cylinder motorcycle racing engine as a power plant, but we could find only a wrecked Honda DOHC 4-cylinder in Agen. It was a cruising bike engine, but at least it was aluminium. That would have to do. Since Philippe had experience with motorcycle engines, he took it apart, cleaned it, balanced its reciprocating parts on our digital scale, and got what new parts he needed in Agen.

Meanwhile, Raoul and I welded the frames very carefully from aluminium tube and the women sewed up the Dacron vanes as usual – they were experts at it by now. But I told Joëlle that this wind-motor was for Jester and to take extra care and make it extra strong. Raoul suggested, and I concurred, that Jester's new 'wind-motors' could also produce usable and useful power if they were coupled by the usual bicycle chain and sprockets to generators clamped onto the masts. This power could be run to a 3 hp motor that could augment the steam engine with chain drive at low speed and could also be switched to supply power at night without having the steam engine on simmer. He said that he could work this out.

Since the X-brackets of the 'standard' wind-motor were the engine mounting and the landing gear struts, it was time that we made the floats. These we fabricated out of light gauge aluminium sheet and light aluminium angle for corner supports. It took all my skill, and about a day, to weld the open seams inside the floats.

Everyone knew that Folderol Jester was something of a special case because it wasn't only a river and canal barge but could go across open water. She also had a more powerful steam engine than the barges of Raoul and Philippe. Even so, the day came when everyone knew that we were not only constructing wind-motors to make Jester somewhat more fuel-efficient. That day came about ten days later after Raoul, Philippe and I spent a long night assembling the aircraft. We tied it down to skids fore and aft, skids weighted down with stacked sacks of flour and grain. We remembered to wrap plastic tarps around the jute sacks of flour. I had made provision to muffle the motorcycle's engine down to Rolls Royce quiet – at the cost of 7 hp – by exhausting into the oversized landing struts which had baffle canisters inserted inside them.

First, Christine came out into the warehouse a bit earlier

than usual to count cartons of pâté for a shipment when the weather permitted. Even she knew she was looking at an airplane, an incipient one, even if it looked more like a Wright Flyer than anything made during the past century. She ran back into the office saying "The boys have made an airplane!" and soon Joëlle, Mélusine and Marie-Thérèse were standing there gaping at the thing.

Joëlle walked up to me, she was smiling but she was also shaking her head. After the O'Shaugnessey adventure, I wasn't about to apologize or explain anything to anyone – not even Joëlle. "What in the world…?"

"It's an airplane," I said. "I hope," I added. "But it is also two wind-motors for *Jester*'s mizzen masts – that's the two rearmost ones. The components are just arranged… differently."

"Jesus," said Joëlle, walking up to it, and as much around it as she could given the skids and the tie-down straps. She peered at it, hands on hips. "Do you think it will work?"

"I won't know 'til I try."

"You're not going up…" and then she bit off whatever she was going to say, presumably remembering our agreement. "When's the test flight?" she asked.

"As soon as the weather breaks," I answered.

"That will be very soon," Mélusine intoned with great import, just like a sorceress should. "Yes… yes… I have been *seeing* visions of… flying… in a great cause and greater desperation. But I expected nothing like this."

I laughed. "I can't blame you for that, my Druid, very little like it has flown before – if it flies at all," I added. "Okay, boys, crank her up." I gave the old thumbs up signal.

The engine's electric starter motor did the cranking and the Honda would have roared to life if it hadn't been muzzled. As it was, sweet Castrol-smelling exhaust escaped from around the landing struts where the rubber hoses didn't catch all of it and the wings inflated smoothly, just as Raoul had intuited.

A strong jet of air came from the slots on the after edge of each wing. The nylon straps tightened dramatically, holding the thing to the skids. I went to the contraption and very gingerly lowered myself into one of the two seats in front of the engine. True, the fearful arrangement of sprockets and chains that spun the squirrel-cage fans *did* have aluminium guards on the people side if not outboard, but I was careful.

I revved the engine and worked all the controls. When the big wing flaps went down and directed the thrust toward the floor, dust (and some flour) flew and the thing tried to rise. After a few times working the rudders between the canard biplane wings, I shut her down.

"How much power are we supposed to be getting?"

"About 60 horsepower at 7500 rpm," said Philippe.

"That *should* do, I guess," I said. I walked back to Joëlle. "It really is a wind-motor, Joey, or two rather, and it actually produces power for *Jester*. The engine was extra and some other bits and pieces, plus a little extra care in making everything."

"Do you mind my asking how much?"

"The engine cost 4000 Euros and the rest about 1500 more."

"It's your money, mostly yours anyway."

"Yes."

"I see much of value because of this," Mélusine intoned.

Joëlle looked at her curiously and then it changed to skepticism, almost as if Mélusine had suddenly turned traitor. "Are you serious, Mélusine?"

"Yes, Joëlle, and very soon now."

Joëlle shook her head slightly in a puzzled way. "Marc, tell me," she gestured at the airplane. "Now I can see that it *is* really assembled from two wind-motors, although they are a bit different from our usual ones. And I see that the engine and the floats will have to be carried separately. But how long does it take to convert the wind-motors into this airplane – if it flies?"

"About two hours for two people who know what they're doing."

"Not bad," she conceded, pursing her lips and nodding her head. "Can I ask what you designed it *for*?"

"I don't know. Just to see if it could be done, I suppose."

"Your mind is wiser than you think, Marc," Mélusine observed portentously. "Your kind of magic is already at work, though you do not know it."

"Hmmm."

"How fast will it go?" asked Christine.

"That's a good question, Chrissy. If it flies at all, it should make about 60 miles per hour, maybe a little more." That was the best answer I could give.

"Is it safe?" Marie-Thérèse asked dubiously.

"As safe as any ultralite," answered Raoul.

"Safe enough… if it flies," said Philippe. "In good weather…"

17

I have described the summit level locks at Carcassonne in very great detail elsewhere, but the view has never failed to excite me, even on a dull January day early in the year 2012. If you are moored near the Canal Police Station and the public boat ramp, as I was for both safety and convenience, and moored facing the long flight of locks down to the level of the Aude River, the Narbonnais lowlands open out before you like a gigantic fan. If you are lucky and it is a clear summer day instead of a grey winter one, you will see a distant haze of azure that is the Mediterranean.

To starboard and down is the reconstruction of medieval Carcassonne designed by the eccentric architect Viollet-le-Duc in the late 1800s. Even in his own time, his vision was criticized as a romantic fantasy. It looks like a fairy tale Disneyland dropped down in the middle of nowhere. Nonetheless, in the 1930s the American travel writer Richard Halliburton wrote: "See Carcassonne and die." You can take that any way you wish, as a contradiction of Viollet-le-Duc's critics or as an independent confirmation of their opinion.

Jester was tied up with her two mizzen wind-motors working and supplying enough power on this high summit level to provide lighting and some coffee-making and cooking capacity without having to keep the steam engine ticking over at about 50 rpm. Nonetheless, this change from my usual practice made me a little nervous because it naturally took more time to raise a head of usable steam with a cold boiler. I had to admit, however, that the savings in coal oil fuel was noticeable. It amounted to about 50 Euros between Aiguillon and Carcassonne and about 50 Euros on the return trip. Raoul and Philippe would be saving proportionally more with their wind-motor barges and this meant more profit for the commune or corporation or whatever you want to call it.

We had managed to test the airplane configuration back in Aiguillon as soon as the ice in the inlet had melted. Indeed, the long inlet out to the Lot River had been perfect for my many take-off runs before I actually tried a hop off the water. True, the inlet was over 10 feet narrower than the wingspan, but the floats raised even the lower wing comfortably clear of the low banks. We had already removed the small trees and bushes that encroached nearer than 10 feet from the banks on each side.

I wanted to get the feel of the thing and also to see if my calculations of the size of the rear floats and the smaller front one were anywhere near accurate. It may be my imagination, but I thought that the floats were a little too large. The aircraft-to-be seemed content to remain a boat and water- bound, but this proved to be only because I felt some trepidation about actually trying to take off. I've never enjoyed flying. I have always preferred travel by land: trains, buses or my own vehicles… or my own boat over water.

I had planned things carefully. I took one run at much higher engine rpm and pulled gently back on the wheel-on-the-stick that lowered the wing flaps. This not only increased the lift, but also ducted the squirrel-cage-fan-motivated thrust downwards. The contraption rose rapidly from the ribbon of water and I flew for fifty yards or so and set down again. I tried it again; a longer hop, and this took me into the little bay on the Lot where I turned around to go back to the warehouse in two longer hops. But this was where things got tricky because the bridge gave bare clearance – about two feet – to either side and turning in the corner pool beside the silo meant that Raoul or Philippe had to grab the wings and pull the thing around while I idled the engine.

I tried longer and longer hops and finally I took off just past the bridge and flew all the way to the bay at an altitude of about 50 feet, turned in a lazy and nearly stress-free circle and headed back toward the warehouse. This time I gradually climbed to an altitude of about a hundred feet in order to clear the wind-motors on the roof and the silos and turned lazily over the anxious group below. Joëlle and Marie-Thérèse had their hands to their mouths.

The aircraft seemed stable enough to me in the turns, it seemed to take off quickly and it seemed to land with fair stability. So, I flew back and forth all afternoon, about three hours, and dared gentle swoops from side to side and a little greater altitude, say 200 feet. I had a cheap altimeter for cars based on air pressure squeezing a rubber diaphragm, but I didn't really trust it. It did say 300 feet at one point, and perhaps it was correct. One thing was apparent. If I wanted any comfort at all some sort of windshield had to be devised to curve down from the upper wing to my feet resting on the fibreglass tubes of Jester's masts.

As I went higher, the women covered their eyes and then just went inside. I did stay close to the inlet, except for the turns, because I knew I could set down there. Raoul and Philippe stayed to the end and they were a lot less cold than I was by the time it was late afternoon. I landed on the Lot end of the inlet and taxied down to the bridge with Raoul and Philippe guiding me past the shore fixtures associated with it. We left it moored for the night in the corner pool.

Now, although serious trading was an urgent necessity as soon as possible after the weather moderated, I had negotiated two days of testing with Joëlle using Raoul and Philippe because I needed them. Also, everyone really knew that ice deposits could build up, and had accumulated, during winters like this one – at least according to local lore and old newspaper stories. These ice deposits broke off a few days after the real thaw had set in and floated down the rivers in fairly large chunks. So, what I was asking wasn't outrageous since damage to any of the barges could actually occur until all the ice had truly melted.

That meant that Raoul, Philippe and I would really have to work to refine the aircraft since we had to allow most of a day to re-rig Jester, including putting the forestay fittings on the new main masts (which had once been the mizzens). During part of the afternoon when I was flying back and forth at higher altitude, Raoul had disappeared. I thought probably that he had gone aboard Jester to re-route the Decca radar cables and this proved to be correct.

Since we had not been able to find the two plastic chairs that had immediately come into my mind, Raoul suggested two thin aluminium-sheet full length 'chairs' that were more like metallic chaise longues. These we had pop-riveted together in about two hours, but we made one slightly smaller so that it would nest in the larger one. I had not originally wanted any cushioning, but after I struggled out onto the wharf I had changed my mind. Accordingly, we asked the women to make two Dacron-covered 2-inch foam cushions to fit into these chairs and tied onto or into them with holes we would cut with a hole-saw attachment on a drill.

"How does she feel?" asked Raoul.

"Quite solid. Easy to manoeuvre and she takes off like a dream – if you use enough revs. I was chicken at first, as you saw, but when you get the hang of it, it is easy."

"The floats?" This was Philippe.

"I think they may be a little large… and I hope they don't leak at those welds. Not much metal there."

"We have a couple of cans of urethane foam mix. Maybe enough to blow it in through a hole and keep the floats so full they can't leak," said Raoul.

"What does that stuff weigh?" I asked.

"Like feathers," Philippe said.

"Okay. Let's try that. But one thing we have to do is make some sort of curving windshield from the motor mounts down to the feet of the seats."

"One more item to carry aboard Jester," Raoul said.

"Can't you wear goggles?"

"No, that is yes, I can, but my concentration will be put off that much more. And I'm new at this."

"You can get used to goggles, surely?" Raoul again.

"I don't know why, Raoul, but I think I may have to use this thing before I have time to dicker around with it or get used to goggles."

So, we took measurements there at the wharf and I agreed that with the chairs reclined so much, we didn't have to have a curved windshield. We could have a flat one that extended from the motor mounts at the top of the upper wing down to the feet of the chairs. "Good," Raoul said with emphasis, "then it can fold twice and be smaller and flat for storage on Jester."

"It has to be wide enough to shield both chairs, not just mine, and none of the folds can be in the line of vision." More measurements at the wharf.

"Right," said Philippe, "I think that, folded, it will fit snugly right on one of Jester's upper bunks."

So, we worked to make the windshield from 1/8-inch Perspex plastic and light aluminium angle, pop-riveted. The folding joints had aluminium alloy pins. Mélusine brought us dinner in the warehouse. A little later the cushions came in and we drilled large-diameter holes in the appropriate places in the chair-forms we had taken from the aircraft and had brought inside. Raoul, Philippe and I used standard and needle-nosed pliers to round out the edges of these holes. The chairs were held in place by aluminium alloy backpack pins through wind-motor structural members.

Once the windscreen was done and would quickly attach to our satisfaction to both the upper wing and to the footrests with bungee cords stretched tight, we tried out Raoul's idea with the blown-in urethane foam. The temperature had fallen to about 40-degrees Fahrenheit or roughly 8-degrees Celsius, the lower limit for the foam to mix and set. But it seemed to work and bubbled up out of the 3-inch diameter hole we had cut in the top of each float.

Philippe, with infinite care, hand-scored threads into two cylinders of pine and then scored the threads more deeply with the Dremel. He then hand-cut gaskets, out of soft leather, to fit on the rim of each plug. After that, he cut off the protruding tail of urethane foam, cored out the hole, and screwed the pine plugs down solidly onto the top of the floats. Then, taking handfuls of water, he wet the pine. "When that wood swells up, they're not going to unscrew very easily."

The women had already sewn us square bags of Dacron filled with 25-pounds of grain. These, placed in the 'passenger's chair were supposed to represent a body. We would start with a body of exactly my own weight. Then, we would add to both sides with 25 pounds under my knees and perhaps elsewhere and piled appropriately on the grain-dummy. Eventually, we would discover the payload of the aircraft and how critical balance of the total weight might be. Me, I thought that with forty-odd feet of wingspan, balance might not prove as crucial as everyone seemed to think. But at 2 o'clock in the morning we finished what we could do and were dead tired.

The next day soared up to a balmy 10-degrees Celsius, normal seasonal for the Midi, instead of the 10 to 20 below zero Celsius it had been for almost three weeks. Since the days were short in January, we were all up at sunrise. The windshield was affixed and I clambered into my aluminium chaise longue, now moderately padded. The dummy was added in 25-pound increments up to my weight of almost exactly 180 pounds – a 175-pound dummy, in short.

Raoul and Philippe turned the aircraft around in the corner pool and I replayed the short hop procedure of the afternoon before. Take-off was a little more sluggish, but not as much as I had expected with twice as much weight. Turning out over the Lot bay was just a little more tricky. Landing was definitely trickier because I discovered that the aircraft came in more quickly.

On the first attempt at landing, I tried to brake with the wing flaps, the plane rose up instead, I raised the flaps too quickly out of fear and instinct, and so I came in rocking a little from side to side. This time, I was glad that the rear floats were just as large as I had designed them and as far apart as I had designed them. They took the landing, dampened out the rocking quickly, and I was able to steer straight down the inlet with only minor swerves.

The second time I tried landing with this weight, I came in at a shallower angle, barely any flaps, and cut the revs on the engine from the beginning and progressively. This landing was much better. I did take-offs and landings all morning and quite methodically until I had gotten the technique down pat. I found that reaching my altimeter's putative 300-foot altitude was no problem, although it took a little longer.

Now came the real test. We loaded her up in 25-pound increments that were distributed as equally as possible between my seat and the dummy's. She started to be reluctant to become airborne at 425 pounds and also very skittish to turn as the wings lost lift with the craft's 'heeling'. I also heard protests from the structure of aluminium tube and wire. At 450 pounds, she would barely lift off the water and I didn't want to try anything except landing – very carefully and very slowly. We had one answer. A total payload of 380 to 400 pounds was the absolute maximum. And 350 pounds was a lot better. I also discovered, and Raoul and Philippe could plainly see, that the floats were almost submerged on initial contact over 425 pounds.

So, back at the wharf, we unloaded 50 pounds and added some few pounds of priceless gasoline. This time, I took her up and went out to the Lot bay, turned around, and came back toward the warehouse as quickly as possible at 7500 revs. Christine and Philippe (Joëlle wouldn't watch), standing exactly a half-kilometre apart, from the Lot mouth of the inlet to the corner pool, registered a speed of 67 mph in level flight. We measured it the other direction, since there was a mild westerly breeze blowing and got 62 mph. So, we were happy to call the top speed at something around 65 miles per hour.

At the wharf, we went over every tubular strut, wire and control hinge or pivot for wear. There didn't seem to be any, but I explained that I had heard complaining noises from the structure at 450 pounds. So, we examined the Nicopress sleeves for the 3/16-inch guy wires with, literally, a magnifying glass. Not one wire was frayed or looked like becoming so, but some of the steel eyelets at the ends of the guy wires appeared newly scraped. That must have been the noise.

The weight of the two wind-motors was about 120 pounds. The weight of the two fibreglass masts from Jester was 82 pounds. The weight of the Honda engine was 207 pounds and the weight of all the wire, Nicopress sleeves and attachments was 33 pounds. The chairs weighed a total of 13 pounds (with bungee cords). The three floats weighed a total of 37 pounds. A full (aluminium) tank of gasoline 50 pounds, giving the Honda a running time at 5000-7500 rpm of 10 hours. All this weighed in at 542 pounds, plus the 400 pounds of absolutely maximum load gave 942 pounds. Against this was about 360 square feet of wing area and about 65 horsepower. This worked out to about 2.6 pounds per square foot of wing loading, well within the strength of Dacron cloth – with excellent sewing, that is.

On the other hand, according to the two books I had about ultralites and the information that Joëlle pulled from the Internet, most of these figures were well in excess of those regulating ultralite-type aircraft that could be flown without a license by any enthusiast-pilot adhering to VFR (Visual Flight Rules). On the other hand, well, I didn't care a great deal about these rules.

Without the aerodynamic drag of the floats, Raoul and Philippe opined that she would do 70 mph. Perhaps this was true enough, but what was the use of an aircraft that was confined to land… for use from a boat?

But they did suggest, and I listened, that some thick plastic sheet bent around the wires and struts with the help of heat would reduce the aerodynamic drag considerably. Once bent, these plastic streamliners could be clipped on around the wire or strut. Raoul and Philippe started on this task, but I confess that I was so exhausted by the tension of the day that I simply fell into my bed, in my now draft-proof room, and fell asleep.

The next day we re-rigged Jester with the wind-motors and their incipient aircraft, taking the engine, folding windshield and chairs below. All this did fit, but the other three bunks were completely filled with paraphernalia. We hung the four squirrel-cage fans from Jester's cabin ceiling.

Thus I moored, as I have said, with the wind-motors turning and producing almost enough electricity for my needs, but with a disguised aircraft aboard. And, as Joëlle had not been so forward as to ask (but I did), what was the use of it?

I had arrived in Carcassonne with a mixed cargo of Calvados, Moroccan four, some pâté, some upland clover honey and some potatoes. Joëlle and Christine had discovered that these commodities were supposedly in demand by Carcassonne restaurants. They were right.

Within a long day at Carcassonne, most of the cargo had been offloaded to predominantly upscale restaurants in both the new and the mock-medieval cities. Ivory made selling and distribution much easier, but I had known this for seven years. I sold most of the Calvados at Le Cheval de Septimanie, my first call, as I thought I might.

Finally, by about eleven o'clock that first night, I had sold the rest of the cargo at prices that would have made Joëlle's spread sheets fairly wriggle with passion – had they not been decently constrained within a ledger.

Thus ended the Calvados once bought in far-away Cherbourg in Normandy. And at an average of 4.5 times its price, or something over 40,000 Euros profit. Raoul's instincts last summer had been correct about getting a warehouse. There, within the warehouse, commodities could incubate, as it were, until they had reached the maximum market price anywhere else where we could transport them.

"Well, well, isn't it a small world?" I have said that most of the conversations would be in French, but this one was in English, and I recognized the voice.

I turned, smiling, and extended my hand to Inspecteur Bernard Gabereau of the Canal du Midi Police. "Inspecteur Gabereau," I said, "this is truly a pleasure." And it was, too, because, in truth, he had possibly or probably saved the lives of Mariko O'Shaugnessey and myself out on the mudflats of the Vilaine River only six and a half or seven months previously.

"I hear you are now tamed and... ah... domesticated by marriage."

"Well, I wouldn't say that," I equivocated.

"It happens to us all in the end, boy. Well, those of us who aren't gay..."

At that point, Gabereau's homely homily was cut short by sharp exclamations of terror. "Aidez-moi!" screamed a male voice beyond the canal wall that began the downward flight of locks. I whirled, hearing two small-calibre 'phutts', and saw the shadow of a man staggering up this stonework wall. He made it over, barely, rolling over the top, but he staggered and slumped down onto the decorative stonework walkway on our side.

In the dim lock-side lights I saw two man-forms looming on the balustrade and knowing that Gabereau was no match for me, I shoved him to the ground as two more 'phutts' sounded along with accompanying small muzzle flashes. I dropped to one knee with the Walther somehow in my hand. The Walther bucked, but just twice, and I saw the two forms jerking floppily back before they had ever surmounted the stone wall of the lock. I hardly felt the Walther's recoil. "Stay down, Gabereau" I yelled and ran toward the lock's stone balustrade. I was rewarded with the sight of two prone bodies sprawled out on the far side of the wall down the steps. They weren't going anywhere.

I turned back to the victim just before Gabereau arrived. I bent over him and I heard his final whispered words quite clearly "Egadi... Maritimo".

It took me a few moments to gather my wits. "Gabereau, what ammunition do you use?"

"Nine millimetre."

"Great." I said. "Want to fire say five or six shots in the air, just to get nitrate on your hands? That would simplify matters a lot, as well as add to your reputation."

Finally, it got through and Gabereau did fire five or six shots straight up. This brought the gendarmes from the Police Station out like ants from a ruined nest... presumably they had been waiting for the violence to subside... and brought answering whistles from gendarmes nearby on Carcassonne's streets.

18

Two days later at eleven in the morning of a beautiful bright winter's day in southern France, I was sitting in Inspector Gabereau's office alongside the canal in Carcassonne. As befitted an encounter with officialdom, I was dressed à la mode Grand Capitaine, as I had been on my previous visit to Gabereau's office.

I knew I was in no trouble because I had already signed a statement asserting that yes, although I had shot at the assailants, it was much more probable that the trained policeman I was chatting with at the time, Inspecteur Gabereau, had actually brought them down. He had fired some shots too, and about the same instant I had. Gabereau himself had witnessed my statement as the truth.

I had deposited the money from my trading in our communal bank. Jester was empty of cargo and my conscience was light as well. True, I should have been back in Aiguillon, or at least nearing the place by now, but I had spoken first to Christine because she happened to be on duty with the corporation's ever-ready 'emergency' cell phone, and then later personally to Joëlle, and they knew where I was.

"The reason I asked you to stay, Marc…" he hesitated, then shrugged at the familiarity, but smilingly took refuge in wry protocol, "er… Mister… no… Captain Rennsalaer, is that you know something of the victim… deceased, by the way."

So, he hadn't merely been wounded. He hadn't made it. I must have looked genuinely surprised after that moment of brief mourning for I saw Gabereau looking at me with a tight smile.

"Inspector Gabereau…"

"Inspecteur-Général."

I cocked and inquiring eyebrow. "I may be mistaken, but

I don't think I had ever seen him before. Of course, it was dark and without much light from the canal-side lamps." I paused. "Inspector-General…?"

"I know you had never seen him before, at least it is highly unlikely. Nonetheless you know something of him." It was his turn to pause. "Yes, Rennsalaer, Inspecteur-Général des Canals de France… since last September first."

"All of them?"

"Yes, indeed."

"The… ah… affair of the Lorelei – and the Sleipnir helicopter, of course – had something to do with it…?"

"So I imagine." Gabereau looked smug, like the Cheshire Cat. So, he owed me a very great debt.

"Raise along with the title, I suppose?" I said it very respectfully.

"Definitely."

"Where's your… er… head office now? Paris?"

"I float around as I will, Captain Rennsalaer. Wherever I'm needed." He stopped for a second. "The victim's name was Gérard Delorme." I must have looked blank because he said: "Doctor Gérard Delorme…?"

I squizzled my brows, searching memory banks, and finally a dim glow dissociated itself and floodlit Mélusine's discussion in Brest. "Ah…" I said at last.

Inspector-General Bernard Gabereau nodded genially and smiled benignly. "So, you see I thought that you might like to stay and sample Carcassonne's rather tragic and bloody cultural heritage until Pierre Falardeau arrives."

"When's that?"

"Any time now." Gabereau looked down, shuffling papers while he spoke. "Of course, he'll want to see the reports and learn what happened. I suppose," he continued wearily, "that he can identify the body officially, although we've already done that from dental records." He sighed. He looked up at me. "It would very likely be in your interest to meet with him."

"Possibly, Inspector-General."

"So, stick close to Folderol Jester and the Police Station."

"Will do," I said. "I do have one question before I go, Inspector-General." He nodded, so I continued. "The assailants, also deceased, had silencers and used small calibre handguns."

"Twenty-twos. No identification found. No identification so far with Interpol."

"That's not so good, Inspector-General."

"No."

We both knew, too well, what these facts indicated. The use of short-range sometimes-silenced .22 pistols was a trademark of Israel's extremely efficient and equally feared secret service. The Mossad.

I went down the few steps of the Police Station in a pensive mood. I glanced automatically to the left, at Jester, out of long habit. Snugly moored she was, with wind-motors turning merrily.

Death could be so sudden and so quickly forgotten. I glanced to my right toward the stone wall that began the long downward flight of locks to the Aude. There was not even police tape where the victim had lain sprawled on the stone walkway beside the summit level canal. For that matter, as I ambled over to the wall itself, there was no sign or blood and nothing to mark where the two gunmen had fallen back onto the stone steps down to the next lower lock.

I leaned on the wall for a while. I thought I could see the haze of blue in the far distance, the Med. Nearer at hand, the bicycle traffic of Carcassonne passed by and the very occasional taxi.

I went back to the place where I thought Gérard Delorme's body had lain. I knelt and searched the mute stones of the walkway for any signs at all that a tragedy had taken place on them. There was not even the barest trace of blood that I could see, no thread of cloth caught in a crevice of mortared stonework. No scuff of leather. Nothing.

"That ground will take no footprint... All of it is bitter stone."

I stood up quickly and turned to see, as I expected, Professor Pierre Falardeau looking down.

"Euripedes' *Electra*," he said. "Is this where it happened, Captain Rennsalaer?"

"Yes. He was obviously trying to make it to the Police Station. He almost did."

"If I may, I would like to speak with you."

"Not here directly in front of the Police Station," I said. "I happen to know that there's at least one gendarme at the Carcassonne station that cannot be trusted in certain matters. French unions and respect for seniority being what they are, I doubt that Bernard... I mean Inspector-General Gabereau... has been able to get rid of him yet."

So, we strolled along the walkway, past Jester, and looked at the various barges. "That leaves your daughter Danielle, unaccounted for," I said.

Falardeau nodded. "Did Gérard say anything before he died? Gabereau told me you reached him first."

"Yes, but I don't know if I heard correctly. It sounded like 'Egadi... Maritimo.'"

"I know they managed to reach Malta in October and were planning to try to reach Sicily – somewhere on the east coast, probably Catania or Syracuse, they said."

"How did you receive this communication?" I asked.

"By a hand-written almost illiterate fan letter to Mariko O'Shaugnessey. Being hand-written, some of the letters were raised. With a ruler it was easy to pick out the raised letters and the message – in Italian, of course. Or, rather, in Sicilian. It was a common medieval code that O'Shaugnessey would spot right away. In fact, that's probably what caught her eye when she received the letter, and why she didn't toss it in the garbage."

"Why did she suspect a secret message?"

"How likely is it that a Sicilian peasant, by the spelling, would congratulate her on the Gospel when the Vatican had just banned it?"

"Hmmm. I take your point."

"It ended 'Falardeau-Delorme'… but in an anagram, of course."

"When did this get to Mariko?"

"A month ago."

I mused a moment. "So they speak Italian? Or… Sicilian."

"Danielle does. Like a native. Her mother was Sicilian, from Palermo."

"I thought… er… that Sicilian was just a dialect of Italian."

Falardeau laughed. "You know the old joke, of course, Captain Rennsalaer – 'What's the difference between a language and a dialect?'"

"I'm afraid I don't."

"A language is a dialect with an army and a navy. For hundreds of years the Sicilians had an army and a navy. Sicilian is fairly distinct from Italian. Few people speak it any longer, except in small coastal villages but more often up in the mountains." Then, as though changing the subject, "Are there any sea charts aboard your boat?"

"Not of the Med, really, just the coast of France and Spain."

"Where does one buy sea charts?"

"At any ship chandlers."

"Are there any in Carcassonne?"

"One that I know of. In the new city."

"Let's go," Falardeau said.

We went. By first taking the steps down the hill behind

the Canal Police Station and then by taxi. Falardeau kept the taxi waiting. The shop had many copies of the Canal du Midi charts but few of the Mediterranean. Falardeau gave me money and I purchased a large-scale pilot chart of the Western Mediterranean. This included all of Italy and Sicily on the right-hand extremity of the paper, including some inserts for Corsica, Sardinia, the Lipari Islands and Sicily with its associated offshore islands.

"Have you had lunch, Captain Rennsalaer?"

"Not yet."

So, we got into the waiting taxi and Falardeau directed it to Le Cheval de Septimanie in the old reconstructed medieval city. This naturally brought back various memories. Some as recent as two days ago.

I said that we wanted a table where we could watch the door, or at least be seen from it easily. We were expecting a friend, if he could get away for lunch. I opened the large chart as soon as we sat down at a suitable table, folding it to somewhat manageable proportions. "I hear they have gotten hold of some good Calvados here," I said shamelessly, "if you like the stuff." Me, I had had more of it than I ever wanted.

It took only a few minutes for me to find 'Egadi… Marettimo'. "Here," I said, "Look at this." I passed the chart across with my finger pointing to the northwest coast of Sicily.

I had not expected to find 'Egadi… Marettimo' so easily. Perhaps I should order now, and quickly, before Falardeau charged out of the restaurant. It was the best in Carcassonne and pricey. Thankfully, the waiter came at that instant. I ordered cassoulet and Falardeau impatiently ordered coq au vin. He also ordered the house white wine. I asked for a beer, and now please, like a barbarian, which was right in keeping with the restaurant's décor.

The walls were made to look like the interior of a ruined

building and there were panoramas through the 'windows' of barbarians on horses, presumably Visigoths, on the rampage through the 'streets'. Defending warriors were fallen and women scattered. One could almost hear the shrieks as rapes – called peripheral gene flow by anthropologists – were consummated. In the evening, I knew, Le Cheval de Septimanie featured barbarian torchlight from brackets on the walls.

"Yes," said Falardeau. "I see it. That must be what Gérard meant... now that we know they were trying to get to Sicily."

We? "I imagine that their strategy was to go from Sicily to Sardinia and then cross over to Corsica in France – I *think* it is part of France." Corsica was to France what Sicily and Sardinia were to Italy. They were parts of France and Italy – on maps, that is, and the fiction was preserved in the larger towns and cities. But get out into the countryside, especially into the mountains, and they were what they had always been long before France and Italy existed: Corsicans, Sardinians and Sicilians.

"Why such an isolated place?" Falardeau mused.

"Smugglers, I imagine," I said. "That, and the fact that if Danielle speaks Sicilian like a native, as you say, she would attract no attention in a small town. Gérard would. That's probably why they decided that he would have to make the run for France."

"That and the fact that they must be running short of money. Gérard must have been given most of it in order to get here. And that means that Danielle is alone and destitute in Marettimo. We must get to her somehow. A lone woman in Sicily isn't very safe, especially in an isolated place. And how can she live?"

There was that 'we' again. "They've been very resourceful so far," I said. "What is the one kind of woman who *is* safe in Sicily? Sacrosanct, in fact."

"A nun."

"And a nun who comes to a place like Marettimo, who was sent there from the mainland, would be able to make a living. The townsfolk would support her, no matter how little they had themselves, if she established a school – assuming there isn't one there already – or if she just tended the sick."

"That's true enough," Falardeau admitted.

"The problem is, if she's nearly destitute already, that she could never save enough money as a nun to get away. On the other hand, so long as she's there, it is unlikely that the… er… opposition can ever find her."

"I could fly to Rome, then to Palermo and take a bus to Trapani around the coast. It says here on the chart that there's a ferry from Trapani to Marettimo."

"Hmmm." I sipped my beer, waiting for my cassoulet and ruminating on the follies of humanity. "I think you may be forgetting the mainstream of this afternoon's symposium, Professor Falardeau." My watch insisted that it was twelve-thirty.

He put the chart aside as the waiter served coq au vin and poured out the dollop of wine for the customer to taste. I doubted that Falardeau was enjoying the taste of anything very much, but he dutifully smiled and nodded, the ritual was completed and the wine was poured. The waiter served me after Falardeau, naturally.

Not one person had come in after us so far, but now a middle-aged couple entered. I scanned the man for suspicious bulges under his shoulders or funny wrinkles of his jacket in the small of his back. Nothing. Their age wasn't bequeathed by make-up. The woman's purse was red leather and large enough to hold a Tommy gun and for that reason alone I dismissed them. She was too easy to recognize.

"You mean, Captain Rennsalaer, that three deaths in the family would be unfortunate."

"And following so quickly upon one another too."

"Your suggestions?"

"That Danielle is in the place called Marettimo, we have good grounds for believing. That she's a nun there is pure conjecture, but it is a reasonable one. As a nun, she could also have large holy books in her otherwise austere and poverty-stricken room. I doubt that many people in a place like Marettimo can even read. Those who can would simply think that the books must be extra holy because they are old and in a strange language."

"I'm with you."

"Okay. She and the… ah… book or books… can stay in Marettimo almost indefinitely."

"But…"

I raised a hand. "Naturally we don't want *that*." Falardeau was looking at me almost pleadingly, but I wasn't trying to tease him with my recital of the obvious – now that he had re-thought ways of getting to Marettimo. I was thinking. "The maiden has to be rescued in a way that no one knows that she's been rescued. She has to disappear from Marettimo and arrive in France. For all we know, a legend may be born in Marettimo that St. Theresa, Maria or Veronica – or whatever she calls herself there – came among them for a while and then was called back to God. And her holy books must disappear along with her."

"Can it be done?"

"Yes," I mused, "I think it *could* be done." I paused. "I didn't know it could be done when we first spoke in Brest. Certain… er… developments make me think it can be done now." I paused as I sampled the cassoulet again. "Two questions, Pierre Falardeau."

"Yes."

"The first is how much money can you… er… allocate for this… er… project?"

"A hundred thousand Euros."

I cocked a quizzical eyebrow.

"That is all my savings and then some," he said. "There are, though, other interests, mutual acquaintances, in fact, that are vitally concerned with the... book... if not with Danielle's welfare."

"This wouldn't be Mister Stewart and Associates, by any chance?" I asked.

"Indeed so."

"The second question is whether you know of any Italian or Sicilian leather manufacturers."

Falardeau looked taken aback. "No, not offhand, I'm a scholar. I have a friend, an erudite businessman, who is in the leather goods business in Paris."

"Then I suggest that you get in touch with him. Tell him you want him to order some top-quality leather goods from some supplier located on the southern *west* coast of Italy. I need somewhere bordering the Tyrrhenian Sea – Naples, Palermo or Trapani would be perfect. Cagliari in Sardinia would be better yet. A small shipment of purses, vests, dresses, belts and shoes would be best. Fashion boots would also be good. We need your friend to make this purchase *immediately* out of Paris."

Falardeau was making notes and this time I didn't stop him. "Your friend in Paris will then contract with us" – here I gave him one of our new business cards – "to convey this cargo to Aiguillon for shipment to Paris by train. The cargo will be a small sample one, an experimental one if you like, to test the Parisian fashion market with these new goods. The total shipment cannot exceed 20 cubic metres. It must be packed into individual cartons not exceeding half a cubic metre in volume and the whole shipment to be packed on 14 wooden skids at least 6-inches high."

"Got that," said Falardeau, scribbling furiously.

"Now, Professor Falardeau, I want 50,000 Euros up front. That means *now* – or at the very latest, tomorrow. Certified cheque or bank draft from any major bank *in France*. And that's non-returnable. I may not be able to find Danielle. Or, she may already be dead, like Gérard. I may not be able to find the… ah… texts. For all we know, though I strongly doubt it, Gérard may have tried to bring them out. He's dead. And the texts may have been… ah… confiscated."

"I think I can do all this," Falardeau said. "When will Danielle be back?"

"If all goes well, and you can do all that, then if she's still alive Danielle will be back within a month."

"Thank you, Captain Rennsalaer." As we stood up, I rolled up the chart and tucked it under my left arm. That looked natural for a Grand Capitaine and it didn't impede my access to the Walther even a little. I waited while Falardeau placed an exorbitant number of Euro notes on the saucer that also bore the black leather fold-over with the bill tucked ever so discreetly inside.

"Don't thank me yet. Save it until you see Danielle."

"Where can I find you?"

"Just where Jester was today. Moored along the canal a stone's throw from Gabereau's office. It is secure there and I don't have to pay for the mooring."

As we left, I looked around for the middle-aged couple and saw them in a back corner with plenty of their meal yet to be finished. They did not even glance up when we went out through the door into the street. I decided to walk back to the canal. Falardeau hailed a cab. On the other hand, he had a great deal to do and I really didn't.

19

During the round table discussion that supposedly guided every voyage, we had decided that I should try to bring back a cargo of citrus fruit from the Narbonnais or from Spain.

The Narbonnais produced its own citrus fruit in fair amounts, but some additional citrus fruits from Spain were landed by coastal freighters and small traders at Perpignan. Some of this Spanish produce percolated up into the Narbonnais and was considered better than the similar French produce. The Spanish Seville oranges were certainly larger and juicier than the smaller oranges of the Narbonnais. According to Joëlle and Christine, these citrus fruits – especially those from Spain – would fetch premium prices in Carcassonne, Toulouse, Moissac, Agen, Marmande, Bordeaux and even small quantities in Aiguillon.

Therefore, once having sold my cargo in Carcassonne, I was to try to load citrus fruit in the Narbonnais and sell it off as I returned to Aiguillon. Anything left when I reached Aiguillon, Raoul would take to Bordeaux and Philippe would take to Villeneuve-sur-Lot.

Unfortunately, this game plan was put on hold by the developments in Carcassonne. If Falardeau was able to come through with the 50,000 Euros by tomorrow, then my voyage would make five or ten times the profit that could have been expected from Narbonnais or even Spanish citrus. And this didn't count the profits made on the mixed cargo I had already sold in Carcassonne and had deposited to our corporation's account. If I were successful in rescuing Danielle and the text, then the additional 50,000 Euros plus the transport of the Italian leather goods would far surpass the profits from any ten or fifteen wildly successful voyages to Narbonne, Bordeaux or anywhere else.

So, I was content to wait until at least tomorrow and see

what transpired with Falardeau. Passing an Internet Café when walking back toward *Jester*, I sent a brief e-mail to Aiguillon:

Joëlle:

> Must remain in Carcassonne until at least tomorrow night. Unexpected opportunity of exceedingly profitable venture regarding Italian leather ware and other Italian goods of very great value. Will know more tomorrow. No worries.

Marc

I would not like it thought that I ever exactly *lied* to Joëlle. On the other hand, we had our agreement, I had my life, and why should I cause her undue stress? So long as I came home, and came home with money, I figured that what I did was my own business.

So, that evening I sat on *Jester*'s poop and watched the sunset behind me gilding numerous turrets of medieval Carcassonne in unlikely shades of mauve, fuchsia and gold. Philippe would have loved the fish on this summit level that frequently dotted the canal with their expanding rings at evening feeding time. And thinking of Philippe… did I need him, Raoul or Mélusine the most for this operation… or anyone? Philippe was an ex-paratrooper and his soldiering experience might come in handy. Raoul was an intuitive mechanical genius and that would certainly come in handy. Mélusine was – so she said and so I was starting to think – a Druid with special… er… *expertise* in weather magic.

Of the three, I had a hunch that Mélusine would be of the most use to me. I *could* do what Philippe and Raoul could do. I could not replace Mélusine. And it was January, the season of the Mistral. Mélusine could handle *Jester*, at least in port and even under way in good weather. True, the commune or corporation in Aiguillon would have to exist on non-gourmet cuisine for a while, but they had done that before Mélusine had arrived with me. And the other women would have to cope with the twice-weekly soup kitchens in Aiguillon. And Raoul and Philippe were needed for trading.

And, damn it, why had I not thought of that one test of the aircraft that I could have done back in Aiguillon? On that note, I went below as the winter night was coming on early with little or no afterglow. I hate to say it, but I fell asleep like the proverbial log and didn't worry about a thing.

I saw Pierre Falardeau rise like a lanky periscope from behind the Police Station as he climbed up the steps from the street below. I waved, sitting as I was on *Jester*'s poop with a cup of coffee in my hand enjoying another bright morning. Approaching *Jester* briskly and with a smile, I figured that he had been successful in most of his endeavours.

He looked at *Jester*'s hull uncertainly, but finally grasped the gunwale of the forward hull and performed a creditable western roll over the side. He ended up on his feet, somewhat to his surprise because the deck was higher than the water by a foot or so, and came to the steps leading three feet up to the poop and me on the big hinges.

Me, I slid-hopped off the poop onto the deck to meet him half way, as it were. He reached into his inside jacket pocket and extracted some papers. He looked at them, rummaged, and handed one to me. It was a cashier's cheque for 50,000 Euros. He rummaged some more and handed several folded sheets to me.

These proved to be, on inspection, a freight contract for 20 cubic metres of leather goods to be picked up in Cagliari, Sardinia and delivered in Aiguillon, France. There was no date for the pick-up or the delivery specified, so far as I could tell. But, whenever these goods arrived in Aiguillon, they were to be sent by train forthwith to Paris.

"Mister Stewart has a great deal of trust in you," said

Falardeau.

"As well he might," I replied. "Want some coffee?"

"No, thanks." He glanced hurriedly at his watch. "I have to run."

"All right."

"You'll get her back?"

"If it is humanly possible. And if she's still alive," I answered. "By the way, Professor Falardeau," I said, musing somewhat. "Could you compose a very brief encrypted message for Danielle? Like the one she and Gérard sent to Mariko. It has to be short because I want it to be a... er... leaflet. It has to be something that the townsfolk of Marettimo would talk about so that Danielle will come to know about it within a day. It also has to be something that no one else but Danielle would be able to break. Perhaps Latin or Greek or whatever. She must know who sent it by the method of communication itself – you – and know that help is immediately at hand, but she'll have to move at a moment's notice *with the text* to somewhere – I haven't figured that out yet. It depends on the weather and the moon."

"Yes. I can do that. It should be easy enough."

"Good. Format it so that you can print off say six-to-eight copies on a piece of paper. Give it to Gabereau to hold for me and leave a number where you can be reached for the next two days in Carcassonne. And, maybe most important, Professor Falardeau, I need a good, recent photograph of Danielle in colour. I have to be able to recognize her. How tall is she?"

"Five feet five."

"How much does she weigh?"

"I've no idea. She's slim. One thirty? One twenty-five?" He paused. "The photograph is no problem, of course. However, I had planned on returning to Brest tomorrow."

"Don't."

He nodded. "All right. I will stay reachable."

I watched Falardeau go over the gunwale again. And I watched him walking to the Police Station, along the side of the building, and then disappear by downward degrees like a jittering retracting periscope as he jogged down the steps. Perhaps he had another taxi waiting.

After checking that *Jester* was locked tight, and leaving the plastic coffee cup in the lee of the wheelhouse, I followed Falardeau. First, I deposited 20,000 Euros in our corporate account as soon as the banks opened. I deposited 10,000 Euros in Joëlle's personal account. That left roughly 20,000 for my expenses from Falardeau's bank draft. Then, when I got to the Internet Café, I sent another message to Aiguillon.

Joëlle:

    Deposited 20,000 Euros to company account against aforementioned Italian contract. 10,000 to you. Imperative and most urgent that Mélusine joins me immediately in Carcassonne. TGV from/through Aiguillon should arrive sometime today or this evening.

Marc.

TGV stood for Très Grande Vitesse. These trains were the pride of France and so they should be. The 'Very Great Speed' trains sped through the countryside at over a hundred miles per hour and, sometimes, a hundred and fifty. They had accidents about half as often as British trains travelling half as fast. This should say something about the British flair for organization as opposed to the French penchant for unbridled passion.

While I was there in the Internet Café, I pulled up Marettimo Island and town on msn.com and printed out the map, such as it was, that is.

Marettimo was not, as I had expected, the village where the ferry from Trapani called at the island. That ferry landing had no name whatsoever. The village of Marettimo was some distance inland. A kilometre? There was no way of telling. As far as msn.com was concerned, on maximum magnification, there was not even one street in Marettimo.

Nonetheless, on the brighter side of things, there were few places around the Egadi Island group that were not in the lee of *something*. Therefore, there would always be calm water within the Egadi Island group *somewhere*. Thereafter, I went to the biggest library in Carcassonne. I found not one mention of Marettimo in any travel book on Sicily, and there were several on the shelves.

I shopped my way to the train station in new Carcassonne. The 20,000 Euros in my pocket once had a buying power of $1.47 Canadian per Euro and much more now. Of course, prices had also gone up. Currency and commodity value fluctuations were yet another thing that made trading so… interesting. Maybe 'challenging' would be a better word.

Ever since Joëlle had given up her job as a city administrator in Agen to work full-time with the corporation (or commune) in Aiguillon, one of her principle interests and duties was to keep track of the daily fluctuations of currencies and commodities – as best she could, that is. A Euro or Franc would not buy the same amount of *some* commodities in one area as it might in another. Things had always been that way, only they were a bit more so now. So, whether she liked it or not, Joëlle – and to a lesser degree Christine – had been forced to become currency and commodity speculators.

Nonetheless, the 20,000 Euros in my pocket still represented a very great amount of purchasing power compared with, say, an average annual professional income. However that might be, I still shopped carefully on the way to the train station, doing 'comparative shopping' whenever possible because I had some time, about four hours I figured, to kill anyway.

I spent most of one of them in just one store, an upscale sports clothing emporium where, eventually, I bought two medium weight one-piece zippered ski suits, both black. One large – I tried it and it fit – and one medium-petite for a five-foot-five slim lady. I also bought two pairs of clear plastic ski goggles.

After that, I sought about two-dozen cans of black fabric spray paint – guaranteed to be both flexible and waterproof, so the label said – and I had to go to four quincailleries to get them all of the same shade and manufacturer. The flat black enamel spray wasn't so much of a problem and one hardware store had as much as was needed.

I bought a fair amount of dehydrated foods and fruits, some limited amounts of fresh ground beef, pork and vegetables. I didn't forget some cheese, coffee and dried milk. I certainly didn't forget the beer, and this time I actually found some Coors.

Fairly heavily laden by the time I reached the train station in mid-afternoon, I was quite surprised to find Mélusine waiting patiently on a bench. I had half expected that Joëlle and Christine and perhaps Marie-Thérèse would have prevailed upon her not to come at all. I said as much when I walked up to her, or waddled, carrying shopping bags from several stores.

"I am *your* Druid, Marc Rennsalaer," she said. "Do not forget that. I am afraid that I had to tell Joëlle as much today."

"But you're a woman. I was sure you would side with them."

"There are no sides, here. Or only one. I am *your* Druid. I… belong… to no one else. You gave me a life, not Joëlle… or Christine or Marie-Thérèse. And you gave them a life too. I will cook for you all and I will look after the babies that may come. But I will… forever… come at *your* need."

"Did Joëlle authorize payment for your ticket here?"

"She did when I said that I would pay for it myself, if she would not. That's when I had packed a bag and was leaving."

"Your harp?"

"I wouldn't leave home without it." She jiggled the orange shopping bag.

"Let's get out of here, Mélusine."

Extravagantly, we took a taxi to the foot of the steps beside the Police Station and the canal. Mélusine and I managed to get the groceries and her things below, but there was not so much room as there had been. We cushioned the harp up against the Honda engine on what had once been 'Mélusine's' bunk.

The bunk's mattress had been removed so that the engine would not damage it, and the folded-over mattress was in the top bunk above mine cushioning the folding windshield. She could still use the drawers and the closets for clothes, but she didn't have much. She began putting the food away. I had hung the four squirrel-cage fan inserts on the port side of *Jester* so they wouldn't prevent cupboard and refrigerator doors from opening in the galley, but they narrowed the already narrow corridor by eight inches.

"You'll have to sleep with me in my bunk, only the bunk is really too narrow for two. Maybe we can throw that mattress on the floor and one of us can have a cozy nest in that. But it is going to be crowded."

"Whatever you say. What do you want for dinner?"

"I'm feeling terribly North American, Mélusine. Can you lower yourself to the level of hamburgers – there are some onions there somewhere and a head of lettuce. There's mustard in the fridge… if it's still good."

"Certainly. Coffee?"

"Definitely."

I went up on deck, not only to retrieve the morning's

coffee cup but to figure out what I was going to say to Joëlle. I had better train her now, but I had to dissipate some anger first.

So, I sat on the poop looking at Carcassonne's medieval splendour in the late afternoon. On impulse, I walked to the Police Station and picked up a very sealed (with tape) envelope that was waiting for me in Inspector-General Gabereau's mail cubbyhole.

As Falardeau had promised, there were six copies in very small letters printed out on the page and these copies were separated by lines, inviting to be cut out. I saw immediately, however that some of the script-font letters were raised above the others. The letters looked like Greek, Latin and Hebrew all jostled together with some slashes of Ogham thrown in as a seasoning.

I had no idea what the message actually said, however, until I saw the small loose piece of paper inside the envelope. And the photograph.

> Daffodown-dilly went to town
>   with her yellow hair and green gown.
> There she'll be plucked from the ground
>   when this moon be wane or round.
> Be ready for some sign, I know not
>   what or whom will bring you home.
> Carry little but your tome.

05 63 59 35 11 phone

As for Danielle, she was a stunning blonde. Her high forehead ended in a fine, regular nose, perhaps a trifle long that separated oversized blue eyes. Her mouth was wide and her lips upturned full with the smile she was wearing. But the chin, rounded and delicately oval was somehow determined. If one looked deeper into the bright, smiling eyes, you could see independence and stubborn determination somewhere far down in the pupils.

"Officer," I asked a gendarme on duty at the desk. "Could you make ten copies of this? I'll pay whatever it costs." I handed him the sheet of gobbledygook separated by lines.

"Certainly. Inspecteur-Général Gabereau instructed us to give you every assistance." He took the sheet and went to the rather antiquated copy machine.

While it slowly ker-chunked out the ten copies, I asked: "By the way, Officer, is Inspector-General Gabereau still in Carcassonne?"

"No. He had to go down to Narbonne Plage for a couple of days. Some Spanish smugglers apparently landed there."

"What were they landing… or picking up?"

"I think it was Spanish cigarettes and cut-rate jeans."

He came back with the ten copies. "No charge," he said when I rummaged in my pocket.

I had walked off some of my anger. So, by the time I was sitting on the poop, I was composed enough to phone Joëlle.

"Oui. Allo." It was Joëlle herself who answered, for a change.

"Joëlle, it's me, Marc."

"Yes, what is it? More trouble in Carcassonne?" She had just received 20,000 Euros of 'trouble' for the company and 10,000 more for herself. I felt my anger rising again.

"Only for you," I said.

"Go on," she said in a subdued voice.

"Never again during the course of this relationship criticize anything I do in front of our associates in Aiguillon or in public anywhere, as you did with the airplane."

"Yes, Marc."

"And never again contradict or try to obstruct any direct order I give you, like with Mélusine's coming to Carcassonne. Your job, your only job, is to expedite my explicit instructions to the best of your ability and *immediately*. Is that crystal clear?"

"Yes, Marc… but then why am I the manager of our co-operative venture?"

"Who said you were? You're a shareholder and you contribute your skills like we all do."

There was silence. Then she said: "You have let me take over that role."

"You do have expertise that I lack, Joëlle, and I respect it. It can make us more efficient and more profitable. You're the so-called manager only because I have let you take over that job. Just like I am by far the major shareholder in our venture, and just like you are all in debt to me to a greater or lesser degree, my decisions out-rank yours… and anyone else's if push comes to shove. Got that?"

"Yes, Marc."

"Don't go getting it into your head that you're a corporate manager, like in the old days, as you call it. You're just doing the job that you are best qualified to do for the common good. In the end, you do not control anything or anyone. I do. Do you understand?"

"Yes."

"And if you do not like that, Joëlle, I will *hire* someone who can do your job. There are plenty of people out there with your qualifications or better who are looking for jobs. You can then collect your share of the profits but have nothing to do with the company and probably also have nothing to do with me because I can't trust you. Got that?"

"Marc!" She was hurt and angry and I could hear sniffles.

"And if you don't like *that*, then we will make an application to terminate our agreement. Immediately."

"Marc! What are you saying?"

"That I will not put up with your criticism of me or anything I choose to build, I will not tolerate any contradiction of me or any attempts to obstruct a direct order I give. There's only one person in charge of this commune, co-operative or corporation – whatever you want to call it. Me. I was trading when I first met you. I can trade alone again – and cheaper. Got that?"

"Yes, Marc," I heard her sob softly.

"And I don't want to have this conversation again."

"You won't have to."

"Fine. Good-bye, Joëlle."

As I sat there on the poop look down on the Narbonnais and wondering where Gabereau was down there, it occurred to me that Joëlle's 'you won't have to' *could* mean that she wouldn't be in Aiguillon when I returned.

I shrugged. As much as I loved her, and I knew that as truth from seven years, I would rather have no girlfriend at all than one who had delusions of grandeur. Some French women were just born that way, however, and as soon as they got to feeling 'married' they got worse. Their condition could only be treated with a quick application of a whip, a chair and a cap gun – like a circus lion tamer. And if that didn't work, a split was the only answer. They didn't change. Was Joëlle like that?

Falardeau had done his thing, including the message. I hadn't expected it so soon, but perhaps he had been thinking about something similar for a while. There was really no need for him to remain in Carcassonne. So I phoned his number and left a careful message that I would try to meet him in Brest. I looked up at the sky. It was late afternoon, but there was time to drop down to the Aude before the canal closed at seven. My lunch would have to be a quick one.

20

We made it into the Canal de la Robine, a spur line of the Canal du Midi, but not actually into Narbonne by the time navigation stopped at seven in the evening. We were somewhere just west of Narbonne in a rather attractive little village, attractive in a quaintly shabby way. As I was tying Jester to bollards just beside the lock that had stopped our progress for the day, I saw a metal shop across the canal side street and discerned the golden gleam of brass tubing.

Now, in addition to a rough strategy for each voyage as I have described, we all had a list of items to be obtained if possible: steel wire for the ongoing wind-motors, any kind of steel or aluminium scrap that we could get on board, old sails or sailcloth, brass or steel hinges of all kinds, rope in good condition, another old push-model Singer sewing machine – and so on.

The gleam of brass drew me across the street and I discovered several 10-foot lengths of roughly 2-inch and 3-inch inside diameter extremely thick-walled tubes. I got these for a nominal sum because the owner didn't think he would ever sell them. They would replace Jester's missing whistle-tube and make air-cannons for Raoul and Philippe's barges. There were also a few varying lengths of larger-diameter tube and some scraps of brass plate too. I bought these and carried the lot back to Jester in several trips. I wanted them inside, but I knew there was no room, so I lashed them to the inside of the hull with nylon straps.

Down below, Mélusine was cooking a meat loaf. It would serve for dinner, sandwiches and also breakfast meat instead of sausage. But, for an hour and a half there was not much for her to do except to let it bake, so I told her most of everything that had transpired so far, including Gérard's last words.

Then I went over the strategy, such as it was, of the

operation. The idea was to cross the 400-odd miles of Mediterranean from Narbonne to Cagliari at the southern end of Sardinia where we would check on the shipment of leather goods. Hopefully, it would not be ready because the manufacturer was a small one. So, while waiting, we would cross the 225 miles or so from Cagliari to the Egadi Island group off the northwest point of Sicily.

I showed Mélusine the pilot chart and the printed-off msn.com map. Somewhere in that group, sheltered from whatever wind was blowing, I would assemble the aircraft. I had never been there, but there seemed to be no lack of shoreline and very few inhabitants. We should be able to find some seclusion. I planned to fly over Marettimo at night and drop Falardeau's leaflets. Then, the next night I would drop hand-written, but similarly encrypted instructions as to where Danielle should go from Marettimo – this must be somewhere within easy walking distance since she would be carrying a large and possibly heavy book.

In the meantime, I would dismantle the aircraft into wind-motors again, pick Danielle up from the beach in Ivory and we would return to Cagliari to pick up the leather shipment. From there, we would either sail directly for Narbonne, or coast around Sardinia and Corsica into the Gulf of Lyon and get to Narbonne that way.

When I finished, Mélusine looked at me like I was daft and went to check on the meat loaf. "You do not even know she is in this place… Marettimo…?" she said, bending to open the oven door.

"'Egadi… Marettimo' were Gérard's last words and Falardeau knew that they were trying to reach Sicily from Malta. And this Marettimo is about the best place one could hide in Sicily if Danielle speaks Sicilian like a native. Anyway, we have some leads and that is better than what Falardeau had back in September in Brest."

"But you know nothing."

"That is true, Mélusine, I was hoping you could help me with that. Did you ever meet Danielle?"

"Twice. Once in Falardeau's office in Brest at the university and again at Falardeau's apartment in Paris."

"Did you get any reading on her?"

"She is a very determined and willful young woman."

I shoved the chart across the table. I was sitting on my cushioned bunk, but Mélusine had been perched on a pillow on her bunk's plywood surface. "Do you remember what you said on the way to Aiguillon? I believe that it was in Cherbourg or Brest." She shook her head. "You said," I continued, "'there's a woman in the pattern somewhere, but she doesn't know what she is because she's had no teacher' – or something like that."

"I think that was Joëlle."

"But you had never met Joëlle."

"That is true, Marc."

"So, if you can feel Joëlle in a pattern, a person you never met, could you not feel Danielle whom you have met?"

Mélusine laughed. "It doesn't work like that. I just get visions. I cannot make them come."

"Then you're not much help as a Druid, Mélusine," I said brutally. "You cannot be satisfied with letting the visions just come to you. You must discipline yourself to call up at least some of a vision even though it may be only partly true." Our eyes locked across the table. "You close your eyes, or do whatever Druids do, Mélusine, and tell me about Marettimo." I shoved the folded chart and the msn.com map over to her. "I'll tend to the meatloaf."

According to my fork test, there was no pink inside the meatloaf in the three places sampled. This was overdone by French standards, just right according to my less evolved North American ones. I took it out and set it on the top of the stove, turning off the oven and banging the back of my head against fibreglass squirrel-cage fan inserts. I reached back to dampen their motion and mild clunking against the roll-down computer doors.

"I see a dark-haired woman. She is lonely and she is afraid. She is despairing. Long dark hair, and she is très… very… concerned about it for some reason. She wears nothing but a shapeless dark robe… I think it is Arab?" her voice rose in surprise. "But she has a bad cross on her chest."

"Bad…?"

"Rough. Crude."

"Go on."

"It is made only of two sticks tied together with… how do you say…? little thongs of leather."

"How is the cross held on her chest?"

"A thong around her neck."

"What is she doing?"

"She is walking from the beach."

"Why?"

"She was looking for a small round sponge among the pools of the rocks there."

"Why?"

"Because of her period. It has begun and her stomach is cramping."

"Did she find a sponge?"

"Yes, but she is worried. And angry."

"Why?"

"Because it may be too small… and she is not used to this."

"What is she doing?"

"Holding the sponge in her hand, of course, so that it will die." And then, very suddenly… "She wants to die."

"Does she?"

"No, she gets up…"

"Gets up?"

"She had fallen to the sand."

"I see."

"She wants to die, but she cannot."

"Why not?"

"Because she has a heavy…" here Mélusine visibly slumped, "… a heavy burden that must be borne."

"Is she carrying anything?"

"No. The burden she must bear is in the village."

And with that my Druid more or less collapsed on the table, but managed to get one forearm between her forehead and the wood. I waited a decent interval and then brought her a plate of meatloaf and mixed vegetables. I arranged knives, forks and spoons around her as best as I could and poured out a generous glass of vin rouge. "Here, Mélusine, drink this and you'll feel better." I gently held up her head and just as gently held the glass to her mouth. She sipped and swallowed, and then did it again. Presently, she pushed herself upright and I shoved the plate in front of her.

After a few minutes staring at the plate without seeing it, she said: "I didn't know I could do that."

"You done good, Mélusine," I said, eating meatloaf. "How much of it was true, do you think?"

"It was a true vision. I could feel the sand and her cramps…. but it could not have been Danielle."

"Why not?"

"She's blonde."

"I don't imagine she would stay that way, not in Sicily."

Mélusine looked at me and started picking at her food.

"In Malta, she could get some hair colouring, dye – whatever women call it – but probably not in Marettimo. She expected help to arrive before her blonde roots grew out. That may be why she was worried. And I can well imagine that Danielle Falardeau would not be used to using Mediterranean menstrual sponges."

"Do you actually believe in that… vision…, Marc Rennsalaer?"

"I'm inclined to."

"Why?"

"Because, Mélusine, you confirmed something I never mentioned to you. I had suggested to Falardeau that Danielle, because she could speak Sicilian, would probably disguise herself as a nun. That is the only way a woman in Sicily could be absolutely safe. And, because of where they had just come from – Ethiopia and Egypt – she might have a black Arab burnoose. And you were surprised that her gown was Arab even though she wore a Christian cross. A burnoose could easily pass for a poor nun's habit. And that's just the way you dressed the woman near Marettimo."

"I didn't say she was in Marettimo."

"No, but that was the map you were thinking about."

She hesitated, and then tried a bit of eating. She looked up at me. "If you… and I… are right, Marc Rennsalaer, there is one thing you should know."

"Yes?"

"This woman is just about at the end of her strength."

"That came though loud and clear, Mélusine." And that consideration changed my plans, such as they were.

21

Early the next morning, as soon as the canal opened, we dropped down the several locks into Narbonne and entered a stretch that I knew very well. The Canal de la Robine runs right through Narbonne, in fact Narbonne is its raison d'être. We passed quickly through the concrete-sided part of the canal that wends though the city and headed for the étang, or 'pond', that gives out onto the Mediterranean through a narrow channel near Narbonne Plage, or Narbonne Beach.

On the way, just at the end of the canal that leads into the étang, I did stop at the Elf-Antar float and filled two of my deck-mounted metal jerry cans, the red painted ones, with 10 gallons of premium gasoline. This was an expensive proposition at 10 Euros per litre. I locked them down tight.

Mélusine had been doing most of the steerage since Carcassonne. She was really getting quite good at it. Perhaps that was because she had gotten her special nourishment at Carcassonne and again last night after calling up the vision.

I had explained that at the downward flight of locks out of Carcassonne to the Aude and all the way into the Med, the buoy system reversed. Going 'up' was considered 'returning' and since we were going down the rule was no longer 'red to right returning' and she should therefore keep the red buoys to port and not to starboard (right, looking forward). If she saw green buoys, she should keep them to starboard.

After the Elf-Antar transaction, I asked her to just stop and drift in the channel of the étang for a few minutes. But to keep Jester under a tight rein by using all directions of thrust to stay in one place, while I folded the cutwater doors forward and secured the triangular Chinese floor between them. I took special care to make sure all the locking bolts were tight. Once in Aiguillon, my very first priority had been repairing the Bay of Biscay's storm damage to Jester.

Raoul and Philippe would have helped anyway no doubt, but they were all the more enthusiastic because they were awed by my feat of crossing Biscay knowing that an Atlantic storm was waiting offshore. The reputation of the Bay of Biscay frightens even sailors, and Raoul and Philippe were really truckers turned bargees by force majeure. The very thought of the Bay of Biscay terrified them. Raoul had gone to Royan once, had seen the Atlantic rollers from there, and had vowed never to go within sight of them again. So it was Raoul who had suggested fitting cotter-pinned nuts to the locking bolts, and using tapered bolts and tapered holes in the flanges, and though it took more trouble to fabricate and secure, it was stronger. Once the entire cutwater system was as strongly secured at it could be, I gestured to Mélusine to continue with all legal speed (7 knots) along the channel.

I sat on the ramp-door and watched the Chinese floor alternately filling and emptying in the slight wind-swell on the étang. On this 20-kilometre stretch we passed little reed-islands and the mysterious barrows along the shore that had piqued my continuing interest when I had first sailed into Narbonne. Most people think the étangs dull, but they reminded me of what I had read of the Chesapeake. These étangs did not produce oysters, however, but langouste instead – my first commercial cargo in France. The étangs could, though, rival the Chesapeake's variety of waterfowl – only here Mandarin ducks took the place of Mallards.

I was half expecting to run into Gabereau somewhere in the étang, and hopefully he'd be aboard a nice big police cutter with radar. Perhaps I could prevail upon him to test whether the aircraft returned any significant radar echo on police near-military radar sets. But this was not to be, for we saw no sign of smugglers or police cutters. Indeed, in the depths of winter, there were hardly any signs of life at all.

About three hours later we rounded the last curve of the channel and the blue of the Mediterranean spread out before us from horizon to horizon. Today, the water wasn't the bright azure that one associates with summertime, it was a kind of chalky-looking grey-blue and the swells were running about 4-6 feet from a north wind, the Mistral.

I gestured to Mélusine with an outstretched arm to head southeast. After we had splashed easily over the bar at the mouth of the channel where the swells creamed a bit, I made shift to raise the jibs or small genoas, the foresails, and then hoisted the mains. I pivoted all the sails forward on the starboard side so that the portside sails filling with the north wind would not blanket the starboard sails.

The radio had informed me that the wind would hold from the north, from the Alps, that is, for the next several days. I felt Jester's speed increasing almost geometrically once the sails were up, drawing and trimmed. She was lightly laden with no cargo aboard to speak of.

Back aft I could see the wind-motors whirling around rapidly. True, they were feeding electricity to a motor that augmented the steam engine but I couldn't decide whether we were doing any better than with conventional sails on the mizzens. Jester was a hybrid, and a daily more experimental one, what with the wind-motors now a disguised airplane (of sorts). One could not expect too much performance from so many compromises and dual usages.

Raoul had suggested the solution that we finally adopted. A 5 hp electric motor, our third aluminium-cased one to save weight, drove the steam engine by a 1/2-inch chain around the flywheel. The steam engine could be shut down completely and its valves could be levered opened to release any backpressure. Therefore the electric motor from the wind-motors had to crank the steam engine around and this was wasted energy.

On the other hand, the steam engine was already connected to the impeller drive by a 1-inch chain and already turned a generator for lighting – more drag. Nonetheless, even with the steam engine freewheeling, as it were, I could see some rpm driving the impeller, so wind-motor power alone was contributing some thrust, but whether it was significant or equalled the power of two conventional mizzen sails I couldn't say.

Now, given the urgency of my Druid's assessment of Danielle Falardeau's predicament, some people may wonder why I did not do what I had done off the Cotentin Peninsula and off Brittany. After jacking Jester's front hull up with air in the front keel, I had gotten my ten knots from Brittany onward with the full load of Calvados and, before that, had gotten about fifteen estimated knots on a beam reach with the sails up off the Seine estuary. So, why not jack Jester's hull up now, making her a 'semi-multi-hull' and sail with all possible speed toward Danielle Falardeau?

The answer was one of those complex nautical compromises. Jester could be a multi-hull, but she was a heavy one compared to a true Indonesian orembai. Jester was made of welded steel, not bamboo and teak. Also, since the Cotentin and Brittany caper, her conventional Chinese battened-lug sails on the mizzens had been transformed into wind-motors. In terms of absolute speed, I had good reason to doubt, by now, that these wind-motors gave the same amount of power as the conventional sails. But there was also no doubt that they were more versatile by far in producing power all the time and no matter what the wind direction might be in relation to the boat.

I could get my ten knots with the sails, wind-motors and steam engine. I could get useful propulsion and battery-charging power with the wind-motors even if docked, but I could not get 15 knots of speed with them with the additional sails that Jester still carried. Well, that wasn't quite true.

I might be able to get those 15 knots, but only at the cost of possibly damaging the wind-motors revolving around their stationary masts (shafts). And if those wind-motors were damaged, then I had no biplane with which to rescue Danielle Falardeau. In our Joëlle-hurried construction, the stainless steel collars surrounding the stationary mizzen masts as 'bearing races' also carried welded-on steel tabs to locate and distance the two masts into a narrow Vee configuration that defined and gave strength to the entire assembled canard airplane. These spacers were aluminium-tube lengths bolted to the masts via those stainless steel tabs. So, if I risked damage to the wind-motors trying to go faster on the crossing to Sardinia, I also risked a good chance of ever being able to save Danielle Falardeau.

Me, I was more than happy to have ten reliable knots out of Jester with wind-motors on the mizzens. This was more than most modern yachts could boast, plus the advantage of the wind-motors in port to produce electricity. And plus all that, I had the added advantage that these crazy wind-motors could be, but with a lot of work, converted into an aircraft.

Therefore, I decided to get my ten knots with no risk to the wind-motors/aircraft and cross to the southern end of Sardinia, Cape Teulada, in about 48 hours at 10 knots instead of 30 hours at a speed of fifteen knots. This would waste no time at all since if we went faster we would arrive at night and I could not attempt to assemble the wind-motors into the aircraft without light. And I could not attempt to fly until dark. Besides, if this rescue was to be done to anyone's benefit, including Danielle's, I had to touch some bases in Cagliari first. Danielle would simply have to endure a day or so longer, in spite of my Druid's concerns.

I went up to the poop and then down into the wheelhouse beside Mélusine. I shut off the steam to the engine and stooped into the cubbyhole engine room to pull the lever that opened the backpressure valves. I could see the engine increase its freewheeling revs. We must be getting some thrust from the thing because in this breeze the wind-motors must be producing about 3 kilowatts each, 6 kilowatts total.

A kilowatt is about three-quarters of a horsepower (with losses). So, the wind-motors looked to be contributing about 4 hp to the drive of the boat.

I still couldn't decide whether we were ahead of the game, behind, or just breaking even. However, now we were using no fuel for the steam engine. I went back into the cramped wheelhouse and peered at the yachty-type speed indicator that worked off a pitot tube in the bow. The digital indicator varied continually between 9.3 and 10.1 knots, less in the troughs of the swells and more on the crests. More when we accelerated down a crest. I shrugged. We were doing about the same as before under sail, maybe a little less.

I looked at the pilot chart. No dangers on this course, and fathoms increasing by the second. I turned on the Deccas, now on the main masts. There was a distant boat or a small ship off the port bow. I saw it, and the Deccas saw it too, so they were working. The boat, it looked like a fishing boat, was heading north, perhaps for Béziers, and was throwing up a fair amount of spray.

"Are you getting tired, Mélusine?"

"No, not at all. Are you getting hungry?"

"A little," I admitted.

"Okay… I'll go heat up the meatloaf. A beer with it?"

"You got it."

So I took the wheel and folded down the across-wheelhouse seat, folded up the backrest, leaned back and sailed a course just north of southeast, not quite ESE, more southeast-by-east because I figured the north wind would push us south by leeway anyway. I was steering for Cape Teulada at Sardinia's southern tip, about 450 miles away. Cagliari was up around it to the north on the eastern side of the island a short distance. If the wind and our speed held, we should see the light of Teulada in about 48 hours, maybe a little less. Or, rather, we wouldn't see it since we would arrive about now, or noon, the day after tomorrow.

22

Cagliari looked very picturesque in the late sunlight; at least it did to me. It was a port, and a minor one on a minor island, but an island with close and intimate relations with the outside world. Cagliari was a haven for the kind of boats and ships that have always fascinated me more than ocean-crossing liners and super-tankers. The light was fading fast, not because it was so late in the afternoon but because the mountain spine of Sardinia just to the west and which hemmed Cagliari in all around blocked the sun long before it could set in the west.

Most of the crafts in the harbour were local fishing boats, presumably sardine seiners that produced Sardinia's most famous product. And at least a fair proportion of them were painted in the raucous traditional colours. Here were also very small coastal freighters of a distinct type I have never seen before, a high bow and high stern but a very low central section. Some of them wore bright livery too, through most were grey and rust-streaked.

This was my first visit to Italy, even so problematical a part of it as Sardinia. We located the customs shed, for this was a Port of Entry. I didn't know exactly what to do, this being my first visit, but the officer we dealt with, at least, was in a crisp uniform, and was very efficient in a friendly way. He spoke French and some English. I knew that since 2007, the European Community had enacted complex reciprocal legislation that was intended to promote small inter-country trade. I knew that we needed only our French passports to visit Italy, but I didn't know what regulations might cover the carrying of cargo from Italy to France. I explained that I was a small trader and that my boat was more of a yacht than a freighter. I could carry about five metric tons at most, but at home the boat could push a barge to increase the payload.

"Why don't you just take up smuggling, Capitano Rennsa-la-er...?" the Customs Officer said with an engaging smile. "Everybody else does, and it saves us all that official paperwork."

"Renns-ler. It's easier to say than it looks."

"Very well. Rennsler."

"Right." I paused. "But I'm not a smuggler... although I have been tempted, I admit... I carry legal cargo with papers attached." I handed him the papers covering the leather goods haulage.

He read most of it. It was naturally in French. Then he made an appreciative whistle. "This stuff must be very expensive."

"I think so," I agreed. "It is going to a Parisian fashion shop... or several of them. I don't know exactly."

"The manufacturer here must pay an export tax – nothing to do with you."

"And I imagine there's an import tax on the other end, in France. All I'm doing is taking the goods from here to there. Is there a... er... haulage tax? And if so, who do I pay?"

"Not me," he laughed. "All you need is this." And from within a drawer he produced the most magnificent document I had seen in a long time. "*Constituto in Arrivo per il Naviglio da Diporto*," he intoned with the dignity it deserved. At least 18-inches in length and a foot wide, it bore huge gold, red and silver stamps. He handed it to me and I held it up and genuinely admired it.

"Jesus," I said. "It is beautiful. How much does it cost?"

"Fifty Euros."

A gallon gasoline back at the Elf-Antar pump. "What does it entitle me do?"

"Once I fill out the name of your vessel, and the name of the owner – we don't bother with the crew once we've seen their European passports – it entitles you to sail anywhere in Italian waters." I handed the form back to him and he entered the name of *Folderol Jester* as I spelled it and the name of Marc Rennsalaer from my passport. I handed him a fifty Euro note and he stamped it yet again and added his signature.

"How long is this good for?"

"A year. When you leave Italy, we would appreciate your informing an officer at your port of exit." He then typed on a computer for some time. "I am entering your vessel's arrival at Cagliari and the purpose," he nodded at the papers on the desk, "the shipment of leather goods." Soon he looked up. "Anything else?"

"No, I guess not," I said.

He handed me the leather contract papers and the *Constituto*. "Enjoy your stay in Italy, Capitano."

"That's all there is to it?"

"Not unless…" He picked a regulation book. "Have you seen a rat aboard your vessel within the last six weeks?"

"No."

"Has any crew died of bubonic plague since you put to sea from Narbonne?"

"They would hardly have time."

"See what I mean. Enjoy your stay in Italy."

Outside the Customs Office and down the wharves we found a newspaper kiosk that also had phones attached. We obtained some Euro coinage from the newspaper vendor and I phoned the leather manufacturer using the name of the contact written on the contract. This turned out to be the harassed manager and President of the small operation. He was flustered, as I had hoped, to have someone at the wharf ready to take delivery. It wasn't quite ready, he explained in French almost as bad as my own. So I put Mélusine on the line just to be absolutely certain we would understand the situation correctly.

Apparently, they needed three days – and that seemed to be a minimum – to gather together all the disparate items called for. Some were still being produced. It was harder to prepare a selection of samples than to produce numerous examples of just one or two items. I could well understand this, which is why I had specified what I did. We said that we *could* wait around for three days, four at the most, but we would then expect the goods to be delivered as contracted at the proper pier.

On the way around the southern tip of Sardinia at Cape Teulada and up to Cagliari, we had noticed several coves with a sliver of sandy beach at the head before the mountains tumbled down to the sea. In other places, the coast was rocky and ironbound. One of these coves would do very nicely, especially the one just under the loom of Cape Teulada itself. It seemed to be deserted without the usual tiny village clinging to the shore. Unfortunately, however, we could not make it back there in less than three or four hours and I did not want to navigate a strange coast at night. And certainly not the coast of Sardinia.

So, we lay to beside the Customs Shed for the night, for a nominal fee, and had the security of the Customs officers passing to and fro on their shifts. I needed a good meal and a long night's sleep. Mélusine gave me both.

23

The next morning just after dawn I tried an experiment that I had been thinking about for a while. There was a fairly good breeze as the sun came up and so I took Jester out under the bare power of the two mizzen wind-motors alone. This gave about 3 knots to steer out of Cagliari harbour and into the fairway. In the meantime, I fired up the boiler on coal oil to raise a head of steam because I wanted to get back to that cove quickly.

The wind-motors could give steerageway and a trifle more by themselves while the steam built up. No time was therefore lost in waiting to raise steam as had previously been the case, and the wind-motors certainly made it less expensive to have cabin lights and the coffee maker than keeping the boiler and engine on simmer all night with coal oil. The only time when the wind-motors could not do the steerageway job was if a stiff wind and sea had to be countered. But that was seldom or never the case on the canals and only infrequently along the shore.

When the steam came up, I used it because I didn't want to trust the sails as the coast opened up from Cagliari harbour. I'd heard about the sudden squalls that could swoop down from the Sardinian mountains – or from any coastal mountains for that matter. So, I cruised Jester southward at her best ten knots with these Sardinian mountains looking very close abeam to starboard. I kept to the 60-fathom line by the sonar and scanned the chart for any rocks ahead.

About five hours later, say around eleven o'clock, the bay and cove opened up to starboard in a gentle curve about five miles in diameter. The water suddenly turned dead calm, not quite as flat as a millpond, because we were in the lee of everything except an east wind blowing across from Italy. I figured that here even winds from down off the mountains would be rare because the mountains had diminished considerably and could barely be called hills. I took her in slowly with an eagle eye on the Eagle sonar and a hawk's eye on the chart. The bottom shelved up rapidly and it looked to be firm white sand.

I called Mélusine to the wheelhouse. I told her to hold Jester steady as in the étang back at Narbonne and I unbolted the cutwater doors and the Chinese floor. I folded the doors back against Jester's sides and folded the Chinese floor up against the landing-craft style ramp. Then I took the wheel and ran Jester gently ashore on the beach. I lowered the ramp and for safety, I suppose, put two anchors from the bow up the beach, and wrapped the cables around stunted but tough-looking pines just above the sand line. I turned off the boiler and declutched the engine from the impeller. Then it was long past time for a good, long breakfast.

Now, I don't think I'm lazy, but I don't like to remember that day. Of course, there are other and better reasons I don't like to think about it too.

I was just going to leave it that I got the aircraft assembled by about three o'clock in the afternoon but that doesn't do justice to the struggle, some of it needless. The Honda engine, of course, was the hardest part.

For some reason, Raoul, Philippe and I had wrestled it below and onto Mélusine's bare bunk. We had some idea that it should be protected from the weather, I suppose, but it would have done quite well on deck wrapped in a tarp. We weren't thinking straight and I had felt pushed at the time by Joëlle's 'managerial' concerns that the trading should start as soon after the thaw as possible.

For that matter, the engine should have been on deck and tarp-wrapped, all right, but also supported on a metal frame motor-mount that was fastened to a small and sturdy wooden skid, and preferably a skid on wheels. That would have taken another day or so to design, make and test – and I had already 'negotiated' three days to let any ice formations get broken off and carried away.

Therefore, as I wrestled the engine off the bunk and into the wheelhouse, all the time trying not to re-injure the spine that a land mine had already messed up, part of my strength was supplied by anger. I vowed never again to 'negotiate' anything with Joëlle about something I considered important – not that I had known why I felt that way at the time. And if she was no longer in Aiguillon when (and if) I returned, well, perhaps that was for the best.

Getting the engine up out of the wheelhouse wasn't too bad because I used a thick balk of wood from the beach and a come-along ratchet crane lashed to it. Swinging it out through the hatch and onto the poop required Mélusine pushing and me pulling. Getting it into Ivory's truck bed wasn't too bad using Jester's own winch that was bolted very solidly to the top and front of the wheelhouse just in front of the smokestack and whistle-tube(s).

Ivory took the engine to the aircraft in a literal minute through the sand, but placing it in position between and behind the seats called for the come-along again, this time hooked into the rear X-member motor-mount. And then I had to shimmy it in position with several levers that Mélusine collected among the shore pines so that the threaded mounting bolts would get enough bite not to strip the tapped holes. But I finally socketed it snugly into place. And cotter-pinned the bolts. Assembling the chairs in place, rigging the guy wires and jacking the aircraft up to affix the aluminium floats was a comparative piece of cake.

I permitted myself no lapse, knowing that anger was the enemy and exactitude the antidote for it. The guy wires were carefully tensioned. Like almost everything mechanical, one thing affected every other. I didn't want to bind the universal joints at the engine, and I didn't want to bind the squirrel-cage inserts at their outer wheel-bearing ends. I made very certain that the sprockets and chains were as perfectly aligned as our own design of magnified viewing glass could make them.

By three, I began painting the aerofoil vanes of the once-wind-motors black with the fabric spray paint. This was a quick and easy job. Then I spray painted the aluminium floats and struts flat black as well as any other bare aluminium I could see, like tubes slightly revealed by vane cut-outs. As you can see from the drawing, there were a few of these. I was finished about five and it was almost dark. The paint had set, but it wasn't yet dry. I thought it would dry overnight because the weather was relatively warm, or seasonal, at about 10 degrees Celsius.

But that's when Mélusine came hurrying out through the ramp door with an anxious expression on her face.

"Marc…!"

"What is it, Mélusine? You look awful."

"I don't know. Something's changed. Something is happening that could change everything."

"Where, Mélusine, please be a bit more specific. London? Paris? Aiguillon?"

"Marettimo."

"Did she die?"

"No, not yet. But forces… I can't understand." She shook her head. "Forces are converging on her. She does not know."

"Now?"

She shook her head. "A few hours."

"Do you see anything…?"

"Only possible death… for her… and you."

"Possible?"

"Yes. Nothing is fixed."

"I'm glad to hear it, Mélusine."

"But you have to leave now… very soon."

"I'm not going anywhere until it is pitch dark, Mélusine."

I turned her around and pushed her back toward Jester's now downward sloping ramp-door. "Mélusine, go below and make me two meatloaf sandwiches. Take two cans of beer... and a plastic jug of water. Wrap it all up well in a thick plastic bag."

I stopped in the wheelhouse, trying to think. On the wall beside my upper bunk, now cleared of its folding windscreen, was a length of 1/4-inch nylon line. Dammit, I had no anchor for the aircraft – another result of not having time to think things through.

As I took off my clothes and zipped into the large ski suit, I thought of using a two-handled pot with a makeshift bridle of nylon line. After slipping into the suit, I sat on my bunk with the haute-upscale stainless two-quart pot with copper bottom that Mélusine had collected from the galley and carefully rove a stout bridle from each upscale stainless steel handle. I encased each handle in several separate turns of the nylon rope and joined them all to one line with a loop secured by several half hitches.

By then Mélusine was through packing the provender. I put my goggles on and did not forget the medium-petite ski suit and the other pair of goggles. They were in a plastic bag anyway. I added to it the Adidas that Mariko had once worn and a thick pair of socks. I tucked Mélusine's food into the plastic bag with the other ski suit, goggles and Adidas. It was an upscale plastic bag too, good and strong.

It was getting dark, but not as dark as I wanted it. I forced myself to do things methodically, as I should have done in Aiguillon... Forget it... I tied the improvised sea anchor securely to the support for the front float, paid out sufficient line but kept it taut and forced the pot between the two chaise longues. I passed a nylon strap between two holes in the chairs, through the handles of the pot, and snicked the plastic tang-lock home. I strapped the upscale plastic bag with the extra clothing into the passenger's chaise longue.

Mélusine had followed me and I turned to her.

"Violence?"

"Oh, yes."

"Wait here."

I returned from Jester in less than three minutes, remembering to lock my secret cache and drop the key into one of the trendy zip shoulder pockets of the ski suit. I also had a microlight and a map of the Egadi Island group. It was dark enough by then that I didn't mind carrying Stoner's brainchild out in the open. Naturally, the AR-15 was already the flattest black. Charles Stoner had been nothing if not a professional.

With the long and semi-flexible leverage of the canard design in the front, Mélusine and I were able to shove the aircraft off the beach. I was about to wade into the knee-deep water to turn the thing with the front facing out of the cove when Mélusine stopped me and waded out hip-deep in her jeans. "I can get dry within minutes, you cannot," was all she said. She backed the aircraft almost up onto the beach so that I could clamber aboard when a wavelet receded and scramble into the pilot's chaise longue.

Mélusine held the aircraft steady as I started the nearly silent Honda and let it warm up for a minute or two.

"How long do I wait?" She asked.

I had been considering this. "If I'm not back by, say, three o'clock tomorrow… quinze heures… then try to take Jester back to Cagliari. Try to call Joëlle in Aiguillon and get Raoul or Philippe to fly to Cagliari and try to get Jester back to Aiguillon."

"And if I cannot contact Joëlle… or Christine?"

"Then talk to the police in Cagliari. Tell them everything you know, including Falardeau. You will get back to your Brittany, Mélusine."

"That is not my desire, my Lord."

"Nor mine, my… liege? Anyway, shove us off."

24

She lifted off easily from the smooth waters of the little bay beneath Cape Teulada and I thought it was dark enough so that no one could see the craft against the dark of the ocean. I did not gain sufficient altitude to pick out any lights on distant Italy to the east. But I thought I caught, out of the corner of my eye as I turned southeast, a twinkle far off to port that might just be Cagliari about fifty miles north or some nearer village.

The problem was that I was not used to altitude – not used to flying, for that matter – and here I was trying to fly about 200 miles southeast over the ocean at night. I knew that a slight north wind was blowing down the strait between Italy and Sardinia because I could actually feel it.

I knew that disorientation was the major threat. All the books I had read, and they were few, had stressed the necessity of trusting your instruments in order to avoid disorientation. I had a good watch with a luminous dial. I had an altimeter that I had tried to calibrate for sea level. It wasn't luminous, at least not much. I had to lean forward a peer at it. I had a good automotive compass that was luminous and which was bolted with nylon bolts to the aluminium frame of the windshield. I had a map that I had pored over for several nights before, but I could consult it any time with my microlight. Behind the windshield there was very little turbulence.

By my calculations the three-island Egadi group was between 187 and 206 statute miles due southeast of Cape Teulada. At the aircraft's presumed speed at this loading, 65 mph, I would be there – somewhere – in almost exactly three hours. The moon, three days from full, was supposed to rise within an hour. That being the case, it should bathe the Egadi Islands in a fair amount of light.

The problem, actually, was now. I 'trusted', with reservations, the altimeter and I kept its barely luminous needle at 50 feet... and erred on the higher side of fifty. The difficulty was that the waves below did not have white crests and so I could get no horizon line. I took solace in the fact that the 'wheel' I was holding had a perfectly horizontal tube on the bottom and two vertical handles on either side. One of these was the motorcycle-type throttle to the Honda and I kept it at 7500 rpm. I figured that if I could keep the wheel's baseline horizontal no matter what, and kept my eyes flicking from instrument-to-instrument and back to that baseline, I could stay in level flight.

This seemed to work and I started getting hungry, which helped take my mind off orientation. In half an hour, according to my Seiko, a buttery glow showed itself in the east (according to my compass heading). This must be the moon and, keeping an eye on that horizontal bar and the compass, I resisted every urge to steer toward it. I wished I had had time to work out some sort of luminous plumb level swinging or pivoting from the wheel. Fairly soon the moon rose up, more on its back than on edge as in more northern latitudes. Again, I kept my eyes focussed on the compass and the horizontal bar to the wheel, resisting any urge to fly toward the only reference point in the blackness.

Soon, however, the moon itself gave me a reference point. I could see lighter and darker bands of light below and I took these for the gentle swells of the Tyrrhenian Sea. They seemed frighteningly close below, but I trusted (more or less) the altimeter and kept to 50 feet... well, 75.

As the moon rose, I looked at my watch. Halfway. The Honda never missed a beat and as the moon rose higher it began to cast silver shadows instead of golden ones. And very suddenly, I saw the faint finger of Trapani's lighthouse ahead off to port. I had been blown a little southward of my intended course. I altered course to the north or port very carefully and now with the two reference points – the moon and Trapani's light – I became more confident.

After forty minutes more, in the higher moonlight now, I could make out the small, distant shadows of irregular islands in the sea and moon-illuminated channels of water between them. It was still much too early to steer for Marettimo Island in the group of three, the nearest or most seaward of them, but I saw it steadily differentiating itself in the distant group.

Mélusine had said unexpected and sudden danger. In a place like Marettimo, such danger would probably come from the sea, or much more likely come from the sea. I was approaching the now clearly separate island from the northwest. On the north coast of Marettimo, I knew, was a deep bay or cove separated by a fair stretch of island from the supposed ferry landing from Trapani to the southeast. This bay was a place I had earmarked myself for a pick-up because it was so separated from the ferry landing.

Not having any idea whatsoever of the island's altitude above sea level, the safest course was to fly completely around it, a matter of five miles or so according to the msn. com map, and come in again from the northwest to that deep cove. According to the msn.com map, and the pilot chart, this bay was within easy walking distance from the village of Marettimo. So, staying over moonlit water, which was easy to distinguish from land and was at least at a constant level, I went south, west, north and east again around the entire island returning to about where I had arrived. While going north, I saw one or two twinkles off to starboard, somewhere on the island, which should – or could – have been the village of Marettimo.

Then, not far away, I saw it, while on the northern leg of my circumnavigation.

A travelling vee in the silver moonlight. I was seeing the creaming wash from a motorboat. It was coming from the east, from Sicily, and the vee was obviously curving toward the very same deep northern bay I would have chosen myself. I watched the wake until I was certain that it headed deep into the bay. Then I flew around the island again and decided to set down on the western side of the cove's entrance. I knew not whether there were rocks or sand below, but I watched the swells carefully. From my experience as a river pilot, at least, there were no reefs below, only a smooth bottom of some kind. With the moon to help, and trusting my altimeter, I came in shallow and slow just inside the mouth of the bay. And I killed the engine just before I thought we would hit the water.

By the moonlight on the loom of the land, the craft came to a gradual stop about twenty yards off the western entrance to the bay. This was a spit... and it looked like white sand in the moonlight... but Mélusine had spoken of rocky pools where small sponges might be found. The north wind was blowing, but we were in the lee of some small cape (unnamed to msn.com) that projected out from the northeast corner of Marettimo Island.

I rolled gingerly out of my chaise longue, not knowing whether I would be in three feet of water or ten, and was surprised to find it waist deep to a firm sand bottom. I reached over the pilot's chair, unsnapped the pot, and took it forward warily. But the bottom didn't change or deepen appreciably. I took the pot and a deep breath and took it to the bottom where I filled it with sand, and sort of buried it in sand. Going back to the aircraft, I took the AR-15 from its nest beside my pilot's seat – it had been strapped in with a nylon snap lock – and waded toward the head of the bay. I was soaked by now, of course from setting the pot, and was getting somewhat cold, but I made no splash in the water. I went very slowly.

Presently, my eyes also being long since adjusted to the light, I made out a boat drawn up on the beach in the high moonlight. The moonlight showed it to be a horseshoe type of affair and soon I took it for a Zodiac or Avon. Some sort of inflatable, at any rate. By now I was within twenty yards of it and could make out the shape of an outboard at its stern. The bottom was shelving up to beach and this obliged me to squat in the water, holding the assault rifle out of the water but parallel with the surface. Was there a boulder on the beach? It seemed unlikely with all that smooth white sand. I came in behind the inflatable, and saw the boulder rise and assume a short man's height. A short and stocky man. This meant extra-slow going.

To take him now, or later... that was the question. By now, I was up against the inflatable's stern with a left hand on the outboard and saw that it was indeed, a 4-to-5 man Zodiac. Zodiacs are dark grey. Avons are usually red and white. That more or less decided the matter. There were more men somewhere and I wanted to shorten the odds. So, I shoved the Zodiac's stern, making a slight scuffing in the sand with the pivoted prow, and the man came back to the boat to haul it further up onto the sand.

As he bent to grasp the bow or bow painter, I rose suddenly from beside and behind the inflatable and slammed the AR-15's butt into his throat. He went down like he'd been pole-axed and I was on top of him a split second later. However, I still did not know for certain that this man was a lookout and boat-guard for a Mossad hit team on the trail of Danielle Falardeau and her book.

I was gratified to feel a pulse in his Carotid artery, proving that he was alive, though his injury would likely cause extreme discomfort for quite a few weeks, as physicians like to say. Unfortunately for him however, my rapid examination of his unconscious body quickly disclosed a Ruger .22 pistol and a razor-sharp U.S.-issue upside down fighting knife in a shoulder holster on his left side. This indicated that if he wasn't Mossad, and personally I had no doubt of that, then he was still a bad guy with the means and motivation to do harm to the innocent.

Therefore, with no very extreme regrets, I broke his neck there on the moonlit sands of Marettimo with the heel of my right hand under his jaw, hard, and my left forearm beneath his neck. I heard bones crunch. He died without a sound. My conscience was clear, well, more or less. He had been either Mossad and had something to do with Danielle, or he had been a smuggler.

His Ruger .22 automatic in his shoulder holster and a fighting knife strapped upside down to the shoulder holster on his left shoulder had more or less settled matters and my conscience. Not even a smuggler would wear an upside down fighting knife.

Now, I had shopped so long for the ski suits because I was trying to find styles with as many pockets as possible, preferably even knee pockets. I didn't get my heart's desire, but I found a style with at least some pockets, all zippered. It was sort of a combination ski suit and recreational ATV rig. Snowmobiles have never become widely popular in France, but they do exist, mostly in Valois on the margin of the Alps. I had a pocket for the Ruger and its holster, with the knife and its scabbard attached. I took the time to arrange these most usefully in the pocket.

Slinging the AR-15 over my shoulder, I propped the dead man up against the Zodiac's bow with the inflatable's painter piled under him so that it wouldn't glide off the beach. Since he had been waiting, I would wait too. But not near the Zodiac. I found myself a nice sand dune about twenty yards from the inflatable and dug myself into it.

25

It was nice and comfortable there in the sand although I admit to being a trifle cold. I was soaked, of course. I had taken off a few minutes before eight o'clock and landed a few minutes after eleven. It had taken me over an hour just to stalk and kill the man at the boat after I had seen the Zodiac on the beach. It was almost one o'clock in the morning and the moon was as high as it was going to get. At times, I thought I heard the sound of high and argumentative voices from somewhere inland.

But it was another hour and a half before I heard scrunching coming toward the beach from the dunes above. I looked up and saw three forms coming down. One must have been a woman in a long dress or gown because I saw no flash of moonlit sand as I did occasionally between the presumed legs of the two others.

The presumed men said nothing at all, but someone was sobbing softly and the voice had a higher tone. As they came nearer I saw, or thought I did, that the gowned figure had 'her' hands over 'her' face. One of the other figures was not swinging his arms or hands as he walked. I could see no hands or arms. So he must have had them crossed over his chest. He must therefore be carrying something relatively large and perhaps heavy.

They approached the inflatable but, of course, the boat guard didn't stand up to whisper a direction or a greeting. The other two man-forms stopped, but the presumed woman, unheeding, kept on going, until she was roughly pulled back by the only man-form that had its hands free.

Surprised, she lost her footing in the soft sand fell backward. That's all I needed because the two man-forms were now at least three feet higher than her and somewhat silhouetted against the white sand dunes.

I had been planning strategy for what might befall. I decided that I wasn't going to play around with knives with two or three men – I had no idea how many there might be, only that the Zodiac would hold six people – in the near-dark, and presumably trained Mossad types at that. I would cut them down from the safety of my dune. If anyone was alerted by the noise, I would presumably have Danielle Falardeau, the book, and an entire island for hide-and-seek games with me holding the considerable advantage of an AR-15. Sooner or later the gunfire from such games would cause talk, even on Marettimo, and sooner or later the Caribinieri would show up. I might lose the airplane – I'd had time to devise a better one while in the dune anyway – but I'd have what I had come for.

'Her' fall backwards gave me the chance I needed and I didn't hesitate, having thought through the options previously. The burst from my AR-15 didn't exactly cut them down – at this range it threw them backwards in grotesque shapes and a large object flew from the shape of one of them. I'm good enough to know that the man at the Zodiac was very dead and that the two sprawled on the dunes were dead as well. I crouched and ran over to them.

"Don't dare scream, Danielle Falardeau," I said distinctly but softly as I passed by the prone figure on the sand.

To my surprise, the two men had been dressed as priests. They had dog collars and more modern trousers, not cassocks. However, their two pistols and fighting knives convinced me that somehow they had fallen from grace. I was collecting these items and stowing them most carefully and methodically in one of the suit's other pockets when I heard a slight scuffling of sand behind me. I had kept the prone figure in corner's eye vision so to speak, but now it seemed to be crawling slowly over the sand.

"The book is to your left," I whispered.

She moved as I indicated and finally found it. She knelt

on the sand with the object clasped to her chest. When I had finished arranging the weapons in my pocket – fighting knives are usually razor sharp and I didn't want to get one of those blades in my leg, stomach or groin inadvertently – I crouched over to her. I shone my microlight in her face, shielding the sudden light from inland and the bay between both our bodies. Her hair was black but there was no mistaking that nose and those blue eyes. She flinched and turned away from the tiny light. "Who are you?" she said.

"That doesn't matter now. Danielle Falardeau?"

She nodded.

"Are you injured?"

She shook her head.

"All right. Come with me."

I reached down and took an elbow, helping her to her feet. Her 'gown' was, as I had suspected, the thick homespun of a genuine Arabic burnoose or jelaba, to give it its correct Arab name. Once she was standing, I saw that she was clasping a large book to her chest. I bent and whispered in her ear. "We must be very quiet, do you understand?" I thought I saw her head nod emphatically.

I put her in the Zodiac and, making almost no sound pushed the inflatable off the sand once I had pulled the painter from beneath my first victim. His body collapsed once its prop was removed and his head lolled into the water with little wavelets teasing his hair. I towed us along the western spit of the bay very slowly out to the anchored airplane.

Keeping the AR-15 at the ready in my right hand – it weighed only 6-plus pounds the way Stoner had designed it, I pushed gently through the water with some confidence now that I knew the bottom. My eyes scanned the open entrance of the bay ahead in the silvery moonlight and soon I made out the slightly darker shadow that was the plane near the end of the western spit.

When we reached the tethered airplane I hauled the Zodiac

around to the right side of it next to the passenger's chaise longue. "Danielle," I whispered into an ear. "We have to do things slowly, methodically and carefully."

She nodded.

"I'll hold the boat steady. You first put the book into that seat." Even I could barely see the flat black under the black shadow of the wing above. She reached out an arm to explore it, and she did it thoroughly. I felt her nod and then I steadied her as she lifted the book into the seat. It must have been fairly heavy because I could feel her muscles quivering.

"Now, take off the burnoose in the Zodiac. Try not to make any noise," I whispered in her ear. As I heard the thick cloth rustle ever so softly, I took the plastic bag from the seat. The book was laying partly on it, so there was some suggestion of a crinkle. Her head came back to me and I could see the vague suggestion of white flesh in the moonlight, breasts hanging. "Put the suit on. It zips up the front, so go very carefully and slowly." Her head nodded. It seemed to take forever, but I heard absolutely nothing. The head came back. "Socks, dry socks and Adidas shoes, Danielle. You will need them. Put them on and take your time."

Again, it seemed an age, but she was quieter than a mouse.

"Now what?" the barest whisper.

"The hard part… you have to get in the seat. Sit on top of the book."

I held the boat and helped her over, but the barest rustle of nylon was unavoidable. Once she was in, and I could tell by the shift of the craft on the water and by the slightest gurgle-splash of the float on the water, I shoved the Zodiac out into the bay. I worked my way around to the right side of the aircraft and put the AR-15 into the seat. Then I lifted it over to the extreme right side of the seat.

I found the anchor line when I walk-floated to the front of the canard and jerked the pot from the grasp of the sand and hauled it in under water so there would be no drips from the rope. Rather than raise the pot with its inevitable dripping of water, by feel I extracted one of the knives and, very carefully, cut the nylon rope under water. There went a $60 pot, but it went without a sound. There was little or no wind and so I had had little difficulty holding the aircraft steady.

Now, I used all my strength to lift and lever myself aboard and into the seat. I made it, but not without some clunking of the hard objects in my pockets against the aluminium chaise longue. I lay back on the barely cushioned chair and, breathing hard because I had lifted myself in a now-sodden ski suit, and snapped the AR-15 into place between the seats. I tried to compress the tangs of the nylon locks as much as possible, but there was still a slight snick.

I pulled the anchor line up taut along the canard cantilever 'fuselage' that were Jester's two masts clamped together and, holding the line in my right hand, reached up to where Danielle's face should be. I pulled it over and whispered into what I figured was her left ear, more or less. "Hold this rope tight." I waited until her hand came up to grasp it. "Now, don't scream, no matter what happens." I felt her head nodding against our clasped hands. I removed my own hand slowly and felt, rather than saw, the tension in her body as she pulled hard on the rope.

Now, I had to do things by feel, but I had marked where the starter button was clamped onto the right side, the outside, of my seat. I could see the little bay's entrance quite clearly in the moonlight, but the light seemed to have reduced its intensity. I felt carefully and pressed the button. The Honda came to life instantly and made less noise by far than an outboard, but still there was no doubt that an engine had started. Sound carries well over water. The previous noises, except maybe for the slight clunks as I had come aboard, could have been fish feeding or wavelets randomly slurping in a configuration of rocks. We had taken our time.

I'm afraid that I gave the Honda no time to warm up, but increased the revs very quickly up to 7500 rpm and we started to jitter over wavelets at increasing speed toward the mouth of the bay. At that instant, I heard an outboard also start up somewhere off to starboard.

I had never forgotten for an instant that I was dealing with the Mossad. I had assumed that they would have another inflatable in the neighbourhood. After nothing had happened immediately after the AR-15 burst I had figured that this other inflatable must have been making another circuit of the island to check for smugglers or fishermen and luckily just happened to be on the distant western side at the time. An AR-15 makes a sort of loud cough, not an ear-splitting ker-blam like other guns. What with outboard noise, they might not have heard anything on the western side of the island. I still think this must have been what happened.

They had another Zodiac out there at the mouth of the bay to guard against some unexpected visit by a smuggler or a belated local fishing boat. And they must have been getting as curious about the passage of time as I was getting anxious. But, in fairness to me, they must have been more surprised than I was. They could not have expected anyone with an AR-15 and they certainly couldn't have expected an aircraft that they could not see. That did not prevent them, however, from firing at the wake they could barely see in the moonlight and at the engine noise they could barely hear in the night.

But one… or two…? of their shots were lucky, even at what must have been extreme range for their usual .22 shorts or longs. They seldom used the Long Rifle cartridge or else I might be dead. The top panel of the windshield shattered and something crashed into the side of my head. In an instant, blood was running down into my right eye and I wiped it away as we climbed to fifty feet, then (slowly) to 75 and then 100.

I felt my scalp and my fingers came away sticky and, from the taste of them, bloody. I felt no damage beyond the searing pain in the right side of my head. Scalp wounds bleed a lot and I was mostly concerned with blood impairing the vision of my right eye. On the other hand, I could have suffered a concussion from the impact. The compass was a bit blurry and I thought I was steering northwest. But the wind was howling though the cracked Perspex and spreading the blood over my face, even the left eye was becoming blurry. Also, I was cold from being wet and this didn't help.

"Danielle!" I shouted to get her out of her shock. I switched on the microlight with my left hand; my right one was on the wheel and motorcycle throttle. I tried to reflect the light off the Perspex at an angle.

"My God." she screamed. "You're bleeding. All over your face."

I tried to keep my voice calm. "I know," I said. "I think it is only a scalp wound. They bleed a lot. But they're not necessarily dangerous. I need your help, now. Will you give it?"

After a moment... "Yes. What can I do?" She was made of stern stuff.

"In the front of my zippered ski jacket you'll find a plastic bag of food. It's crammed into the inside left pocket."

"Food!"

"Yes. Listen. And there's probably some napkins... serviettes... packed along with it, if I know Mélusine."

"Yes...?"

"Okay. Get them out... quickly... and wipe the blood out of my eyes so that I can see to fly this thing."

Instantly, I felt her scrabbling at the zipper and removing the plastic bag.

"Hang on to it, don't let it blow away."

"Got them."

"All right. Now wipe my eyes out. Do the left one first,

furthest from you." This eye cleared a bit. "Good," I said. "Now do the right one." I felt her wiping. That cleared a bit too. "What does the compass say?"

"Northwest, but it is swinging toward west."

I moved the wheel and the rudders a little to starboard. "What does it say now?"

"Northwest."

"What does this say?" I tapped the altimeter.

"Twenty-five feet."

I tried not to panic. I pulled the wheel gently toward me. "Now?"

"Fifty-five feet."

"Good. Now, Danielle, we have to keep the compass pointing toward northwest. And we have to keep this…" I tapped it again "… above fifty feet but not above 100. Got that?"

"Yes. Steer to the right a bit. There. Northwest."

"That's all you have to do. That and wipe my eyes. Sooner or later the bleeding will stop and the blood will coagulate. I need to be able to see until then, so use the water to wipe my eyes."

"For how long?"

"About three hours."

"Can you make it?"

"If I get one of those sandwiches. Have one yourself."

She wiped my eyes again. I could feel the water. That was much better, but also colder.

26

With the wind whistling through the broken Perspex, it was like trying to talk in a well-muffled convertible. Thankfully – because I was still a bit winded by all the excitement – Danielle said nothing for a long while because she was gobbling down Mélusine's meatloaf sandwich like a long-term famine victim. Maybe she was. But she did not forget to bathe my eyes frequently and regularly. She used water from the plastic jug and before long, my vision was clear. One thing about the cool air blowing through the windshield – it couldn't really be called that now – was that it coagulated the blood fairly quickly. But the wound still smarted, shall we say. More than smarted, it throbbed and hurt like hell.

Before long, it seemed a little less dark all around us. I risked a quick glance at the Seiko on my left wrist. What…? Five-thirty?

"Danielle, look over your right shoulder, – and don't lean out or fall out – is the sky getting lighter?"

"Yes, I think so,"

"Why did they come for you tonight… last night?"

"A peasant, a small farmer and sometimes fisherman, went into Trapani on family business – his old aunt had died – and told stories to anyone who would listen about the Holy Woman they had in Marettimo. And she had a big Holy Book with her that only she could read."

"When was this?"

"Three weeks ago."

"And the men dressed as priests?"

"They said they were a deputation from the Bishop at Palermo. They were to take me back so that I could be examined as a possible Saint."

"I see."

"I knew who and what they really were, of course. The

people in Marettimo did not. How could they? There was something of an argument. Marettimo didn't want their Saint taken away."

"I think I may have heard some of that."

"Being Sicilians, the argument went on quite a while. Finally after the Bishop's men promised to return me so that I could continue my saint's work at Marettimo – and especially after they had distributed the golden crucifixes with amber beads that had been blessed by the Bishop himself, they consented to let me go."

"So you were sold for some pieces of brass. Not thirty, surely?"

"Less," she laughed. "Counting the donkeys, there are only twenty-five souls in Marettimo."

"Danielle," I said, "for reasons I won't explain, I'm going down to between fifty and twenty-five feet now that it is getting a bit lighter and I can more or less see an horizon."

"Radar."

"You got it."

"All right. I'll keep you above twenty-five feet and below fifty now."

"Thank you."

"Can you see the compass clearly now?"

"Yes, thanks. But I'm not used to looking at everything, especially in the dark."

"You haven't flown much?"

"A day and a half."

"Jesus H. Christ."

"If it's any comfort to you, Danielle, me and some friends of mine made this thing in a week."

It was now barely light enough to get a vague idea of the contraption. "Is this some kind of ultralite?" Her voice sounded somewhat horrified.

"My own design, I'm afraid… and not a legal ultralite."

"Oh, God." Then there was a silence, and I thought I knew what was coming.

"Couldn't Daddy arrange anything better, or Gérard?"

"Danielle, I'm sorry to have to tell you…"

"Gérard's dead…" She said nothing and she didn't cry. "I felt it, you know. I knew it… I have mourned for him already."

A more Homeric line had seldom been uttered in plain speech. "When?"

"Less than a week ago."

"When you got your period and were looking for a sponge…"

"How could you know that?" She asked, her voice raising, dismayed. "I never saw anyone – new – on the island. How could you know that?"

"And you wanted to kill yourself when you felt that Gérard had… died."

"Yes, but how could you know? I never told anyone that."

"I knew. That's why I came as quickly as I could. I'm sorry the conveyance is not up to your expectations."

"I'm sorry I said that, whoever you are…" She paused. It was now light enough to see the outlines of the aircraft somewhat clearly. "Where's the propeller?" she asked suspiciously. "I've flown ultralites before. I don't see or hear any propeller."

"I wish you could take my place then. I don't like flying anyway. It has no propeller. It is experimental, like I said."

The light was getting better by the moment and now I could see waves not far, in fact much too close, below us. But I didn't want to climb above fifty feet. I felt her looking at me. "I know you… from all the photographs. You're that man who helped Mariko O'Shaugnessey… Marc… Marc…"

"Rennsalaer."

"That's it."

"So Daddy found you."

"He did."

She now looked around at the aircraft. Mostly black, except where I hadn't sprayed the fabric paint too evenly – in these splotches it was only dark grey – no noise and no thwacking propeller. She could look out at the no-ridge wing stretching out to her right and she studied the clues of the chain guards. "There are fans in the wings."

"You got it."

"So, no noise to speak of, much greater aerofoil efficiency and black."

Danielle Falardeau was a tough cookie, but she'd been through a lot. Now that she was theoretically safe, she broke down as I had figured she would. She sobbed suddenly and buried her face in her hands. She cried bitterly and it wracked her. "Gérard, Gérard, Gérard," she moaned.

Men and women are very different animals. A man may, truly, mourn just once for a fallen comrade, but the hurt will always be with him and up front, though he may push it aside. A woman can never mourn just once for a friend or a lover – it is, for women, a lifelong process, though they can seemingly forget it better than men and accept (better than any man) that someone else may have to take the fallen lover's or comrade's place. That's how three million years of evolution have moulded the differing psyches of the two genders.

When she had finished and was into the sniffle stage, I said distinctly so as to be heard over the air stream: "Gérard Delorme did not die in vain. I was with him. And his last words told us where you were."

Ahead, the grey southern tip of Sardinia was plain to see against the still-darker blue-black background of the sea. I was nearing the coast just south of Cape Teulada and so I steered a bit more to starboard to take us a bit north. Within ten minutes I could see 'our' cove nestled in the ghostly grey predawn and thought that I could see the black speck of Jester at the head of the cove still partly in shadow from the hills above. But a light twinkled from the speck. I figured that Mélusine had not slept. And perhaps she had even sung us home.

I came in slow, shallow and slow, very slow, and finally felt the rear floats jerk with the sound of mildly cascading water. Then the front float floated down, terribly slowly it seemed, like a feather, with the canard front wings seemingly reluctant to let us touch water at all. Once we were afloat on a 'boat' again, I dropped the Honda's revs down to just 500 rpm and we glided toward Jester.

I saw a figure – it could only be Mélusine – wave from the poop beside the wheelhouse. It was only grey crepuscular pre-dawn still, no real sunlight had surmounted mountainous Italy to the east, when I ran the airplane gently up onto the sand beach beside Jester. And Mélusine ran off Jester's open bow to meet us at the water's edge.

27

Once Danielle and the book, of course, had been hustled into Jester and down below into the cabin, Mélusine, like an angel, drove out to meet me in Ivory with a toolbox in the back, and two come-alongs.

"You're wounded," she said at once.

"Nothing serious," I said, grabbing the toolbox out of Ivory, and especially the socket set. "This time, Mélusine, we put the damned engine on deck, on a skid. You can wrap it up in a tarp just as soon as I collapse."

"Yes, Lord," she said.

"And knock it off, Mélusine."

"Yes, my Lord." But she said it so breathlessly and so sincerely that I couldn't do much but glare at her, and I was not at all sure how much weight a glare from bloodied eyes carried. I let it go at that, and concentrated on dismantling the Honda's engine from the motor mount and dismantling the universals and chain drives (and so-called chain-shields).

It required two hours to dismantle the aircraft and by that time it was full light even if the sun had not quite climbed above the mountainous spine of Italy blocking the horizon to the east. The Honda's engine was back on board Jester, thanks to Ivory and Mélusine. And one more load carried the pieces of the aircraft off the beach and onto Jester.

"I would like to have the wind-motors re-assembled and turning," I said to Mélusine, "but I just don't think I have the strength to manage it."

"I think I can." This was Danielle's voice and she was bringing two cups of very strong French coffee. She had not collapsed below as I had expected, but stepped down from Jester's poop deck balancing the two cups. She was still in the black ski suit. Mélusine took one cup and I took the other.

Danielle looked at the bits and pieces balanced on Ivory's truck bed. "It can't be too hard, now that I know the principle."

"Oh, rare for Anthony." I intoned.

"Where do you store the squirrel-cage inserts?" Danielle enquired.

"Down below in the central corridor. Port side," I said, "so they don't impinge upon the stove and fridge."

"Okay," she said. "Leave it to us. You just sit here and watch, or go below."

"One thing," I said. "We've been dismantling this thing for a couple of hours and not one person from that village," I gestured up the nearest hillside to a picturesque collection of sugar-cube houses with red roofs, "has come down to the beach in curiosity or even to offer help. Why not?"

"Malucci."

My Latin was almost up to this linguistic challenge. "Bad eye…?"

"Almost," Danielle tinkled a small tired laugh. "Evil eye."

"But surely someone in that village saw me painting the aircraft yesterday afternoon?"

"I'm certain they did," Danielle said. "So much the worse… or better… A big black bird took off from this bay yesterday evening and has returned this morning. It is being dismembered by sorcerers in the bay right now. Better not enquire too closely into it. No one will come down."

"Surely someone knows about ultralites?"

"Not necessarily in southern Sardinia."

"And in Marettimo?"

"Worse… or better." She paused. "Someone would have seen a big black bird take off, their saint disappeared, but three false priests were left dead on their beach."

"Why 'false'?"

"Because their Holy Woman with her Holy Book has vanished."

"I see." It was hard to believe that this was the year 2012.

So, I watched Mélusine and Danielle assemble the wind-motor frames and vanes around the lightweight fibreglass mizzen masts and carry the wind-motors, one at a time, up to the rear of Jester's poop and insert them into their holes in the corners of the vessel's frame. Danielle then connected the automotive generators that pivoted on the masts. I saw Danielle taking a long look at them, and then she tensioned the chains and sprockets correctly, just as well as Raoul or I could have done. By the time the sun actually rose over Italy, the wind-motors aft were whirling merrily again.

When the women had waved and had gone below, I raised myself from a skid in Jester's front hull and wearily raised up the bow ramp door. I went up to the poop and then down into the wheelhouse. Using wind-motor power and battery power alone, I backed off the beach some hundred yards and slowly turned Jester around so that she was headed into the gentle east wind and could head out of the bay and into the strait between Sardinia and Italy.

Once that was accomplished, I went quickly forward again so that Jester wouldn't drift backwards too much – a good easterly wind had sprung up with the sun – and dropped the two anchors off the bow. I could actually see them on the bottom through the clear water and they bit into the white sand, burrowed in. Jester shuddered to a stop and I went back up on the poop and down into the wheelhouse to kill any drive from the impeller. Now, the wind-motors whirled, but more rapidly than merrily in the gentle breeze, and were producing electricity only for Jester's domestic requirements.

I didn't really want to go below into the cabin because I suspected that Mélusine had the medicine chest out and whatever she did was likely to hurt.

So, to kill time and also to avoid the inevitable, I went to the very aft of Jester's poop and inspected what Danielle had done with the wind-motor bearings around the stainless steel collars on the stationary mizzen masts and how she had tensioned the generators with their sprockets and chains. I couldn't have done better myself, nor could Raoul, who might have made a slightly better job of it than I.

Only one thing had changed, of course, the wind-motor vanes were now black on the outside rather than glaring white. As the vanes moved, at least in slow Savonius mode, the two-toned effect was striking. But whenever, in a stronger breath of breeze, they were whirled quickly enough, just barely, to attain Darrieus mode, the vanes were all black because only the outsides of the vanes were visible. The look of them rather suited Jester and the fabric paint didn't reduce their efficiency at all. Unfortunately, I suspected that the 'flexible' fabric paint would begin to crack and peel off sooner or later and begin to leave an unsightly mottled effect.

On impulse, and probably to avoid the medicine chest, I went all the way forward again and closed up the cutwater doors onto the Chinese floor. This killed another fifteen minutes to get all the bolts tightened with their cotter pins. The wavelets coming into the bay – they were a little larger now – were split in two as they encountered Jester's hull and caromed off to either side. The warps out to the two anchors were taut, but they were good braided nylon shackled to lengths of chain, and would give a fair amount of spring. Besides, I would feel the change of sea long before things got too boisterous.

Mélusine's ministrations weren't as bad as I had been anticipating, mainly because she couldn't figure out what to do or could be done. After cleaning the dried blood off my face with alcohol swabs from my very well stocked medicine cabinet and then with water, she looked at the actual scalp wound itself and held up one of the mirrors from the cabinet so that I could see it too. Danielle helped by holding yet another mirror in front of my eyes.

"The bullet ploughed just under the skin of your scalp from about the temple to the back of your head."

"Is it still under the skin somewhere back there?"

She felt and I winced. "Nothing, no lump."

"Check carefully," I said. "It will be small, a .22, I would imagine."

More gentle probing, more wincing. She was trying to feel things through my hair, which, thankfully, was still decently dense. "There's nothing, Marc. The bullet must have passed on out through the skin where the skull curves."

"Somewhere near the parietal suture," I said.

"If you say so,"

"How does the side look, from the temple to the back? I see a sort of raised and bloody ridge, something like a mole tunnel. There's something wrong at the top of the ear."

"The bullet sort of severed the very top of where your ear is connected to your head," Danielle contributed.

"No wonder the damned thing bled so much," I said.

"What do I do?" asked Mélusine helplessly.

"Not much," I shrugged. "It hurts, but it's not serious. I'm only worried about infection and the ear grafting back where it belongs." I paused. "The first thing is to take one of my good Gillette razors and very carefully shave the hair away about half an inch on either side of the wound. Can you girls do that?"

"Of course," Danielle said. It took them about twenty minutes because they worked slowly. Mélusine collected the locks of hair before they fell on my bunk. Danielle did most of the shaving. "It looks much cleaner," she observed.

"Good," I was holding a mirror and looking at it sideways. "Now, I think you can ignore the mole tunnel, a scab has already formed in it and on it. It'll heal eventually – I hope.

The ear is another matter. Yes, I can see that about a quarter of an inch of it isn't connected to my head."

"That's right," Mélusine agreed.

"Okay. The scab has to be removed from the ear and also from the area where it was once connected. The area wiped with alcohol. And then shove the ear back where it belongs and bandage it up tight." I noticed that Danielle was reading the instructions on a sanitized suture pack.

"What about a stitch to hold the ear in place and then the bandage?"

"I would probably look more handsome that way, if it could be done."

"It says that these sutures will disintegrate in 4 to 5 days."

"Can you put a stitch in?"

"I don't know why not," Danielle said. "One just holds the curved needle in these little plier-things, and sews together what has to be sewn together."

"So, do it," I said.

The cleaning and the stitch hurt, but the wound was already throbbing so the additional discomfort wasn't much, all things considered. "How does the ear look? I can't see it too well in the mirror."

"It's where it's supposed to be," said Danielle.

"Now bandage it in place. I suppose it's best to put the bandage around my head. Very firm, but not too tight." Danielle and Mélusine co-operated and the job took about ten minutes. After that, I looked in the mirror and appeared to be fairly respectable.

"You look like Rambo," said Danielle.

"I don't feel like Rambo," I replied dryly. I looked among the bottles in the medicine cabinet. I took a couple of penicillin tablets and two Tylenol 3s. "Remind me to take two of these a day for the next three or four days," I said to Mélusine. I re-packed the medicine chest carefully, glancing at the expiry dates listed on a sheet of paper taped to the inside of the lid. The penicillin was supposedly still good. I snapped the cabinet shut.

I began to zip out of the black ski suit. "Mélusine, some blood trickled down my neck. I felt it. Could you wash it off, please?" When I was out of the ski suit, I emptied its pockets while she washed. This took some care. I stashed the pistols in one of my drawers after taking the magazines out. They were all identical Rugers, taking the .22 Long cartridges. The knives were all the same too, and standard American issue, and I remembered them fondly.

The round leather-covered handles were hollow with a knurled aluminium cap on a chain. Inside the hollow handle were a fishing line and a package of assorted hooks, plus the smallest of first aid kits. In the aluminium cap was a compass. The knife itself could be rigged on a stout stick or, much better, a length of one-inch bamboo, and it made a formidable spear when it was lashed on tightly using the tangs of the blade-guard handle-hafts.

The blade, in a vaguely Bowie pattern, was 'almost surgical quality' 440 stainless steel, and the cutting edge could be honed to razor sharpness. I heard Mélusine say something. The thick back of the blade featured a serrated length that made a rough saw and semi-barbs to hold speared fish. I was looking at the blade, turning the bright blade and looking at my reflection on that beautiful polished steel.

"Okay, I've said it twice," Mélusine said. "You're done."

I shook my head... and regretted it. "Sorry, Mélusine," I said. "Memory lane and all that." Did I have a slight concussion? I checked the outside of my vision for yellow blobs, 'floaters' some doctors had called them. Nothing. But I decided to rest a bit for the next days. I stripped all the way out of the ski suit and took a brief shower – brief because there was almost no hot water.

I came out into the cabin towelling myself. "That was

brisk," I said.

"I'm afraid I used a lot of hot water," Danielle explained. "I felt filthy."

"I can imagine," I sympathized while dressing in clean jeans, another plaid shirt and my faithful and none-too-reputable Nikes.

"There are some women's clothes in that drawer there." I pointed to one of the drawers under Mélusine's bunk.

I went out to turn the boiler onto simmer. After all, I wanted a long hot shower at some point, and I was certain that Danielle would want another. Was there some way of getting warm water with the wind-motors? Possibly. Why not put automotive winter block heaters into the boiler? They could be on-switches so that the current they produce could be re-channelled to propulsion and lighting after the water reached a certain temperature. A thermostat-type switch of some sort, would that work? I would have to talk with Raoul about this. There could be a lot of refinements, but we were all new at this.

When I came back into the cabin, Danielle was dressed into the Jordache jeans and horizontal striped top that Mariko had once worn. She had put the Adidas shoes back on, too. The table was down and Mélusine had set down a bowl of vegetable soup for each of us. Mélusine must have made it last night. It had had a long time to cook and it was delicious. We also had sliced bread and butter and cheeses. There was a cold Coors on my side of the table, a glass of red wine opposite me.

"I thought a soup would be best for Danielle – and probably for you too," Mélusine explained.

"I think you were right," I smiled.

"What's the plan," asked Danielle. "I'd like to tell Daddy I'm safe."

"Who says you're safe?" I asked mildly.

"I'm off Marettimo, thanks to you, and you killed the

three men who came for me." Mélusine glanced sharply at me when she heard this.

"And who shot at us, I wonder? After we had taken off…"

"Listen to him, Danielle. This is his… ah… field of expertise. One of them."

"Here's what I think we should do," I began, musing somewhat and sipping Coors as I did so. "We have to go to Cagliari tomorrow to pick up the shipment of leather goods."

"Leather goods…?" Danielle queried.

"The one your father arranged in Paris. It's genuine and it is our cover for being here. Mélusine will explain if you ask her. I will contact the Parisian buyer by e-mail or phone in Cagliari as soon as we have loaded the shipment. He will contact your father, at least he will the way I will phrase things. Then we sail from Cagliari back to Narbonne and west along the Canal du Midi as far as Aiguillon."

"How long will all this take?"

"About a week." She started to protest and I raised a hand. "Now, Professor Falardeau – Daddy, to you – may want to meet us in Narbonne, Carcassonne, Toulouse, Agen or somewhere short of Aiguillon in order to collect you and shepherd the leather shipment by train to Paris. That may cut the time to four days. I hope so."

"Once we get to France, at least, I'm home and safe."

"Danielle, I've heard from several sources that you are a willful and determined young woman. But I'm in a bad mood, Danielle – some domestic discord, scalp wound, some slight weight on what's left of my conscience from killing three men. That sort of thing," I had finished the soup and so I sipped the Coors. "Delicious, Mélusine. Thank you." I turned my full attention to Danielle. "So, if I have any trouble with you whatsoever, Danielle, I'm in a mood to knock you ever so gently and professionally unconscious, tie you up and deliver you to Daddy like a trussed chicken."

Mélusine giggled. "I believe the Tylenols have not yet taken effect," she said.

"Daddy will… will…"

"Probably thank me," I said. "He's already paid me a great deal of money."

"I'm not used to people talking to me that way."

"Then start using that head of yours. Gérard Delorme died within metres of the Carcassonne Canal Police Station. About twenty metres to be precise. I was there, as I related. You are not safe anywhere… and neither, by the way is Daddy… until that book is in a guarded vault at the Bibliothèque Nationale."

She looked at me. I looked at her. She took a long swallow of wine. I took a long swallow of Coors. Finally, she lowered her head and nodded. "I take your point," she said, "and you're entirely correct."

"Mélusine has black hair tastefully streaked with grey," I continued. "In Cagliari, she will go and purchase some appropriate hair colouring so that you can disguise the blonde roots that are growing out. But you had better stay below when we're not actually at sea or in some secluded place." I sipped again. "And it would also be better if you and Mélusine both dressed in jeans and the same general kind of top. It's not much of a disguise – or disinformation – but it might confuse things. From a distance, you look roughly alike."

"I have two black turtle-necked shirts," Mélusine contributed.

"Good. Then both of you put them on now. And, Mélusine, buy two more identical shirts tomorrow. Something garish and horrible to confuse the eye with colour."

The Tylenols were starting to kick in, thankfully. Just for kicks and old times' sake I put on one of the knife strap-scabbards again with the Walther's shoulder holster over that. The other two knives would make good presents for Raoul and Philippe. The weight of the upside-down knife on my left shoulder felt good, the weight of the Walther better. I stretched into my old windbreaker that covered most of the weaponry anyway and all of it if it was zipped up a bit. I left it open, though, and went up on the poop beside the wheelhouse.

The wavelets had become no larger, the day was bright and the sun was shining. The two nylon anchor warps stretched out from the bows. I reckoned the temperature at 15 or 16 Celsius, but I still tended to think in Fahrenheit – call it about 55 or 60 degrees. Winter in southern Sardinia. The wind-motors were still turning well, and still in Darrieus mode, so there would be more than just a trickle of charge to the batteries. I looked up at the village on the hill, but without *too* much suspicion. After all, the Mossad was ruthless, everyone knew *that*, but they did not have unlimited manpower and they were not omnipotent.

If I were they, I would tend to think that the Holy Lady of Marettimo had been taken off the island by a much-muffled and black-painted seaplane of some kind, but not an ultralite monstrosity. This could be anything from a Grumman to a Cessna to one of the Pipers. They all had sufficient range to reach destinations in Sicily, Italy or Sardinia. Much modified, a smuggling plane, perhaps an old Grumman Gulfstream, could reach the Costa Brava of Spain, Majorca or Minorca – or even maybe Perpignan or Narbonne in France.

Therefore, if I were the Mossad and hotly after this book that undermined the historical raison d'être of modern Israel, I thought that I would *assume* that Danielle Falardeau and the book were already in France by now. Or at least on the borders of France with Italy and Spain. I would pull all my 'assets' back to the immediate Paris area where Professor Pierre Falardeau could be kept under the closest surveillance – for sooner or later he, Danielle and the book must converge.

In that case, Falardeau was in potentially grave danger. But I didn't think the Mossad would kill him out of hand. He was a fairly prominent academic in his own right, and more so after all the hoopla about the Magdalene Gospel.

The obvious thing to do, if I could, would be to get me, Danielle and Pierre Falardeau arrested and get the leather consignment confiscated by the police in, say, Agen. From there, under a substantial police guard, everything and everyone except me would be taken by overnight train almost due north to Paris. The Falardeaus' reputations might be temporarily sullied by allegations of impropriety – smuggling, in this case – but if the book arrived safely, then the romantic story of getting it into the Bibliothèque Nationale would be worth a book in itself and would only enhance the stature of the Falardeaus and the value of the ancient text.

I would have to speak with Danielle about this, now that it seemed she had come to her senses.

Trying to work out this plan, I went down the steps to the deck and ambled up into the bows, gazing thoughtfully over at Italy. I could see no actual land, of course, but I did see the clouds rising up from the mainland as the ground heated up in the sun. Presently, I heard steps on the deck and Danielle joined me at the ramp-door.

"I'm sorry," she said. "I *can* be a brat," she admitted disarmingly. "Daddy… that is, my father… spoiled me a little after my mother died." She paused. "And now, after what you said, I'm very worried for him. He's in danger too, isn't he?"

"Some," I admitted, "but I don't think the Mossad will kill him outright. Only if they feel they have to in order to get the book."

"So, when Dadd… father, the book and I come together is the most dangerous time."

"I think so." I stopped for some moments. "Listen,

Danielle. I've been thinking about that…" And I told her my plan, such as it was. She heard me out and thought through both the short and long-term ramifications. "It would be delicious," she said. "'Prominent Professor and Daughter Arrested' and then, a little later, the real story comes out to everyone's credit."

"That's what I thought."

"But how can you do it?"

"I think I know a man who can help," I said. "I'll talk with him."

"Maybe I can repay you in a way too, now that I think of it," she laughed. "Mélusine told me that you're originally American and have a weakness for acronyms. Mariko O'Shaugnessey said the same thing to… my father… not that she doesn't love you dearly," she said quickly.

"Oh…" I said warily.

She was looking at the wind-motors and pointed. "Given what you did with them, what about DARE…? 'Dual Aeroturbine Recovery of Energy.'"

"That's not bad," I said.

"It's better, a double acronym – 'Disguised Airborne Retaliatory Expedient.'"

"I *like* that," I said.

"I thought you might." And that was just what Mariko had once said.

"And it's particularly appropriate because my first idea was just a conventional airplane with a propeller in the front and a tail assembly in the back. That would be DARE I. But the configuration that I finally decided on was the canard in which I plucked you off Marettimo… DARE II."

"Oh, God. I can't take any more. I really can't." And she walked away laughing with her hands over her ears… just like Mariko had done.

28

The next morning I saw at least sunrise colours high in the sky to the east over Italy and, again, there was a modest easterly wind to keep the wind-motors twirling. But having kept the boiler on simmer last night to provide hot water, mostly for Danielle, it was no trouble for Mélusine to edge Jester gently forward until the anchors broke out of the sand while I handed the warps in hand-over-hand as quickly as I could.

I like to think that I am neat and methodical, so I set the Danforth anchor flukes into their welded steel brackets, one on either bow. I looped the coiled warps around the revolving drums mounted at deck level just below the anchors.

While I was doing this, I thought about Danielle and her showers. She must have had at least four, it seemed, and once had called Mélusine in for an extended visit. For the better part of four months, as near as I could figure it, she and Gérard had travelled from Lake Zwai in Ethiopia to Cairo (presumably) and thence to Malta and then on to Sicily. From Sicily, Gérard had been sent with the last of their money to try to get to France and help. He got to France, but was killed.

Thereafter, Danielle had hung on in Marettimo as a Holy Lady with a Holy Book. She had gotten, or had been given, barely enough food to survive. She had lost weight. That was clear from a comparison of her face with the photograph. And I imagined that she had picked up lice, too, as befitted a traditional Holy Woman. I imagine that all the washing had mainly to do with her long hair and that Mélusine had combated the lice with alcohol. I knew only that my ski suit and Danielle's were both washed and hung up to dry, *inside out*, and smelled a bit of alcohol. I was too gentlemanly to ask the personal details of Danielle's four-month ordeal. I hoped only that she was and felt cleaner now and was relatively free of at least the larger and more obvious parasites.

I went back up to the poop and then down into the wheelhouse.

"Thanks, Mélusine, I would like to steer now, if you don't mind."

"Right. I'll go put some more coffee on. That carafe is small for three."

"And the bunks are a bit cramped for two. Did you get any sleep at all, Mélusine?"

"Yes. It was quite nice. Of course I've never slept with a man... ah... habitually," she said. "It was cozy, but I wouldn't like to do it all the time."

I have said that *Jester*'s central hull was eight feet wide and that's accurate enough to give a general idea of the size. But the precise truth was 7-feet and 6-inches wide because, when I built her, I had a vague idea of visiting some of the English 'narrow canals'... someday. And they are 'eight feet and no more', as James Brindley put it when he made a fair number of them. The 'no more' part is absolutely correct, but so is the equally important but un-stated 'no less'.

Therefore, *Jester could* shoehorn her way into a *well-maintained* narrow lock – with her outriggers folded up from the gunwales and into the front hull. These 'narrow canals' wended through half-forgotten towns in all-but-forgotten pre-industrial England. I had discovered by accident last summer that some of the small Brittany canals were almost as narrow as the English ones, and so *Jester*'s somewhat cumbersome versatility had come in very handy in Brittany too.

When you subtracted two feet (and no more) for the central corridor and two inches more per side for the steel angle flanges of the hull and the 2-inch foam insulation between them, a bunk width of only 31 inches remained to either side. This was completely adequate for one person – even though

I had fold-up safety railings on the outsides in case anyone rolled off – but it was 'cozy' for two. At least, it was better if the two were very good friends. Given all those showers, Mélusine explained tactfully that perhaps it would be better if we slept together. I didn't demure and I am not particularly modest. Besides, I was fast asleep before Mélusine finished her ministrations with Danielle and was finally able to join me.

"Mélusine," I said, guiding *Jester* out of the cove and into the sunny strait between Italy and Sardinia, "would you ask Danielle to join me in the wheelhouse? I want to have a word with her."

"Certainly, Marc." She hesitated. "She did some very rough travelling and that's harder for a woman than for a man, of course." she said. "But everything is taken care of now."

"I'm sure it is," I acknowledged. "That's not what I wanted to speak to her about."

After the mouth of the cove had been decently passed, I turned gently to port heading for Cagliari and kept a steady eye on the sonar. The radars weren't so critical since the morning was bright and the visibility excellent. I fancied that I could almost see Cagliari and, whereas this could not be true, I did see the brilliant distant flash of wings in the sun high above Cagliari as an airliner took off from the airport there. The wings banked into the east, probably heading for Rome. There could not be many flights, these days, out of Cagliari. And they would all be local, that is, to some larger city in Italy.

I heard the cabin door suck open from its seals. Danielle came up to my right, under the open hatchway. I could smell the slightly astringent scent of her – my – shampoo mingled with the slightly fishy tang of salt air from the strait.

"Danielle," I began, "What sort of… er… *provenance* do you have for the text?"

"A bill of sale from Bishop Luke of the Coptic Ethiopian Church."

"Signed?"

"Signed, dated and stamped in rather gorgeous red wax with his signet ring."

"To your knowledge, Danielle, are there any Ethiopian restrictions on the export of verified antiquities?"

"None that would apply to this text. We thought of that, Gérard and I."

"Why not?"

"Because whether this text actually belongs to Ethiopia, Eritrea or Somalia is a very moot point. It came originally from Eritrea, spent some time in Somalia and ended up on the island of Debra Zion in Lake Zwai in Ethiopia. Besides all that, the governments of Eritrea, Somalia and Ethiopia are all presently technically at war with each other, and are also all being opposed by rebels at the same time. They are in no position to claim anything."

"Not to mention that they are all being challenged by chronic famine."

"That, too," she agreed.

"Now, with a duly executed bill of sale from the last… ah… *legal custodian…* of the text, could you make a case for preserving a world heritage treasure from a chronic war zone and thereby saving it from potential destruction?"

"Yes. Indeed. That was why Bishop Luke agreed to sell the book to us in the first place. Ethiopian rebels – and Somalis – were both advancing in the direction of Lake Zwai when he agreed to give us the book." She stopped. "By the way," she said, "there are two little holes all through the book from the front wood-and-leather cover to the back one."

"Unavoidable, I'm afraid, by the nature of how you and the text were… er… recovered. But you'd better make a mental note to remind Professor Falardeau to clean those holes very carefully and to remove any nitrate residue, plus any microscopic pieces of brass plating. Got that?"

"Yes. Definitely."

I paused in deep thought. "By the way, Danielle, I hope you didn't swim in Lake Zwai."

"Not on your life. You think I would risk getting Bilharzia?"

"Good." Bilharzia was a tiny worm that was normally a parasite on freshwater snails. The worm would abandon the snails at the first hint of mammalian urine in the water. Most of the indigenous mammals of the region had developed a greater or lesser degree of immunity to the worm, but human resistance was much lower. Perhaps this was due to the fact that humans and human-like creatures had evolved in East Africa and had done so relatively recently – only within the last 1-3 million years or so. So human beings were the prime victims of Bilharzia.

The horrid little worm swims up the urethra and lays its eggs in the urinary tract of people. This causes tumours, swelling, indescribable agony and inevitable death. Most of the lakes of Ethiopia host Bilharzia but because of the thick reeds in Lake Zwai that are home to numberless snails, Lake Zwai is infamous for its Bilharzia.

"I've had enough trouble with ordinary, time-honoured and harmless parasites like lice," she said.

"So I... er... gathered from Mélusine." I changed the subject, or rather returned to the text. "The plan, then, was to present the book to some French institution..."

"The Bibliothèque Nationale has already agreed to accept care, custody and responsibility for the relic."

"You have this in writing?"

"Yes, of course."

"Do you mind my asking *where*?"

She laughed. "A very strong cotton money-belt around my waist. That's all I could wear under the burnoose without anything showing. And the money belt is right where it always was… Only now it's clean," she added.

"I was just… er… wondering," I said tactfully. I paused. "And so you have these documents with you? On you? Now?"

"Always."

"Good. Keep them safe… but I don't have to tell you that."

"No."

"Okay. Here's the plan I have in mind. I know a Customs Officer in Cagliari, that is to say I have met him. I know nothing really about him except what an open face and an open smile may reveal. I spoke with him at some length and, well, I have a hunch that he would be co-operative."

"In what way?"

"I'm going to take him to lunch today, as soon as we get into Cagliari, and ask him to send a routine dispatch to Interpol advising that, perhaps, *Folderol Jester* is carrying some contraband from Cagliari to Narbonne. Perhaps drugs, perhaps smuggled leather goods, blue jeans. I will ask his advice."

"Okay…?" Danielle dragged the question out.

"That should get to Inspector-General Gabereau of the Canal Police of France. He knows me. He also knows your father and, because of his meeting with Professor Falardeau, I assume that Gabereau knows the entire story about you, Gérard and the text. In fact," I added, "Gabereau was right behind me when Gérard was shot and reached the body just too late to hear Gérard's last words."

"What do you hope to accomplish?"

"That Gabereau will meet us on the étang into Narbonne, arrest us, put us under strong police guard, and escort at least you, Professor Falardeau and the book direct to Paris."

"Why don't you just inform Gabereau yourself?"

"I could do that."

"Why don't you?"

"Because I want the medium of communication to be a message in itself to Gabereau. Marc Rennsalaer and *Folderol Jester* are not to be involved. If anything, me and my boat were only dupes for carrying a contraband cargo. I will be arrested, initially, perhaps but I will be released and I will be cleared. When it does become clear that Professor Falardeau and his daughter have actually smuggled a controversial religious artifact into France, Marc Rennsalaer was as innocent of that knowledge as of the so-called contraband."

"So, you want none of the eventual credit?"

"Absolutely not. My name is already rather too well associated with controversial religious texts. I have a life to lead and a business to run."

"The unsung hero."

"Definitely unsung and preferably unknown."

"I will respect that," said Danielle.

"Get your father to respect it too."

"I will."

"If we can get the book into the Bibliothèque Nationale, then I think you and your father will be safe. I'm in a more vulnerable position working along the canal and headquartered out of a small town like Aiguillon."

"Won't *some people* recognize the name *Folderol Jester* and put two and two together?"

"That's likely. More than just likely, it is inevitable. But there will be no absolute proof of my involvement. The leather cargo out of Cagliari is completely legitimate. If I shipped out of Cagliari with another crew member to help with the crossing to Narbonne, there's no proof that I knew much about that crew member or what she was carrying."

"An obvious book, some two feet high and a foot wide?"

"Well, Danielle, *that* will get sewn up in a leather dress, won't it?"

Comprehension dawned. "That might work," she admitted.

"By the way, do you carry your passport in that money belt?"

"Of course."

"Then be so kind as to dig it out and give it to me, if you don't mind. I will need it to sign you aboard as crew in Cagliari."

With evident misgivings, she finally undid the belt of her jeans and pulled up a few inches of her black turtleneck. She had to un-strap the belt in order to get anything out of the several pockets. I saw a minimal and anemic reflection in the bright wheelhouse window. Starved or not, Danielle Falardeau, had a luscious belly. Finally, she extracted the passport and went through the whole performance in reverse. When she was safely girded again, she handed the French passport to me. "Don't lose it," she admonished.

"Not a chance, Danielle." I paused for a moment. "Danielle, would you mind knocking on the cabin door and asking Mélusine to steer for a while? I want a private lesson in Ethiopian history out on deck."

29

Out on Jester's front deck the breeze, mostly made of our own speed, offered the tang of salt from the Tyrrhenian Sea spiced with the pines of Sardinia's mountains looking very close abeam to port. They were really five miles away but so abrupt and high that they seemed much closer.

Jester was jittering northward in these protected waters over waves that could be bettered in most bathtubs. Close to the starboard gunwale and looking down, as I was, one could see that this water was really crystal clear, but a broader vista looking out to the east toward still below-the-horizon Italy filled the eye with that dazzlingly brilliant cyan for which the Tyrrhenian Sea is famed.

I glanced astern and probably fooled myself into imagining that a small cloud just above the southeastern horizon was a volcanic puff from Stromboli in the Lipari Islands north of Sicily. It might have been, I suppose, but Sicily was probably too far away for that.

I had been listening to Danielle's history lesson for about half an hour and had learned a great deal. What I had known of ancient Ethiopian history previously would have fitted into a small thimble. She was taking a well-deserved breather while enjoying the sea and scenery from her seat atop a few wooden skids. Her not-black-enough dyed hair was streaming freely, and I hoped, louse-free, in the breeze. She looked fresher anyway.

According to what she had so far related, the essential problem or difficulty began about 1400 BC with the accession of Amenhotep III, the seventh or eighth ruler of the Eighteenth Dynasty, to the throne of Ancient Egypt. Because Egypt had a semi-matriarchal system, Amenhotep had to marry his little sister, Sitamun, in order to be proclaimed Pharaoh since he had to marry a supposed descendant of Isis in order to become divine himself. But Sitamun, it is thought, was only about three years old at the time of this dynastic union.

A few years later, no one knows how long, Amenhotep III issued a Scarab proclaiming a girl called Tiye as his 'Great Royal Wife', not little Sitamun. This meant that Tiye's children would be eligible to become Pharaohs and supposed descendants of Isis. This was a decided departure from Ancient Egyptian tradition. Various bits of evidence indicate that Tiye, 'daughter of Yuya and Tuya', was a Hebrew girl from the long-established Hebrew residence around the city of Zwar in the 'Land of Goshen'.

This 'Land of Goshen' was just outside the recognized Egyptian boundary, but close enough so that the Hebrews could easily partake of Egyptian bounty as biblical Joseph had arranged. There is some slim evidence that Joseph either was Yuya (to become 'Yusef' in time), or may have been Yuya, and was the father of Tiye.

According to Danielle, the Hebrew 'One God', then known as Aten, had certainly been conceived by this time and Tiye seems to have been a believer in this divinity. The evidence for this is that Amenhotep III gave Tiye a pleasure barge as a wedding present and the name of this vessel was Aten Gleams. Further, Amenhotep III enlarged Lake Zwar to give the barge larger scope for pleasure cruises. It was probably aboard Aten Gleams that Amenhotep's and Tiye's son was conceived.

Knowing that he had departed from proper Ancient Egyptian practice, Amenhotep III gave orders that the child was to be killed if it was a boy so that he could not claim the throne of Egypt as Pharaoh. But Tiye hid the child among her Hebrew friends and relatives in Goshen and he grew up to claim the throne of Egypt as Amenhotep IV at the age of nineteen. This was legally possible because his father, Amenhotep III, had, after all, proclaimed Tiye as the 'Great Royal Wife.'

In order not to ruffle the feathers of proper Ancient Egyptian succession too much, Queen Tiye cleverly arranged a temporary Co-Pharaoh rule with the aging Amenhotep III and her son, Amenhotep IV. Tiye also arranged a marriage between her son and a proper Egyptian princess, the exquisitely beautiful Nefertiti. And things were stable for some years, no one knows how many.

When Amenhotep III finally died, Queen Tiye's son gave up the name Amenhotep IV and styled himself Akenaten. He also immediately outlawed the worship of the traditional Egyptian gods and goddesses, tearing down their temples and killing their priests and priestesses, proclaiming that Aten was the only God and the only one that could be worshipped.

This was a highly unpopular move with the vast majority of Egyptians and they rebelled. After six or seven years of ongoing and increasing rebellion, Akenaten was deposed and fled into exile with his mother, Queen Tiye. It is thought, and there is some very recent evidence to support the idea, that Akenaten's wife, Queen Nefertiti, was killed in the popular uprising.

Sigmund Freud was the first to propose in Moses and Monotheism (1939) that Akenaten and Moses had been the same historical personage. Akenaten's deposition and flight out of Egypt was the 'Exodus' of the Bible. But the 'Israelites', or loyal followers of Akenaten, could not have fled into Palestine. It was too strongly held by the Philistines. The modern word 'Palestine' derives from 'Philistine'.

Both linguistic evidence and Arabian and North African traditions converge to argue that the 'Promised Land' was in western Arabia along the Red Sea coast. The first known 'proto-Hebrew' inscriptions have been found in modern Hijaz and Yemen; the ancient polity of Saba or 'Sabaea'. Bernard Leeman has shown that Jerusalem, Gaza and many other biblical sites were actually first located there. After the

Queen of Sheba (Saba) visited Solomon, her Queendom was annexed by the Israelites and claimed as the Kingdom of David and Solomon.

Around 600 BC, the climate of Arabia began to change to become drier and Saba was cut off from the rest of the world and finally just disappeared. The few Sabaean Hebrews living around Kadesh in Palestine, who had trickled in as traders and herdsmen before the desert choked Sabaea, decided to transfer the entire Israelite history from Saba to Palestine. They renamed Kadesh 'Jerusalem', still called 'Al Kuds' in Arabic from the earlier 'Kadesh', in this deception along with many other 'biblical' place-names, and decided to canonize this false history in a book attributed to Ezra, a scribe of the Babylonian captivity. Daniel managed to convince the Persian conqueror of Babylon, Cyrus the Great, of this false Hebrew history and the Hebrew claim was enforced by Cyrus and his eventual successor, Artaxerxes.

The big volume containing the first five books of the Old Testament, signed by Akenaten with his Ancient Egyptian cartouche and recovered by Danielle Falardeau, vindicated the scholarship of Sigmund Freud, Ahmed Osman, Kamal Salibi, Chaim Rabin, Bernard Leeman and many other archaeologists and linguists. The Old Testament was a purposeful geopolitical hoax to claim Palestine as the Promised Land and traditional home of the Jewish people – a hoax that was still causing much of the world's conflict.

The true history of the Jewish kingdom had been preserved, and as Arabia began to dry up, was taken across the Red Sea to Ethiopia. That was the basis of Ethiopian Emperor Hailie Sellasie's claim to be the 'Lion of Judah'. And later, when Paul concocted the New Testament out of the concocted Old Testament, grafting the Egyptian Osiris and Isis religion of ancient Christianity onto bogus Judaic roots, the Ethiopians had become 'Judeo-Christian' too.

So, when Islam, conceived by Mohammed in AD 622,

began its bloody expansion across North Africa, these Judeo-Christian Ethiopians began their long retreat along the Rift Valley, carrying their precious religious works with them. They found it was safer to settle on islands in the large Ethiopian lakes of the Rift Valley and to keep their holy books there. There, on these obscure islands, they and their books were well protected by water and Bilharzia from the Moslem onslaught. And so ancient Sabaean tradition had been preserved until 2012.

But the problem was that the Ethiopian Coptic Christian lore masters themselves had long forgotten how to read their own holy books. They reverently copied and re-copied them in a script they could not understand (Sabaean) and which preserved a history that belied their own Judeo-Christian beliefs based on the Hebrew bible.

I turned around at the gunwale and looked at Danielle Falardeau on her sunny wooden skid. She blinked at me and smiled in the overhead sun and the Sardinian mountains gave her an indescribably beautiful backdrop.

"Jesus," I said at last, "what an unholy conglomeration of a mess." I paused. "But it does clear up a minor mystery of relatively modern history… the major problem, Israel, is still causing headlines, of course."

"What's that?" said Danielle.

"Italy invaded Ethiopia, of all places, in 1895. It also explains why Mussolini, goaded and backed by the Vatican, invaded Ethiopia again in 1935… aside from it's being just about the only place where the Italian army had a chance of winning."

"My God, you're right!" exclaimed Danielle. "Daddy was told by Mariko O'Shaugnessey not to underestimate you."

"Hmmm. The Vatican had just as much reason as the Mossad to get hold of those books and to get rid of the Lion of Judah. Now I understand why. Never did before, but somebody always knew the truth."

"It is really ironic, isn't it?" Danielle mused.

"You'll have to be more specific, I'm afraid" I grinned. "There's been a hell of a lot of irony recently with regard to holy books."

She laughed. "Yes, I see what you mean." She paused. "I was just thinking that it is ironic that Rastafarian believers actually preserved a better grasp of true Western religious history than our best university professors – until this text turned up, of course." She hesitated, "and yet even they had it a bit garbled too."

30

About two hours later, coming into the outskirts of Cagliari harbour from its modest roadstead, I espied on a wharf to starboard a sign reading 'Sardiniacciaio'. Since I wasn't quite certain what this meant, I was gratified to see it reproduced in French as well as German and English. 'Sardiniacier.' Sardinia steel. It was obviously either a shipping terminal or one with a factory attached right behind it.

Two things about its wharf caught my eye. The first was a number of young people, of both genders, working among the goods stacked on the dock. And the second was the number of rolls that looked suspiciously like coiled steel wire. On impulse, I nudged Jester toward the wharf that happened to be about the height of Jester's outrigger decks. Since I had asked – or told – Danielle to remain below while we were in Cagliari, it was Mélusine who came into the wheelhouse when she felt the sudden and rather abrupt change of direction.

"Mélusine, take the wheel and nuzzle up to that wharf there."

I scrambled up and out of the wheelhouse, flinging back: "And don't let Danielle in the wheelhouse or anywhere visible until we can do something about her hair." Danielle's blonde roots were definitely growing out and had only been concealed on Marettimo by purposefully cultivated grime on the part of the Holy Lady who must have worked it assiduously into her scalp. Since I could vouch for the fact that much of Marettimo was pristine sand, I suspected that this darker earth must have derived from garden plots that had been fertilized by the manure of the few sheep, many more goats and the very rare cows that belonged to the village. No wonder she had picked up lice.

On deck, I uncoiled the 1-inch diameter braided nylon

bow mooring line and snaked the end of it up to the somewhat sturdily-built, although it was difficult to tell in her bulky sweat pants and winter windbreaker, short-haired blonde girl who called out cheerfully, "Werfen sie hereunter." Her hair was actually golden and its short curls made a halo around her head in the midday sun.

"Bitte schön," I replied, and walked astern to repeat the performance with the identical aft mooring warp. I watched her muscular frame wrap the lines most competently around the loading dock's bollards.

Jumping onto the wharf, "Deutsch?" I asked.

"Nein. Aber ich spreche nur ein wenig Deutsch."

"English?"

"A little more. I'm Dutch."

"Can I speak to a manager, or the foreman? I want to buy some steel wire."

Taking off her workmanlike gloves as she went, she led me into a fairly grubby office that boasted one window looking out over the loading dock. Behind the desk was a harried-looking portly little man with a bedraggled moustache. But he smiled most engagingly at me as the girl said "Inglisi."

"Canna I helpa you," he said with a thick Sardinian or Italian accent. The sign on his cluttered desk read 'Jacomo Iotigolo.'

"I saw your steel wire and I would like to buy some. Is that possible?"

"Of course. That's our business." He handed me a catalogue. "What size?"

I was amazed at the prices. They were about forty percent lower than anything I had seen in France. "Well, I was looking for 3/16ths, but I see all your sizes are metric, of course."

He finally persuaded me that since 3/16 of an inch was 4.5mm, more or less, that I could get either 4mm or 5mm, depending on the application. By now I had noted a table of breaking strength for each diameter of 1x19 wire. It was also much lower than anything I had seen from France, Britain, Germany or the United States. I pointed this out, and the little man shrugged.

"Our steel in Sardinia is not of the best," he said with disarming honesty. "Everybody knows that. There's too much sulphur in our iron."

I was thinking of the twenty wind-motors on the roof of the warehouse in Aiguillon. They weighed only 70 pounds each, or a bit less, and there was never enough stress on them with three guy wires to come anywhere near the breaking load of even this poor quality 4mm wire. But I wouldn't trust the wind-motors of the barges and Jester to Sardiniacciaio's products.

"Do you make open-barrelled turnbuckles and thimbles for the wire... Mister Iotigolo?" I peered at his sign.

"Yes, we do," and he handed me another catalogue. "They are all only galvanized, but thickly. No stainless." Again, the prices and strengths listed were about forty percent less than what we'd been paying.

"Are these strengths accurate?" I asked.

"Absolutely. After all, you can't get much lower strength with steel wire and still call it steel wire, can you?"

"And the quantity of wire per roll?"

"There's actually a couple of metres more wire per roll than it says in the catalogue there," he said. "Pick a roll at random out there," he gestured through his window at the loading dock, "and I'll have one of the kids measure it for you."

I had to admit that he had a point about the strength of the wire and I was already close to being enchanted by Sardiniacciaio's simple honesty and lack of sales pitch. From the amount of wire the catalogue said were on one roll, I calculated that the wind-motors on the warehouse roof would require 8 rolls of wire and 60 turnbuckles and ninety...

no one hundred and eighty... thimbles. This would also free up some of my stainless steel wire, turnbuckles and thimbles. "I'd like to buy 10 rolls of your 4mm wire, 80 turnbuckles and 240 thimbles to fit," I said. "Can you load them now?"

I went back aboard *Jester* and, once in the cabin, told Mélusine and Danielle to go into the... bathroom. I quickly collected the necessary Euros from my secret cache and, because of the nippy but sunny winter's day, I also donned my windbreaker with the Walther and upended knife beneath it as previously. When I had re-locked the cache and was closing the cabin door I called to the women that they could come out. On the way, I transferred Danielle's passport from the pocket of my jeans into the zipable upper-arm pocket of my windbreaker.

By the time I was on Jester's front cargo deck, two girls and a boy were handing down coils of wire. I counted ten, three already on deck and seven waiting on the dock. "Just put them on the deck," I said, "I'll put them where I want them." I said it in English, but the kids nodded. Sardiniacciaio obviously had a multi-multilingual labour force. This intrigued me. On the way to the office to pay the man, I passed the well-toned Dutch girl counting turnbuckles and galvanized thimbles.

"Greta? Gretchen?" I tried.

"Liedewei," she said. "Leed-a-vay," she pronounced it for me, slowly.

"Okay. Liedewei, how many kids work here?"

"They come and go."

"Why do so many... er... kids work here?"

"Because Sardinia's the cheapest sunspot in Europe. Cheaper than Greece, now. Cheaper than even Croatia. A winter's work here and you can live all summer in the sun and sand."

"I see."

I paid the manager... or whoever he was, Mister Jacomo Iotigolo... and received a stamped receipt for the goods, a receipt and itemization that had already been spewed out of the computer's printer. I checked the manifest carefully and, while doing so, casually handed the man Danielle's passport. "By the way," I asked, "have you ever seen that girl? She says that she worked here, but now wants to go back to France… to Narbonne… and I'm headed there. She wants to help crew. I just wanted to know if you remember her, if she was any trouble or anything like that?"

He peered at the passport photograph carefully. "She looks familiar. Of course, so many young people do work here for a month or two. No, if she was here I don't remember any trouble with her, but she couldn't have stayed long."

"Thank you, Mister Iotigolo." I took the passport back from him and re-zipped it in the windbreaker's pocket. "Just wanted to check on references."

"No trouble." He walked out to the loading dock where Liedewei was double-checking galvanized wire thimbles. Iotigolo tousled her blonde hair. I thought there was genuine fondness in the gesture and not much, if any, lechery. "Now, Liedewei here is a regular. Every winter for four years she's been with us and she is one of the best workers we've ever had. She could have a career here, as far as I'm concerned."

"But I like the sun and sand too much…" She was still counting out thimbles two-by-two. Finally, she was satisfied and dropped them with a modest carillon into a box. "Ten rolls, four millimetre, two hundred and forty 4 mm thimbles and 100 20-cm turnbuckles." I had decided to buy some extra turnbuckles. She handed the box to me. It was heavy, but manageable. I nodded and she gave me a careless two-fingered salute from her halo. Her smile was priceless, all sincerity and love-of-life with dimples in the corners of her mouth. Liedewei was very hard to forget.

Down on the deck, I arranged a few wooden skids along the rear of the deck next to the break of the poop where the Honda engine also lurked, tarp-wrapped, on its skid. I rolled and lifted the rolls of wire until they made a compact mass against the steel of the very rear of the front hull and a convenient step up onto the poop. After noticing that the wire was, indeed, adequately protected with grease of some sort, I took care to wrap the spools, some made of cheap wood and some made of thick cardboard, in a plastic-weave tarp against rain and potential Mediterranean waves. Then, I lashed the spools securely in place with several nylon tie-down straps.

By my calculations, I had not only made a good capital investment for our Aiguillon establishment, but had taken up sufficient deck space with the purchase of steel wire to force at least some of the leather consignment into the cabin.

This proved to be the case when we arrived at Wharf 4 in Cagliari harbour. The leather goods were waiting, as promised, but everyone agreed, on looking down into Jester's cargo deck, that all of the shipment wouldn't fit. I said that the most expensive items should go into the cabin for greater safety on the crossing to Narbonne. Thankfully, all of the boxes were well marked with the contents, so we decided that the leather dresses and the fashionable high boots were the most valuable items of the consignment and we separated them out then and there on the dock. The dresses and boots amounted to four cartons that would barely fit through the wheelhouse hatch and through the cabin door. Mélusine took them and then she and Danielle stacked them precariously in the upper bunks, one of which already held the aircraft's folded and inadequate windshield.

As we stacked the rest of the cartons on skids in the front cargo deck, Mélusine, as arranged, escaped from Jester's increasingly crowded hull and went into Cagliari in search of hair colouring and some provisions.

Finally, all of the leather consignment was aboard and the cartons of it completely filled what was left of the front cargo deck almost to the 4-foot high gunwales. But, for all its bulk, the cargo weighed a good deal less than a ton. Possibly because of their tardiness in having the consignment ready to begin with, the leather manufacturers stayed around to help me secure the cargo under one of my biggest plastic weave tarps with numerous nylon tie-down straps.

This, I reflected, was a much safer cargo than the Calvados had been and we were crossing a much safer body of water. Not that I underestimated the Mediterranean. It can get very rough, especially in winter. This time, I was taking no chances with the weather. I would sail only with three or four days of good weather in the forecast. After about an hour, the cargo was stowed to my satisfaction. I checked the manifest and signed for it, giving the date and everything was counter-signed by the leather manufacturer's shipping manager.

The owner made a brief appearance to see us off and was somewhat chagrined to see the size of Jester. It was obvious that he thought the buyer would have entrusted the goods to a larger vessel, but I assured him that larger coasters seldom called at Narbonne any longer and that Jester was the quickest transportation to France short of airfreight. After muttering something about insurance, he wished me a good voyage and conveyed his hope that the Sardinian styles would do well in Paris. Since I could see Mélusine coming down the wharf with packages, I said that I hoped for the same success although I knew little about the fashion business.

I scrambled down into the cargo deck to double-check, once again, that the leather goods were securely protected with the tarp against the weather and securely strapped down against slippage. The problems with this load were the opposite of those with the Calvados. This load would try to float if a lot of water came aboard, so it had to be kept down on the skids and not just secured from slippage. I did this with a webbing of nylon from gunwale to gunwale as well as tie-downs to the wooden skids themselves. When I was satisfied, at last, I followed Mélusine down into the cabin.

It was crowded down there because the cartons extended off the upper bunks and encroached upon the standing headroom. I could still sit on the lower bunk with cartons barely caressing my head. The place smelled of leather. I was gratified to hear water running and I figured that Mélusine was assisting Danielle with the delicate business of hair colouring.

Presently, the women emerged from the… bathroom… and Danielle wore a towel turban style.

"No more blonde roots?" I asked.

"All done," Mélusine replied.

"The last rinse I could buy was in Palermo," Danielle explained. "And that was almost two months ago. I was sure that Gérard would be able to return long before, but…" She let it trail off.

"All right," I said. "I want to go into the Customs Office. I may be away for a couple of hours – if the man I want is on duty, that is. Danielle, I think it would be better if you remained out of sight for a while. When we get under way, you can come out on deck so long as you're dressed like Mélusine."

"I was able to buy a couple of cheap turtlenecks," Mélusine contributed. "To give us a change from black."

"Good. Make sure you look like the Bobsy Twins," I said.

"What?" Danielle said.

"Never mind. Dress alike." I paused. "Now, Mélusine and Danielle, when I'm gone and when your hair is dry and you're dressed alike, I want you to look in these cartons," I gestured above my head. "Pick out one with dresses inside and sew the book inside of one of the leather dresses. Repack everything so that the book is nestled in the middle of a carton somewhere. And be careful opening the cartons and re-closing them so they don't seem suspicious or tampered with. All the boxes are numbered on their labels. Remember the number of the box where the book is."

"That seems simple enough," Danielle said, drying her hair.

"Do it carefully. And then mix up the cartons a bit on the upper bunks so that the book isn't in the first box anyone would come to." I hesitated, afraid to ask. "By the way, girls, do you suppose there's any hot water left?"

"Certainly," Mélusine said in a tone that sounded somewhat harsh to me.

"Good." I undressed where I was, except for my underwear, and tossed the Walther and knife on the bunk. I padded off to the head and showered… briefly… managing to get most of the grease from the steel wire and most of the sweat from the stowage of the leather consignment off me. Then, returning to the cabin, I dressed à la mode Grand Capitaine with the Walther and knife hidden decently beneath my blazer and the ubiquitous windbreaker.

I was not lucky in the Customs Office because my friendly and extroverted official from a couple of days previously wasn't there. It was his day off, but his replacement, although not so friendly and extroverted, was nonetheless competent and courteous. I added Danielle Falardeau to the crew's list of Folderol Jester, offering her passport for scrutiny. As the previous Customs official had said, that was all there was to it. When the passport was handed back, I said: "Now, I was told to inform you when the boat was leaving Italian waters."

"Yes. We appreciate that, but not everyone takes the trouble."

"Well, I've taken on a consignment of leather goods here in Cagliari and I'm bound immediately for Narbonne. But, depending on the weather, I may stay in the lee of Cape Teulada for a day or so to wait for better conditions. There's a cove there that I know that gives shelter and good anchorage.

Is that all right?"

"Yes. Of course."

"The weather forecast seems reasonable and we will probably be out of Italian waters today."

"I can check the latest weather bulletins for you."

"I would appreciate that."

He came back in two or three minutes reading a computer printout. "The Gulf of Lyon and the Western Mediterranean, winds Force Two to Three from the Northwest with seas running from four to six feet for the next three days". He handed the sheet to me and glanced at his watch. "That came in at 13:00 hours local time. Just now."

"Can't get much better than that," I said and smiled. "We'll clear Italian waters this evening then. And thank you."

He nodded. If he noticed the bandage around my head, and I'm sure he did, he didn't mention it. But I saw him writing down something about Jester on his Departures sheet.

After being unlucky at the Customs Office, would I be lucky in love? That was Plan B. I called Aiguillon on the 'emergency cell number', wondering if she would be there.

"Oui. Allo." It was Christine. Apparently, she had phone duty again, or…

"Hi. Christine. It's Marc. Is Joëlle there?"

"Of course. Hold a moment?"

After a moment, a carefully neutral "Yes, Marc?"

"Hi, Joey. Listen, I'm in Cagliari… that's in Sardinia…"

"Sardinia…!" Then, another carefully neutral "Yes, Marc."

"I've just picked up a valuable consignment of leather goods here and I'm heading back to Narbonne tonight. The weather's supposed to be good so I'll be there in about 48 hours from this evening. Everything is fine. Very good, actually."

"Yes, Marc."

"Now, I want you to do something for me. Exactly what

I say, no more and no less."

"Yes, Marc."

"Tomorrow morning, but not before then, I want you to call… write this down, Joey… Inspecteur-Général des Canals de France, Bernard Gabereau," I spelled the name out for her. "Tell him who you are. Tell him you're calling on my behalf. Tell him the following… I have reason to believe there may be opiates in the leather consignment aboard Jester. He should try to intercept us off Narbonne if he can, but certainly in the étang from Narbonne Plage."

"You mean drugs…?"

"I mean what I said, Joëlle… o-p-i-a-t-e-s," I spelled it.

"I will say opiates, Marc, I promise."

"Do that, Joey… and I'm rather surprised that a student of mass economics like you would mistake mere drugs for opiates in casual remarks."

"Oh." Then, "Oh…"

"Hmmm." I paused. "Now, Gabereau is the police chief of all the canals of France. He has an office in Carcassonne, but he also has an office somewhere in Paris. Call Carcassonne first, maybe, but then call Paris if he's not there. But whatever you have to do, get that message to Gabereau."

There was silence, but I thought I heard writing.

"Joëlle?"

"Yes. I was writing all that down."

"Your copy of Mariko's book. Do you remember the dedication she wrote to you?"

"Yes, of course."

"Read it again. And read who wrote the concluding Afterword."

"Yes, Marc."

"Tell Gabereau that I'm with his daughter."

"Yes, Marc."

"Now, are you still supplying the soup kitchen every day?"

"Yes, but tomorrow's the last day. The weather is back to normal."

"Good. Try to call Gabereau from the Hôtel de Ville, or from the Police Station, not from your own cell phone. But if you cannot... if you cannot... then call him tomorrow anyway from the company's cell phone or from yours."

"Yes, Marc."

"Now, Joey, have you got all that?"

"I do."

"Aside from all that, how are things?"

"Philippe managed to make two trips to Villeneuve-sur-Lot. Raoul should be on his way back from Narbonne with the citrus fruit. The wind-motor barges are very cost-efficient. Our profits are substantial... in projection, of course, but we can actually see it now."

"Good. But I think you will be happily surprised by the income from this present venture of mine – as with Mariko's book."

"I believe that I have the picture, Marc. I'm not absolutely certain, of course."

"Think books." I paused before continuing. "Now, I'm thinking of something else, but I don't want to complicate things for you. Getting in touch with Bernard Gabereau is the most critical item on the agenda right now."

"I have that. You can go on."

"All right, your operation of the soup kitchen in Aiguillon must have brought you in contact with some... er... consumers."

"Yes..."

"I would like you to think about four or five people... they have to be youngish, in good health and of both genders... who might make good and honest employees for us. Not necessarily live-in employees, as we are now, at least not at first."

"I've been thinking about that too, Marc, and I have a few

people in mind. But I'll make a list for you."

"Good. It may be that we'll soon need some help and there may be some expansion of our organization, commune, co-operative… whatever. That's all. I better go now. This is long distance four ways and must be costing a fortune."

"Marc… before you go… I'm sorry. I was out of line. I can get that way."

"I know you can, Joey. I've known you for seven years, remember? It's all right, Joey, but I had to put my foot down."

"I know you did. But it hurt."

"I'm sure I did."

"It won't happen again."

"So you said, Joey. I'd better go now, this call is costing a fortune."

"I love you, Marc."

"And I love you."

31

When France was yet a smudge on the distant horizon in the late afternoon, I opened the cabin door and asked Mélusine to ask Danielle to go into the… bathroom… and lock the door. She went without question or hesitation, especially when Mélusine gave her a sharply meaningful glance. Then Mélusine came into the small wheelhouse.

I would soon need Mélusine at the wheel and, anyway, she knew almost all of Jester's capabilities. Nonetheless, there were some things I wished to keep even from Mélusine, so I asked her to take the wheel for a moment and I went to my secret cache in the cabin. The… bathroom… door was closed and Danielle was pointedly running some water so that I could hear it.

I removed the AR-15 from the cache and the magazine of only six remaining air-cannon projectiles. Something would have to be done about making more projectiles, especially because I had this uncomfortable feeling that we might well be needing them soon. Mélusine already knew about these, but she didn't have to know that I also kept some money (secret even from Joëlle) in the cache and she didn't have to know where the mechanical and electronic key to the cache was itself hidden.

Now, knowing that with favourable conditions and using the steam engine as necessary, it would take almost exactly 48 hours to sail from Cape Teulada to Narbonne Plage and the entrance to the étang, I had planned to arrive just after dark. True, there was some risk of running aground if I didn't hit the étang entrance perfectly, on the other hand, I had two radars and sonar and I figured I could avoid these hazards. Much more did I fear the stab of a boat's searchlight somewhere out on those dark twenty kilometres of the étang by a boat that was not a police boat. For that would mean a good chance of ending up just like Gérard Delorme.

"Mélusine, steer with the waves for a few minutes. I need as much stability as possible." Before I disappeared up and out of the wheelhouse hatch, I unlocked the whistle-tube from its solid wheelhouse roof mounting.

"Aye, aye," she grinned.

I affixed the magazine – sadly depleted – into the air-cannon. As before at the humpbacked bridge, I kept the now single whistle-tube upright with bungee cord stretched forward and attached to the magazine flange, and not yet to the magazine itself. I closed my eyes and felt the flanges and bungee attachments in the dark so that I could memorize how they were arranged.

Back in the wheelhouse, I took the wheel again. "Mélusine, tell Danielle she can come out now and to come to the cabin door. I need to speak with you both."

The waves were, as forecast, only four to six footers and I slowly turned Jester back toward a course for the entrance to the étang. Her motion was steady because I had already doused, furled and strapped down the sails. Only the wind-motors continued to revolve and very slightly offset the fuel I was using. I flicked on the two Decca radars and could discern the étang's entrance on both screens. The Eagle sonar proclaimed 122 fathoms so I glanced at the chart once more to orient myself and then forgot about it. I already knew there were no rocks or reefs between Jester and the étang's entrance on this course. I had sailed it several times when I had first come to France more than seven years back and I have a good memory.

I felt the door of the cabin open because of a gentle buffet of air, and heard the customary sucking of its seals against the metal flanges. I didn't turn around from the darkening wheelhouse window. "Mélusine and Danielle," I said, "there may be some trouble within the next couple of hours. Mélusine, I want you to go around the boat and batten down all the storm covers of the portholes. Make sure they're tight. Then come back here to the wheelhouse. I will need you. Right?"

"Right."

"Danielle, once you and Mélusine have battened down the storm covers… she'll show you how… I want you to come back to the cabin door and close it from the inside with that wheel in the middle. You'll have to pull it very tight toward you as you turn the wheel. Now, that means you're sealed in. That doesn't really matter. Jester won't sink whatever happens, even if there's a hole in the bottom. There's enough foam flotation and the air inside will be trapped at the ceiling and will also act as a float."

"Jesus," said Danielle. "You're expecting something that bad?"

"No. Not really," I said. "It is just a precaution."

"What about you and Mélusine?"

"Don't worry about us. Jester is stronger than she looks. Much stronger, virtually bullet-proof in fact, at least the wheelhouse and the cabin."

"I'd rather take my chances with you two."

"Please do as he says," said Mélusine in a voice that surpassed firm and was leading to harsh.

"Yes. All right. As you two wish."

They left and I heard the sounds of the steel storm shutters coming down over the portholes, tight against the hull, and the clank of the locking levers. There were ten portholes and ten covers and I counted them all. Mélusine and Danielle came back to the cabin door, Mélusine stepping through without hesitation and Danielle pulling the heavy door shut and I heard the scrunch of the steel tangs as she wrestled the wheel to dog the door tight. Maybe I should oil them. Or would a light coating of grease be better?

We were now about five miles offshore and I doused all of Jester's lights, including (illegally) the navigation lights. It was not quite dark and I could see no small craft, nor wooden craft, anywhere near us or the étang entrance – or between us and it. The Deccas would show me anything larger, especially if it had radar because I had long ago mounted one of those questionably legal devices that identified a radar signature.

"Are you armed, Mélusine?"

"Yes." That reminded me to check, once again (it does no harm), whether the Walther and the upside down knife were beneath my own windbreaker.

"Okay. Here's the plan." I paused for a moment to think out exactly what the 'plan' was, insofar as one existed. "I'll take Jester into the étang. There's a slight outfall there and a bit of a bar. The waves may be a little higher there, not much, but it might throw you off. Then, I'll give you the wheel. You should be safe enough down here in the wheelhouse because it is all polycarbonate and steel. Virtually bullet-proof. Keep the hatch open so that I can call down to you and ask for lights if I need them. Close the hatch and lock it if I say so." I hesitated. "Got that last bit?"

She nodded, then said yes. "And I remember where the switches for the navigation lights, the deck lights and the searchlight are," she continued.

"Good. But here's the tricky part. You'll have to steer through the étang by the buoy lights and radar. All the buoys are metal, so they should pick up on radar very well. And remember it is red to right returning now. We are 'returning'".

"Got it." Then a pause. "What do you expect?"

"I'm not certain, Mélusine. I've tried to cover our voyage with very legitimate cargoes, and I have all the papers for them," I patted my windbreaker. "I've informed the authorities back in Cagliari of our crew and cargo. Also, I do not think that even the Israeli secret service, the Mossad, can suspect that I snatched Danielle Falardeau away from Marettimo a few days ago. They know it was done and they know they lost three men. They could also know that she's aboard Folderol Jester bound for Narbonne. If they monitor Sardinian and Italian customs communications, that is. I registered Danielle as a crew member for the sake of legalities."

"So, maybe nothing will happen."

"Maybe not. On the other hand, Gérard Delorme died not too far from here. So, I tried to deal myself an ace in the hole."

"What…?"

"An advantage."

"Oh. American slang."

"I have informed the canal police, who have jurisdiction here, that Folderol Jester may be, unknowingly to the captain, of course, carrying contraband. That is, Mélusine, I have informed them if Joëlle did exactly what she was told to do."

"She will have. You can rely on her. She loves you very deeply. More than that, she needs you."

"Yes, Mélusine, but both love and need are four-letter words."

"Four letter words…?"

"Swear words… in Anglo-Saxon."

"Oh."

"So my ace in the hole… our advantage… is that the canal police should show up sometime, somewhere between here and Narbonne."

I looked at the oncoming entrance to the étang painted on the radars. We were heading right for the middle of the opening and I could see small breakers creaming in the last of the evening light.

"Mélusine, quick, take the wheel. I forgot something important." I went into the engine room and took the old, brass Very pistol from the wall and checked to be quite certain that I took two red flares. I took the time to put the

Very pistol and flares into my left windbreaker pocket and zipped it up. I grabbed the small flashlight bracketed to the wall and zipped it into my right windbreaker pocket with the folded bundle of all the cargo manifest papers. I closed the door carefully and took the wheel just as Mélusine, biting a lip, was preparing to go into the small combers at the bar. I took the wheel from her and she edged behind me.

Jester sea-horsed gently over the bar with two comfortable fathoms beneath the keel and entered onto the rather inky waters of the étang. Only some stars reflected in the dark mirror because the sun had sunk behind the huge limestone outcropping that separated Narbonne from the étang. The étang's twenty kilometres curved around this buttress of the Languedoc. "Buck up, Druid. Nothing like the Gironde, was it."

"No. It reminded me of the situation."

I didn't bother to add that it reminded me a little, a very little (but enough), of it too. Instead I asked: "Does your Druidical seership foresee anything special for tonight?" I stepped aside and she took the wheel again and turned Jester gently and deftly to port, scanning the radar screens. Way ahead, a red light winked, a buoy, and I pointed it out on the radar screen – a star of greenish light as the beam swept around. I saw her head faintly nodding in the darkness.

"I have it." She paused. "Strangely enough, Marc, I see nothing in the way you mean. I feel danger, but perhaps that is only because of your talk."

"Fair enough," I said.

As I have described, the étang (the inadequate English translation is 'pond') at Narbonne, like all the others, is a brackish lagoon behind the actual shoreline of the Mediterranean. These étangs form a kind of inland waterway of their own and are sometimes interconnected with each other by the Canal du Midi. Aside from offering small boats shelter from the open Mediterranean, they are the abode of langouste, mussels and many other kinds of shellfish. As such, they have their own economy, sort of, and people harvest these shellfish from small wooden skiffs.

When I first arrived in France, the étangs fascinated me, possibly because they resembled the Chesapeake area in so many particulars. I have already referred to the reeds and waterfowl. I began my working life along the canal by buying langouste and mussels from the étang-people and selling these products in the larger towns further up the canal – Carcassonne, Toulouse, Agen. This enterprise had proved almost immediately profitable and encouraging because I had originally planned Jester and Ivory for the Inland Waterway and Chesapeake. And I had also anticipated the fuel shortages that affected both places in roughly the same way. Jester was shallow-draft, drawing only two feet ordinarily and her impeller was specifically designed not to be fouled in reedy places. Ivory was even then amphibious, although not as efficient back then with the old air-powered Norton single cylinder 500cc motorcycle as now with the modified and all-aluminium air-powered Kawasaki.

Since on the étangs as on Chesapeake, roads seldom ran around the entire shoreline because of the marshy nature of the terrain, Jester and Ivory between them were able to purchase the products of the brackish waterway directly from isolated rickety wharves and sometimes directly from skiffs. This ensured much lower initial prices. Ivory could then haul this live cargo directly aboard Jester and Jester could take it directly to cities that coveted the shellfish. Ivory could drive off Jester and take the product, still living in plastic tanks of aerated water directly to the back doors of upscale restaurants where profits were highest.

The only difference was the product. Temperate zone Chesapeake produced oysters, quahogs and many sorts of clams. The sub-tropical étangs of southern France produced langouste, mussels and demoiselles. The profits were about the same, I would suppose, in proportion. I have never even seen the Chesapeake although I had planned Jester for working there, because I discovered that I had a claim to French citizenship before I ever got to Chesapeake.

The riches of the étangs had attracted people long before me. There were barrows along the shore of the Narbonne étang, and even more along the larger Béziers étang to the north. These barrows had caught my eye when I first came into Narbonne and, after I had met Joëlle about a year later, we had often discussed them. According to her, the earthworks had been built by the first semi-civilized people to arrive at the Mediterranean coast after the end of the Ice Age had allowed them to journey from the Atlantic, through the Garonne River corridor, and on across southern France to the Mediterranean.

Joëlle had called these people 'Elysians' and insisted that they had come from Atlantis originally and the islands off Brittany called Lyonesse. They had settled around the rich food sources of the étangs before they had pushed on out into the Mediterranean.

The name of these migrants aside, Joëlle's viewpoint had received powerful scientific support in August 1999 when the site of Viols-le-Fort was discovered about 100 kilometres north of Narbonne. The stone-built houses of these people featured figures and characters that were identical to ones incorporated into Dordogne cave paintings. They were a form of alphabetic writing, though no one has deciphered it. They raised sheep and goats. At the same time, their domesticated crops of peas, some wheat and some emmer were radiocarbon dated to 10,000 BC in November 1999... older by a thousand years than any Neolithic site in the Middle East – at that time, the site of Jerf-el-Amar in Syria.

Modern science calls these people the 'Cardial Culture' after the shells of a certain kind of étang mussel they apparently loved and ate in huge quantities.

So, at least some of the more important aspects of Western culture had come from the Atlantic west to the Middle East across the Mediterranean and not the other way around. One of these aspects was religion, and specifically Christianity. The original Neolithic Good Shepherd was the son-and-husband of the Great Fertility Goddess. This has now been proved with too many artifacts to ignore. It is easy to trace the development of the Good Shepherd into Jesus and just as easy to trace the development of the Great Goddess into 'Mary'.

This transformation was most evident in Ancient Egypt as many pre-Christian sculptures of the Madonna and Child show. In short, the New Testament's Paul hijacked a very old Christian tradition and gave it a purposefully Judaic twist.

And this brought me back with some surprise to the present situation, probably because that first red-lighted buoy was almost abeam. If the New Testament was a distortion, what about the Old Testament?

"Red to right returning," Mélusine intoned.

If, as Sigmund Freud argued in his 1939 Moses and Monotheism, the Pharaoh Akenaten had really been Moses, then the Israelites did not just leave Egypt in the Exodus, they were expelled from Egypt. And equally, anyone who looks carefully at a map sees immediately that the Israelites' 'Promised Land' could not have been in Palestine. It could only have been in Western Arabia near the Red Sea Coast. And that's just where the archaeological evidence of inscriptions says it was, according to both the Christian-Arab linguist Kamal Salibi and the Jewish linguist Chaim Rabin.

My problem now was that in those early days of being in France, I hauled produce from the étangs and had been fascinated with the ancient barrows of the almost forgotten Elysians along the shores, but I had neglected to get to know these brackish 'ponds'. I knew that they were a maze of waterways between islands that grew thick reeds. Some of these islands were real mud banks attached to the generally shallow bottom, but some, I suspected, were floating mats of reeds. I never learned the maze like an étang native. Why should I have? I remembered a few marshy channels rather vaguely where I had loaded shellfish from marsh skiffs, if these channels still existed.

The buoy was just off our starboard bow. "Mélusine," I said urgently. "Dead slow. Come to a stop."

"Do you see anything?"

"No, and that's the trouble." My little radar-beam detector had not indicated any radar source throughout its diameter of sweep. That was 10 miles. If the Mossad was out there, they should have been detected by now... *if their radar was one of the more common frequencies like unto police radar.* But what if they had military radar?

"Softly, softly to starboard, Mélusine."

"But that means leaving the channel."

"I know." I glanced at the Eagle sonar. As soon as we turned to starboard, it began flashing *feet-feet-feet* at me instead of fathoms. But there were presently ten of them, feet, I mean, and soon reeds passed by on either side. I could barely see open water by starlight and the waning moon wasn't supposed to rise for several hours.

"Do you see that open water, Mélusine? It curves off to port."

"I think so." The reflections from the radar screens and the sonar on the wheelhouse windows could confuse matters.

"Okay. Try to follow the water until the depth is only six feet. I'll watch the sonar, don't worry. Go slowly." About a minute later the Eagle flashed 6 *feet-feet-feet*. "*Now*, stop." Jester, barely moving anyway, shuddered only slightly when the thrust was reversed.

"Now what?"

"Now, we wait," I said. "Anyone out there has two radar signatures and an IFR... infrared... return. If anybody's there, they will come for us. If not, we wait for dawn and go into Carcassonne behind the first boat that comes along the channel."

"Is this a change in the … plan?" she asked.

"Yes. But I want to tell any police that we're here."

I scrabbled up out of the wheelhouse and onto the poop. Aiming straight up and averting my face, I fired the Very pistol once. High above us, and high above the étang, a red flare arced upward and exploded in a burst of red star like sparkles. A red flare is the international sign for a vessel in distress. After a minute by the illuminated face of my Seiko, I repeated the performance.

"And anyone else knows that we're here too," said Mélusine from the wheelhouse.

"True enough." Standing on the poop, I thought that the nearby reeds were very nearly as tall as the wheelhouse was above the water… about six feet. But, of course, the polished brass smokestack, masts and wind-motors were much taller yet. "Mélusine, rap on the cabin door… softly… and tell Danielle that I've decided to just stay hidden in the reeds until dawn… or until the police come, whichever comes first. Tell her to try and get some sleep if she can."

32

I was two hours on the poop before I thought I heard something. Whatever it was came from the direction of the channel through the étang from Narbonne. And at first I wasn't at all certain what it was. I had been expecting a large boat or maybe even, though I very much doubted it, a helicopter. This distant gnat-like buzzing puzzled me until I remembered I had heard something fairly similar and very recently. Then I had it: the curving wake in Marettimo's moonlight and the whining outboard of the second Zodiac off the coast of Marettimo.

It was wintertime now, so unfortunately there were no frogs singing in the reeds. Frogs, being ultra-sensitive to vibrations in their muddy and watery amphibious environment, stopped singing abruptly when anything caused vibrations from fifty to a hundred meters distant. Frogs had, indeed, saved my life on several occasions, most notably in East Timor and even in the interior of Somalia. I was fond of them.

These sounds were, in any case, still in the far distance. My friends, the frogs, would not have ceased their singing yet even if they had not been in hibernation. So, I fell back on that old standby, listening for and counting the numbers of, rotors, as it were. I had gotten fairly good at this too, also in East Timor and Somalia but also in Desert Storm and the Philippines. Knowing the difference between a Huey, Apache and a Tupolev, or between a Saab Sleipnir and an Apache could be the edge between life and death.

I thought that I could distinguish two smallish outboards. From my Marettimo experiences, I figured that they would be pushing Zodiacs. They were not doing it very quickly. Two Zodiacs meant up to eight men. I could not hope to take all these, especially if they came from two directions at once. Then, what if the men weren't Mossad after

Danielle Falardeau and the damning Ethiopian text, but were gendarmes in search of Marc Rennsalaer? It would do no good, therefore, to open up with the AR-15 at a range where I could not distinguish the target. And I would have no choice but to do that if I chose the option of killing whoever was coming. Therefore, the AR-15 was useless. I glanced down at Mélusine. She was sitting on the padded bench that folded down across the wheelhouse.

"Mélusine," I whispered. She was instantly alert and turned her head toward the open hatch. I handed her down the AR-15, its banana clip detached and separate. "Someone's coming. A long way off yet. I don't know if they're friend or foe. I want you to go into the boiler room with this assault rifle. Dog yourself in there like Danielle did with the cabin." She nodded. "And this is very important... turn off any Calor gas that may be on. Make sure there's no leakage at all. But just make the valve hand-tight, no more. It's brass and if you force it too hard you'll make a leak."

She nodded, having already taken the banana clip carefully. She took the assault rifle just as carefully. "What do I do?" she asked.

"Nothing. Just wait. They may not find us at all in these reeds and we're buying a lot of time for the police to come. Don't come out whatever happens. I'm going to close the hatch now. Lock it tight. That makes two doors between you and whoever it is.... and both are very strong. I'll bang on your roof when things are okay."

"Good luck," she said. I slid the wheelhouse hatch shut.

Me, I sat up on the poop with the familiar hinges beneath my knees and listened. The outboards had come nearer, but were still perhaps two hundred metres away or more. They sounded like 3-5 hp motors. A four-man Zodiac would take a lot more, as any viewer of Jacques Cousteau's documentaries will know, but maybe this meant that the Mossad had limited resources allocated to Carcassonne. I checked the Walther and its extra 9mm magazine in my left upper arm zip pocket and checked that the knife could be drawn quickly.

I reflected that we had not done badly by going off the channel and into the reedy boondocks. They must have come from Narbonne or nearby and my red flares had alerted them, perhaps. In any case, whoever it was had had a fair distance to travel. That took time and sooner or later dawn or the police would make an appearance. The more time they took to find Jester, the better.

Finally, I could hear the outboards nearby in the channel and caught a snatch of softly uttered conversation. Then the two Zodiacs began searching along the channel and short distances into the reeds on both sides. The more time I could use up, the better, so I just kept quiet up there on the poop.

Sooner or later, the almost inevitable actually happened and one of the boats found Jester among the reeds. I will record what happened with the understanding that it may not be wholly accurate. Some of the language was French and that is rendered accurately enough. Some of the language was, I think, Hebrew or Yiddish and that was impossible for me to understand, except for inflexions of emotion and inferences from what actually took place.

Someone said: "There! A boat. Hidden in the reeds."

"We've found it," a muffled shout. And I heard the other outboard rev and come in the direction of the summons. Finally, two inflatable boats bumped and thumped gently along Jester's hull from the stern up to the outriggers and decks where I could see them in the light of their own flashlights. And they did a stupid thing. Instead of coming up on both sides at once, the boats crept up along the starboard float. And both boats were that non-reflecting grey that denotes Zodiacs. By the time the men had good reason to notice me, I saw they were wearing dark ski masks over their faces. So they were not police, but smugglers, pirates, bandits or worse.

I counted seven men, three in one Zodiac and four in the one behind it. I wasted no time. That was why barge captains and crews were allowed to carry small arms. The Walther crashed three times from the portside behind the wheelhouse and I saw, thanks to the light of their torches, three bodies thrown over the rounded gunwale of the Zodiac and splash into the water. A 9mm at a range of about 10 feet has all the dramatic impact of a brick through plate glass. I knew my abilities well enough to know none of the three would breathe again. Their torches went flying too, and one of them stayed lit on the shallow bottom of the étang, illuminating its motionless former owner in about four feet of clear water.

The four in the other Zodiac opened up with a fusillade directed at the wheelhouse, which they could be pardoned for thinking, was mostly glass. The whines off the polycarbonate and steel were gratifying, but I noticed a deeper voiced gun among the soprano .22s. A 9mm by the sound of it, and at point blank range, that might just penetrate polycarbonate.

I'd left the radar screens and the sonar on in the wheelhouse in order to give some confusion with light and shadow. I thought I saw the far window on the starboard side of the wheelhouse cracked in a web-like pattern. I felt rather than heard, the Zodiac backing away because they were desperately using Jester's outrigger to push against. I risked a shot from behind the wheelhouse down at the grey shape of the Zodiac itself and was rewarded with a gratifying 'flap' sound and the rapid escape of air.

"My God, we're going down!"

"Shut up! The water's not that deep."

I lay prone on the poop deck and wriggled over toward the starboard side. I could barely make out the darker shadow of the Zodiac in the dark water. I fired the Walther again, not quite straight down, aiming at the other inflatable sausage that comprised the Zodiac. Another flap and another explosive hiss. Then the water on the starboard stern splashed as the men tried to walk-swim away. There were a few wild shots in Jester's direction and I heard them clanging off the steel hull. Presently, the splashing receded back toward the channel. What they planned to do there, I couldn't guess and couldn't care, but for the sake of professionalism if nothing else, I kept a prone position on Jester's cabin and scanned the reeds back toward the channel.

It was a good thing that I did because two of the men managed to come upon a reed island that was actually a bare hillock mostly out of the water, although it must have been muddy. Two men? Then I heard some further splashing some way off past the tiny island. I listened carefully and thought I could make out two sets of splashing.

Very carefully, I shined my small but powerful flashlight onto the tussock, but carefully through a pane of polycarbonate. I saw parts of two bedraggled forms caught in the beams. They shielded their eyes.

"If I were you," I said, "I'd toss your guns in the water. You both are too easy to pick off from here." After a moment, I heard two definitive plops and when the beam next pinned them in its light, I saw pale hands raised.

It was about that time that I heard a distant thwacking and glanced toward Narbonne to behold a searchlight shining down and coming closer over the étang. Another sound also made itself evident, the throaty growl of a diesel-powered boat also coming from the direction of Narbonne. I waited, prone on the cabin roof, until the chopper was overhead.

I continued to pin the two men on their hummock in the beam of my flashlight until I was certain that the helicopter crew could see them too. Although I did not look up to verify it, I was morally certain that the helicopter was a police one. If the Mossad had attacked in two Zodiacs because they had no other assets available in the Narbonne area, they would not now send a chopper and a launch. Since the tussock of reeds was much too small for the helicopter to land on, my reasoning was vindicated by the dim sight of several man-forms descending rapidly by ropes from the helicopter's wide doors. French paratroopers, then, or Foreign Legion.

The chopper itself then landed on the water among the reeds, its amphibious virtuosity proclaiming it for a Kestrel AT-200B. France is a small country, as major powers go, and has to make all of its military equipment extremely versatile. The helicopter could be used to land paratroopers in Côte d'Ivoire, for example, but was equally suited for snatching civilian refugees off rooftops during Rhône floods.

I banged on the cabin roof and said: "Okay, Mélusine. Open up. All clear." She ran out of the tiny boiler room and was sliding the wheelhouse hatch back before I could raise myself from the cabin roof.

I dropped down into the wheelhouse and turned on the navigation lights as well as the over-deck lights on the main masts. Yes, one of the polycarbonate panels had taken a direct hit from a projectile powerful enough to leave a web-like pattern of fractured plastic. Knowing quite well from the Lac des Doigts that Bernard Gabereau did not like either helicopters or getting his feet wet, I backed *Jester* slowly, watching the sonar, out into the buoyed channel. The big police launch was right there and I could see that some of the crew were engaged in fishing the remaining two men of the second Zodiac out of the channel. While doing this, the wheelhouse was temporarily flooded with light as Danielle Falardeau opened the cabin door to Mélusine's urgent thumping and soothing assurances.

I brought *Jester* to a stop near enough to the launch so that Gabereau could step from it directly onto the port outrigger deck and had light from the main mastheads with which to do it. Behind Gabereau came Professor Pierre Falardeau… and Joëlle, much to my surprise. Then I scrambled down over the leather cargo to the bow and tossed a Danforth lunch hook into the étang.

Gabereau came up to me just as I got back to the poop. "Hurt...?" He asked, looking at the bandage on my head.

"Not this time, thankfully. A welcome change from Glastonbury."

"So I would imagine, Rennsalaer." He paused and perhaps smiled, but I couldn't tell in the uneven lighting. "The... ah... opiate." Here I felt Joëlle squeeze my hand. "I take it is somewhere in this cargo?"

"I suspect so, Inspecteur-Général. But my guess would be that it may be so cleverly hidden – you know how smart those drug smugglers can be – that you'd better take the whole cargo back and go through it with a fine tooth comb."

Gabereau made an abrupt gesture to some gendarmes on the launch and then negotiated his way over the tarped cargo up to the poop deck and down into the wheelhouse. "A good deal neater than with Bouchard's wine last summer," he called down. "Your merchant of vinasse," and he chuckled again at his own terrible pun.

Gabereau's gendarmes from the launch, four of them, swarmed down onto *Jester* while, after I disentangled myself from Joëlle's hand, I worked hard to free the nylon tie-down straps and peel the tarp back. The leather cartons were loaded onto the launch from *Jester*'s port outrigger deck by being tossed from hand to hand. In a very few minutes, the deck cargo had been transhipped.

Down through the wheelhouse hatch and the open cabin door, I could see Gabereau, Danielle and Pierre Falardeau in earnest conversation. Danielle was very close to her father and he had his arm around her.

"There's a bit more cargo in the cabin," I called to the gendarmes, "all of it wouldn't fit on deck." And I fished the cargo manifests from my pocket. I sorted the leather from the rolls of steel wire and handed the leather consignment's paper to one of the policemen. "Inspecteur-Général Gabereau will want this," I said.

Not thinking of anything I could do for the moment until Gabereau noticed me again, I took Joëlle's hand and gently led the way to the port gunwale beside the police launch.

"You are hurt, Marc," she said looking at the bandage and touching it gently.

"Not bad, though, Joey. Just a scalp wound from a bullet off Mare… Never mind. I imagine it is already healed. By the way, can I ask why you're here?"

"Well," she said, "Gabereau kind of invited me. He sent a helicopter to Aiguillon. At first I was afraid that something terrible had happened to you, but he put my mind at rest about that as soon as he could. I think he just likes me… and I didn't want to refuse, knowing that you have a… delicate… relationship with him."

"Fair enough."

"Marc, what's wrong? Why are you looking like that?"

"I don't know, Joey. It's just that all this has seemed too easy. I can't believe this is the end of it," I waved an arm at the launch, the helicopter and Gabereau with Pierre and Danielle Falardeau in tow coming down the poop steps and dodging the coils of steel wire under their tarp.

"Why can't something go easy for you?" Joëlle asked. "For a *change*," she said definitively.

"Like Glastonbury…?"

"Yes, Marc. You were in bad shape even when you arrived in Aiguillon. Aches from the broken ribs, headaches from the neck injury, pains from the ruptured spleen and so tired."

"Was it that bad for you?"

"For me! No. For you, my love."

"Didn't I hide it well? Did I complain too much, Joey?"

"You hid it well. Maybe too well. Perhaps you should have reached out. I would have been there."

"You're sure?"

"Don't you know… by now?"

I looked around at the police. "Now I do," I said. "I

was never quite certain before. We never had a close relationship."

"Haven't we? There are many ways of being close."

"Well, Captain Rennsalaer." Pierre Falardeau came up to us, extending his hand. I shook it. "I don't have the second half of your... ah... fee with me at this moment. I'm sure you can understand that with all the recent... excitement."

"I can."

"Do you mind if it is deposited directly into your account? Tomorrow. Our... er... mutual acquaintance apparently knows your account number very well."

"That account, yes."

"So it will be done. And perhaps you've forgotten, he told me to mention it to you, but your royalties are also due about now on the... ah... other book."

"Thanks, Professor Falardeau. To tell you the truth, yes, I had forgotten. I gather you've met my... er... good friend and companion, Joëlle?"

"Yes, indeed. Although I wish we had met under less urgent circumstances."

"They were fine with me, Professor," said Joëlle, shaking Falardeau's hand. They were exchanging some words in French when Danielle, without warning, came up to me and grasped my head in her hands, giving me a long and very thorough kiss.

Joëlle and Falardeau looked on until she was finished. Danielle turned to Joëlle. "I hope you don't mind," she said.

"Not at all, Danielle," Joëlle replied. "Marc seems to inspire that reaction in many women."

"Not surprising," Danielle said. "You're a very lucky woman."

"I know it."

"If the last of the knights errant is quite through," Gabereau said and not without a touch of wry, "I would like to have a

meeting with you as soon as this…" he waved an arm, "…
business is concluded in Paris."

I cocked an eyebrow.

"Oh," said Gabereau, "Madame Rennsalaer and I have
had some chance to compare… er… dedications." He
quoted: "'For Bernard Gabereau whose patience, astuteness
and intelligence helped preserve an ancient truth.' Number
00042," he said.

"I'm not really Marc's wife, Inspecteur-Général," Joëlle
said. "We have an arrangement and legal agreement, that's
all. I wouldn't want you to get the wrong idea."

"No matter, stability is the thing."

"I'm impressed with Mariko's dedication to you… and it
was well deserved. About a meeting. Certainly, Inspecteur-
Général." I paused. "Carcassonne, Aiguillon… Paris?"

"Perhaps Aiguillon would be more appropriate for the
subject at hand," he said seriously.

"As you wish."

"I'll give you a few days notice, of course, Captain
Rennsalaer."

"We will certainly look forward to your visit," I said
sincerely. I liked Bernard Gabereau.

Gabereau turned to Joëlle, taking her hand and bending
over it. "Enchanté, Madame. À la prochaine."

"Bien sûr." Joëlle gave a little curtsey.

"And Rennsalaer, please do drop by the Carcassonne
cop shop tomorrow and sign a statement about how you
first suspected that there might be contraband hidden in the
leather cargo… and add a few words about what transpired
in the étang tonight," he added, a bit dryly, I thought. "I do
enjoy good fiction," he added.

"Yes, Inspecteur-Général."

"Madame." Gabereau gave a suggestion of a curt bow
toward Joëlle and managed to surmount the gunwale with
some dignity.

33

We made the top lock at Carcassonne by about noon the next day – or, rather, probably the same day. After a discussion about it, Joëlle and Mélusine agreed to take the TGV train back to Aiguillon along with the ten rolls of steel wire and fittings. Christine verified that Philippe was currently in Aiguillon and would await their arrival at the train station with his on-board vehicle. Even without his full complement of scuba tanks, his version of Ivory could manage the bare four kilometres into Aiguillon and back.

At first, Joëlle and Mélusine had not wanted to go, arguing that Mélusine at least should stay to help with *Jester*. I reminded them that I had to make a statement for Gabereau and this might take some time, because there might also be questions. It was no good to tie up three people's time for the business that only one person had been asked to do. This was true enough because both Joëlle and Mélusine could better occupy their time in Aiguillon.

So, we all three helped load the wire and fittings into Ivory at the concrete wharf next to the Police Station at the summit level lock. I did not mention that Gérard Delorme had been killed within a stone's throw of us. Ivory wuffled off *Jester*'s bow and around to the nearby boat ramp. We set off for the train station after I went back to *Jester* to raise the ramp back up and check *Jester*'s moorings.

I had already double-checked that she was locked. And the polycarbonate window *was* well and truly shattered, but not broken. Where could I find another sheet of the stuff in France? I had just left the whistle-tube vertical, hoping that no one would come aboard to inspect it too closely. The AR-15 was still in the minuscule 'boiler room', but there were some things I wished to keep hidden even from Joëlle and my secret cache was one of them. That was *another* reason I wanted them on the train to Aiguillon.

As we went down the rather winding road from the canal to the street below the Police Station, we breathed in the magnificent sight of medieval Carcassonne below us.

"My God," said Joëlle, pointing down toward the battlements. "Pterodactyls…?"

"Mother of God," murmured my Druid, and somewhat incongruously, I thought.

I laughed. Everyone has the same reaction. "Those are fruit bats, girls. Perfectly harmless."

"Don't bats fly at night?" Joëlle insisted.

"Yes, dawn and dusk?" Mélusine contributed.

"The little ones do, the *Microchiroptera*. They eat insects. These are called *Megachiroptera* and they eat fruit. Citrus fruit, in fact. They aren't strictly diurnal – dawn and dusk. They can fly at any time during daylight, although I admit they usually come out at dawn and dusk. It's pretty rare to see them at high noon, but it happens."

"They look just like flying dragons," Joëlle insisted.

"Especially with that scene down there. Medieval Carcassonne. Like something out of Tolkien or a painting by Gustave Doré or Frank Frazatta." I paused, remembering. "We lived in Narbonne, Joey. There are fruit bats there too. I saw them occasionally."

"Well, I never did… and I would surely have noticed *those* things!"

"There are many more of them here in Carcassonne. You can blame Viollet-le-Duc."

"Who's he?" They asked almost simultaneously.

"The architect who reconstructed medieval Carcassonne in the 1870s. You see all those crenellations and overhanging battlements…?" I pointed down at the improbable version of the medieval town that was now almost level with us as we wound down the hill toward the train station. "Well, those architectural features provided convenient and shady roosts for the local fruit bats. So, I suppose that most of them in the Narbonnais must have moved to Carcassonne. Superior accommodation and all that."

"Did Viollet-what's-his-name plan *that*?" This was a disconcerting question from Joëlle. I had learned over almost seven years that she came to a curious, but significant, focus on many matters.

"That's a very interesting observation, Joey. One that I never thought of and have never heard before – but you may well be right."

Surely, Viollet-le-Duc had known that some large fruit bats did live in the Narbonnais region, even if they were not terribly common because it was the northern limit of their natural range. *Megachiroptera* were really species typical of the tropics. The largest known species, for example, is called the 'flying fox' and inhabits Malaysia.

Joëlle's question was an interesting one. Viollet-le-Duc must have *known* that there were some few fruit bats in the Narbonne area. Had he *purposefully* planned so many extravagant overhanging battlements in his medieval Carcassonne in order to provide roosts for them so that the size of the colony would increase? He was criticized even in his own time for his over-dramatic vision of medieval reality. Reconstructed medieval Carcassonne was called a fantasy even in his own day. Now, did the eccentric architect *plan* a natural and self-perpetuating dawn and dusk (mainly) scenario that would vindicate his fantasy with an unforgettable event?

That possibility became more likely particularly when one remembers that Viollet-le-Duc's vision was not intended to be the real medieval city of Carcassonne, but an allegory of a Cathar or 'Elysian' stronghold. It was under perpetual attack by infernal forces of the Judeo-Christian Tradition –

in Carcassonne's case, the Vatican armies of the Albigensian Crusade under Simon de Montfort (initially). Was the diurnal vignette of dragons swooping daily over his reconstruction *intended* as a perpetual reminder of what was really at stake in the ongoing religious war beneath our thin veneer of mass demographics and mass democracy?

Joëlle's question had aroused a troubling question about the purpose of Viollet-le-Duc's medieval reconstruction of Carcassonne in my mind. And my mind was still partly occupied with the small part that Gérard Delorme, Danielle, Gabereau, Pierre Falardeau, Mariko O'Shaugnessey and I were still playing in the great and never-ending struggle against the religious distortion and propaganda that had twisted the soul of the West.

"Pardon?" I said, aware that Joëlle had said something else.

"I was reminding you," she said patiently, "to check your bank account about the fee… whatever that is… and the royalties due on Mariko's book. Like Professor Falardeau said last night… or this morning."

"Right."

"Marc…? How many accounts do you have that I don't know about?" Then she stopped for a long moment. "I forgot, didn't I, that I'm not supposed to ask that kind of question. I'm only a girlfriend."

"I could ask you the same question, Joey. And I know you have at least 10,000 Euros in one of them. I deposited it."

"Touché."

"Have you always been provided for?"

"Yes."

"Are you my sole beneficiary under French law?"

"Yes."

"Have I ever cheated you… er… financially, that is?"

"He wouldn't," said Mélusine, my Druid. "Marc Rennsalaer is not the kind of man to cheat you ever financially,

Joëlle. There are some things you have no right to know. He has his own life. You do not own it just because you two have a relationship."

"I see," said Joëlle, but she was careful to keep her tone neutral. "And do you, Mélusine, know more about... certain things... than I do?"

"Yes. Only about certain things. Marc has *never*" she emphasized it, "told me *anything* of your relationship." She paused, hesitated. "I will tell you this, Joëlle. When he was frantically concerned to get to you and Aiguillon last September, at no matter what risk or cost, I did my... work... to get us to Aiguillon."

"That's why Mélusine knows some things I do not." It was a flat statement.

"Yes," I said.

"I have some skills that you do not, Joëlle. This is not a criticism. It is only a fact. Marc needed those skills to cross the Bay of Biscay against all odds and get to you that much faster. Do you remember what happened in Aiguillon that September?"

"Yes. Marc found me in the Police Station in the basement of the Hôtel de Ville because the woods were on fire at the Aiguillon warehouse... and there was a riot."

"Marc arrived in time, before you could ever have expected him to."

"Yes."

"So it was that Marc thought he needed me in... er... Sardinia a week ago."

"You've nothing to be jealous of, Joëlle. Your role and Mélusine's are... ah... complementary," I said with complacent male satisfaction. This proved, and rapidly, to be a mistake.

"But I'm your companion," Joëlle almost shouted it. She certainly said it, well, definitively. "Surely, Marc, I should know *everything*."

"And Mélusine is my Druid, Joëlle. Don't cross that threshold again until you've earned it. And a legal agreement doesn't mean a damn to me," I said. "I've got more important things to deal with than even you. Don't force me into a choice between my life and the dictates of your ego. You don't have to remain my companion, as you put it. We can easily dissolve our agreement. It's entirely up to you. And, besides, the oceans are wide and *Jester* can sail many of them. Got that? Remember that?"

"Yes, Marc."

We were approaching the train station by now. "That's what I want to hear… and a lot more of it since I ever met you in Narbonne. The world is changing, Joëlle, in case you haven't noticed. It is no longer the twentieth century. It's a cross between the twenty-first century and maybe the fifteenth… for all I know."

"Earlier," said Mélusine.

"Try to fit in, Joëlle. I have to try, and it is very hard to do."

"So," Joëlle said at last. "I sit back, accept. And am a legally-protected companion."

"And a lucky one," Mélusine said. "One whose husband has never, and will never, cheat on you emotionally or financially. One whose husband is chastely kissed and called a knight errant by women much more physically attractive than you."

"Mélusine, did you have to put in that 'chastely' part?" I asked.

Joëlle laughed. "Okay, I get the point. I'll hold the keys to the castle… with a gentle hand… and trust my knight-errant. And his Druid. Is there anything else I can do, besides playing the chatelaine?"

"Yes, there is, Joëlle," I said seriously. "It comes under the category of chatelaine, I guess… with a gentle hand."

She looked a question at me across the width of Ivory.

"Really think. *Think*. About some young people that can work for us and who can gradually be integrated into our community. It is of great importance."

I pulled Ivory up in front of the train station. I hopped out over the doorless side and went to get a heavy-duty cart. When I returned to the vehicle with it, Joëlle and Mélusine had almost, between them, offloaded the rolls of wire and the boxes of fittings. I helped with the last bits. Joëlle was never one to hang back from work. I had to give her that.

We had to hustle to catch the TGV train to Aiguillon and points east all the way to Bordeaux. I admit that I was about to turn away and just go when Joëlle grabbed my arm and turned me around. She entwined her arms around my neck and rose on her tiptoes to give me a long kiss. "I'm learning, Marc Rennsalaer, mon ami. Have some patience."

"I love you, Joëlle," I said honestly, "and I have loved you for seven years. We both have small time for patience, Dearest. Talk to Mélusine on the way to Aiguillon."

"I will."

"And I will try to find a partial cargo, at least, of citrus fruit."

Joëlle laughed.

"That was your master plan, wasn't it?"

"It was indeed."

"Then I will do my best, even if I have to buy it down in Narbonne on the Rue Gambetta."

"Don't you dare go back, Marc. Not to Narbonne or anywhere else. Bring *Jester* to Aiguillon empty if you must. But get there soon."

"By the way," I said, indicating the wire, "tell Raoul and Philippe that all that stuff is earmarked for the wind-motors on the warehouse roof. And here…" I fished the Sardiniacciaio manifest out of my windbreaker pocket. "I suppose that someone will want some import tax or duty on that stuff."

She took it and, for the moment, stuffed it down her ample bosom.

"I will look after it, Marc, and I'll tell Raoul and Philippe." She kissed me again, and just as the announcement for the TGV to Toulouse, Agen, Aiguillon, Marmande and Bordeaux came over the loudspeaker. I watched Joëlle and Mélusine jostle down the ramp to the platforms. They had a decided advantage versus the other passengers with their heavy cart carrying steel wire.

My next stop was a branch of my bank and I came away from the ATM machine just a bit stunned. I had a balance of 174,957.27 Euros. There had been three separate bank transfers.

One was for 50,000 Euros and that must have been Falardeau and associates. The largest deposit, I finally, figured out, must be royalties on Mariko's book – my 25% of 10% on the beautiful leather-bound presentation edition of 10,000 copies. Stewart and associates must have sold about 9900 of them at about 500 Euros apiece. A deposit of 1,200 Euros bothered me a little until I finally remembered that I had quoted that much on the haulage of the leather consignment from Cagliari. I had forgotten *that*.

This balance sent me scurrying to a real, live teller in order to make some transfers of my own. I transferred 150,000 Euros into the corporation's account... a homecoming present for Joëlle just as soon as she could get back to Aiguillon and online. I kept some in my own account and took a little cash to go along with the better part of the 20,000 Euros I had in my cache. I had some hedge against unforeseen expenses, boat repairs, possible domestic dissolution and a fund of emergency capital.

Having done my duty, so to speak, I wuffled back toward the canal and the Police Station. I looked around for bats buzzing Old Carcassonne as Ivory climbed upward, but saw none this mid-afternoon. Like good fruit bats, they were presumably feeding in the orange and grapefruit groves of the Narbonnais some miles to the east.

After much consideration along the way, I had my obligatory statement for the Canal Police and Gabereau more or less figured out. I would keep it short and sweet.

When at Carcassonne about a week before, expecting to find a cargo of local citrus fruits if possible, I had unexpectedly received the opportunity of loading a consignment of leather goods in Cagliari, Sardinia for a select chain of Parisian fashion retailers. I had informed my wife and partners in Aiguillon, France of this opportunity by cell phone and e-mail.

Arriving in Cagliari, I had noticed Sardiniacciaio at the entrance to the harbour, but had not stopped then, although I was interested in buying some steel wire and fittings, because I believed the leather consignment to be waiting.

First complying with Italian shipping regulations at the Customs Office, including the registration of my sole crew-helper at the time (copy of *Constituto* attached), I discovered that the leather cargo was not yet ready for shipment. It would be ready in two or three days, or so I was told.

On the wharf, however, I had met a young French woman who was willing to crew in return for passage back to Narbonne. As a reference, she said that she had worked at Sardiniacciaio during the summer. I explained the situation and took her name and a phone number where she said she could be reached. If she had still not been able to arrange passage back to Narbonne when I returned for the leather, I would contact her.

She gave a counter-offer of coming aboard immediately and crewing for the two or three days so that I could assure myself of her seamanship. I accepted this in return for her accommodation and board and went south along Sardinia's eastern coast to a cove I had seen just north of Cape Teulada.

We stayed there a couple of days making minor adjustments and tests to the two experimental wind-motors, or vertical axis windmills, I was trying out in lieu of conventional sails. We stayed at anchor or ashore most of that time, taking measurements and making some modifications. We also swam, even though the water was a bit cold, and fished.

When we returned to Cagliari for the leather cargo, I did stop at Sardiniacciaio and bought ten rolls of 4mm steel wire, with some fittings (copy of manifest attached) and verified that the young French woman had apparently worked for Sardiniacciaio for a time. Messire Jacomo Iotigolo had a recollection of her passport photo, although he couldn't be absolutely certain because the firm hired many foreign young people as summer and winter help.

After picking up the leather consignment… and some of it had to go into the cabin because the steel rolls had consumed some deck space… I again complied with Italian shipping regulations by adding the new additional crew member and declaring my intention to leave Italian waters that day. A weather forecast supplied by a helpful Italian customs official at the Cagliari office was favourable and I confirmed that we could depart for Narbonne that day.

To me, some of the sealed cartons brought aboard seemed too heavy for leather goods alone and I suspected that some contraband cargo might be mixed in with the leather goods. Although this vague suspicion had been growing, I did not really act on it until we had cleared Cagliari. Since we were bound for Narbonne non-stop, I arranged to have the French Canal Police informed while we were en route for Narbonne. Again, this was done by cell phone to my wife and colleagues in Aiguillon.

Soon after entering the étang at Narbonne Plage, I made a mistake in navigation, in the dark, and missed a buoy. This put us into the reeds off the channel and into shallow water. I was afraid of actually running aground, so I stopped the vessel to await the dawn. I fired two red flares hoping to attract assistance that could lead us back to the channel.

I surmise that smugglers, bandits or pirates must have seen the flares and decided to investigate, possibly hoping to steal cargo. I have heard that Narbonne Plage and the immediate area had experienced very recent trouble with smugglers.

Approximately two hours after going into the reeds, seven men in two outboard-powered inflatable boats came up to *Jester* wearing black ski masks or something similar. I could not see their faces. They spoke French, but also some other language that I could not understand. They fired on *Jester* and I returned fire with my registered handgun (copy of registration attached), deflating the two boats and hitting one or more of the attackers. I could be certain of nothing in the darkness.

Two of the men did reach a marsh island when their boat sank and I was able to pin them with my flashlight. Since *Jester* was made of steel, and therefore impervious to their handguns, they dropped their weapons. Perhaps one or two other of the attackers tried to swim away toward or in the channel. I could hear some splashing.

Then, Inspecteur-Général Gabereau of the Canals of France arrived with the police in both a helicopter and a launch. Perhaps he had been alerted by my warning, but perhaps he had also been on routine patrol over the étang. When I had previously been in Carcassonne, when I got the leather cargo, Inspecteur-Général Gabereau had similarly been away near Narbonne Plage after smugglers. I was told by a gendarme in the Carcassonne office that the illegal smuggling of clothing (denim jeans from Spain?) was involved in that case too.

The police confiscated the leather consignment and took the young French woman into custody, and I saw another man in custody who seemed to know her, perhaps an accomplice. I was told to make a statement this morning.

Now, this was bad fiction because the all-important events at Marettimo were expurgated. Someone could possibly discover this if close attention were paid to the actual *time* spent in that cove north of Cape Teulada. I had kept this purposefully vague and had bracketed it on both sides, as it were, with official documents that were stamped with specific dates and times. And, if anyone ever bothered to enquire, the inhabitants of the village above the cove would certainly verify that I had, indeed, played around with the wind-motors.

However, with all the attachments I proffered, I didn't think anyone would pick up on the vagueness of the time spent in the cove and the gendarme who took the statement did not. I signed it, he countersigned it, and he gave me a stamped copy. I hoped that the statement would give a hint to Gabereau: I wanted no mention of me or *Jester* in whatever transpired, no part of the considerable fame – or infamy – due to the preservation of the Ethiopian text.

About dusk, I finally got back to *Jester*. I found enough food to make myself a small and informal dinner and marvelled at the space I had to myself…. for a change. I ate the couple of sandwiches on the poop with a cup of coffee and watched Viollet-le-Duc's pterodactyls coming home to roost. When it was full dark and no one happened to be walking along the canal side, I took the air-cannon magazine below, collected the AR-15 en route and attended to making matters right in my secret cache.

Manor House Publishing Inc.
www.manor-house.biz   905-648-2193